Sophie Sullivan is a Canadian ~~...~~
Diet Pepsi-drinking, Disney ~~...~~
writing romance in almost equ~~...~~
day job as a teacher and spen~~...~~
family watching reruns of *Friends. Ten Rules For Faking It was*
her romcom debut novel, but she's had plenty of practice writing
happily ever after as her alter ego, Jody Holford.

Visit her website: **www.sophiesullivanauthor.com** and find
her on Facebook **/SophieSullivanAuthor**, on Twitter
@SophieSWrites, and on Instagram **@authorsophiesullivan**.

Praise for Sophie Sullivan:

'A refreshing romance with a strong sense of setting and a
charismatic cast. Readers will fall in love right alongside
Grace and Noah' *Publishers Weekly*

'I adored this book! Sophie Sullivan has written a fast-paced,
sweet romance full of heart and truth. Once you start
reading, you won't be able to put it down'
Lyssa Kay Adams, author of *The Bromance Book Club*

'Impossible to read without smiling – escapist
romantic comedy at its heartwarming best'
Lauren Layne, *New York Times* bestselling author

'A wholesome, slow-burn romance that will warm your
heart and offer a glimpse into social anxiety disorder.
This is a Hallmark movie in book form'
Helen Hoang, *USA Today* bestselling author

'A funny, sweet rom-com from a fresh, sparkling new voice.
Everly's social anxiety was instantly relatable, and I was rooting
for her every inch of the way to her happily-ever-after'
Andie J. Christopher, *USA Today* bestselling author

'I loved this sweet, funny story! Fun, refreshing premise that
had me wanting to make a few lists of my own and an ending
that had me choking up and happy clapping'
Kira Archer, *USA Today* bestselling author

By Sophie Sullivan

Ten Rules for Faking It
How to Love Your Neighbour

How to ~~Hate~~ Love Your Neighbour

SOPHIE SULLIVAN

HEADLINE
ETERNAL

Published by arrangement with St Martin's Griffin,
An Imprint of St Martin's Publishing Group.

First published in Great Britain in 2022
by HEADLINE ETERNAL
An imprint of HEADLINE PUBLISHING GROUP

2

Cataloguing in Publication Data is available from the British Library

ISBN 978 1 4722 8074 9

Offset in 10.80/13.44 pt Adobe Caslon by Jouve (UK), Milton Keynes

Printed and bound in Great Britain by Clays Ltd, Elcograf S.p.A.

MIX
Paper from
responsible sources
FSC® C104740

Headline's policy is to use papers that are natural, renewable and recyclable
products and made from wood grown in well-managed forests and other
controlled sources. The logging and manufacturing processes are expected
to conform to the environmental regulations of the country of origin.

HEADLINE PUBLISHING GROUP
An Hachette UK Company
Carmelite House
50 Victoria Embankment
London EC4Y 0DZ

www.headlineeternal.com
www.headline.co.uk
www.hachette.co.uk

To Alex,
for more reasons than I can list, but mostly
for being you

How to ~~Hate~~ Love Your Neighbour

1

If she'd had to lay down money on which of her motley crew would cause the most trouble, Grace Travis would *not* have picked the Chihuahua. As she waited for Tequila, one of the two bullmastiffs, to finish sniffing an apparently odorous swatch of sidewalk, she looked toward the water. She loved it here.

She took a deep breath of her own, inhaling the scent of salt water and sun. Harlow Beach was probably her favorite place on earth. The little pang of longing in her chest warred with the guilt of making the leap. The little house she'd inherited had sat empty for months now. Glancing in that direction, she swore to herself it wouldn't be much longer. She honestly didn't think she could stand many more nights of sleeping under a roof that wasn't hers when there was one right off the beach holding little pieces of her past.

She gave Tequila and his brother, Lime, the second of the mastiffs, a tug. "Let's go, guys. One of us has things to do," she said.

The five dogs got on board, rushing forward at varying speeds despite the limits of their leashes. They made an oddly adorable mosh pit of fur and ears. Technically, she could get by, thanks to student loans, with just her coffee shop job, but walking these dogs brought her exactly where she wanted to be. *Even if you can't be here for real. Yet.* Plus, it built exercise into her overscheduled days, with the added benefit of pocket money. Plus, plus, she'd grown attached. As a kid, she'd always wanted a dog.

Brutus, the nine-pound Chihuahua, led the pack. They descended the cobbled steps onto the sand to get out of the way of the few passing runners and cyclists that made it out this early. The salty air filled her lungs as she scanned the beach.

No jury of peers would blame Grace for the way her mind blanked at the sight in front of her. With the steady, gentle waves lapping onto the beach, the sun rising like a slow yawn, and the hot dude in the bright swim trunks emerging from the surf, droplets of water trickling down his chiseled chest, anyone's hand would have slackened on the bundle of leashes.

In those next few seconds, time spun out. Brutus's bark was followed by a determined yank that freed his leash from Grace's fingers. He shot off toward the dark-haired surfer dude, whose face registered surprise at the yappy little guy coming in hot. Brutus went straight for the paddle in the guy's hand, jumping with a stupid amount of determination given his size.

The other dogs had their buddy's back, pulling Grace along without consent until they surrounded the man. She thanked every deity she could conjure in those seconds as the dogs frolicked around him that none of them had a vicious bone in their furry bodies. They weren't after him. Nope, they just thought his paddle was an oversize toy they deserved to play with. *Good lord, do not follow through on thoughts about his paddle.* Her feet slipped in the sand, the dogs pulling her farther off balance as Poppers and Pepper, the miniature poodles, joined Brutus's enthusiastic barking and jumping. Pepper connected with the paddle. Grace winced even as she reached to stop the pup from playing with it like a stick. Which was her downfall, really.

Tequila and Lime cushioned Grace's fall. Somewhat. Really,

Lime assisted her tumble by collapsing at her feet and knocking her the rest of the way down onto the sand. Her groan morphed into a nearly giddy, completely embarrassing laugh, which gave gorgeous surfer guy the green light to laugh his sexy face off as he stretched a hand out to Grace. Tequila wanted in on the action, jumping to lick right up one side of the guy's cheek.

Her phone buzzed in her pocket, her head swimming with that unreal sensation of something that couldn't be happening but was. Her heart galloped in her chest like a runaway racehorse.

She took advantage of surfer, or more accurately, paddleboard guy's momentary shock at being loved on by a mastiff and stumbled to her feet without his help. The dogs bounced and pulled between them, overcome with the pure joy only dogs can feel over absolutely nothing. At the moment, Grace wished she had the canine gift of not feeling any shame. Her cheeks were hotter than the afternoon sun promised to be.

"Are you okay?" He wiped his cheek with his palm as he spoke.

Brutus continued to bark at him but at least Grace got a firm hold on the leash. All the leashes. She tugged, sliding her feet backward. Of course, he had to have a sexy, rough voice to go with the live-action *Baywatch* thing he had going on.

"I'm good." She laughed loud enough to startle a couple of pigeons. "So good. I am fantastic. Sorry about that. Brutus must have thought you looked familiar." *What? What the actual hell are you saying? More important, why are you saying it out loud?*

Her phone buzzed again but she just kept backing up.

"Brutus, huh? Funny name."

"The funniest." *Stop making it worse.*

She was going to strangle herself with the leashes. *Just keep backing up. Say nothing else.* "Sorry about the dog breath." *Disappear. Keep moving until he can't see you anymore.* "Tequila's not mine."

Hot guy chuckled. No. No chuckling. She wasn't trying to be funny.

"That's his name." She pointed to the dog, who whined about leaving.

"Nice to meet you, Tequila and Brutus. You could stick around, introduce me to the others."

He took a step forward. Her heart lurched with his movement, surprising a gasp from her lungs. Until this moment, moonwalking through the sand, with five dogs making her unsteady, she hadn't known such a thing actually happened. The organ in her chest *jumped*.

It was supposed to be a turn of phrase. One of those clichés that brought her endless happiness in the novels she hoarded. Her phone buzzed one more time, finally pulling her out of her stupor. She shifted the leashes into one hand, pulled her phone out of her pocket with the other, glancing at the screen.

Morty. She stifled the next groan. If he was calling for her to pick up ice cream this early, while he knew she was working, she was going to throttle him. *He's been through a lot. Don't be so harsh. In fact, he's giving you the perfect excuse. Be grateful.* Grace waved her phone in the air.

"No time, sorry." There was never any time. Not for the things she hoped and dreamed about. Not for stopping to talk with a good-looking guy on the beach when she had to be at the coffee shop in less than an hour. No time to swing by the little bungalow and gaze at it from the street, wondering when she'd get the nerve to tell Morty she needed to move out of his home and, finally, into her own.

He lifted his hand in a goodbye salute as Grace swiped her thumb on her phone and made herself return to real life. The one with a lot of dogs and no men. Well, no others she wanted to see shirtless, anyway.

By the time she put her phone to her ear, the line was dead. Damn. What if he was hurt? *He's a grown man who doesn't need mothering. He probably wants you to pick him up a burger because he refuses to believe there's nowhere close by to get a burger at seven A.M.*

Guilt at her flustered irritation lodged in her side. Dropping the dogs off at their respective homes, she reminded herself Morty gave her a job and a roof over her head when she'd needed both. She couldn't just abandon him because she was ready to claim a part of her life she'd never even known.

Originally, she'd walked Brutus as a favor to Morty's neighbor, but he'd insisted on paying her, then referred her to a friend. Things tended to snowball around Grace. At least, in this instance, it was good money.

She knocked on the door only three down from where she lived. Brutus clawed at the wood, excited to be home. John Dade opened the door in a robe, leaning heavily on his cane. "Hey. Come on in. Coffee is on," the elderly gentleman said. His pompadour hair that never seemed to move reminded her of Jay Leno.

Grace let the leash drop and was backing down the steps before she answered. Brutus darted inside. "Not today. Thanks anyway."

"You stop by your house?" John stepped onto the small stoop.

Didn't she just say no time? "I couldn't. Not today."

"Well, when you're ready to get in there, my son is happy to help you with any of the renos."

She nodded, her throat going thick. "Morty's moving around better every day. Hopefully soon."

John looked toward Morty's house, shaking his head. "Fool. At our age, riding a scooter is just asking for a broken foot."

That's exactly what her boss—roommate—pseudograndfather had done. Which had delayed Grace's plans by several months. Her skin felt too tight as she moved down the steps, looking back over her shoulder.

"Hopefully, he's learned his lesson." Doubtful, but a girl could hope.

"Girl your age ought to be starting a family of her own, not looking out for Morty. He's my best friend but he's taking advantage of you."

"It was my choice to stay," she reminded John, who was another pseudograndfather. Yup. Grace's life was full of men. Just not the ones that would help her with the whole family of her own dream. "Also, don't say a woman of my age."

John barked out a raspy laugh. "If I were your age . . ."

She held her hand up, picking up the pace. "Don't say that either. See you tomorrow."

She walked/ran down the sidewalk, checking her phone as she went. Harlow was an older neighborhood of California, about an hour from Los Angeles and close to the beach. The street she lived on with Morty was a time warp compared to the surrounding area.

The one-level homes were an assortment of once-popular colors. Morty's place was off-white with faded blue trim. She'd moved in four years ago, when she'd started her degree. Bounding up the single step, she turned the knob, only to find it locked. She never locked it when she went for walks.

Digging her key out of the inside pocket of her yoga pants, she fumbled with it, her heart racing faster. When she'd seen the ad to assist an elderly gentleman after hip surgery, she'd figured it was easy money. She had no idea how much more it would turn out to be.

She pushed the door open, and called out as she closed it. "Morty?"

The living room was empty, though the television was on, muted. Her pulse skipped once and *not* in the delicious way it had on the beach. Here she'd been lamenting her inability to move while he could be lying flat on his face. Which was how she'd found him six months ago after coming home from the lawyer's.

She headed to the right, down the hallway that led to the bedrooms and a bathroom. His hip had healed well all those years ago, but they'd become friends, so Grace rented a room from him. She'd planned to move out after graduating from design school.

Inheriting the house on the beach from grandparents she hadn't known was a shock. Finding Morty on the sidewalk, hurt, had pushed everything else from her mind. He was seventy-two years old but acted like he had the body of a teenager. Which his body was constantly proving to him, he did not.

"Morty," she called again, outside his bedroom door. Her brows crinkled. He was moving around in there. She could hear something. Leaning forward, she rapped her knuckles on the door.

Rapid cursing was followed by a woman's voice. Grace groaned. *Seriously? I can't do this.* Several thumps told her he was using his cane, but when the door swung open, it was confirmed. So were too many other things. His hair was a mess; his pajamas were askew. Grace slapped a hand over her eyes.

"Why don't you listen to your messages? What's the point of having one of them stupid phones if you aren't going to use it? I'm going to start putting a sock on the front door."

"Morty. Be nice. Hi, Gracie. Sorry to startle you, dear."

"Hi, Tilly. Sorry to interrupt." Grace backed up as she spoke to Morty's longtime lady friend. He refused to call her his girlfriend because he wasn't "a damn high schooler."

"Not interrupting, dear. Don't let him make you feel bad. I was just forcing him to do his exercises."

Eyes still covered, Grace pointed in the direction of the bedroom, hopefully at her roommate. "I *knew* your foot was bugging you." The doctor said it had healed well but he needed to take it easy.

"Don't need a damn mother."

She dropped her hand to look at him. She sighed, trying to quell her longings, but they bubbled up. Maybe it was exhaustion or the fact that she hadn't gotten to see the house today or the hot guy on the beach or Morty having more of a social life than she did. Whatever it was, she broke. "You're right. You don't. I have to get ready for work but I wanted to let you know I'm going to be moving into the bungalow. It's time."

His face registered shock. "I thought you might sell it and stay here."

Tilly turned, giving them the illusion of privacy.

She stepped closer. "I don't want to sell it. My grandparents left it to me. It's the only link to family I have." She regretted the words instantly.

"Guess I'm sour onions." He harrumphed. For real. Like some comic-book character.

"You know what I mean. It's time. I want to be there." She glanced at Tilly. "You don't need me."

Something she couldn't read came into his gaze. "You just going to go live your own life now. Done with me? Just like that?"

Tilly turned back, frowning. "Don't guilt the girl, Morty. She's been more than patient enough with you and your silly behavior."

Grace smiled, stepped into him, and pressed a cheek to his wrinkly cheek. "I'll only be a few blocks away. You're not getting rid of me that easy."

"Gonna come back and mooch off me?" His attempt at grumpy bravado was undercut by the crack in his voice.

"Every chance I get." Grace's heart felt like a balloon being released into the air, no longer restricted or tied down.

Morty nodded.

"I'll let you get back to your . . . uh, visit," she said, her cheeks warming again.

"I was just stopping by on my way home from work, honey," Tilly said, joining Morty in his doorway. Sure enough, she was dressed in her nurse's scrubs, her white-blond hair tucked up into a tight bun. She wore her sixty-odd years well.

The fact that they'd found love in their later years gave Grace hope that she might one day find her own.

"I'm glad he has you," Grace said, her own voice feeling thick.

"Ask one of those barista boys you work with to help out after work. We'll get you all loaded up in my truck." Morty's crooked smile was a balm to her heart.

He was going to be just fine, and she was finally going to start living her dreams. In her very own house.

"Thanks. I'll see you later. Be good or be safe."

She turned to go down the hall before she did something silly like cry over making a decision she'd wanted to make for months.

"Good and safe are both overrated," Morty called.

She laughed on her way into her room. She'd miss living with him but couldn't wait to have her own space. A home she could truly call her own. She might not have a past worth dwelling on, but her future was wide open. Her life was about to begin. Right after her eight-hour shift.

Grace made it to the Coffee Stop with barely enough time to don her apron. Her boss, Ellie, was flexible and sweet but couldn't stand tardiness. Which was more than fair.

"Hey, sweet girl," Ellie said, coming out of the storage closet just off the serving area.

Grace tried not to appear winded as she took the box of napkins from her boss's hands. "Hey. How's it going?"

"I cannot complain," Ellie said, grabbing her own apron from the hook by the display cabinets.

Grace finished the sentence for her, saying, "Because no one would listen if you did."

Ellie chuckled, going to the machines, getting them started. They opened in thirty-five minutes. Local college students kept Saturday mornings busy, almost from the get-go. They'd file in, order their drinks, look at Grace like they knew her but couldn't place her—*yeah, I go to school with you and now I'm serving you coffee.* Not for much longer.

In three months, she'd graduate, finally, with a degree in design. The road she'd started on years ago was coming to an end. Grace was as excited as she was scared. More so, now.

Grace stopped uncovering pastries for the display case when she realized Ellie was standing beside her, staring expectantly.

Her stomach growled at the scent of chocolate and pie crust. "Pardon?"

Ellie's dark eyes sparkled. With the jet-black hair she refused to let gray pulled into a tight ponytail, the barely-there wrinkles were more visible, but so was the shine. "I asked how you were doing. Something on your mind?"

Her grin probably went from ear to ear. "I did it. I told Morty I'm moving out."

Ellie lifted her hands, stared up at the ceiling. "Hallelujah." She looked at Grace again. "It's about time."

Grace checked the napkin dispensers, storing the extra packages under the counter. "You know I needed to make sure he was moving around okay before I left."

She felt Ellie's gaze. "Or maybe you were afraid to take something you deserve? Afraid that mama of yours was going to try and take it away."

Grace rearranged the napkins, turning the packets sideways so more could fit. "Still seems weird they'd leave the house to me instead of their own daughter."

Ellie grabbed another box of napkins, opened it, and started handing packets to Grace.

"Or they knew their daughter was as selfish as the day is long. Makes it all the more amazing you're such a sweet thing."

She glanced up at Ellie. "You're biased."

"Doesn't mean I'm wrong."

Grace stood, about to break down the boxes, but Ellie pulled her into a hug. "Proud of you," Ellie whispered.

She swallowed around the lump in her throat. "Thanks."

Ellie let her go, looked up at the clock over the chalkboard menus.

"I'm going to work on payroll. Call me if we get slammed before Hugo shows up. That boy better not be late."

Grace nodded, unable to wipe the smile from her face. She

hummed under her breath as she cut assorted squares, arranged pastries, and checked supplies. She liked the routine, enjoyed the mundane tasks of setting everything up just right.

She did her best not to let thoughts of her mother dampen her spirit. Tammy Travis never let her know grandparents who'd cared enough to leave her a freaking house but she'd waxed poetic about the life she deserved. As Grace got older, she wondered how her mom planned to achieve that life without putting in some damn effort. She'd never understand why her mother had kept family from Grace's life. Why she'd let them struggle to the point that Grace couldn't wait to escape her mother's trailer. Coming to Harlow was the best thing she'd ever done.

Hugo, a twenty-one-year-old college student who made Grace feel ancient despite her being only seven years older than he was, burst through the swinging door from the back.

"Sup Gracie-girl." His long dark hair was tucked into a ponytail.

"Not much, Hugo. Good thing you showed on time. You want to unlock the door? We're ready to go."

"I'm always on time." He winked at her exaggeratedly, pointing his index finger her way, making Grace laugh. His serious lack of flirting skills made him endearing. The customers loved him.

Grace laughed, lifting her brows in question.

Hugo chuckled. "Yeah. That's fair. But I'm charming."

"You are that." Which was why Ellie let him get away with his perpetual lateness.

Hugo lowered his chin, focused on attaching his name tag to his apron. "Big plans tonight?"

He asked it every shift, teasing her when she told him she was curling up with books or a design program. This time, she waited until he was looking at her. "Moving into my place. Any chance you could help? I don't have much but my bed and dresser are heavy."

He clapped his hands together. "Yes! Finally. I will help in exchange for you letting me plan the shindig to end all shindigs."

Grace laughed. "First, you're not old enough to use that word. Second, no parties. Too much going on. I just want to get in there and get settled." She didn't have the cash to do most of the renovations that needed to be done but being able to call it her home would offset her impatience about that.

"Fine. Small, simple gathering to celebrate then. I'm not budging." He crossed his arms over his chest, lifting his chin in the air.

Shaking her head, she patted his arm. "Deal. But not until I'm ready."

Hugo gave an exaggerated fist pump. "I'll take it."

Grace shook her head, starting an espresso order for the customer who'd be walking through the door shortly.

On cue, Mrs. Kern, Grace's favorite professor, walked through the door, smiling at Grace. "Morning."

"Morning. How's your Saturday?" Grace pushed the espresso across the countertop.

"The girls were still asleep when I left so it's been blissful," she said, pulling a wallet out of her oversize purse.

During the week, Mrs. Kern was all business, her blond hair in a tight braid, makeup expertly applied, her attire a great blend of classic and functional.

On the weekends, however, she wore sweats, her hair loose, face makeup free. She was Grace's idol, and though she couldn't be more than thirty-five, Grace wanted to *be* her when she finally grew up.

"Sounds nice. You marking our papers today?" Grace leaned on the counter while Hugo helped the two teens carrying backpacks who approached the display cabinet.

"Actually, I'm finalizing some exciting news I'll share Monday." She hesitated, her easy smile sliding into something . . . different. "Listen, Grace, I have a favor. A big one."

Her excitement over whatever her teacher was finalizing fizzled. Grace was horrible at saying no to favors. It was how she ended up walking five dogs when she didn't even own one. How she'd ended up telling Morty of course she didn't mind staying at his house longer. How she ended up working this Saturday at the shop when she'd had the day off and could have spent it moving into her house. *Or chatting with a hot guy on the beach.*

"Sure." Stretching her mouth into a smile, she hoped it looked genuine. She should have made herself a double shot of what she was serving.

"The girls have their birthday party next Sunday. Our face painter canceled. She's got shingles, of all things. I'm in a bind."

Pulling her lip between her teeth, Grace pictured dozens of squirmy seven-year-old girls asking for butterflies and unicorns to be drawn on their cheeks. If she could go back, she wouldn't use her summer painting faces at a carnival as one of her truths in the icebreaker, two truths and a lie, her first class this semester in Mrs. Kern's course.

"You're a great artist," Grace said weakly.

"Not on skin!" Mrs. Kern picked up her coffee. "Please. I'll pay you three hundred dollars."

Whoa. This favor was looking up. She had a small nest egg but that much money would let her splurge on a few extras.

"I feel bad taking your money," Grace heard herself say.

"No reason to. I'm happy to give it if it means I don't have to do it."

"Then, I guess I'm in."

"You're a lifesaver."

Today had taken a series of detours she couldn't have predicted. It took all of her brainpower to focus on her job instead of twirling around with the excitement of it all. She was moving into her own house. Tonight. She thought about that weird saying about the first day of the rest of someone's life. Tonight was the first night of her dreams coming true. *Look out, Harlow Beach. Here I come.*

3

Noah Jansen waited outside of the fitness club for his younger brother, checking his watch again. He hated the restless energy coursing through his body and wanted to get inside, hit the punching bag. His phone buzzed with a text.

"Shit," he said, looking at the screen.

Something came up at the radio station his brother owned—well, technically, the station *he* and his *two* brothers owned. Typing out a quick "that's fine" text, he spun around, thinking he'd go for a run on the beach. He'd already gone paddleboarding but that hadn't settled anything inside of him either.

If anything, meeting the sexy dog walker had only pumped him up more, made him feel like a kid on a sugar high.

"You lost, man?" Rob, the owner of the gym and friend of Noah and Chris's, walked up to him, a gym bag slung over his shoulder.

"Nah. Chris was supposed to meet me here but bailed."

"Can't work out without your baby brother spotting you?"

Noah huffed out a laugh. "Bite me. Just trying to figure out if punching a bag is enough today."

Rob arched his brows. "You okay?"

Fuck. Now what? You want to stand out here dissecting your feelings or something?

"Fine. Just a little restless. I'm waiting to hear back from a Realtor. I'm trying to buy the house next door to me. It's been empty since I moved in but I'm getting the runaround about the owner." His brother's words from months ago still haunted him. *You jump from one goddamn thing to the next wondering why you're not satisfied. Stand still and maybe you will be.* He was *trying*.

Rob shook his head, dropped his gym bag on the ground between them. "Uh-oh. Poor little rich boy." The grin took away the sting.

"I repeat, bite me."

"So, go buy something else. Work on the house you have," Rob said, as if both of those things were as easy as walking into the gym.

"I am. I've been jotting down ideas, calling and arranging contractors. I've got a crew coming by soon." Noah pushed both hands through his hair. "Never mind. Ignore me. I just need a distraction."

Rob eyed him a moment longer, then picked up his bag. "I have something that might work but you'd need to be a hundred and ten percent in."

Noah flashed the smile he'd used in the media when he'd been the face of his father's company. "As opposed to the half-ass effort I usually put in?"

Rob's laughter rang through the air, reminding Noah it'd been too long since he'd felt as carefree as he was known for being.

A few people waved at Rob as they headed into the gym. "Not saying that. This is just something if you give your word, something else can't come up."

Irritation crawled up his spine. That's what he was known for: a cameraworthy smile and his inability to stick around. Which was bullshit. He'd worked his ass off for his father in New York. Saw everything through to the final signature on the bottom of the paperwork. He'd even tried to have a serious relationship. That had gone three kinds of sideways.

Bailing on drinks or a couple of workouts so he could meet up with some possible network connections wasn't the same as being unreliable. Rob should know that.

"If it's important enough, nothing will get in the way."

Rob eyed him carefully, making Noah want to squirm. Which only irritated the hell out of him further. "Let's go."

Without another word, he walked into the gym, waved to his employees—Noah did the same, as he'd seen them often enough to know some of their names—then headed for the back exit.

"You taking me out back?" Noah's grin came easier.

"You'll see. I want you to meet my friends." He stopped at the exit door, turned to face Noah with a far more serious expression. "I work with a group of kids who get bused in here from surrounding counties. It's something I've been working on. We play basketball and I'm trying to set up a three-on-three tournament to fundraise for a community center. You'd know, since that's part of what you used to do, it's a hell of a long road. But these kids don't need a place to hang as much as adults they can turn to."

Noah's brows furrowed. "Okay. I knew you were doing some stuff with the local school districts."

Rob nodded, his jaw clenching. Whatever he was thinking got under his skin. Something Noah could appreciate and understand.

"Spit it out, man."

"These aren't just elementary kids learning about fitness and health. Most of the kids are between twelve and sixteen. Some from broken homes, some from families just doing the best they can. They're not always easy to connect with."

Noah's heart tugged sharply. His grandfather's final legacy ended up being a rec center in the neighborhood where he'd lived most of his adult life. It was the first time the company had built anything from the ground up. The last time, as well.

"You already know how charming I am. Let's go." He knew,

better than most, how to work a crowd. He could handle some kids.

"They can see through bullshit, so just be yourself."

Rubbing the back of his neck, Noah tried not to glare. "Jesus, man. You don't sound like you think too highly of me. You sure you want me around them?"

He was sort of joking but truthfully, Rob's hesitation was pissing him off.

"Sorry. I'm protective of them. They've been through enough. I just want to show them there are people in their lives that will show up. Whether we raise enough money or not, they need to know they matter."

"I can do that. Let's go. Unless you want me to give you some pointers on basketball?"

Rob's laugh evened out the tension in Noah's shoulders. "They're going to eat you alive."

He pushed open the door, letting the sunshine and heat in. On one of the two courts out back, two kids were hunched, one with a ball in hand, the other waving his arms around, spewing a bunch of trash talk. Oh yeah, he could do this.

The kids turned, saw Rob, smiled. Their gazes landed on Noah, and though they looked nothing alike, their snarls were nearly identical.

"They don't love newcomers," Rob said under his breath. "Hey. I brought a friend. This is Noah. Noah, meet Leo and Danny."

Danny gave a small wave, then pushed his hand up into his long blond bangs, tucking them behind his ear. "Hey."

Leo grabbed the ball from Danny, started dribbling.

Rob grimaced. "Where's everyone else?"

"Busy," Leo answered, not looking at them as the ball sailed right through the hoop. Good shot. Bad attitude. He could relate.

Stretching out his shoulders, he let Rob take the lead, updating the kids on the event he was planning. Noah listened, seeing how Leo's gaze kept landing on him, like he was just waiting for Noah to make a wrong move. He couldn't help but wonder what the kid had gone through to be that distrustful at such a young age. He didn't even look old enough to drive.

"We'll play two on two. Leo, no cheap shots," Rob said.

"Scared I'll hurt your friend?" Leo's smile was a little mean.

"Play fair or don't play," Rob returned easily, whipping the ball out of his hands and taking a jump shot. When it went in, he strutted around under the hoop. Danny laughed outright, grabbing the ball. Leo's lips twitched but he didn't crack.

"Come on, dude. Let's whip their old asses," Danny said.

"Whatever," Leo said, taking Danny's pass. "Nothing better to do."

~~~~~~~~

Noah pulled into a drive-through after the gym, surprised at how hard he'd had to work to keep up with a couple of kids. He and Rob had won, barely. Leo hadn't spoken to him the entire time, but he didn't cheap-shot.

After ordering a burger and large Coke, Noah headed for the freeway. The drive from San Verde to Harlow Beach was a good one. Gave him enough time to think. In New York, he'd rarely driven. Once Chris had pulled up stakes for good, leaving New York behind for the California sunshine and the love of a woman who, no shit, completed him, Noah's restlessness had begun.

He thought a relationship was the answer and tried to make a serious go of it with a former flame who'd . . . well, flamed out. He realized a few weeks in that there was a reason they'd been on only two dates, both of them to high-profile events. Still, he'd worked at it, telling himself he wasn't his father, who was on his sixth engagement.

While he'd been trying to find the good in his so-called relationship with Belle—short for Belinda—she'd been telling mutual friends that she wasn't sure Noah had deep enough pockets for her liking. It'd been the final straw. He'd leased out his penthouse apartment, told his father he was headed west, ignored the laughter his old man had thrown at him, and cut his ties.

Tapping his fingers along to the music playing on the radio—96.2 SUN, the station he'd gone in on with Chris and their brother, Wes—he made a mental list.

A quick flash of Leo's scowl reminded him he had lots to be grateful for in this life. He just needed to feel productive again. Then he'd feel like himself. Since he'd moved to a sweet corner lot by the beach, the little bungalow next to it had sat empty. The tiny shack was begging to be razed so Noah could use the land to make his dream property. The house he'd purchased needed work. It was a monster of a thing that took up most of the land it sat on. Which meant that he needed the property next door to truly turn the space into a place he could call *home*.

"Time to make things happen," he ground out, turning off at the freeway exit for Harlow Beach. He could commit just fine. When it was warranted. He told Siri to phone his assistant, Josh.

"What's up, boss?" Josh's phone came through the Bluetooth.

"You hear back from the real estate agent?"

"Yes. He said he contacted the owner and it isn't for sale." Noah heard the sigh in his assistant's voice. Noah was persistent. So what? It was what made him good at what he did. Or it used to.

"Bullshit." Noah squeezed the steering wheel. "Everything is for sale when given the right price."

"Maybe not this one," Josh said tentatively.

"No one even lives in it."

"Maybe we could find the owner, set up a meeting. You're pretty convincing in person. When you turn on the charm anyway. I'm not basing that on your personality lately."

Noah laughed. "Shouldn't you be nice to me since I'm in charge of your paycheck?"

Josh's chuckle answered. "Probably, but no one else applied to run your errands and buy your groceries. The mood you're in lately, you couldn't pay someone else to put up with you, so I think I'm safe."

Jesus. What happened to the charming guy who had a packed social life? Had he completely forgotten how to be around people?

"Second time today someone has commented on my mood. Sorry, man."

"I'm just giving you a hard time. You need to get out, go on a couple dates, go surfing, something. I'll try setting up a meet with the owner. See you tomorrow?"

"Yeah. See ya."

Noah hung up thinking about how he was turning into exactly what he didn't want to be: his father. Unappreciative of his employees, always wanting more, not being grateful for what he had right at his feet. "It stops now."

He had a house to make into a home, contractors to set up, ideas to see through. Starting with the house next door.

He nearly slammed the brakes when he pulled into his driveway and saw a rusty old truck sitting in the drive next door. It was piled high with a dresser, a bed frame, a covered mattress, and other odds and ends. His heart hammered so hard he wondered if it could break his rib cage.

"Are you kidding me?" He makes a vow to get this property and the owner moves in *today*?

He got out of his truck, locked it, and walked next door, across the small lawn at the end of their shared fence.

The man leaning on the truck looked old enough to be his grandfather. There was no way this man was going to be able to lug that bed and dresser into the house. He looked like he might pass out.

"Hey, there. You the neighbor?" the old guy asked, the weight of his body slumped against the edge of a rust spot.

"I guess so. I didn't think anyone was going to move into this place," Noah said, pulling out the smile he reserved for pushing a deal in the direction he wanted it to go.

The old guy pulled an actual handkerchief out of his jeans pocket and mopped his forehead. "Me neither, boy. Me neither."

Noah's senses prickled. Everyone had a price. He didn't want to be his father, but that didn't mean he hadn't learned from him.

"I was actually trying to contact the owner," Noah said.

The guy pushed off the truck, attempting to straighten his naturally curved shoulders. "Oh yeah?"

Interest? Noah smiled. "Yeah. I'd be interested in buying the place from you at a more than fair price. Above market value."

The guy's furry brows moved together, a gray caterpillar over suspicious grayish-blue eyes. "Why's that?"

Noah pointed to his place. "I'm looking to settle in. I like it here but I need more land than I have."

The old guy shook his head. "Kids these days always want more than they got."

Doing his best not to frown, Noah put both hands in his pockets, holding the man's gaze. "Just looking to improve what I already have, is all. You'd make a great profit. Everyone wins."

"Except me," a voice said from his left.

Noah's gaze landed on the woman who'd hovered at the back of his thoughts all day, standing with her hands on her gorgeously curvy hips, giving him a cutting glare.

"It's you," he said.

She tipped her head and he had the pleasure of watching the recognition roll over her features. She sucked in a sharp breath.

"You know this guy? He wants to buy your house," the old man said.

She looked at the old guy, frowned even deeper, and put a hand on his arm. "You should sit down. Go inside for goodness' sakes. Hugo will be here soon."

"Name's Morty. Good luck convincing her. She's as stubborn as you are pretty," the guy said to Noah.

Noah's jaw dropped at the very odd exchange and watched the man—Morty—limp toward the house.

"Your . . . dad?" Noah asked, looking down at the woman watching him. Jesus. She had a pair of eyes on her that lit his insides up like fire. Which was not helpful, considering she had what he wanted. What he *needed*. It felt like it'd been so long since he'd made a deal that gave him the energy-spiking adrenaline he craved.

"No. Good friend," she said.

Noah arched his brow, waiting for her to explain, but she didn't. "I'm Noah Jansen. You're the dog walker."

Her lips quirked. "That and more. I'm Grace."

She didn't offer a last name but shook his hand when he extended it. He had to grit his teeth to keep from responding to the feel of her palm sliding against his. Josh was right—he needed to go on a date. He wrote off the sizzle that traveled up his spine as eagerness to convince this woman he could make her financial dreams come true.

Grace pulled her hand back, shoved it into the pocket of her jean shorts.

"Guess we're neighbors," she said, looking over at his house.

"Unless," he said. No point in hesitating or beating around the bushes he wanted to haul the hell out of his yard. Her things were still in the pickup. What better time to make a move? Timing was everything. Not just in business but in life.

She turned her head, looking at him with those dark brown eyes that he was certain were sizing him up. "Unless what?"

"I'd love to buy your property."

"It's not for sale."

He grinned. He loved this part. "No? Not even for double the value?"

"Not even," she said as if he'd just asked if she had a cup of sugar.

"I'm not joking," he said. Eyeing her closely, he looked for a *tell*—that thing that showed a hint of intrigue. He was dressed to work out, not negotiate. Usually, when he was working on or closing a deal, his three-piece Armani did a lot of the talking for him. *Maybe you're off your game, Jansen.*

Grace's smile came in small degrees, feeling too much like a damn punch to the heart.

"Me neither. Nice to meet you. Officially."

With that, she turned on her heel and walked into the house. Noah stood there staring after her, wondering what the hell had just happened.

4

Grace all but vibrated her way into the kitchen. *Of course beach guy with the shredded abs and wicked smile was an ass. Why wouldn't he be?*

Morty was helping himself to a glass of water when she came into the kitchen, leaning heavily against the counter. He turned when he heard her, set his glass down with a smack.

"Moved for the view, did you? Hell of a view," he said around a raspy snort-laugh.

Grace's lips quivered but she fought the grin. No need to encourage him. "Aren't you in love with Tilly? He seems a little young for you."

His bark of laughter eased the tension from her shoulders. "You're better at deflecting than I am."

She grabbed her own glass from the box of twelve she'd purchased after work and rinsed it out. "I learned from the best. Why don't you sit down? I put lawn chairs on the back porch."

Morty shook his head. "Hugo should be here already."

She rolled her eyes. "They probably stopped for a bite to eat.

Just think, if they hadn't helped me load it up and weren't bringing it over, it would have taken me a lot longer to move."

He was quiet for a moment then said, "You ought to think about Mr. Fancy Pants' offer. Above asking price? You could buy a new place, not have to worry about the work this house is going to need."

Grace sipped her water, then set it aside. Without looking at him, even though she could feel his old judging gaze, she unloaded the glasses, taking the time to rinse each of them and set them to dry in the farm-style sink.

"I want to live here. I want to make it my own. It'll take some time but I'm looking forward to restoring it and making it my own." She couldn't bring back the grandparents she'd never known, but maybe bringing the house back to its glory days would make her feel, somehow, connected. She planned to restore the original moldings, paint the walls, find some retro lighting that could replace the sixties style with more efficiency.

"You're starting a new career soon. You should focus on that," he said.

Grace dried her hands on a paper towel. She needed to wash all the windows and started making a mental list of items to purchase. "You're going to be fine without me. If that's what this is about."

He was no better at diving into his feelings than she was, so it wasn't a surprise when he made a rude noise and waved his hand dismissively in her direction. "Hell. I know that. Just don't want you burying yourself in a money pit when you could have so much more. Especially if you took that guy's offer."

She stiffened her shoulders, stepped toward him. "I won't. Let it go. Go sit down before you fall down." She didn't mean to snap but she didn't know how to explain the sense of family she was hoping to unearth through fixing up this home. Maybe it was silly. *It's yours. Your choice. It can be silly if you want.*

"Calling me old?" He lifted his chin, a slight smile tipping up one side of his mouth.

"Nah. Just weak," she said, poking him in a bony shoulder.

He laughed, patted her cheek. "You're a good girl when you aren't being sassy."

Grace winked at him. "So, never?"

~~~~~~~~

Hugo arrived with his on-again-off-again boyfriend. When Grace saw him hauling the mattress out of Morty's old truck bed by himself, his tank top showing off his biceps, she was grateful they were currently *on*. She hated calling in favors but her other choice was hauling a few things at a time and that wouldn't work for her bed or bigger items. Besides, she considered always being willing to switch shifts for him a good trade.

Her things got deposited fairly quickly, and though the guys offered to stick around, help her set up the bed, she told them she was fine. The truth was, she wanted to be alone. When she said goodbye, thanking them all profusely, promising a pizza-and-beer get-together very soon, she shut the door and leaned against it. It rounded at the top, which she absolutely adored. Turning, she ran her fingers along the scarred wood planks. She'd need to redo it. Excitement swelled through her whole body. Turning in a circle, she walked through each of the rooms, taking them all in.

The entryway had a little coat closet and a recessed nook she'd like to put a bench in for putting on her shoes.

She stared at the space a minute. The whole place needed a thorough painting. Inside and out. "I need a beach picture right here." That would be the first thing people saw when they came in.

To the left was an archway that led to a living area. A wall with a window-size hole revealing part of the kitchen separated those spaces. All of the appliances needed to be replaced but would do for now.

She ran her hand along the wainscoted cupboard doors. They were beautiful.

"Coat of paint and they'll be like new." She wanted to play around with Chalk Paint and figured these would be a good canvas.

There was a small laundry off the kitchen, a mudroom of sorts with a door leading out to the porch. The house was small but she liked the coziness of the one-story layout with two bedrooms and a den the size of a closet. It might actually be a storage closet but she'd done a design project on tiny spaces and wanted to see what she could do with it. Her bed was set up and made; she had only clothes, some linens, and toiletries to unpack, so she took her phone to the deck and sat in one of the two lawn chairs she'd brought.

She could see the beach, though she had to sit on the right side of the porch to look past Noah's hedges. *Noah Jansen.* Sinking into the chair, she cast a quick glance around, and then she did a quick little toe tap dance in her seat.

"This is my view from now on," she whispered. She thought about her grandparents, wondering what they were like. Had they sat out here every night? Maybe with a cup of tea or a beer? Had her mom played in this yard? She couldn't imagine her mother playing innocently. Tammy was a master player but not in a way that held any fond memories.

Maybe her grandparents had read to her mother sitting on this deck. *A porch swing. That's what this needs. One of those wooden ones.* She wasn't sure how much they cost but maybe she could use the bonus money from face painting toward that splurge. Maybe. She needed to take a look at payment plan options for home insurance and taxes first.

Looking down at her phone, she texted John Dade, asked for his son's contact information. There was no more waiting. All the things she'd patiently been putting aside were right here, within her grasp. Her life right now was a series of boxes she was checking off and the feeling was pure bliss. Finishing up school? Check. Settling into a home you own? Check. That one was still a shock. Without her grandparents leaving it to her, she wouldn't have that box checked. Good friends? Check. Job prospects? Check. Life was moving along just fine, thank you very much. It was like she could see her lonely, rootless self slipping farther away in the rearview mirror.

She heard a sharp snipping sound to her left. Her home had been built on the west side of the property, which allowed for a nice expanse of yard between her and the right-side neighbor. Due to the size of Mr. Money's house though, which was the newest on the street, her proximity to him—or at least, his home—was a lot closer. If he trimmed the overgrowth properly, she'd benefit from the view. The tops of his shears came into view. *Has to be on a ladder.* He was tall—easily over six feet—but not that tall. The blades swished almost aggressively. She'd taken a course in landscape design two semesters ago and decided it was not for her. *Interior only, thank you very much.*

"Your scissors sound angry," she called over the hedges. She honestly wasn't sure if he'd been serious about his offer. Not that she was interested but it made him somewhat intriguing. One of those boxes had long been left unchecked: someone to love and share life with.

The creak of a metal ladder answered her and then she saw Hottie McMoney Pants peering over. She winced, hoping he was steady and not holding the shears blade-up.

"Not angry at all. Just doing some trimming."

"Oh? You have a background in pruning?"

It was a lot trickier than people thought. She could see his face from the nose up. His hair was messy, like he'd gone in and showered while she'd unloaded. His forehead crinkled.

"Is there a degree in such a thing?"

"Actually, yes."

He laughed but it wasn't the one that made her stomach swirl deliciously like the cresting waves in the ocean he'd walked out of. No. It was harder. Sharper.

"Afraid not but I've been holding scissors since I was four so I think I've got it."

"There's actually a real art to pruning," she said, trying not to sound condescending. She didn't mean to be but knew that doing it wrong could wreck the shrubs. "Most people hire someone to do it if they haven't done it." If he was serious about buying her house, he could definitely afford a landscaper.

"Believe it or not, I don't have to hire someone for everything I do."

Grace frowned, then walked down the steps and along the side of her house where the hedges tapered off. She peered over the fence, leaning her upper body over the waist-high white wood. The flat top dug into her stomach while her hand rested on the support beam running lengthwise.

He was standing on a ladder, wearing shorts that showed off muscular legs and no shirt. *Oh. My.* He might not be Edward Scissorhands but he looked damn fine doing it. She leaned a little farther over and into the wood to get a slightly better peek at Captain Grumpy. He'd just glanced her way when the wood cracked where she put her weight. She wasn't exactly top-heavy but the angle, the surprise, and the break sent her tumbling over right onto his lawn like a comedian tripping over a half door.

She heard his curse, the thump of the scissors on the ground, and him hurrying toward her, but closed her eyes, rolled to her side.

"Are you okay?"

She opened one eye. He leaned over her, hands on his thighs, peering down at her.

"Pretty good. Thanks for asking. I think your fence needs some work."

He shook his head, his lips quirking. "You fall a lot."

Glaring, she ignored his hand, *again*, and rose to her feet with as much dignity as she could muster. Which was *not* a lot.

Instead of answering him, she wiped off her shorts, ignored the stiffness in her leg, and went to inspect his hedges.

"They're crooked."

"They are not," he said.

She stood back from the ladder, hands on her hips, and stared at them. He gave a sexy little growl when she tilted her head to the side.

"They're definitely crooked."

"You probably have a concussion from fence diving."

Turning, she stared at him, trying not to focus on how good he looked with no shirt. Worth the fall, for sure. But the scowl detracted from the view.

"You should hire a gardener. You'll want to for the palms anyway," she said, pointing to the other side of his property, where the overgrown trees blocked a lot of his beach view.

"I don't need a gardener," he said.

A small smile tilted her lips up. His jaw was granite, like his stance. Touchy subject? "Okay. Well, good luck."

As she walked away—let's face it, with no dignity, because falling in front of the same man twice in one day did not warrant such things—she felt his gaze.

"You know what? I think you're right."

Grace turned at the end of the fence, immediately suspicious. "I am."

He huffed out a laugh, ran his hand through his damp hair. "I'm going to call someone and have them taken out completely. Better view that way."

Now why did that sound like a thinly veiled threat?

"You want the view in the other direction. Toward the beach. Not my place." She shrugged because if he thought it was a threat, he was wrong. She'd benefit from the view.

"Yeah but when I convince you to sell, the hedges have to go anyway."

She shook her head. She didn't grow up in circles where people were rolling in money. Most everyone she'd known was rolling in debt and bad choices. This guy didn't wear his in slick suits—though she had no doubt he'd look good in one—but in his very essence. Polish. Confidence that bordered on ego. Things that didn't impress someone who worked their ass off to get to this very point.

"Like I said, good luck."

It wasn't happening. She'd finally received a little piece of family—though the word was mostly foreign to her—and she wasn't letting it go.

"Everyone has a price," he called after her.

"Not me," she called back, her earlier calm replaced by a restlessness that made her wish she had paint so she could start on the living room.

"We'll see," he called back.

Grace ignored him, went into the house and grabbed her keys, her purse, and headed for her car. Paint. This agitation she felt could be rolled out as easily as a feature wall.

Before pulling out of the driveway, she checked her phone to see if John had replied about his son. He had. But there was another text.

Tammy
Why don't you ever text me back?
I need to borrow some money.
I'll pay you back.
Not much.
I could always borrow some from the guy I'm seeing. Enough to buy a bus ticket your way.

Grace was surprised her jaw didn't crack from how hard she clenched her teeth. She sighed, closed her eyes briefly. Why couldn't she just tell her mom to go get lost? Part guilt, part useless hope that she'd change, part certainty that the woman would do as she pleased.

Grace
I don't get paid for another week.
Tammy
I can wait that long.

Grace sighed, leaning her head against the seat. Shit. Tammy did that often—threatened to come live closer. Grace had worked most of her life for two things: to get away from her mom and to not turn out like her. Now that she was in the house her mother had grown up in—the one she'd run from at sixteen—Grace was even more determined not to let the woman tarnish the life she wanted to build. She thought about the three hundred dollars Mrs. Kern had paid her in advance.

Grace
I have $200. That's it. You can't keep doing this.
Tammy
This is what family does. Thanks.
xoxo

"Family." Their definition of the word was vastly different. Grace wanted to toss her phone but reminded herself she couldn't afford a new one. She set it on the passenger seat, started the car, and backed out of the driveway. The earlier satisfaction she'd felt, the sense of *home* she'd wanted to lap up as she walked through the rooms, had disappeared. So much for porch swings. *Silver linings, Grace. You have enough for paint.* Grace had been making the best of things her entire life. She wasn't about to stop now just because of a grumpy neighbor and a selfish parent. There was always a silver lining. The paint store being open despite the hour was hers for today.

5

Noah leaned against the upstairs wall, keeping his body angled so he could see out the window but wouldn't be noticed. Grace was mowing her lawn. She had headphones on and a smile so wide he could see it from his second floor. Who smiled while doing yard work? He sure as hell hadn't felt like smiling while he was trying to grapple with the stupid hedges the other night. Well, not until she fell ass over head across the fence. Once he knew she was okay, he'd still bit back the laughter. He wasn't sure if she was clumsy or just unlucky.

Whatever she was, the old guy was right. She was stubborn as hell. He'd seen her twice in passing the last two days. Once, the next day, when she'd simply waved on her way in from her car, and then last night while he was making use of the freestanding basketball hoop he'd had shipped to his place. She'd watched him for a few minutes from the front porch after washing windows. The woman had more energy than those dogs she walked, which he'd also seen her doing at the crack of dawn this morning.

A tiny little piece of him admired her grit—he had some of his own, coming to the surface more in the last week than he'd felt in a while. *Thrill of the chase.* Glancing at his watch, he saw he had a bit more time before he needed to head out to the rec center. Plus, closing a deal that took no effort wasn't any fun. Since moving to California, he'd purchased a couple of corporate properties that were fully leased out. They were moneymakers and didn't need him. He and his brothers owned a few other companies, but Noah was eager to do something completely on his own. This house was just the start.

His phone buzzed. Moving away from the window, he swiped his thumb across to answer.

"Hey," he said to Wes.

"Hey, back. How's it going?"

Noah shrugged, even though his brother couldn't see him. "Fine. The house next door? Someone moved in."

"Someone like an owner?"

Forcing himself not to look back out the window, he walked toward the master bedroom. He didn't have much furniture, but he'd bought a kick-ass California king bed. Sitting down on it now, he rolled his shoulders. "Inherited, I think."

"So, now you can make an offer face-to-face."

Straight to the point. That was Wes. The thoughtful, optimistic one. Chris was analytical, serious. Noah was the fun one. The fly-by-the-seat-of-his-pants, carefree one. Supposedly. No one knew how much thought, planning, and work went into choosing his deals, seeing them through, and fighting for what he wanted. Not much of that was carefree. He just didn't bitch about it. They had a sister as well, but Ari was in a world all her own. She was the princess of the family, not held to the same expectations as the others. Which was likely why she was the only one who could put up with their father.

"Already did. She dug her heels in but from what I can tell, she's a paycheck-to-paycheck girl. Once she sees how much work owning a total fixer-upper is, she might change her mind. Pretty sure her roof needs to be redone. Her siding is shot. That's just the outside." She had a hell of a yard, though. He could picture a pool, cabana, maybe a small guesthouse for his mother when she was stateside. He could see himself flipping burgers while his brothers hung out, conversation and laughter surrounding him. *Like when Gramps was alive.*

"Maybe you have enough to focus on just with your place."

Noah gripped the phone, smoothing out his frown. "I am. I'm focusing on making that part of it. You wait, man, it's going to be awesome. Remember when Gramps used to rent out that property upstate? We'd all hang out and swim, eat until we couldn't breathe?"

He heard Wes's sigh in the background. "Of course I remember. I loved those summers. Before everything went to shit." His brother laughed, but it didn't feel funny. "You okay, man?"

"Just lots on my mind. Lots to do. We need to have a meeting about the corporate acquisitions I just made for Squishy Cat." Their youngest brother had named their company. "Demo crew is coming tomorrow. We're taking the wall down between the living room and kitchen. Open it up. I'm trying to get ahold of some press contacts, see if I can get a spotlight on this which will build my credibility out here. Maybe back East, too, since I heard Dad's trashing me."

"Ignore that. It's a tantrum. He'll get over it. He knows he lost a huge moneymaker when you said you weren't coming back."

"Well then, he should have let me actually do something while I was there."

"I know. So? You're going to swing a hammer on this one?"

Irritation bubbled inside of him. His brothers liked to give him a hard time, but he worked his ass off. Maybe he didn't literally sweat when he was making a buck, but neither did they. "It'll be a good way to get my aggression out seeing as beating up you or Chris would be like picking on a toddler."

Wes chuckled. "Whatever, man. You're all talk."

Not this time. This time, he was all action. From start to finish.

He was hiring people because he knew his limits, but he was all in on this one. He was going to grow old here while he built an empire around him and showed his dad, himself, that he could stick. That he could succeed without any hand-holding. Like his grandfather, he'd build a legacy of his own. One day, maybe he'd have a son and that kid wouldn't rip apart his work piece by piece while simultaneously destroying his family.

He rolled his shoulders again, rose from the bed. He needed to get going.

"I gotta go. I'm meeting up with Rob. Then I have some landscapers coming to rip out the hedges between our yards." He hadn't told his brothers about the kids or the three-on-three tournament. He wasn't sure why.

"That's a nice gesture," Wes said.

Noah glanced out his bedroom window at the crooked freaking hedging. "They're a nightmare, man. It's a necessity."

"Maybe, but it might look like an olive branch to the owner next door. You know what they say, good fences make good neighbors."

An idea sparked quick in his head, making Noah smile. "Fences. Yeah. They do say that, don't they? Talk soon, bro."

He hung up, got ready to go out, and left the house, heading toward Grace's front door.

When she answered, his brain went momentarily blank. Sweaty tendrils of hair stuck to her forehead. Her tank top was damp and she held a glass of something ice cold in her hand. She looked tired but happy. Weird. He hadn't felt happy trimming the hedges. Nor had he felt any great thrill pulling out the mower last week.

"Hey, neighbor," she said, taking a long drink.

His brain fritzed as he watched a droplet of water fall from the glass onto her skin. *Jesus. Focus, man.* "Hey. I'm just headed out."

She lowered the glass. "Big meeting?" Her smile was cheeky.

He didn't smile. It would be false advertising, and he knew she was joking, since he was in gym shorts. "I've got someone coming to fix the fence. I was thinking in addition to reinforcing it, it should be repainted."

Her pretty brown eyes smiled innocently. "Okay."

Good fences might make good neighbors, but broken ones—especially those broken by an adorable and stubborn woman—cost money. Money he was betting she didn't have.

"You want a say in the repairs and repainting? I was thinking white again because it goes with the trim of my place. But I didn't know what you had planned for yours."

The softening of her gaze, the way her lips turned up in a sweet smile snagged at his conscience. "That's sweet of you to ask. White is great."

His pushed his conscience back and made the next move. *That's all this is. A series of moves to close the deal. Feelings, including guilt because of a damn smile, don't rate.*

"I'm not sweet, Grace. It's the fair thing to do since you're paying half."

The glass in her hand nearly slipped. "What?"

Steeling himself against responding to the stricken look on her face, he kept his expression neutral. "The fence is shared. I'll let you know the final price. I gotta run. Your yard looks good."

He turned and hurried down the steps, not waiting for her to recover from the surprise. That should give her a nudge in the right direction. Namely, out. People thought the idea of fixing up a house was fun, like they saw on TV. The truth was, it could cost a fortune. More than once, he'd seen people burn through their savings and come out of the purchase more in debt than ever. It wasn't a *game*. It was a business. Even when it was personal.

6

Saturday nights at the coffeehouse turned into a Nashville-style open mic. Poets, grifters, and seriously talented people stopped by, grabbed the house special—a vanilla-caramel chia tea—and listened to others pour their hearts and songs out. It was usually pretty cool, sometimes painful. Hugo had begged her to take his shift, plying her with promises of taking any shift she ever needed him to. He knew she never bailed on a shift, though, so he wouldn't have to pay up. Besides, her Saturday nights usually consisted of textbooks and design software. Ellie kept the place open until midnight, which wasn't an unholy hour.

By the time she'd arrived home, taken some time to decompress and tweak a couple of design ideas she had for a project she was almost finished with, then showered off the smell of coffee, it had been almost two, and she'd fallen into bed.

At which point, she'd stared at the ceiling, willing herself to think about designs, paint colors, and floor plans. Instead, she'd thought about how Noah Jansen was two people. His first persona was a hot, charming surfer dude with a laugh that stuck in a girl's dreams. The second was a stubborn, entitled elitist who got what he wanted one way or another. She'd finally fallen asleep dreaming about fences piled high with money.

She woke Sunday morning with less vigor than usual listening for the sound that woke her up. She groaned, sat up as she heard it again—a loud, awful whir of a noise.

What the actual hell is that? Not worrying about the fact that she was dressed in sleep shorts and an oversize 49ers T-shirt, she stormed out of the bedroom. In bare feet, with a deep scowl and some serious bedhead, Grace kept going, through the house, out the door, and to the fence.

Several work trucks bearing contractor names were parked in Noah's driveway. Guys in jeans, T-shirts, and baseball caps littered his yard, music playing loudly from someone's speaker. Some guy was pressure-washing the side of the house, which would be the racket that woke her up.

Since no one would hear her if she yelled, she picked up a rock and tossed it near the spot where Noah chatted amiably, like it was a decent hour in the day, with a couple of other guys. He turned when the rock landed near his running shoe.

God. He had absolutely no right to look sexy in running gear at this time in the morning when she woke up like a bear two weeks early from hibernation. He left the guys he was talking to and sauntered over, amusement etched on his stupid-gorgeous features.

"Trying to break something else of mine?" One side of his mouth quirked up even as he tipped his chin down.

Grace clenched her fingers into fists at her sides and tried to push her temper down. "Why are you making this much noise at this hour on a *Sunday*?"

Noah had the nerve to laugh. "Wow. You do not wake up friendly."

She pointed to the pressure-washing dude and gestured to the others, who were looking their way. "Not when I'm woken by a herd of steel-toe-booted elephants, blasting music and water when

I've worked all night." Okay, slight exaggeration. She tended to wake up on the grumpy side anyway, but he wasn't helping.

"All night? Pretty sure I heard your car roll in just after midnight." He leaned closer, his gaze more intense. "What kept you up all night, Gracie?"

You. Wondering where I'm going to get the money to paint my half of the fence. She poked the air, just short of jabbing him in the chest. "It is too early for all of this. There are laws against this sort of thing. Plus, it's unneighborly."

There. That ought to put him in his place. Instead, he crossed his arms over his chest. "Correct. *Bylaws* that state I can make noise after eight on a Sunday." He looked at his fancy watch, then back at Grace. "It's almost ten. Speaking of being unneighborly, are you always this grumpy in the morning?"

Her retort died in her mouth. No. Not to this extent. "I need coffee."

Without a word, Noah turned on his heel and walked away. Disappearing behind a truck, he was back in under a minute with a white to-go cup bearing her favorite logo. Yeah, yeah, she craved the competition. What Ellie didn't know about wouldn't hurt her.

Noah handed her the coffee. "Untouched. It's mine. One of the guys brought it. There's cream and sugar in it. Maybe not the way you take it but consider it a peace offering."

The stiffness went out of her stance, her lungs deflating, as her pulse did a double beat. *Which Noah is this? Please don't have a third persona. It's too hard to keep up.* "You don't have to do that." The fact that they took their coffee the same way did *not* mean anything.

"I wouldn't do it if I didn't want to. Take it," he said, smiling as he extended his arm.

A peace offering. Did that mean he was willing to negotiate on the timing of the fence painting and repair? Grace took the drink, brought it to her lips, taking a generous sip while telling herself the actual glow inside of her was from the sweet taste in her mouth, *not* the way Noah's fingers brushed her own.

"Hmm," Noah said, leaning a hip against the fence.

With both hands around the warm cup, she glanced at him through lowered lashes. "Hmm, what?"

"Just making mental notes. The way to calm Gracie in the morning is coffee. Noted."

She narrowed her gaze. "Grace."

"Grace before coffee but Gracie after. Your whole body softened with your first sip."

Holy hell, she did not need this man noticing anything about her body. That didn't stop the full-body awareness his voice prompted. The noise carried on behind him, and even though the guys were working, she felt their not-so-subtle glances.

But while he was being so amenable and *friendly* . . . "Thank you for the coffee. I appreciate it. Sorry for being so grumpy."

"No worries."

She couldn't shake the feeling he was placating her, and she didn't like it. "About the fence."

His brows rose, and he hooked a thumb over his shoulder. "I'm going to have my carpenter look at it. He'll give me an estimate."

Grace was more than a little intrigued by all the people and what changes he was making to the house and property. Keeping her focus, she walked around the fence, to his side, to the spot where she'd busted the wood.

She crouched, looked at it. "It just needs two slats replaced. I could do that myself. A little paint, it would be fine. Doesn't mean we have to redo the whole thing."

Noah wandered over, crouched beside her. She took a drink of coffee so she didn't inhale the scent of his cologne or soap or whatever made him smell like the ocean at night.

"It's old. It needs to be fixed."

Grace stood. "Perhaps, but it doesn't need to be right now."

Noah stood. She wished she were taller so she didn't have to tip her head back.

"You damaged my property. I don't think it's crossing a line to want it fixed." His tone was equal parts reasonable and authoritative.

Grace's grip on the cup tightened. "I'm offering to fix it. One portion was damaged. That doesn't mean I should have to foot the bill for a paint job on the whole thing."

"Half. Half the bill."

The more reasonable his tone, the more irritated she became. "You have more than enough happening right now. I just moved in. I need a bit of time. Let me fix it myself and in a couple weeks, I'll get some paint and take care of both sides."

There. He absolutely could not refuse an offer like that. She didn't know where she was going to find the time to paint it, but she'd shift things around, hold off on the rooms inside.

"It's nice you feel confident, Grace. I appreciate the offer but I'm not looking to wrap some duct tape around the post and call it a day." He gestured to the guys. "As you can see, I have plans for my place. I like pleasing aesthetics."

If she didn't need the coffee so bad, she'd be tempted to pour it on him. "First of all, I could fix this fence faster and better than any of these guys you're paying. Second, do not talk down to me about how things look. If you were that concerned, your hedges would be out by now rather than having them look like misshapen sloped blobs."

A guy in a backward baseball cap had started to approach but stopped when Grace's voice rose.

Noah's jaw tightened but he glanced toward the guy. "Sorry, Kyle. I just need a minute to resolve something with my *neighbor*."

His attitude was fuel on her agitated fire. "No. We're done. Take it or leave it. I can fix this myself and paint on my own schedule or you can forget me chipping in."

He shook his head, lowering his arms so his hands rested on

his hips. "I don't think you want to go head-to-head like this." He leaned in, his gaze animated. "You're in over your head. There's an easy fix to all of this. We forget about the fence if, say, you sell me your place at a tidy profit?"

She shoved the coffee at his chest. He stepped back with an "*oof*," taking the cup.

"I'm not selling my house." She whirled on Kyle, who looked incredibly uncomfortable. "Do you have some extra two-by-fours? A saw I could use? Whatever you'd use to fix this little break in the fence here? Could I borrow those items?"

Kyle's gaze widened and he looked back and forth between her and Noah. She turned to Noah.

"Let's make a deal. I'll fix this *my way*. If Kyle thinks he or one of his guys could have done better, thinks I did a half-ass job, or that it looks like crap, you win. I'll pay for half the fence painting and repair."

Noah regarded her carefully. Kyle just looked like he wanted to run in the opposite direction.

"If," she said, "it's professional-looking enough that you can't cry like a spoiled child about it, then we're even. You paint it if you want but I'm not paying. Also, you stop asking about buying my house."

She heaved out a breath, feeling like she'd run around her yard several times.

"I just wanted to run something by you," Kyle said, his words stumbling over one another.

"What would you use to fix the fence here, Kyle?" Noah pointed.

The worker's heavy sigh permeated the air. "Couple of two-by-fours cut to fit. Sander to smooth them out. Some primer, matching paint on those two slats. Might not be a perfect match but it'd be damn close."

Noah nodded, held Grace's gaze. "You fix it to my standards."

"That's not fair. You'll just say it isn't good enough to get your way."

"Fine. You fix it to Kyle's standards. If he says it's as good as he could have done, I won't ask for your half if I decide to paint the whole fence."

Her chest was tight; her limbs were jittery. "What about my house? Will you stop asking to buy it?"

His smile snuck up on her with its charm. "Where's the fun in that?" He held out a hand. "What do you say? Deal?"

Because she knew better than to shake without being sure, she clarified. "Kyle, you'll be unbiased?"

The guy took off his hat, swiped his hair back, and readjusted it on his head. "I'm getting paid either way so yeah. Though I really did need to ask you something, Noah."

But Noah didn't respond. Grace grasped his hand, hating the spark that soared up her arm like a missile.

"We have a deal. I just need to change."

7

Noah took stock of his emotions. Definitely a bit pissed off. Intrigued—was that an emotion? He couldn't hide the impressed. Grace had a temper and going toe-to-toe with her made him feel almost energized. Which likely made him an ass. His mother had forced him and all of his siblings to do counseling when she'd divorced his father. In Noah's opinion, feelings were better left undiscussed. Talking about them only muddled them up. But he couldn't deny he was feeling myriad things when it came to his next-door neighbor.

After finishing up an email that laid out the agenda for his next SCI—Squishy Cat Industries—meeting with his brothers, he headed downstairs, checked out the progress on the wall between his kitchen and living room. Kyle was nowhere to be seen, and neither was the wall.

"Damn. That looks great," Noah said, staring at the place where the wall used to be. See? He could do this. He didn't need some expert telling him what looked best—though he still planned on seeing about design help. He'd walked into this room the first time and just felt like . . . he was holding his breath. *Now, I can breathe*. He loved the open concept.

"Pretty easy demo," one of Kyle's guys said. Josh should be there soon. He'd know everyone's name.

"Great." What else could he say? He went in search of Kyle, leaving the guys to finish cleaning up the debris of making his ideas come to life. Wes's teasing about getting his hands dirty nagged at the back of his brain. *What am I supposed to do? Offer to sweep up? I couldn't take down the wall. Probably would have brought the house down. I'm paying these guys to do it and it's not like overseeing the entire project isn't work.* He'd never been on-site for a job from beginning to end.

Kyle was pulling a block of wood off his saw setup. Noah wandered over. "Hey, you don't mind letting my neighbor use a bit of wood for her attempt at proving a point?"

Kyle turned, set the wood down. "You underestimated her. She's done."

Noah's head snapped up, turned in the direction of the fence. "What the hell?" He stalked over to see Grace standing up, brushing off her jeans. She pushed a pair of safety goggles up and onto her head.

"Hey, neighbor," she said.

Noah glowered at her. He'd returned ten emails, made himself a sandwich, talked with the guys. She'd become a carpenter in that time? Who the hell was this woman?

"Who helped you?" He leaned in to inspect the work. The damage had been minimal. Really, he was just trying to nudge her over the cliff. He figured the money would appeal to her—money appealed to everyone. But no, she'd gone and issued a challenge and infused him with . . . what? Life? Energy? Indignation?

"No one helped me. Are you always like this?" She picked up a hammer and Noah stepped back, making her grin. "I'm not going to hit you with it no matter how irritating you are."

His grin came out of nowhere. "Guess I should be thankful. I wouldn't put it past you. So far, in our brief history, you've sent attack dogs after me, insulted my hedging skills, and broken my fence."

A subtle pink glow lit up her cheeks, and something twisted in Noah's chest. He ignored it because it wasn't the focus here.

"Tequila and Lime are hardly attack dogs. They just wanted your paddle."

He started to speak and she put up a hand, that shade of pink deepening. "Don't. I heard it as I was saying it. Also, you have no hedging skills and your fence is now fixed by me."

"So, you're a dog walker, hedge expert, and carpenter?"

"I told you, I'm many things. But mostly, I'm an interior designer. I'm just about finished with my degree in design. But this?" She pointed at the fence. "That's simple maintenance. It's fixed. I'll throw some paint on. Dion thinks he can match the shade."

Noah looked around, then back at her. "Who's Dion?"

When she shook her head, a pitying look in her gaze, his shoulders stiffened.

"He's one of the men working for you. I think he's inside right now."

He did *not* like the way she was looking at him. He hadn't met every person here yet, so sue him.

"Hey, Grace, thanks for the recommendation. My wife got us reservations for tomorrow." Kyle joined them, taking the hammer from Grace.

"Reservations for where?" Why did he feel like he'd stepped out of his own life for days?

"It's Kyle's anniversary. He wanted to suggest somewhere unique for dinner because his wife is a foodie. I was just telling him about a farm-to-table restaurant that cooks the food tableside."

Noah's head spun. She'd fixed his fence, made friends with his workers, and looked like she stepped out of a sexy reality television show about home renovations.

"So? Are we good? We can forgo you trying to gouge my bank account with your silly painting nonsense?"

Jesus Christ. I've dined with heads of state and this woman just called me silly. Where am I? Noah needed a run, a stiff drink, and ten minutes alone with this woman, without his staff peering over his shoulder, to talk her into just moving the hell away.

"Fine. We're even."

She tilted her head. "Not quite."

"Excuse me?" He put his hands on his hips.

Kyle covered a laugh, poorly, and slipped away.

"I want a tour of your house. You can give me that in exchange for being a grumpy old man."

He felt like steam might come out of his ears. "There are so many things wrong with what you just said. I'm thirty-three. Nowhere near old."

"Is that a no?"

"Why do you want to see my house?"

"Because I love seeing different spaces and it looks like you're doing a lot of work. Seeing the before and after is my favorite. Well, that and all the steps in between. I love seeing what something can become."

She shrugged and Noah's heart tugged. He felt like she'd just opened a little window to herself and slammed it shut as soon as she realized it.

"Never mind. I have to get going. I don't mind painting these pieces but I have to do it later."

"You can see my house." He spat the words out like he had no control over his own speech.

"Yeah?" Her gaze lit up and he thought of deep, rich chocolate.

His stomach tightened with unfamiliar feelings. "Yeah. Just knock on my door when you have time."

She grinned. "Come and knock on your door?" She sang the words.

He stared at her.

"Seriously?"

"What's happening?"

"Theme song for *Three's Company*?" She stared, her lips parting.

"Never seen it."

Grace rolled her eyes. He was pretty sure he'd never had some-one show so much exasperation with him in such a short period of time. "Don't get out much, huh?"

"You don't make any sense," Noah said, unsure if that was a good thing or not. "Why aren't you painting the fence now?" He didn't mean to sound demanding and he actually didn't care, but for some reason he sort of liked talking to her. Even when they were arguing.

"I have to go paint faces."

The guys started cleaning up behind them after Kyle hollered that it was time to close down for the day. Machines stopped and he could just barely hear the waves rolling again. One of his favorite sounds.

"How many jobs do you have?"

Her smile lifted something inside of him that was equal parts interesting and annoying. "As many as it takes. But hopefully, one day soon, just one. You?"

He chuckled when he thought about it. "Just one I guess. But it's varied. I buy, sell, renovate, and reconfigure buildings, com-panies, and corporations."

She nodded, leaned against the fence she'd fixed, comfortable in her own skin. It was soft, sexy skin. *Do not go there.* Maybe he should ask Josh to set him up with someone.

"Ahh. That makes sense. I thought I smelled some sort of ex-ecutive scent on you."

He was pretty sure that was an insult. "I think that's the scent of success."

She pushed off the fence. "Everyone has a different definition of that word. See you later, Noah."

She strode around the fence, once again leaving him staring after her and questioning himself.

8

Grace got into her vehicle and laid her head back against the seat with a very heavy sigh. Her best friend, Rosie, a fellow design student she'd met one day four years ago, did the same. Their moves were choreographed like synchronized swimmers'. Grace would have laughed but she was too tired.

"How can seven-year-old *children* be so exhausting?" Rosie asked.

Grace turned her head to see that her friend's eyes were closed, her black curls surrounding her rounded cheeks. "There were just so many of them."

"If I have kids, they'll be allowed two friends max at a party," Rosie vowed, opening her eyes but not lifting her head.

Grace, not having the same option, started her vehicle and backed out of the driveway, casting one last glance at her teacher/mentor/idol's beautiful suburban home. Joanna Kern had it all: the career, supportive husband, beautiful home inside and out, and mostly human children. Okay, the kids should be cut some slack due to sugar highs and whatever child pheromones they had that made them ask *so many* questions.

"I want two I think but I'd really prefer they come several years apart," Grace said, though the thought of being someone's mother terrified her to her soul. She did not want to repeat Tammy's mistakes, and it was a struggle every day just to get up and make sure she didn't turn out anything like her mother in every other aspect of her life.

"I'm so glad you're driving. Sorry if I fall asleep while you're talking," Rosie said around a yawn.

"That's what he said," Grace said on a weary laugh. Between getting woken up earlier than she wanted, the stress of dealing with her neighbor, and then the party, she was looking forward to a shower, cozy jammies, and a glass of wine. Maybe a home-reno show.

"Speaking of things he said, did your neighbor back off on the fence?" Rosie fiddled with the radio, bouncing around from station to station before landing on 96.2 SUN.

Grace had texted Rosie last night, upset about the idea of paying for the cost of the fence right after she'd sent an e-transfer to Tammy. "I fixed it today actually. Even he couldn't complain about the job I did. He tried. I still have to paint the two slats I replaced but he'll have to wait."

"What an entitled jerk," Rosie said.

Something in her tone told Grace there was more coming. She switched lanes so she could jump on the freeway that would take them back to Harlow Beach.

"Have you googled him?"

Grace snorted. "I try to get to know a guy before I do that."

Rosie's laugh filled the vehicle. It was loud and infectious. "I'd actually be okay with that if you did, in fact, let yourself get to know guys."

This again. "I've told you, I'm not looking for flings. I want to find the guy that complements the life I'm building."

"Despite your mom's less than stellar example, you know you can date and even have sex without falling into a man's clutches, right? You're in control. It's okay to have some fun before you find the one. In fact, it's pretty hard to find the one without dating."

"Did you have a point?" Grace took the exit, adjusting her hands on the wheel. She wanted one of those cars that drove themselves. Or a car service for when she was tired. *Noah Jansen probably has a driver. And a butler. Probably doesn't know either of their names.*

Rosie dug through her purse, pulled out her phone. Grace saw her touch the screen from the corner of her eye.

"Noah Jansen of the New York Jansens, thirty-three, is an American real estate developer, socialite, and the son of business magnate Nathaniel Jansen. Jansen's grandfather is best remembered for his contributions to a variety of New York City neighborhoods including the Wells Street Community Center in Harlem. Noah works for his father's corporation along with his two brothers. He's been linked to several well-known women but remains single."

"*Pfft.* Probably because of his attitude. He might have money but he thinks women can't fix fences and that he can buy whatever he wants."

"Dude is rich. And hot. You failed to mention that."

"Did not," Grace said, whipping her chin in her friend's direction. "My first description of him was sexy, hot surfer dude."

"Okay. That's fair but you failed to follow up on that after saying he lived next door."

"It's not something I want to dwell on."

Rosie put her phone away. "He's likely not used to having anyone stand up to him."

Grace agreed but only nodded. She couldn't figure him out. He had a multitude of personalities, not all of which she liked, but there were hints of something underneath. Like a bedraggled cabinet, stuck in a corner, waiting for someone to put in the time and effort to peel back the layers, see what it once was or could be.

"Want me to come help paint this week?"

"I'd love some help but you have the same projects I do. I don't want to take up your time. I appreciate you coming today. Especially once I got there. I thought those kids were going to take me out."

Rosie's laugh was interrupted by another yawn. "They were pretty excited to see the paint lady. I don't mind. I want to see the house now that you're in it. I want my stamp on it, too."

Grace's chest warmed. "You're the best."

"I've mentioned that before," Rosie said.

Once she dropped her friend off at her apartment, Grace was itching to get home. She pulled into her driveway, surprised to see Noah outside, at the fence, on his knees. The sun was halfway to setting, casting gorgeous colors through the sky. Was he painting?

She got out of her vehicle, leaving her supplies in the back but grabbing her purse.

"Hey," she said, approaching him. As soon as he looked up, she had to bite her lip to keep from laughing. He had white paint across his probably very expensive T-shirt, on the underside of his jaw, all over his hands, and a bit on his jeans. She glanced at the fence. "Looks like you got some of that paint in the right place."

His gaze narrowed and he set the brush he was holding down with a splat. More paint spattered onto the handle. "Laugh if you want. I thought I'd be done in a half hour. Instead, I've been at it for hours, I painted part of my backyard white, and I've already changed once."

She bit her lip again. He was about halfway on his side. She crouched, picked up the wet rag he hadn't used, and used two fingers to pick up the brush and clean it with the cloth.

"Is it your first time painting something outdoors?" He'd need to wash his hands or the handle would get covered again. She glanced at him when he remained silent, his lips pressed firmly together.

She set the brush down on the edge of the paint tray gently. "Wait. Is this your first time painting?"

"So?" The one word was filled with heat, and she would have gotten up and walked off, left him to his fence finger painting, but it was also easy to hear the fatigue and frustration.

She settled on her knees. "So, nothing. It was a question, not an accusation. Painting is harder than people think. It takes practice and something awkward like this isn't the best start. Usually, people start with a big wall or something."

He stared at her, and even though it made her heart jump around like an ADHD bunny, she held his gaze. "You fixed those slats in less time than it took me to reply to some emails."

She offered a smile. "My mom wasn't the best at household chores. We didn't have money to get things fixed. I learned to . . . tinker." And make do.

"I still own four properties in New York. I have several holdings here in California, including this house. I'm a little pissed off to learn I can't paint a fence without looking like I poured a can of it over me."

"I only own that house and my car. Both were gifted to me. Everyone has their skills."

One half of his mouth tipped up. "Nice spin on it. I should clean up. Start over."

"I could help you if you want." The words popped out of her mouth before she remembered the shower, the wine, and the home-reno show. Plus her homework.

"Why would you?"

She stood, didn't hide the eye roll. "God, you're so skeptical."

He stood as well, his gaze going between her and the fence before staying on Grace. "You were right about it not needing to be replaced. Kyle agreed with you. You were also right about the hedges."

She looked toward the place where the hedges had been, pushing aside the reasoning he'd given her when he talked of removing them.

"Thanks for the view," she said, inexplicably excited about a glass of wine on her back porch.

"I could pay you to finish the fence."

Grace's jaw dropped. She pulled herself together with a deep breath. "I don't want your money. I said I'd help you. Maybe if you didn't hire someone to do every little thing, you'd know how to do something as simple as paint."

She started to walk away, thinking a walk on the beach, barefoot, might soothe her more than wine.

"Hey."

She turned, met his irritated glare. "What?"

"You said painting was hard."

"I lied to make you feel better," she snapped.

Noah's gaze widened. "You . . ." He broke off and surprised the hell out of her when a laugh burst free. He bent at the waist, messy hands leaving prints on his jeans. When he straightened, his features had softened with happiness. The sight of him stole her breath. Which also pissed her off.

"You lied to make me feel better."

It wasn't a question, so she nodded, pointed to the fence. "Smooth, even strokes back and forth. Pretty simple."

His gaze heated, and Grace realized that her words could be . . . misconstrued. Her pulse sped up. With the laughter still visible in his gaze, the easy set of his jaw from his smile, he was more than just attractive. He was the kind of guy she'd pin on her "Dreams for another day" board on Pinterest. Liam Hemsworth coming out of the waves. Henry Cavill comfortable in his own skin. *Noah Jansen, socialite and elitist. Don't forget those parts*, she told her wonky heart.

"The paint," she said sharply. "You need to have enough on your brush but don't let it drip."

"Good advice," he said. Was she imagining his voice had gone husky?

"Well, good night."

"You said you'd help," he reminded her.

She probably shouldn't waste time on a guy who annoyed her as much as intrigued her, but she wanted to be a good neighbor. The truth was, she wanted to be a great everything. Student, designer, person, friend. Neighbor. Daughter. Some of those weren't attainable, but maybe she could ease the tension that usually sat between them. Then, the next time she toppled over her fence, he wouldn't try to make her pay for it.

"I did. But I don't want your money."

"I get that. You wanted to see my place. A tour for a paint tutorial?"

She fought the grin. "You already agreed to the tour."

He nodded, wiped his hand over his mouth, and Grace had to hold back the laughter when she saw that the paint had smeared farther across his cheek.

"You show me how to paint, help me out and I'll help you paint something."

Hmm. Grace looked at the damage he'd done to the fence. Uneven strokes, gaps where he'd missed spots entirely. "Is that a fair trade?"

He laughed. "You're a hard-ass. And I've negotiated with more than my fair share of them. What do you want?"

She didn't *want* anything, but, somehow, the act of negotiating rather than accepting a simple kindness made him a nicer person. Weird.

"Okay. I'll help. You have to clean all the supplies and help me stain my back deck."

He hesitated. She arched her brows.

"That works the same as painting, I'm guessing?"

She laughed, grabbed the packet of brushes he'd tossed to the grass. "Yes. You know you could watch YouTube videos to learn this stuff, right?"

He picked up his now-clean brush before she could tell him to wash his hands first. "That doesn't seem nearly as fun. Or educational."

Grace wasn't sure who was getting the better end of the deal, and she never got that glass of wine, but maybe she got something better: on her neighbor's good side.

9

Noah was looking up the cost of jerseys when Rob texted him to tell him the kids were practicing at the rec center not too far from his house today. They switched up locations to better accommodate the kids. Apparently, most of the guys skipped last time because they figured the tournament wouldn't happen.

Noah might not know how to paint a fence—well, he did now—but he knew how to help organize charities and bring in money. He sent Rob a text confirming the time, then sent his mom a text to ask for some ideas.

She texted back quickly.

Mom
I'll think on it. I like knowing you're thinking about ways to make the area better. Means you're settling in. I hope California does for you what it did for Chris.

Noah rolled his eyes but had a smile on his face when he texted back.

> Noah
>
> Unlike your youngest son, I didn't need any help loosening up. Things are good. I just want to help a friend.
>
> Mom
>
> How's your house? Send me some pictures of the work you have people doing.

He knew she didn't mean anything by it. It was his standard operating procedure—he'd swing by projects, take some photos, send them to the art directors or publicity for his father's company, and move on to the next thing.

> Noah
>
> I painted my own fence last night. Should have taken a before and after picture of that.
>
> Mom
>
> Sorry. I need to sit down.

Noah smirked. He came by being a smart-ass naturally.

> Noah
>
> Funny. Have some faith in me. I'm really diving in this time.
>
> Mom
>
> Glad to hear it, sweetie. I'll get back to you on ideas.

Once Grace taught him to stain, he might even do his own. The thought of Grace filled him with mixed feelings. While she dug her heels in on the house, would it be such a bad idea to cozy up to her? Learn a little? Design was her forte after all. *She might suck at it.* He had a feeling, though, that Grace Travis did well at anything she put her mind to.

He had to admit, only to himself, that he'd been more than a little shocked at the ease with which she'd wielded a hammer, paintbrush, sander. It wasn't a sexist thing—it was just that he *hired* people to do these things. He enjoyed seeing the before and after but watching her *during* made him want to experience it for himself. She had a dozen jobs he could see just from the outside that needing doing on her house. It hadn't occurred to him that in addition to everything he already knew about her, which wasn't that much, she was a regular handywoman as well.

The knock on the door pulled him out of his thoughts entirely.

Pulling the door open, he grinned at his assistant, Josh, who held up grocery bags. "Hey, man. How's it going?"

"Better now. I haven't eaten since this morning," Noah said, shutting the door behind them.

"You've heard of home delivery, right?"

Noah grabbed the bags, held them up. "Yup. Just got it."

Josh whistled behind him. "Damn. It looks awesome without the wall."

He set the bags on the kitchen counter and turned, leaned against it. Yeah, it did. The counters, stove, and sink formed a U shape in the kitchen. From where he stood, he could see clear to the bay window in the living area. It was all one open space. He had some thoughts on what to do with the kitchen to open it up even more. It needed serious updating.

"I'm happy with it. I'm thinking about doing something similar upstairs with two of the bedrooms," Noah said.

"Not my area of expertise but I definitely like the open space better." Josh started to put the groceries away, pulling all of Noah's favorites out of the bag. "I printed out the New York contracts for you to go over. Once they have your signature, all of your real estate holdings are officially on the West Coast."

It was bittersweet news, since coming here had caused a bigger rift between him and his dad. Well, a more visible one. Instead of slowly releasing more opportunity and trust in Noah, his father had started micromanaging the acquisitions department that was supposed to be Noah's. The constant second-guessing and overrides of solid deals pushed Noah toward facing the truth:

he couldn't work under his father even if it meant starting from scratch. *Let's face it, your idea of starting from the bottom is pretty cushy.* He didn't take his advantages lightly, but, like anyone else, he didn't want to be dismissed or made to feel like he couldn't contribute. At least if he failed out here, no one would rub it in his face.

Against his father's loudly voiced opinions, Noah sold the buildings he'd purchased solo—buildings he'd tried and failed to get his father's support on—to fund his California ventures.

"That's great news."

"It is." Josh carried on. "The yard looks way better without the hedges but California law is pretty strict about their palm trees so I brought paperwork for that."

Noah grabbed the bag of bagels, popped one into the toaster. "You get ahold of the land surveyor?" He wanted to make sure the fence lines were accurate all the way around the property. If he could nudge over on Grace's property a little, if the lines showed inaccuracies, it would be a consolation prize for not getting his way. *Don't give up yet. You're only in the beginning stages of negotiating with her—it's the best part.*

"Done. They're backed up. Can't get here for another couple of weeks. Just curious, why don't you leave the lot next door for a later time? It's not like you don't have a ton going on."

He didn't want to get into the personal sentiments that made him envision what he was trying to build. "If I leave it too long, she's going to settle in. Plus, I've got the woman from the magazine considering me. If I tell her those plans, make her realize it's not just an interior job, there's a better chance of me getting the magazine spread."

Josh passed him the cream cheese. "Okay. That's fair. You're banking on that spread being your introduction to the real estate world on your own terms."

"Exactly. It'll showcase both my acquisitions capabilities and the development piece. People love a personal story. The fact that

I'm making this into a place to live will resonate. I've got a few of those designers you researched for me coming by to take a look, share some thoughts."

Grace popped into his brain again like one of those animals in that game Whac-A-Mole. She just kept appearing no matter how often he tried to push her from his thoughts. She was equal parts demanding, stubborn, and absolutely gracious. The time she'd taken last night, when her exhaustion was clear, had left him feeling very . . . unsettled. He didn't like the burst of affection he'd felt for her in those couple of hours they'd worked. There was no room for that when he had a big-picture objective.

"I'm looking into office space for you and your brothers. I've got a list for you to take a look at. For now, though, I thought you should set up an actual home office. Not that your island countertop isn't efficient." Josh grinned at him.

Noah pointed to the kitchen window. The palm trees blocked most of it but there was a hint of the ocean in sight. "Great views."

"They are. Want me to order furniture?"

The toaster popped out his bagel. Josh helped himself to a soda. His assistant in New York had recommended Josh when Noah announced his move. So far, the guy was great. He'd judged Josh based on looks—much like Grace had judged him—when he first met him. The guy was a poster child for the California surfing scene. He'd shown up to the house for his interview in board shorts and a loose Hawaiian shirt, with two surfboards on the roof of his car. Despite appearances, he was organized as hell, his résumé was solid gold, and Noah felt lucky to have him in his corner. *See. You have more friends than just your brothers.*

If he was paying him to be around, did that count? He could put in more effort, but like Josh said, why search for something that's right in front of you? The way he'd snapped at Rob still grated on his nerves. He wasn't usually the kind of person to take things out on other people. Going head-to-head with, say,

Grace? That was fine. But he didn't make a habit of pushing people away. Maybe he'd forgotten how to make a circle of friends because in New York he hadn't needed to.

"You okay?"

Noah looked up from his bagel. "Yeah. Fine. Just wondering where your favorite place to surf is."

"I have a friend who owns a place at Laguna. It's busy because of tourists but if you hit the right time of day, there's nothing else like it."

Noah swallowed his bite while Josh sipped his soda. Clearing his throat, determined to build a life for himself on the West Coast, he asked, "Maybe we could go together sometime."

Josh paused in the act of lowering his drink from his mouth. "Sure."

There. Surf plans with a buddy. Sort of. His gut swirled like the waves he was asking about hitting. "Or maybe we could just grab a beer or something. Whatever. When you have time. No pressure or anything."

Josh set his can down, then swept a hand over his slightly-too-long hair. "Right. Listen, man. Sir. Noah. I'm flattered—"

Noah choked on his bagel, cutting Josh off. His brows furrowed and he came closer, slapping Noah on the arm, which wouldn't have been at all effective if Noah were actually choking, which he wasn't. Not really. He'd just swallowed wrong because he realized he'd pretty much asked his assistant out.

Shaking his head, backing up, he grabbed a glass and filled it with water. It was lukewarm but he didn't care. "I'm fine. I'm fine."

Josh lifted his hands. Noah took a deep breath, swallowed down some more water, then forced himself to meet Josh's gaze.

"I'm not into you," Noah blurted.

Josh folded his arms over his chest. "Okay. Why'd you ask me out then?"

Every curse word he knew flew through his head. "I didn't.

Well, I didn't mean to. I'm just trying to make some friends, get to know California. As I was saying it, I heard how it sounded. Then the look on your face. Seriously, man. I'm sorry." Shit. Was he making it worse? "Not that you aren't a good-looking guy and all that."

Josh's eyes widened. "Jesus Christ, man. Shut up. With all due respect, seeing as you pay me." Josh burst out laughing.

Noah winced. "I'm into women."

Josh laughed harder, bending at the waist. "Noted. Me too." Fortunately, the awkwardness pressing down on him released when their gazes locked and both of them laughed their asses off to the point that Noah's eyes watered.

"Okay, then. I'm going to get going. Text me with a list of what you need to get done," Josh said when the laughter tapered off.

Walking him to the door, pushing down the embarrassment, glad as hell his brothers never had to find out about this, he thought about what Josh had said. "I'll make a list of office furniture. Don't think I need any design ideas on that front. Just needs to be functional."

"Sounds good." Josh opened the door to reveal Grace and another woman standing on his doorstep.

"Hey," Grace said, her gaze landing on Noah. A zip of pleasure ran through him like a fuse being lit. Her dark hair was in a ponytail, her face makeup-free. She looked happy. Carefree. *It's nothing. Too long alone, that's all.*

"Hi." He wasn't quite sure where they stood on the status of their back-and-forth with each other. She'd wanted to throttle him the other day, but last night she'd taken pity on his pathetic painting skills.

Josh stepped back, his mouth slightly open. Grace looked at the woman beside her; then both of them came in. Josh shut the door.

"This is my friend Rosie. Rosie, this is Noah, my neighbor. And?" She looked at Josh, who was looking at Rosie.

"Josh. Josh Langston." He extended his hand to Rosie, who was staring equally as hard at him. His surfer hair and vibe were a contrast to the tan-skinned woman with black hair, sharp cheekbones, and bright red lips. She was easily six feet tall, making Grace look petite among the three of them.

The air nearly crackled between the two of them, which made it less likely that anyone would notice that Noah couldn't help looking at Grace, who bit her lip. She arched her brows, her lips twitching. At least he wasn't imagining things.

Noah clapped his assistant on the shoulder, ending the staring contest. "Did you say you were leaving?"

Josh turned his head long enough to glare at Noah. "No. I thought we were making a list of what you needed."

Noah didn't even try to hide his grin. "Right. I forgot. Come on in, ladies. Josh just stocked me up on groceries. Can I get you some coffee? Juice? Soda?" There. He might have stumbled making new friends but he knew how to host. He was a damn good host.

"No, thank you. I wondered if we could borrow the ladder Kyle left in your backyard. Also, Rosie knew you owed me a tour. If you don't have time now, it's okay, but if you do, then she wanted to see your place, too."

There was an odd feeling pressing against his rib cage. He couldn't explain it. Sharp but not entirely unpleasant. "I have time for a tour. Are you a designer, too, Rosie?"

"I am. I'd say I'm the best in the class but I'm tied with my best friend here," Rosie said, nudging Grace's hip.

When Noah glanced at Josh, he saw that his assistant was still in a state of . . . lust? Awe? What the hell was the goofy look on that guy's face? He'd only ever seen it on Chris's face before. *Uh-oh. Watch out, buddy.*

"She's just saying that so I'll take it easy on her in the design contest."

"Interior design, I presume?" Josh asked, finding his voice.

Noah gave him a thumbs-up on his speaking efforts, earning him another glare. "What contest?"

Grace looked at Josh. "Yes." Then at Noah. "Our teacher pulled some strings to offer one to two students an internship at a prestigious LA-based firm. We have an extracurricular design opportunity if we want to compete for it."

He might not know her well but he knew that Grace would be all over a competition.

"That's really great. You're in school?" Josh asked, leaning one shoulder against the wall, looking far too cozy for a guy who claimed to have things to do.

Rosie stepped closer as she answered him. "We're finishing up. I cannot wait to be done and start my real life." Rosie turned in a slow circle, glancing up where the stairs curved to the second level. When she lowered her chin, she met Noah's gaze and he *felt* the assessment. Clearly, Grace had mentioned him.

"Tour?" Josh said a little too loudly. Noah lifted his brows at him.

"Is that okay?" Grace asked.

"Sure." Noah gestured toward the living area. He wondered if she and her friend would have any preliminary thoughts. He could take them under advisement, but the firms he worked with on design back in New York had more than a few years under their collective belts. They definitely weren't newbies not even done with their degrees yet.

"The ladder?" Grace asked as they followed Noah into the open space.

"Right. What are you doing?"

She eyed him curiously. "Does it matter?"

He grinned, feeling that push-pull feeling again. "Is it a secret?"

"Gutters."

Josh and Rosie moved farther into the mostly empty room, but Noah stopped in front of Grace. He heard them chatting like reunited best friends behind him.

"Problem?" Grace crossed her arms over her chest, her mouth turning down on one side.

He ran a hand through his hair. "No. Not a problem, per se. Just wondered if you have your gutter-cleaning license as well."

Grace's gaze went a few degrees cooler. "Why? You want to hire me to do yours?"

He sputtered out a breath. Jesus. She twisted everything he said. "No. I just don't know if it's a good idea to lend you a ladder I don't own. If you get hurt doing your gutters, I could be liable."

"I don't think you would be, technically," Josh said from beside them.

If Grace were a cartoon character, she'd have plumes of smoke coming out of her ears. He lifted his hands in retreat. "Sorry. Forget I asked. Just be careful."

"Sure thing, Dad." Her smile was not friendly.

Josh snickered. "As you can see, this is the living area. Noah had that wall removed. It's opened the place up considerably."

Noah turned, shoved his hands in his pockets. "I take it you're giving the tour?"

Josh mimed zipping his lips, making Noah laugh.

"What he said. That wall really made it feel smaller. I like open spaces."

Grace let out a sigh that made his blood run hot. She and Rosie walked side by side, surveying the open kitchen, talking in some sort of hushed code. When they came back near the guys, Grace's expression lit up.

"I love the bay window. It's gorgeous. It would make a perfect seating area; put in a bench, built-in shelves, you'd have a reading nook. You read, right? The financial section or something?"

Josh's laughter cut through any tension that might have existed. "Don't paint him into a box. He also likes to surf."

He was oddly pleased to see that gentle flush spread over Grace's cheeks.

"The rest of the tour?" she asked.

Pulling himself together, he showed her the four bedrooms, including the master that had a kick-ass tub.

Rosie let out an exaggerated sigh, putting one hand to her head. "I'd marry this tub."

Josh snickered. "I think he's partial to it."

Noah cleared his throat. "I never said I took baths." His brothers would have a field day if they knew that.

"Nothing wrong with loving them," Grace said, eyeing him with amusement.

"No one said love." His tone came out far more clipped than he intended.

"This place kicks ass," Rosie said. They made their way through the house, and Noah was surprised that Grace didn't offer more commentary on her thoughts. He didn't want to ask. He wouldn't ask. She was a student. Not even a professional.

"I'm surprised you don't have more furniture," Grace said when they went back to the kitchen.

"I'm interviewing designers. I have the essentials," he said, nodding toward the big-screen TV and couch.

"Interviewing *interior* designers?" Rosie's voice rose an octave.

Shit. *Way to put that out there. Not awkward at all.* Josh was trying to send some sort of weird-ass signals with his eyes and eyebrows.

Rosie looked back and forth between Grace and Noah, her chin moving up and down in a gentle nod. "Right. Okay. Well, I should go." She looked at Josh.

Josh's gaze locked on Rosie's. "Me too."

"What?" Grace looked at her friend. "You said you were helping me paint."

Rosie looked flustered for all of two seconds. "Rain check? It's not going anywhere."

"Cold, Rosie. Cold."

Her friend winked, and she and Josh left like their asses were on fire. Noah stared after them, a little dumbfounded.

"What the f—"

"My thoughts exactly." Grace's tone was the kind of irritated he'd heard directed only at him. It was kind of nice not to be the reason.

They looked at each other and laughed at the same time. "You think they'll hook up immediately or just exchange numbers?" Grace started for the door.

"I honestly don't want to know. You're leaving?"

"Gutters, remember."

He didn't like the thought of her up on the ladder but he didn't like the thought of *him* up on a ladder either. He especially didn't like the thought of either of them breaking their necks falling off said ladder.

"You should wait until . . ." He trailed off.

She turned at the door. "Until? Some big, strong man can do it? Until I can hire someone?"

"At least until you have someone holding the ladder." He wondered if she was too stubborn to ask. The strain of silence stretched between them.

He broke first. "I'll hold the ladder."

The grin she gave him made him feel like he'd won a prize he didn't even want. "That's very neighborly of you."

Frowning, irritated to be helping her, at the fact that he *wanted* to help her, he just shook his head. "Don't get used to it."

10

Grace wanted to shove the debris she yanked out of the gutters in Noah's face. If she weren't on a schedule of chores that needed doing, she might have told him to shove his offer of help. But beggars fell off ladders when they climbed them without a spotter. *Not exactly the saying but whatever.* Damn, her mood had taken a serious dive. Seven texts from Tammy, Rosie ditching her for her own hot surfer guy, and Noah's attitude created a ball of irritation she wanted to take a sledgehammer to.

The gutters actually weren't that bad, but it was something she wanted done before she borrowed Morty's pressure washer. Less mess overall was her way of thinking.

"You're leaning too far to the left. You're going to fall," Noah shouted up.

"You are stomping all over my nerves," she muttered.

"What?"

"Nothing."

Just a little more. She still couldn't believe the chemistry between Rosie and Josh. Had there been kindling close by, a fire would have ignited. *You don't want that.* She wasn't looking for an I-want-to-tear-your-clothes-off relationship. Though, maybe if she let herself have one, she wouldn't feel like she was going to poke Noah with a rake. *You could tear his clothes off. Argh. No. No thank you.* There was sexual tension, then there was supreme irritation brought on by my Neighbor Know-It-All.

"Seriously, Grace. Don't lean so far over."

She looked down, tossed the tool she was using to clean the gutters. The thump on the grass made Noah jump, shaking the ladder.

"If I fall, it'll be because you can't even hold a ladder." She started climbing down, not realizing he'd stayed in his spot until she felt his presence at her back.

"Got down safely, didn't you?"

She turned on the ladder, glaring at him. "Yay. You have ladder-holding skills. Too bad I don't have any stickers left from the birthday party." She winced. Why did he make her lose her temper when that really wasn't her style?

"Ouch." He stepped back.

"Why did you offer to help if you were just going to complain?" Grace asked, pulling the gloves off and tossing them on the ground.

"Because you would have done it anyway." His voice rose and Grace glanced around, grateful no one was out on their own lawns. The beach was pretty packed today, but their yards were removed enough from the crowds.

"News flash, Mr. Money, people can and do do things alone. Some people, myself included, are very capable of getting chores done without hiring people to do it. You might be shocked to hear this but," she said, leaning in closer. Which she'd realize was a mistake. "I have a full fridge of food that I bought all by myself."

He stepped forward so their toes and noses nearly touched. "Stop being crabby because I didn't want you to fall."

"This isn't about falling," she spat back, her breathing going heavy and shallow at the same time. Or maybe her heart got heavy. Something weird was happening in her chest.

"You are the most stubborn woman I've ever met."

"Awesome. You're the most irritating man I've ever met. And I *lived* with Morty."

When he reared back slightly, she expected a scathing remark. Instead, he laughed.

Grace's lips quirked. Talking to Noah Jansen was like being on a Tilt-A-Whirl. *What would kissing him be like?* Nope. Hard stop sign on that one. What was she thinking?

"I'm getting compared to a grumpy old man; I asked my assistant if he wanted to grab a beer sometime only to have him think I was hitting on him. I used to be the charmer in the family. Maybe California isn't so good for me," he said, all of the fight going out of his stance.

Her heart did that funny thing where it took pity on him. Like last night with the fence.

"You're just adjusting. Clearly, you're used to bossing people around."

"Ha. Yeah. I'm good at that part." An unpleasant expression came over his face, making her wonder what he was thinking.

"I should go. I need to get the den ready to paint."

His jaw dropped open. "You just finished the gutters."

She laughed. "Yes. I did. Now I have to paint or I won't be able to until next weekend. Kind of got a lot going on right now."

He looked down at the ground, then up through enviable thick lashes. "You want help?"

It was her turn to laugh. "No thanks." She looked over at the fence, which had actually dried nicely, but she couldn't help but remember how flustered he'd been when she showed up.

"Because you think I'll mess it up?" His shoulders stiffened again.

"Because I think you'll slow me down." She grinned.

"I could probably do it faster than you." His brows rose in challenge.

Why the hell did that piss her off and intrigue her at the same time? Maybe something was wrong with her libido. *It's called not-getting-any-atitis. It's making your vision skewed. No. Nothing wrong with your vision. No one could say this man isn't gorgeous.* She was only human.

"Wanna bet?"

His grin widened. A kick straight in the stomach. That smile. It erased all the fatigue and frustration she'd carried all day.

"Unless you're scared to lose?"

Grace stepped forward. "To you? No."

He eyed her in a way she hadn't seen before. A way that made her skin heat. A way she liked way too much.

"What's going through that brain of yours, Grace?" he asked, his voice low. Had she really met this man only just over a week ago? The way he said her name felt like a caress.

"Wondering what I should ask for when I win the bet," she lied.

He chuckled. "*If* you win."

"Sure. Sure. That's what I meant."

She continued to watch him, pretending she wasn't dying to know what he was thinking.

"I say we do the neighborly thing and help each other out while still making it a challenge." He folded his arms across his chest, leaned a shoulder against the wall. She did her best not to stare at how it made his toned biceps appear bigger. She really needed to get a grip on her libido. *Or his biceps, which would solve both problems.*

"I'm listening."

"We do one house at a time. Yours then mine. We each take a wall, see who can get it done quicker. Bets out of the way. Then we help each other finish."

Wow. Her brain had totally gone somewhere else with that. Which made her stomach do a swirly thing. She should lean against the wall, too. All nonchalant and totally not impacted by the way his gaze was locked on her own.

Slowly, deliberately, she folded her arms across her chest, right under her boobs, tucking her hands in the crooks of her arms. Then she, oh so slowly, hopefully sexily, let her body relax against the wall. The effect would have been so much better if she'd made sure there was actually a wall to lean on. When she fell into the empty space, she nearly toppled over her own feet.

Noah's bark of laughter was quickly replaced by concern as she righted herself. Her arms unfolded on reflex to break an impending fall. If there was anything to be thankful for, it was that she didn't actually fall flat on her face or her ass.

"You okay there, neighbor?" He stepped forward as she rolled her shoulders, wishing she could have an instant do-over. His hands came to her shoulders, squeezing gently.

"Fine." *Shake it off.* "Totally fine. Guess I thought there was a wall there."

His lips twitched. Damn him. "If only you'd pulled the same move a few days ago."

She refused to give in to the urge to duck her head. "The bet." Redirection was the best distraction from her own clumsiness.

Noah dropped his hands. Grace kept her hands at her sides, standing tall. No leaning whatsoever.

"Okay. We measure the walls, make sure they're the same size. One coat each, though we'll probably have to do seconds. Winner gets to name their prize."

Her gaze narrowed. "No way. Clearly defined boundaries. I win, you stop trying to buy my house. You win, you can keep asking but I'll still say no."

"You need to work on your negotiating, Gracie." His eyes heated when he said her name, which confused the hell out of her. She almost started to correct him, despite liking the delicious swirl in her belly that resulted from his tone, when he held up a hand. "Sorry. Grace."

"You win, I'll stop asking. I win, you help me choose some office furniture."

"Why would you want my help?" That almost seemed like a double reward for her, win or lose.

He shrugged. "It's not an important room. I'll answer emails and read contracts in my office."

Did he know he had a knack for turning a good thing into an irritating one? *Whatever. You still win either way.*

"Fine. Deal." She held out her hand.

"Deal."

Several clichés popped into Grace's head on the way back to her place to change and get ready. The most prevalent one was about keeping her enemies close. That's all she was doing.

11

There was no reason to be nervous about *some guy* coming over to help her paint a room. Maybe if it was a guy she could see herself with, a guy who didn't have more moods than she had fabric swatches, she'd understand her less than steady hands. Smoothing out the tarp to protect the floor, she looked around for her phone. How could she misplace something that she used so often? She spotted it on the coffee table.

Rosie had at least texted, which only slightly made up for bailing.

Rosie
Oh. My. God. It's hard to say which of them are hotter.
Girl. How are you going to live next door to him without drooling?
Josh asked for my number. We're going out tomorrow.
Where are you?
Text me back, damn you. I want details. All the details.

She deleted the text she saw from Tammy without reading it. She'd reply to Rosie later. Right now, she needed to chill the hell out, because if she wasn't careful, she'd end up developing a crush on her grumpy neighbor and he might have plans but Grace had plenty of her own. He wasn't getting in the way.

When her phone buzzed again, she was setting up a second tarp along the wall with the window. She smiled, wondering if he'd call her a cheater or appreciate her cleverness.

He should be there any minute. She glanced at her phone again, wary of it being Tammy. Her mom didn't seem to understand the whole connection between actions and consequences. *Ignore your kid for most of her life, putting yourself first, your child becomes an adult who doesn't want much to do with you.*

It was Morty. She smiled at all the errors. Whenever he texted, he muttered and swore, cursing big thumbs and small gadgets.

Jus becuz you mooed don't mean you cant call a duh

She pressed on his number. He answered on the first ring.

"You coulda texted me back," he said instead of hello.

"I could have. But I wanted to hear your cheery voice."

"Ha." After a winded breath, he asked, "You doing okay?"

"Yes, just trying to decipher your text. I'm guessing you don't think I moo and you meant to call yourself a guy?"

"What the hell are you talking about?"

"Nothing. Just check your text when we hang up. How are you?"

"I'm alive."

She rolled her eyes but couldn't help the smile. "This would be a weird conversation if you weren't."

"Be better if you didn't pretend I don't exist anymore."

"I've been gone under two weeks."

"Tilly wants you to come for dinner."

She turned her head when she heard the knock, watched Noah walk in carrying supplies.

"Tilly wants that?"

"What can I say. She likes you for some reason."

Grace laughed. "I miss you, too. Tomorrow good?"

"Good as anything else. Not like our schedule is jam-packed. You need anything?"

Noah set his things down before looking around. His gaze brightened when it landed on Grace.

"Nope. I'm good. See you tomorrow."

She hung up, watched Noah wander around her space. The house wasn't large. It'd probably fit inside of his. But when she walked around, she could almost picture her grandparents living there. Christmases in this very living room, cooking breakfast in the kitchen. Tucking her mom in down the hall in a small bedroom across from their slightly larger one. Her mother never talked about growing up in a way that let Grace picture it. But being here, it was almost like she *felt* more connected to a life she'd never been allowed to know. One that included a family that might have loved her.

"Great bones but it needs a lot of work," he said, slowly turning as she slid her phone into her pocket.

"Excuse me?"

He gestured to the living room. "The house. It's got great bones. The original moldings, the hardwood floors. There's a lot here. But there's also a lot to do. You ever renovated a whole house?"

She arched her brow, thinking of all the differences between them. "No. Can't say I have. This would be the first one I've ever owned. Lots of my classmates work fixing up places or doing construction but I've only ever ventured into the interior aspect. Doesn't mean I can't learn."

"You are a very curious and capable woman."

She beamed at him. "Thank you."

He just laughed. The women he usually hung out with liked different compliments. "We're doing the living room?"

The evening sunset was casting a glow through the uncurtained picture window. Dust motes danced in the soft rays.

"We are. We don't have much in here because, like you, I plan on taking the wall out between the kitchen and living room." She walked forward so he could see the galley-style kitchen that was far too narrow for her tastes.

He walked in, turned around. He was almost too big for the space. "This wall is all cabinets so you won't have to worry about plumbing but what will you do for storage?"

She pointed to the wall beside the door that led to the back porch. "I'll install cupboards along that wall." She turned. "I'm going to put an island here to separate the spaces. I'll be able to move the fridge to that wall, add more counter space there, and the island counter will have storage underneath."

He nodded, a smile lifting one side of his lips. "Smart." He walked through the doorway, back into the living room. "So, we aren't painting this wall. Just that one, the front, and the bits on the side over there?"

She smiled at him, trying not to make it too obvious that she was about to play him hard. "You got it."

With a frown, he put his hands on his hips. His loose board shorts could easily distract her, but she had her game face on now. At least externally.

"How are we going to race?"

She took a deep breath, smiling as she exhaled. "I measured and it turns out that this wall"—she pointed to the one with the window, the very large window—"and this one"—she pointed— "are the same size."

There was a small window on the wall he'd paint that peeked out to the side yard between their homes.

His jaw dropped open and he stepped forward, making her tip her head back. "You're going to cheat."

She laughed, enjoying this more than she had anything else in a long while. "It's not cheating to outmaneuver your opponent. *Neighbor.*"

"You'll paint the one that's mostly window and I get what equals about one and half times the wall space?"

Putting on a pretend sad face, she nodded, then made the mistake of patting him on the chest. Good lord. She could lose chunks of time running her hands over that chest. Pulling her hand back, she went to retrieve the stool from the hallway. When she came back, he was still scowling.

"If it makes you feel any better, I have the disadvantage of height. It's going to be a lot harder for me to trim the edges and do it right."

"Fine. Game on. When you lose, you'll have no excuse."

"If I win, you can't claim it's because of the window. The walls are the same size."

His grin should have scared her with how it made fire dance in his gaze. Instead, all it did was spur her on. Mr. Money thought he could beat her at this? She had something, in this case, he didn't—experience.

"Just remember, you started this."

She couldn't remember who'd started it but at the moment, she didn't care.

They didn't say go until the paint had been poured, they were each set up, and music was blasting through her Bluetooth.

Whether it was the feel of his gaze on her from time to time, the energy between them, the spirit of competition, or just the unsettling attraction she felt for him, Grace felt like she'd drunk a case of Red Bull with a Jolt Cola chaser.

Sweat dotted her neck where little hairs escaped from her bun. She heard him rolling, moving, whistling but stayed focused on her own wall.

She hated doing the edges, around the windows and outlets, but it was a necessary evil. Moving up and down the ladder was going to have her thighs screaming tomorrow; advantage *him*. Stupid tall people. She glanced out of the corner of her eye to see he was adding more paint to his tray. And . . . his wall was almost finished. What the actual hell?

"How did you?" She stopped to stare.

He hadn't cut in anything. He'd taken the damn roller and covered most of the wall. *He* wasn't sweating.

"How did I what?"

Sure, the rolling didn't take long but cutting in was first. It was always first!

"You're supposed to cut in the edges!"

His toothy grin made her stomach tumble. "Says who? My wall is almost done. I'll get the edges. Don't you worry."

He would but it'd be supereasy because between the length of his arms and the extender on the paint roller, he had hardly any area to cover.

She turned back, refusing to give in. Grabbing a roller, she worked to beat him at his own game. Which would have worked better if she'd remained calm and cool. Collected. Instead, she rolled over the window ledge by accident and lost valuable time cleaning it up.

Even with her switching to his method, he was finished before her. He never said a word about being done, just moved on to the small fragments of wall that divided the routes to the hallway.

When she set the paintbrush down, pushing her hair out of her face with the back of her hand, she turned in a circle. She might have lost but her living room was painted.

"Looks good," he said, his voice low as he all but stalked toward her. The heat in his gaze pushed everything else away. The challenge, the paint, the small room, and life in general.

"It does," she agreed when he stopped right in front of her, so close the tips of their toes touched.

"You've got paint on your cheek." He brushed his thumb over it but all she felt was the way the rough pad of it felt on her skin. His fingers curved around her neck, tilting it just enough that they were at the perfect angle.

"Is it gone?" Why the hell was she whispering?

"I have no idea," he said, not breaking eye contact.

No. Nuh-uh. Just because he was sexy didn't mean he could smooth . . . what? Gaze? Smooth-gaze her and she'd flutter her damn eyelashes. How had he beat her?

"You look mad," he said. His lips remained flat but his eyes smiled. They might have even laughed.

"Not mad. A deal is a deal." Really, she hadn't lost anything. As far as bets went, this one wouldn't make her lose any sleep. He could keep asking all he wanted. She'd just keep saying no.

Her breaths were more ragged than they should be and when Noah's gaze landed on her mouth, a look of interest mingling with heat, she backed up.

"I'll help you with your office." *Because it's not an important room. Jerk.*

They cleaned up in silence, working side by side. She was glad he didn't gloat and sort of wondered if she would have. *You so would have.* But he didn't, and even though he could be bristly about a lot of things, this earned her respect.

When she walked him to the door, he turned, hesitating in the threshold.

"That was fun."

She let out a huff that could have been a laugh or a sigh. "Sure."

"I'll stop asking," Noah said.

It took her a second but when she realized what he was saying, she was too surprised to comment.

"Night, Grace."

She stared after him, wondering how long she'd have to live next door to him to actually understand Noah Jansen.

12

Noah waited in the back corner of Baked, a bakery run by a good friend of his brother's girlfriend, Everly. Tara, the owner, was cute as hell, funny, and a Goddess with chocolate and flour. He looked over at her, smiling at something a customer said, wondering if he should ask her out. He needed to get out on a date, get his mind off business and this restless feeling spinning in his chest. *Would also help with the weird pull you felt to your neighbor last night.*

Grace was . . . nearly indescribable. In truth, he didn't entirely know what to make of the woman. She was fierce and funny. She went toe-to-toe with him literally and figuratively. She had a temper that he apparently brought out, but he'd seen the softness, the wistfulness, and kindness in her actions and her eyes.

Last night, he'd been overwhelmingly attracted to her, and it scared the fuck out of him. He had end goals. He always had end goals.

"What's got you looking so down on a gorgeous morning like this?" Chris asked, sliding into the chair across from him, a latte in hand.

Noah grinned at his younger brother. He'd missed him while he was in New York. All three brothers were close but he and Chris had another level of close. Mostly because their oldest brother was usually stuck in a virtual world and didn't need to bounce things around verbally like they did.

"Just thinking I should ask Tara out. I haven't been out much."

Chris looked back at Tara like he was seeing her for the first time, then turned a hard glare on Noah. "No."

Noah laughed. "Not sure I need permission, little brother."

"Nope. You don't. But she's off-limits. No friends or relations of Everly or Stacey's." Stacey was Rob's girlfriend as well as the DJ at the station they owned. Everly produced for her.

"Since when?"

"Since I want to marry this woman and don't need my brother breaking the hearts of the few friends she has."

Everly was painfully shy. Once a person got to know her, she was awesome, funny, and witty. But it took time. Noah wouldn't ever do something to upset her on purpose. But his brother's words grated on his already unsteady nerves.

"Noted. Not good enough for anyone Everly knows."

"I didn't say that," Chris said, taking a sip of his coffee.

He didn't say it but he didn't *not* say it either.

"How's the reno? You find a designer?"

There's one next door who keeps getting under my skin. "No. Josh has some meetings scheduled for next week. The living area and kitchen are now one great room. We want to get the big stuff done first before we start the surface finishes."

"How's it going with the neighbor?"

Why did thinking about her make his skin feel too tight? "I've been approaching her wrong. I realized that last night."

Chris leaned back in his chair, as at ease in his suit and tie as Noah was even though he'd opted for a more casual look today. He was heading to the rec center after coffee.

"How so? What was last night?"

Noah described the strange evening to his brother. "She thinks she's ready to take on all that house needs. She's going to get halfway in and realize she's over her head. I need to let her do that then swoop in with an offer that'll feel like a lifeline."

Chris stared at him, tapping his index finger against the side of his cup.

Noah shifted. His own cup was empty. "What?"

"You painted with this woman?" Chris's lips twitched. "Rob says you're playing basketball with him and some kids."

"So?"

"You painted. Played with kids. Who are you?"

Noah huffed. "Yeah. I painted. That's what you do when you want something a different color. And what the hell? I like kids. I like basketball. What's your problem?"

Chris took a sip. "No problem. Just surprised. You're really doing shit on this one. Like rolling up your sleeves, fixing fences, painting walls."

He bit down on his frustration. "I'm going to live there. *Yes,* I'm getting involved."

To his credit, his brother leaned back, eased off, giving Noah a few minutes to breathe through his frustration.

When Chris leaned forward, he met Noah's gaze squarely. "You don't need a pool, man. Why are you making such a big deal of it? The ocean is literally at your back porch."

Why was it so important to him? There were his summer memories with his brothers and grandparents. "It's such a simple acquisition. She's being stubborn."

Chris laughed. "So, your business ego is bruised because someone said no? Is that a first?"

Noah stiffened, the cup in his hand scrunching a bit in his grasp. "You know what? I'm tired of everyone saying shit like that. I work damn hard, I've had plenty of losses professionally and personally. Just because I was the face of Dad's company and look good in a fucking magazine doesn't mean everything has been easy."

Chris's gaze widened. He leaned in, pushed his drink away and rested his forearms on the table. Someone laughed loudly as a few more people shuffled into the bakery.

"Where'd that come from?"

Noah grunted. "Gee, I wonder. You know how many times it's been alluded to in the last couple weeks that I don't commit, I'm not serious, or I'm not invested? More times than I can count. I lost out on three deals last month. Every one of them should have been mine. Two of them came right out and said they wanted Dad's name on the deal. The other one was quieter about it but I know that's what they were waiting for, too."

Nodding like he understood, Chris said, "Okay. Sorry. It's a tougher transition than you thought it'd be but come on, you're a third owner with us, you have the house, will probably have the house beside it because you're bullheaded, you've got the office buildings downtown, with full rental income. What's going to be enough? What's it going to take for you to feel successful?"

Damn. He almost wanted to punch his brother for getting to the heart of the restless spinning. What the hell was it going to take to make him feel *good enough*?

"Maybe that's something I should figure out. I gotta go." He stood, needing the fresh air, the space.

Chris stood as well, clapped him on the shoulder. "Hey. I'm here. I wasn't trying to piss you off. I know it's hard to get out from under Dad's foot. But you're doing it. So what if a few deals didn't pan out. Let's do dinner. Forget about business for a bit."

Noah nodded as they waved to Tara and walked out together. "That sounds good. Sorry I snapped."

"I get it, man. You know I do." Chris held his gaze. Sometimes Noah felt like he was the older one. "Right?"

Noah nodded again, gave him a one-armed hug, then shoved

him just because he felt like it. Chris laughed. "You're such an ass."

"Takes one to know one."

Chris laughed harder. "Good to see you're all grown up."

He didn't feel less restless when he got in his truck, but he did feel happier.

～～～～～～

Noah might not be entirely sure what was going on with him lately but he knew, as he parked his truck in front of the worn-down recreation center about twenty minutes outside of Harlow, that this place brought up a lot of memories and feelings. Good ones.

Grabbing the huge duffel bag from his backseat, he had a wide smile on his face when he met up with Rob in the parking lot.

"Hey. Sorry about last time, man," Rob said, coming up beside him.

"No worries. It was fine. Relationships take time. Think the kids will show up?"

"I do." Rob jutted his chin toward the duffel. "I told them there was a surprise. Thanks for doing that. I really didn't tag you into this for the money."

Noah knew that but had some ideas about it anyway. He'd been invited to enough things in his life because of his financial status or his family name to know when something was genuine.

"It's all good. I'm happy to do it. I'm not above a little bribery to get them to let me in a little."

He also knew that it took more than some nice jerseys to actually make headway. He just hoped they'd let him try. Noah and Rob found four kids waiting for them on the basketball court behind the rec center. They were an eclectic mix of heights, ethnicities, and ages. If he had to guess, he'd say the youngest one was about ten, the oldest just about done with high school.

"This guy again?" Leo said, making a derisive noise as he grabbed the ball from the youngest kid to start dribbling.

"I know," Rob said. "With your moody teenage hormones, I didn't think he'd want to come around again either, Leo."

Noah looked at Rob. "I grew up with two brothers and a sister, a little attitude can't scare me." Noah smiled at the other kid, tossing the duffel on the ground. Two more boys came out from the center doors.

"Who's this?" an older kid with an Afro bigger than the basketball asked.

There was a pale blond kid, slight thing though he was tall, walking alongside him. "Probably Rob's lawyer."

The others laughed, but Noah didn't know what made something funny to teenagers.

Rob put up his hands. "All right, bunch of comedians, get in here."

To their credit, the ragtag group of kids listened, standing in a semicircle around them.

"What did you think of me when we met?" Rob asked them, then held up a hand again. "The PG version."

The kids snickered. Even Noah grinned, wondering what they'd said.

"Thought you were lost," the pale blond kid said, showing crooked teeth when he smiled.

"Thought you were a lawyer or some schmoozy politician," the Afro-haired kid said, another smirk.

Rob glanced at Noah. "I was wearing a button-down, collared shirt. Unless you never want to hear the end of it, don't wear one."

"Noted." Noah glanced around, caught Leo mean-mugging him.

"We thought you were just another sucker who had to do some community work for some program so you could get a fancy degree," the little guy said.

"You were all wrong about me. Whatever perceptions I had

about you guys were wrong, too. We talked about that, judging people at first glance."

"Happens all the time," Leo said.

"To more people than you'd expect," Noah said, holding the kid's hard gaze.

He scoffed. "Oh yeah? Someone judge you on sight, rich boy?"

"Leo," Rob said in a warning tone.

Noah patted his shoulder. "It's okay. I get judged all the time. Not as much here as in New York where I'm from. Nothing you can do about what people say or think except be yourself and walk away from anyone who doesn't like it."

His words were met with silence, and for about three point two seconds, he felt like he'd imparted some strong wisdom to today's youth. Until they started to laugh. Leo doubled over, holding the basketball to his side while he let out deep chuckles. Even Rob laughed, shaking his head.

"What?" Noah said, holding his arms out. "What?"

"Dude. You brought a motivational speaker?" a kid with one half of his head shaved, the other half sporting shoulder-length hair, said.

"Something like that," Rob said, opening the duffel. "He's also a friend of mine and when I told him about you scoundrels and us needing another player, he jumped at the chance. Which you'd know if you showed last time. He also brought us some swag." Rob tossed out bright blue jerseys with each of the kids' names and numbers on the back.

Five out of six of the kids took those jerseys, stared at them with some reverence, then whipped them on over their heads. Leo, however, held his in a tight-fisted grip.

"Why'd you bring these?" He stared directly at Noah.

"Because Rob said you needed jerseys."

"So you got money? You're gonna flash it around, make yourself feel like a Good Samaritan, give us some gifts, maybe get some tax breaks."

Rob sighed, stepped toward Leo. Noah put a hand on his shoulder and stepped forward instead.

He went toe-to-toe with the kid, seeing that he was only a few inches shorter than his own six feet.

"Leo."

The kid gave him a "duh" look that almost made Noah smile. Instead, he held his jaw tight, kept his gaze free of emotion. Every negotiation required a different approach.

"The jerseys are a gift because I heard you needed some. I have money but I'm hoping you don't hold that against me. I came to play some basketball. Whether you wear that jersey or not won't affect my ability to beat you."

They stared at each other, and more than that, he could feel the others staring at them. The sound of the ball hitting the court stopped.

Leo's chest puffed out. "Like last time?"

Noah pursed his lips, did his best not to grin. "I was being nice."

Something almost friendly sparked in Leo's dark eyes. "Hope you got insurance, old man."

Noah laughed, stepped away, and bounced the ball out of the youngest kid's hand. "Should the rest of you tell me your names before Rob and I school you on how it's done?"

The kids whooped and hollered, called out some trash talk that reminded Noah how much he'd missed this sort of thing. On the court, on the water, pounding his feet on the pavement during a good run . . . everything else fell away. His focus was pure and easy. He wasn't his father's son or a brother. He was just a guy who loved what he was doing. Like when he was closing a really great deal, in the middle of an awesome negotiation. When his grandfather had smiled at him like he believed Noah could change the world.

"You two against the six of us."

"They can't handle that."

"They'll be limping away crying."

Rob and Noah exchanged amused glances, then dove in, spending the next hour getting their asses handed to them by a group of kids who had a hell of a lot of skill when they worked as a team.

It was one of the few times since he'd arrived in California that he felt like he'd made the right decision.

13

"You've been gone almost two weeks and all you've done is paint a room?" Morty set his fork down, his irritated scowl burrowing under Grace's skin.

"Sorry I'm not moving fast enough for you," she replied, picking up a crinkle fry.

"Don't you say sorry, honey. You have a life. You just moved, you're finishing up school. There's no rush, is there? You're making a home not winning a race. You leave her alone, Morty, you old grump."

"Not what you called me last night," he said with a harrumph.

Grace set her fork down and covered her ears. "Gross."

Tilly laughed, reached out and pulled Grace's hand away from her ear. "He's all talk, sugar. Now. Tell us about the neighbor Morty mentioned."

Grace narrowed her eyes in his direction. "You told her about my neighbor?" Whom she'd been doing her best not to think about even while finding office ideas for him.

"What? I just said the guy who lived in the fancy house next door to yours wanted to pay too much for your place and was eyeing you up in a way I didn't like."

Grace laughed, using her napkin to wipe her fingers. "Is there anything you *do* like?"

"Half price at the movies," he said, smacking his hand on the table.

Tilly shook her head, getting up to clear plates. Grace stood up to do the same, putting a hand on Morty's shoulder as she passed. His grouchy persona was mostly bluster. Though his cheapness was the real deal. He loved to save a buck. When she'd first started working for him, he'd had no problem sending her clear across town to save forty cents on a can of something he wanted.

Morty patted her hand, his weathered skin brushing over her own. When she started to pull away, he squeezed, looking up at her. "You've got some mail."

"Thanks." She smiled at him, thinking the look in his eyes was more emotional than the moment called for.

It wasn't until they were settled in the living room with dessert, an unnecessary fire adding an extra glow to the room, that Morty cleared his throat, sat up straighter like he was about to give a speech.

"Tilly moved in," he said, folding his hands on his lap.

Tilly ducked her head almost shyly, reaching out to put a hand over Morty's.

When Grace burst out laughing, both of them looked up at her, mouths hanging open.

"Sorry. Was that supposed to be a news flash? When I went into the bathroom, her laundry was hanging over the curtain rod. Unless you've started wearing bras, Morty, and I'm not judging, I picked up on your little secret."

Guilt nudged her when Tilly's cheeks went a deep shade of pink. Jumping up off the chair, setting her chocolate cake aside, she rushed to Tilly, wrapping her arms around the woman.

"I didn't mean to embarrass you. I'm sorry."

Tilly accepted the hug, laughing as she returned the embrace. "I forgot all about that. I'm so sorry."

Grace leaned back. "Don't be. I think this is great. I expected it. I mean, I don't know why you'd want to live with this cranky human but I admire you for it."

"Hey. You had no complaints for four years," he said, fighting his smile.

Grinning, she reminded him, "I did. You just ignored them."

"We're going to get married," Tilly whispered.

Now Morty's cheeks darkened, and happiness blossomed like quick-grow flowers inside her chest. This time, she hugged them both.

"I'm so happy for you two." Not at all jealous that a man three times her age had found his match before she did.

"Ought to be. Want you to officiate the wedding," he said. "You like having weird jobs."

Grace laughed and went back to her seat. "Don't think that qualifies as a weird job but if it means something to you two, I'll happily get ordained. I'm honored you'd ask."

"Only going to say this once because it shouldn't have to be said more than that," Morty said, picking up his own cake, staring at it intently.

Grace's stomach twisted. "Okay."

Tilly's smile reassured her, but it wasn't until Morty lifted his gaze that she actually took a breath.

"You're like a daughter to me. Family isn't what you were born with. Well, that's not all it is. It's what you want it to be. You and Tilly are my family. Love you both. No way of knowing why things happen the way they do but I'm grateful for whatever led the two of you to me."

A lump lodged itself in Grace's throat. She could only nod as she widened her eyes in an effort to keep tears from falling.

"Aw, Morty. You're such a softy."

"Not what you said—"

Both women yelled at once. "Don't!"

Moving into her grandparents' house was supposed to make her feel like she belonged, but maybe she didn't need a *building* to do that. Maybe she just had to let herself accept that it was a feeling. Not a place. Wasn't it? Renovating her grandparents' house wouldn't bring them back or mend things with her mother. Not that she wanted to.

"What are you thinking so hard about?" Morty licked his fork clean, setting his plate down on the coffee table.

"Just, Noah offered to buy the house and I'm hanging on to it, thinking maybe that's my link to family, but it isn't. My link is right here. You guys, Rosie. It's just . . . the connection matters to me. I *want* to live there and not just because of its past. I want to make it a home but am I foolish not to take that much money?" He had it to spend. The man had more dollars behind his name than she'd known existed.

"Course you're foolish not to take it. Not sure why he'd offer so much but people who've always had money spend it like it's nothing. The house is yours but you could build a whole future on what he's offering. Don't punch a gift horse in the snout."

Tilly rolled her eyes. "Could you have butchered that expression any worse?"

"Knew what I meant, didn't ya?"

Noah wasn't foolish. He said he'd stop asking even though he won the bet. She wondered why it mattered to him. From what she'd seen online, he didn't get attached or involved with his investments. This was clearly different. For both of them.

"It does sound like a great opportunity, honey, but be careful. Sometimes things that look too good to be true, are."

That was her thought. Shifting the topic to her graduation, she pushed Noah and her house to the back of her mind. On her way out the door, Morty reminded her about the mail. In the car, as she was giving it a minute to warm up, she looked through the pile. Bill. Bill. Junk. Bill. Letter from her mom.

Grace closed her eyes, leaning her head against the seat. Tammy never followed through on her word. Why had she thought she would? *She didn't promise not to write. She said she wouldn't ask for more money.* She was tired of running from her mother. The woman hadn't wanted her around the whole time they lived together, but now that she was gone, Tammy needed someone to whine to, someone to blame.

It made her wonder if she even knew what she was hanging on to with her grandparents' house. Maybe the happiness she'd envisioned never existed. Whatever had, included her mom, the very person she wanted to ignore. Tammy told her sob stories about how she hadn't been listened to or understood. To the point she'd lit out at sixteen and never looked back. Grace left her mother at eighteen, but history was definitely repeating itself. Right down to location. Was she doing the right thing? Did she really want to bring the past into the present? Noah might have a reason for offering too much for her place, but sometimes good things happened to good people at the right time.

Chucking all her mail into the passenger seat, she started for home, waves of uncertainty washing over her. She questioned which would be better: Take Noah's offer and lock the door to the past, leaving the future wide open? Or follow through on her plan because she knew exactly where she was going? As long as nothing got in her way. Like snippy neighbors, broken roofs, or unwanted letters that came with even more unwanted feelings.

14

Having projects due, getting résumés ready, and having multiple jobs really messed with a person's schedule. Grace didn't see Noah much for the next week, which she told herself was a good thing. Her feelings were, at best, mixed. More than ever since Rosie told her she'd seen Noah at the rec center where her nephew played basketball. The more she learned about him, the more confused she grew.

As she came back from a last-minute walk with Brutus—which paid double—her mind was mostly on studying for her Theory in Design test. She had a list of furniture to run by Noah for his office, a couple of sketches to give him choices. She just needed dimensions for the room to make sure whatever he chose would fit.

She walked across the sand, away from the gathering crowds, loving the fact that she could see her house even with Noah's mass of palm trees. Her house was worth what Noah was offering for the view alone. That was something else that had settled on her mind like an unbalanced weight. It was a good deal, but would the money from it fill her with nearly the same joy as walking up to her back gate did? It was funny, in a way, that he'd asked her a half dozen times but now that he'd stopped, she was considering it. *Because it's your choice. You do like your control, Gracie.* A subtle warmth traveled over her skin, remembering the way he'd said her nickname that few people used. The way she'd told him not to.

She played with the finicky latch. Another thing to fix on her to-do list. She'd found a YouTube video but hadn't watched it yet. Moving the latch up and down, she was trying to get it to release when she heard Noah's laughter.

When she glanced up, he was stepping off the porch with a man who looked very much like him and a pretty brunette. The woman saw her first, giving a small smile. Grace lifted her hand in greeting, doing her best not to swear out loud at the gate.

Noah noticed her a second later. "Hey. You okay?"

"Fine, thanks. The lock is stuck again."

"Need some help?"

"Nope. Got it." Thank goodness. She didn't need to be rescued in front of Noah's guests.

Closing the gate behind her, she smoothed down her hair, wondering why her heart rate had accelerated. The walk hadn't been taxing. She refused to believe it was just proximity to Noah. She wasn't even entirely sure she liked him. Or that he liked her.

"Noah lacks social graces so I'll introduce myself. I'm Chris, his brother. This is my girlfriend, Everly."

She smiled, liking him already. Extending her hand over the fence, she shook Everly's first. "I'm Grace."

"Nice to meet you," Everly said. She wore a pair of jeans and a plain T-shirt but managed to look comfortable and chic at the same time.

Grace noticed her shoes. "I love your Converse."

Everly glanced down at the striped black-and-white shoes. "Thanks. I'm a bit of a Converse addict."

Chris stepped into her, putting his arm around her shoulder with a sweet familiarity that made Grace's heartstrings tug sharply.

"There are definitely worse habits," Grace said.

Noah's gaze burned into her skin. Feigning a nonchalance she did *not* feel, she looked his way. "Good week?"

He nodded. "I got a lot accomplished. I'm waiting on the list of office furniture you owe me." His gaze sparked with amusement. She wondered if he'd told his brother about their bet.

"I have it. With some sketch ideas."

She felt curiosity from Chris and Everly.

"You're in design school, right?" Chris asked.

"Just finishing up." Normally, she didn't mind idle chitchat, but everything about talking to Noah, with his family no less, made her feel like simple conversations could go sideways.

Chris looked at his brother with an overly wide gaze. "Aren't you looking for a designer?"

"Chris." Noah all but growled the word, making Grace's back stiffen.

"No luck?" she asked with more of a bite than she intended.

"Something will work out," Noah said.

Cue awkward tension. She was planting herself firmly in the "don't like him" camp at the moment.

"Sorry, just to clarify, you're a designer; Noah, you're looking for designers, and Grace is doing your office for you?"

"That's right. Grace is doing my office because all it has to do is be functional and because she lost a bet. I'll be going with a professional firm for the rest of my house."

Did he realize how insulting he sounded?

"You sound like a dick," Chris said.

Grace coughed to cover her laugh. *Well, he knows now.*

"What?" Noah looked completely confused. "What did I do?" He stared at Grace.

"Nothing. Just stop saying I'm only doing your office because you'd trust a blindfolded toddler to do it. It was *your* idea. Maybe you're just too lazy to pick out your own furniture, I don't know. It might surprise you to know, but I have serious skills. I'm top in my class."

His frown deepened. "That doesn't surprise me. I wasn't slighting your skills. I didn't mean to."

Noah's genuine tone shifted the tide in his favor. What was it about this guy?

"This is why you have to *think* about what comes out of your mouth," Chris said, teasing. Everly leaned into him, rolling her eyes adorably, because clearly she was beyond smitten, even when the brothers acted like this.

Noah ran his hands through his hair. Something he did when he was nervous or unsure. "We're going to BBQ some burgers. Why don't you come over and join us?" Noah said.

Exam. Painting. Planning her life. Plenty of reasons not to. *A girl's gotta eat.* "I need about a half hour. Can I bring anything?"

"Just you," Noah said, stepping closer to the fence.

She looked at his brother and Everly, noting the way they stared curiously. "You sure?"

"Join us, please," Chris said.

She could drop off his office ideas, double-check the room, and get a meal out of it. Those were her reasons. *Not because you're curious about him and his family.* "I'll see you in a bit."

She heard their murmurs behind her as she let herself into her house. She wouldn't show up empty-handed. Inside, she changed, praised herself for picking up wine and *not* drinking it, and started to tidy up before leaving. Her mother's letter slipped out of the pile of papers she was moving. She stared at it, tapped it against her palm.

She could take Noah's offer and cut ties to her past. Her mother wanted a piece of what her grandparents had left despite wanting nothing to do with them when they were alive. Grace looked around the kitchen. It needed updating, new appliances. She wanted to put in a barn door to separate the laundry/mudroom area. The irony was, if she took Noah's money, she could make the house exactly what she wanted.

You've never needed the quick fix before. The truth was, she liked coming home to this house. She felt like she belonged here in some sense. Even if her mother felt like she hadn't. She set the letter down.

She'd worked her ass off, gotten out of the trailer, away from her mom's life and toxic brand of parenting. She'd done all of that without Noah's help. It might take a lifetime but she could make this place her own. Make her own path in the design world. Hell, she'd even found a way to make corporate badass Noah Jansen back off on asking her to sell. From what she'd read, that was a contradiction to his sharklike business nature. She didn't need to sell to grow. She needed to plant roots.

~~~~~~~~~

Grace got caught up in Chris telling stories with the sole intent of embarrassing Noah. Over burgers, salad, and ice-cold colas, Chris did everything he could to turn Noah's cheeks red.

"He did not," Grace said, glancing around the table for confirmation.

Everly shrugged her shoulders. "It wouldn't surprise me."

Noah's scowl deepened. "Next time, I'm only inviting *you*, Everly."

Chris tossed his napkin onto his plate. "Don't be a suck. He absolutely did, Grace. Instead of admitting he didn't study for the exam, he went ahead with the experiment and set the chem lab on fire."

Her laughter started all over again. "Your stubbornness knows no bounds."

"Says one stubborn person to the next," Noah said, poking her in the shoulder with his index finger.

He did that now and again when they were together—simple touches that suggested he maybe liked her more than he meant to. The simple graze made her wonder about more. *Because you aren't confused enough about all the things you're chasing in life? You want a fling to complicate it.* Her only thought after that was . . . *Maybe?*

She decided, watching the two of them interact, that having a sibling could definitely have improved her life.

One day, you'll marry someone who has a family and you'll be part of that one. Morty's words came back to her. *Family is what you want it to be.*

When they'd cleared the table, she pulled out her sketchbook. "Did you want to see the ideas I had for your office? I have three sketches based on price line. You can mix and match if you want unless you have a preferred store. I figure if Josh buys your groceries, you could get him to order these things since that wasn't part of the bet."

"Wow. She has you pegged," Chris said.

She wasn't sure what to make of Noah's expression. His gaze was suspiciously blank when he met hers. "Pretty sure I can handle ordering online."

Nerves ran around in her belly, but they were the good kind. She felt good about what she had to show. The three of them pored over the designs she'd sketched. She'd gone high-end with one, figuring he could afford it. Sleek furniture that hid its efficiency was expensive. The room would be masculine but subtle, closed cabinets giving the feel of more space but opening up to create a usable work space.

"This is gorgeous," Everly said, tapping her finger near the first design.

"It should be for what it costs." She looked at Noah. "But since you insist your office is a throwaway room, it isn't what I'd choose." She set down the second design. It was the middle line between the three. Functional and efficient but also homey. It would be her choice if she had the money. As it was, she couldn't even afford sketch one.

"This is really great," Chris said. "I like the functionality paired with personality in this one."

Everly grinned at him but Grace laughed, her surprise obvious. "Taken some design courses, have you?"

Chris's cheeks went a soft pink. "I just like what I like."

Noah laughed, nudged his brother's shoulder. "I like this one, too. The other one feels too stark. Even with the darker colors."

Grace smiled. She liked this. No, she loved this. She loved making people's ideas come to life, and she'd pictured Noah choosing this one. Design, probably like in his business, involved reading people.

"You want high quality with function and a homey feel," Grace said.

"I want that in every room of my house," Everly said.

"There're only three rooms total in your house, babe," Chris said.

Everly nodded. "True. But one day . . ."

The way she let the words trail off, the way the couple looked at each other, as if they could feel the unsaid words between them, made the longing twist inside of Grace like a sharp stitch.

"Okay," she said a little too brightly. "Last one, all function, low budget."

Chris's smile grew. "Grace, you're skilled."

She gave an awkward laugh. "You can't know that based on a few sketches."

Noah stood straight. "Judging people's skills with little background information is one of my brother's specialties."

"It is. Just like Noah's is knowing when to press and when to idle."

She shared her smile with both of them. "What does that even mean?"

"For me, I've been in lots of positions where I've had to take someone's measure, if you will, with not a lot to go on. You get good at it. For Noah, he's able to gauge a client's interest like a pressure point. He eases up at just the right time to make them want more. Makes them think what he wants is their idea."

A little buzz hummed in her ears as she thought about those words.

Everly added to the conversation, but Grace didn't hear what she said because she was too busy thinking about how odd it was that as soon as Noah stopped asking to buy her house, she'd seriously considered selling it to him.

"You were making a power move, not being kind," she said, more to herself than to any of them.

"What's that?" Chris asked.

All gazes landed on her.

"You okay, Grace?" Noah asked.

"You won the bet." She pointed to the sketches. "You didn't have to let me win, too."

Noah's smile was phony. It was too wide. Too happy. It didn't touch his intense brown eyes. When it did, she felt like she could fall into his gaze. "You didn't win. I did."

"But you said you'd stop asking," Grace said, her stomach tightening.

The silence said everything. He didn't do it because he felt the connection growing between them or because there were more check marks in his "I like her" column than his "She drives me nuts" column. He'd made her think it was her idea, therefore almost getting exactly what he wanted.

"It's manipulative," she whispered. For some reason, she thought of Tammy and how she never wanted Grace around when she was. But the second she was gone . . . different story.

"Maybe we should go for a walk on the beach, Ev," Chris said. The two of them stood, but Grace was already backing away.

"Grace, I wasn't manipulating you."

Even his tone was phony, or maybe she'd just gotten through his shell enough in the last couple of weeks that she could tell he wasn't being truthful.

"You were playing me. It's all a game to you." She spread her arms out, looked around the kitchen he could make state-of-the-art without one care for cost. "It's all a game to you. I read about you. Your family. You guys are business giants. You say you want to settle in this house but it's just walls and wood to you. You have no idea what it means to have something *mean* something to you."

Everly and Chris started for the door.

"No. Please. Don't go. I need to go." She stared at Noah. "Don't ask about my house again. I won't sell it. Because *I don't want to*. Because it matters to me. I get that you don't understand that but you will respect it. No more games either. You won the design from me but no more fence fixing or trading off. Stay away from me."

She wasn't even sure she meant that last part and maybe she was being irrational but her emotions were tangled like shoelaces and if she didn't get out of there *now* she was going to trip on them.

She'd fallen flat on her face in front of this man enough for one lifetime.

15

Noah's breath caught in his lungs painfully as he watched her go. He didn't go after her. He had no right. She was right. He'd manipulated her. His brother had called him on it in the bakery. Because he'd seen her house as a target he wanted to hit. He'd been chasing after deals he could close, thinking it would make him feel something. He walked into the open area of his living room.

But what actually made him *feel* was the woman who just walked out the door. How was that for some fucking irony. Whether he was fighting or flirting with her, she made him feel alive. The way an amazing deal *used* to make him feel. He'd hurt her. Even at his worst, when he was just another corporate lackey for his dad, he'd never intentionally hurt anyone. Business was business. Grace was . . . pure and sweet and *real*. And he'd hurt her by being himself.

Chris and Everly joined him. "That got weird fast. Sorry for saying that shit about how you do business."

Noah turned to face him, noticed Everly's tight-lipped grimace, the pity in her gaze. "For telling her the truth? That I'm an asshole?"

"You're not," Everly said, her quiet voice emphatic.

Noah locked his fingers in his hair. "I'm him."

"Don't do that," Chris said, his tone sharp. "You're not Dad. Look, clearly you've got some mixed feelings for that woman. I'd say it's mutual. There were a lot of heated looks I'm okay with never seeing between my brother and a woman."

Noah gave him a wry smile. "Wouldn't know what that's like." He winked at Everly, making her smile.

"You didn't mention how much more this is than business," Chris said.

"What are you talking about? She's my neighbor. She's fought me on most things since I got here."

Chris smiled knowingly. "When you talk about her, you light up like you used to when you found a wicked property you could flip. Whatever the reason, this girl is lighting something back up inside you. I'm happy to see it. I'm tired of watching you pout, being wishy-washy about properties and companies."

"Screw you, man." He said it with a laugh. Wishy-washy. Whatever. He just hadn't found anything to sink his teeth into.

Chris clapped him on the shoulder. "Let her calm down. Talk to her."

"And say what? 'Sorry for being a product of my father'? 'Turns out I'm more like him than I thought. Business comes before people without me even realizing it'?"

Chris squeezed his shoulder. "It's a choice, man. We choose who we end up being. Good or bad, you don't get to blame him. He may have laid the groundwork but we're paving our own path."

Noah walked away, paced the empty living room. He needed some damn furniture. He needed to start his life here rather than choosing random jobs to chip away at. He needed to focus. To figure out what he truly wanted.

From the corner of his eye, he noticed Everly tapping her fingers against her thigh. When he looked at her face, her lips were pressed into a thin line.

Noah sighed, his lungs deflating like a balloon. "What?"

Her eyes widened. "I didn't say anything."

His brother looked at his girlfriend, reached for her hand to thread in his own. A sharp pang hit Noah in the sternum. He didn't want *that*. Did he? Chris got lucky when he found Everly but that kind of forever was absolutely not for everyone.

"You don't have to. I know you're thinking something. Tell me. I want to know."

When Everly sat on the bottom step that led to upstairs, Chris sat beside her. "Chris's right. It's all your choice. Your father isn't here making decisions for you. You need to trust yourself. Trust your feelings even if they surprise you. If you don't like how you made Grace feel, change it. Let her see you. Not who you think you have to be. There's obviously a connection between the two of you. Whether you acknowledge it or not is also your choice. It sounds like you're going to be neighbors for a long time. You don't want this between you. You've been restless since you got here. Stop running in circles. Make things right with Grace."

Noah shook his head, not sure whether to laugh or bang his head against the wall. "So, what? Follow my heart?"

She just laughed.

"You don't say much but when you do, you make it count."

She beamed at him. His brother was a lucky guy. "Back at you."

They stood to leave, but something had been circling his brain for days—since the last time at the rec center. He looked at Chris. "You remember the park we used to go to?"

Chris nodded. "Sure. With Gramps?" He glanced at Everly. "Our grampa used to take us to this park. We'd go for walks, he'd tell us about his plans. He liked to get out of the boardroom, see the city we were part of. He wanted to build a community center at the entrance of that park. We'd stand in the spot he chose, listening to his vision. We stopped going when he got sick. Then we grew up and he was gone. I went back to that park when I was nineteen. Just to . . . walk."

Everly put her hand on Chris's back. "That's a nice memory."

Noah picked up the story from where Chris left off, painfully aware of the lump in his throat. "They built condos on it. It's not a park anymore. I was in college when Chris phoned to tell me it was gone. We hadn't been there in years but in the back of our minds, it was there when we wanted it to be. Until it wasn't."

He tipped his head back, closing his eyes as it thudded against the door. "I'm tired of slapping down money and walking away like what I bought doesn't matter. I want something to matter. Like that rec center did. Like this house does." Like Grace's house mattered to her. The one he'd tried to buy just because he could.

"You'll figure it out. Sounds like you already have for the most part," Chris said.

Maybe. Now the question was, what did he do about it?

———

He dialed Josh's number, putting the phone on speaker as he worked on cleaning up the rest of the kitchen.

"Hey. I was just about to phone you. Kyle and the guys will be there at nine tomorrow. They'll finalize anything that needs to be done but at this point, we need to put them on hold until you hire one of these designers. Did you talk to any of them yet?"

Washing the counter, he replied, "Yeah. I've narrowed it down to three. They'll come see the space, give me some ideas, and I'll be able to choose the one that fits what I'm imagining." He eyed the sketches Grace left. He'd need to return her sketch book. He wondered if she realized she'd left it. She was really good. It was too bad she was still a student. Not that she'd want to work with him anyway. Not now. Plus, he wanted to be in that magazine, and that meant big-ticket names.

He blurted out his question before he lost his nerve. "What's the best way to apologize to a woman?" Noah asked, squirting soap into the stream of warm water.

"What'd I do?"

"Hurt her feelings." Even saying it, never mind imagining the look in her eyes, made him feel like he could be sick.

"Hmm. Dick move."

Noah bit back his growl. "Thanks, Captain Obvious."

"This is going to sound radical but if you're serious . . ." Josh said.

Noah stiffened, stared at his phone. "I am." He held his breath.

"You look her right in the eyes and you say, 'I'm sorry,'" Josh said, his voice cracking with laughter at the end.

"Why do I pay you again?" Noah asked, but his lips were twitching with amusement.

"To answer weird-ass calls at all times of the day."

"I was thinking a bracelet or something. My dad always bought women jewelry." He had an account at Tiffany's just for apologies.

"Unless you're in a serious relationship or you *broke* her bracelet, I would not go that route."

Could it be as simple as saying, "I'm sorry. I was insensitive"? That didn't seem like enough.

"Okay. Thanks." Noah turned off the water.

"No problem. Funny, though. You've got this reputation as a ladies' man but you're asking for advice."

"Well, that reputation is mostly bullshit. I hit any event with a woman, no matter who it is, and some tabloid says I'm marrying her. Fortunately, my brothers and I don't make much of a splash in the New York society pages anymore. My sister is still pretty good at it, though."

She could have it. That was a spotlight he didn't need.

"I'll see you tomorrow then. I have a surprise."

"What is it?" Noah washed the pan he'd used to grill onions for the burgers.

"A surprise is a thing you don't tell people."

Noah laughed. "An employer is a person who controls a paycheck."

"Touché. You'll see. It's a good one."

"Better be or it's a sucky surprise."

"As long as you don't do a sucky apology, everything should work out fine."

He dried his hands so he could press End. Hopefully, Josh was right and everything would be fine. It occurred to him, as he finished up the dishes, that he was so worried about making things right with Grace, he'd forgotten that he wanted her house in the first place. Maybe Chris and Everly were right: it was a choice. He was *choosing* to shift his priorities. It wasn't too late to figure out what kind of man he wanted to be. He hoped.

16

Grace finished the online practice test with a score of ninety-three percent.

"I'll take it." She shoved her books aside, looked for her sketchbook before remembering she'd left it at Noah's.

She'd probably overreacted, leaving without even saying goodbye to his family. Over the last several years, she'd prided herself on reading people—which was part of why she hadn't told Noah to take a hike. There was intrinsic good in him, a connection she hadn't felt with anyone else, even if he could be a jerk. She sensed there was a reason behind it. But last night, she'd felt like her supersenses were off.

She didn't need anyone else in her life who put themselves first. Her mother had given her enough of that. She picked up the letter again. *Read it.* She didn't want to. Avoidance was a cool strategy, right? *Sure. Works every time.*

Rolling her shoulders, she finished the last of her coffee. She was debating another cup when the doorbell rang. She hoped it wasn't Noah. She wasn't ready to see him or talk to him yet. She did need her book, though.

As she walked to the door, she muttered under her breath, "You're hurt because you thought he was starting to feel something back." Let's face it, she'd been drawn to him from first sight.

Grace swung the door open. She was greeted by a middle-aged man in a red uniform. Bright red. Red shorts, shirt, socks, and hat. She blinked, her gaze zeroing in on the patch on the right chest pocket. RED'S FLOWERS. HERMAN. Okay.

"Hi, ma'am." His wide grin showed slightly crooked teeth.

"Hi . . . Herman."

He laughed, tapping his chest where his name was stitched. "That's me. Are you Grace Travis?"

"I am."

He passed over a clipboard. "Sign here. I'll grab your flowers."

"Okay." Her chest tightened. No one had ever sent her flowers.

She handed the clipboard back after signing, then watched Herman head to the red van. Since it'd never happened before, she didn't know what to expect. Maybe a bouquet? Some roses? Grace did *not* expect Herman to start lugging blossoming flowerpots out of the vehicle. The clay pots he set down on her lawn were beautiful with their bold colors. The flowers inside each one were different. Every color of the rainbow shone out of the arrangements. When he finished, there were twelve pots in her yard.

Herman, who wiped his forearm across his brow, glanced up. "You want these up there on the porch?"

"Who are all of these from?"

Going to the van, Herman grabbed something before coming toward her and passing her a small white envelope.

"The porch, ma'am?"

Blinking rapidly, she looked from the porch to the pots. They wouldn't all fit. There were enough to edge all the way around her front porch.

"No. They're fine where they are." Feeling slightly dazed, she jolted when he slammed the van door shut. "Let me grab my purse for a tip."

"No need. It's all been taken care of. You have yourself a great day. Enjoy those beauties."

Holding the envelope like it was a precious secret, Grace waved as he drove off. She stared down at it a moment before tearing into it.

Hurting you was never my intention. I was wrong.

Noah.

She frowned. Wrong about what? Manipulating her? Hurting her? All of it? Without thinking it through, she walked around the fence and up to his front door, knocking before she could back out.

He opened the door quickly enough that she'd bet he was watching from the window.

"Hey."

That was it? "Hey."

He smiled at her. It wasn't the usual disarming smile but one more humble. "You got your flowers?"

She glanced back at them, then gestured with her hand. "What *is* all that?"

Noah stepped out onto the porch, surveying the pots. "Flowers." He looked down at her, his forehead creasing in confusion.

"Flowers? That's not flowers. It's . . . *landscaping*. What are they for?"

Now he put his hands on his hips, turning to face her. "To say I'm sorry. It's what people do. It's a gesture. An 'I'm sorry I was a jerk' gesture." He rubbed the back of his neck, his gaze darting over her. "I didn't mean to play you. Actually, that's a lie. I fell back on a business strategy that I shouldn't have tried with you. It was wrong. I won't ask to buy your house again. Because you asked me not to."

"Okay. But couldn't you have just said that? Did you need to buy all of California's flowers?"

He looked incredibly uncomfortable, even shifting his stance, which did not suit the man she'd come to know. "It didn't seem like enough."

Grace could only stare. Too many thoughts collided in her brain, so she started at the beginning. "What you said would have been fine. I appreciate it and can see that you mean it. But for future reference, if you're doing flowers as a follow-up, it's typically a *bouquet*. You know, like, twelve roses? Not twelve huge potted plants."

He smirked. "Given a lot of apologies?"

She narrowed her gaze, making him put his hands up in a surrender gesture.

"Just asking. I'm new to this. Cut me some slack."

Grace threw her arms up in the air. "How can you be *new* to apologizing? Are you that much of a jerk that you just stomp on people's feelings without ever regretting it enough to say so?"

The look on his face stopped her before she said anything else. Surprise registered first, then worry. His mouth opened. Closed. He rubbed the back of his neck again.

"I don't make a habit of hurting people, Grace. Regardless of what you think of me."

Part of her problem was that she didn't know *what* she thought of him. Not clearly. Being around him made her brain and feelings resemble a shaken snow globe.

She shook her head. "I think you have no idea the impact you have on the people around you. Everyone hurts people, Noah. Intentionally or not, there's no way around it."

He stepped closer. "I didn't mean to hurt *you*."

God. It was *this* right here that kept her coming back despite her uncertainty. That look in his eyes, the way her body hummed from the tips of her toes to the roots of her messy updo. No one had ever made her feel this way with just a look.

"Thank you," she whispered.

Something shifted inside of her, pushing common sense to

the side and leaving her with a whole lot of wanting to know how his mouth felt.

He took a deep breath in and when he let it out, the warmth of it fanned over her skin. When had he moved closer? Or had she? "You confuse the hell out of me."

Her throat tightened. "Then we're even." In the back of her mind, she heard her own warning: *Do not venture down this rabbit hole.*

Noah reached out, brushed the backs of his fingers over her cheek before tucking a stray lock of hair behind her ear. She felt like she had a hundred heartbeats and he was controlling every one.

"This is a bad idea," she whispered, right before she stepped into him, ran her hands up his chest and met his waiting mouth. His arms clasped around her, pulling her closer into him. He stood in the same spot, rooted to his porch, but Grace felt like she was spinning, falling, twirling, losing control of her carefully scheduled program.

When his tongue touched hers and one large hand roamed over her body, she didn't care about anything other than getting closer. This was how people ended up broken. *And healed.* She couldn't let a man do either of those things to her. She had no room in her life for an unscripted fling. At least not one with this man, because she knew, just from this mind-blowing kiss, that he could wreck all her carefully laid plans.

She pulled back in small degrees as if it would ease the ache. It didn't. Their combined breaths echoed in her ears as their foreheads touched. Her eyelids fluttered open, reality seeping back in.

"We shouldn't have," she whispered even though she'd never be sorry she had. Just once. She'd needed to know. Now she did. Now she knew the kind of desire that probably set her mom's path on fire. The kind that made her leave a home with people who loved her to follow a man who hadn't stuck around past Grace's birth.

That's where this kind of passion went. It was uncontrollable. Unpredictable.

"Gracie," he whispered, his lips finding hers again. She arched into him, not wanting to let go. Because she knew, when she did, she'd have to walk away. Noah Jansen was the kind of man she could lose herself to. Something she'd promised herself she'd never do.

Her feet touched the ground, she pulled her fingers from his hair, fidgeting with them, unsure how to shift her universe back to pre-Noah.

At least Noah looked as poleaxed as she felt. "That's some serious chemistry." His voice was rough. She shivered.

"I'll say," she whispered.

They both started to speak at the same time. She shook her head. "This is a bad idea. For so many reasons."

"Right. Obviously," he said, one side of his mouth lifting halfheartedly.

"We're neighbors." Who was she clarifying for? What she should have said was, "We're worlds apart and completely different and want different things out of life."

"Complicated," he muttered.

"Exactly," she said, more excitedly than she should. "We don't want this to be complicated."

"We could be friends." He stared at her like he wanted to pull her into his arms again.

It was a careful in-between that she wanted to believe she could manage. "We could."

He held out a hand. She laughed, taking it, wishing she didn't want to feel the slide of his palm over every inch of her body.

"I'll grab your book," he said.

She watched him go, whispering to the flower-scented breeze, "I'll just stay here and pretend this is going to end well."

17

Grace fiddled with her 3D design program, moving furniture around. She'd been able to plug in her dimensions to basically re-create her home. Her teacher had told her about a student laptop buy-as-you-go option through the school. It wasn't the top end but it was far better than what she'd had and could actually run the programs. She couldn't afford to make all of the changes, definitely couldn't afford the furniture all at once, but seeing it, even on a screen, infused her with energy. Drive. She wanted this. She'd work her ass off until she got it.

She was averaging a pretty good Noah ratio today, about three-to-one. Three thoughts about something else, one about him. It was better than the night before, reliving the feel of his mouth and dreaming about more. When she'd woken up with his name on her lips, she'd had a firm talk with herself, a reminder of what she was working toward. Noah was not part of her picket fence, two-point-five-children, happily-ever-after plan. A man like that . . . how many places did he own? This was the first he'd actually hung on to.

She wanted a man who held on. Someone she could hold on

to when the storms blew. Her mother had spent her life looking for the right man to make her feel good about herself, to help her achieve whatever she wanted to achieve in any given moment. She used men like a crutch, solidifying Grace's determination to make it on her own before sharing her life with someone else. That someone else, whoever he ended up being, would be her equal. Someone who assumed she *could* handle a hammer rather than being surprised by it.

As she poured her coffee, the best possible incentive for staying on track sat, mocking her. She grabbed the letter from her mother and tore it open.

One hand clutched the envelope while the other shook slightly.

Grace,

You never return my texts. I get that you're probably mad at me. What kid doesn't grow up mad at their parents? Maybe now you understand me a little better. I guess this is some kind of karmic kick in the ass for walking out on my parents. But I had a reason. You don't. I never tried to hold you back from anything.

I don't want to be alone my whole life. I have no one. Really, neither do you. I'm your family. Maybe I didn't get that before but I do now. I could come out there. I know you're living in my parents' house. The house that should have been mine. There's no point in me paying rent on the trailer when I should be there, too. I have every right no matter what some stupid lawyer says.

Taking care of you until you were old enough to do it yourself made things hard on me. I couldn't do the things I wanted to do to have a better life with a kid hanging on my hip. I think that warrants a little compassion on your part. Or, at least, a place to stay. I never wanted to go back to California but if that's where you're going to be, that's where I want to be, too. We could try to fix our relationship. Try to make things better. Think about it. Maybe text me back sometime so I don't have to mail you letters like we live in another century.

Mom

Grace crumpled the letter, tossed it onto the counter. Her breaths sawed in and out rapidly. Gripping the counter, she closed her eyes, forced herself through the alphabet. By *m*, ironically, she was calmer.

Some things never changed. Tammy Travis was one of them. Passive-aggressive bullshit that ultimately laid all of the blame at Grace's feet.

When Grace had been notified about her grandparents' passing and the will, her mother hadn't been mentioned at all. Grace was already in California at the time. She had no idea if her mother had been notified, but clearly she knew Grace had inherited the house.

The letter served its purpose; her priorities were back on track. School, graduate, job, and then she could think about a man. One who would complement her life, not confuse it.

"Enough," she said, pushing back from the table. No dwelling. She had plans for today. She went out the back door, noticing that Noah had someone working on his palm trees. In her shed, which needed fixing, she grabbed some gloves and gardening tools. She was going to plant his apologies.

Going back through the house, grabbing a bottle of water on the way, she bit back a scream when she opened the door and came face-to-face with a stranger.

He was tall with dark hair, good bone structure, and a decent physique. Attractive. Grace immediately decided he didn't have a serial-killer vibe, which was backed up by the fact that he didn't bite back *his* scream.

Grace laughed. He pressed a hand to his chest.

"I'm sorry," he said. "Damn. That scared the hell out of me."

"Same. Can I help you?"

"Do you know CPR?" He grinned, his dark eyes joining in.

"You're still breathing so I think it'd be a bad idea."

"Good point. Okay. Let's try this again. Are you Grace?"

He might not be a killer but she was still standing in front of a strange man who was a foot taller than she was, *alone*.

"Who wants to know?"

"Me. I'm your housewarming gift." He spread his arms wide. His thin jacket opened, revealing a pale gray T-shirt and, fortunately, no guns or shady weapons. Maybe a little conceited but still no killer vibe.

"Excuse me?"

"Just introduce yourself already before she knees you in the goodies. I taught her how, you know," Morty said, coming up behind her "gift."

Grace rolled her eyes. "You did not." She looked at the guy. "But I do know how."

He swallowed, looked back and forth between them, and stepped to the side. "I don't doubt it."

Morty ambled up the steps, slower than usual, making Grace worry. Of course, if she asked, he'd blow it off, so she'd just observe and see if his hip or foot was acting up.

He gestured to the guy with a thumb. "This is Shane. He's my gift to you."

Grace crossed her arms over her chest. "While that's very kind of you, I was hoping for a puppy." She smiled at Shane. "No offense."

He laughed. It was a good laugh. Like his smile. "None taken. Puppies are definitely cuter but I have a few skills they don't."

Her forehead creased. Morty barked out a laugh. "Attaboy! Some things are worth bragging about."

Shane's cheeks went a pale shade of pink. "Not what I meant. Can we please have a complete restart?" He stepped forward. "I'm Shane Dade. John's son. I'm in construction and renovation." He pointed to his truck, which clearly read DADE FOR YOU. "Morty's asked me to take care of your back porch, knocking out a wall, and any minor repairs that need to be done."

Grace looked at Morty, her grin widening. He waved his hand at her. "Don't make a big deal out of it. I plan on being over here and don't want to fall through that death trap back porch."

"Uh-huh. How very self-serving of you."

He nodded, smiling at her. "That's right. A man's gotta do what's best for himself."

She stepped forward, despite his look of worry, and wrapped her arms around him. "I won't try to talk you out of it since you won't listen, so instead, I'll just say thank you."

He patted her back. "Good girl. Thank me properly by making me some coffee now while Shane unloads his truck and regains his composure."

"Hey. I'm composed."

Morty shook his head. "Kids these days have no game. Telling her you're her gift. Sheesh."

Grace put a hand to her mouth to cover a laugh. Morty's tone was so disappointed that even Shane laughed.

"I'll try to do better, Morty."

"Don't want to end up alone, you'll need to."

Before Grace could head indoors, Morty stopped her with a hand on her arm. "Glad you aren't being too stubborn to agree."

She smiled, her heart full of love. "I'm growing as a person."

~~~~~~~

While Morty chatted Shane's ear off as he worked, Grace dug holes along the fence that separated her yard from Noah's. It seemed like a good place to plant the flowers, which would bloom gorgeously. She measured the space between each hole, taking her time because she wanted to enjoy the project. It might have been overkill as far as apologies went, but she never would have spent this much money on flowers.

Between that and Morty footing the bill for the deck repair and the wall removal, she was nearly giddy with ideas. When she'd played around with designs this morning, she'd had the wall dividing the kitchen and living room in place because she thought it'd be a long time before she could make that change.

She was feeling so good about her yard, about her decision to keep things platonic and neutral with Noah, about Morty doing something so sweet. Basically, she was walking on plenty of sunshine when she went into the house, grabbed some drinks, and brought them out to the guys.

Across the fence, she saw two guys working on the palms. They had a truck parked outside the back gate. Another guy was strolling up the side of Noah's yard, paying particular attention to the fence.

"About time. I'm dying of thirst out here," Morty said, grabbing a can of soda from her hand.

She gave him a wry smile. "You keep saying your feet work just fine. You know where the fridge is." She passed the other soda to Shane.

He smiled, used his forearm to wipe his forehead. It was going to be a hot one today.

"Thanks. Appreciate it." He popped the top, drank half the can down.

Grace looked at Morty. "See? That's how manners work."

The old guy just snorted out a laugh and leaned back in the lawn chair.

Her gaze wandered to the guy strolling her fence line. Curiosity wrinkled her brow, making her miss what Shane said.

Doing her best to refocus, she asked, "Pardon?"

Shane looked over at the guy who'd pulled her attention, then back at Grace. "I was just saying, this is a great place you've got here. I won't be doing the wall today. I'll bring a couple guys back with me for that but the bones look good."

She grinned, oddly pleased that he said so. "I'm really happy with it." She couldn't *believe* she'd thought of selling for even a minute. Unlike Noah, money didn't make her world go round. Guilt nagged at her as soon as she finished the thought. There was more to him than that. She'd seen it. She'd *felt* it.

Her cheeks heated and she broke eye contact with Shane.

Grace pointed. "What do you think that guy is doing?" Maybe he was checking the fence for any damage where Noah had the hedges removed.

Shane looked again. "Looks like he's surveying the property lines."

Something way too close to panic gripped her gut. Why would he do that? Morty sat up, looked over at the guy, who was consulting his clipboard.

"Hey there. What's that you're doing?" Morty yelled.

The guys all looked over. Grace wanted to hide. *"Morty."*

He shrugged. "What? You wanted to know."

The guy adjusted his baseball cap. "Just surveying the land," he called back.

The tree cutters went back to work, and ball-cap guy went back to his clipboard.

"Can he do that?" Grace asked.

Shane looked down at her. "It's his land. He can do what he wants."

"What if part of my land is his?"

"Then you'd have to move the fence line. I'm sure that won't happen."

She shook off the nervous tingles in her stomach. Funny how one man could produce such a wide array of feelings within a twenty-four-hour span.

Smiling overly bright, she focused on the deck. Shane had repaired the rotted boards, fixed the railing. "This looks awesome. I'm so excited. I'm going to get a couple of Adirondack chairs for out here."

"Those chairs swallow you whole," Morty complained.

Grace's nerves wouldn't settle down. When Noah came out of his house, locked his gaze on her, it didn't help. It was possible she was an almost-thirty-year-old with a teenager's reactive reflexes. Damn. So much for her resolve. It was just a kiss, she'd told herself repeatedly.

When Morty and Shane started talking about chairs, Grace casually leaned against the edge of the porch so she could watch Noah walk toward his front yard.

A car pulled into his driveway. She recognized Josh when he got out of the car but not the woman he helped out. Interesting. Rosie and Josh had been inseparable for days.

Josh gestured to Noah, who shook hands with the woman, glanced Grace's way once more, then led them toward the house.

"You okay?" Shane asked. He finished off his soda.

"Fine. Um, I'm going to go finish the planting."

Shane leaned over the rail. "Looks awesome. You picked some beauties."

With a tight smile, she nodded and headed off the porch, trying to hear what Noah and his guests were discussing.

Fine. She couldn't help herself. She approached the guy at the fence line. "Hey."

He looked up, smiled at her. "How's it going?"

"Fine. I'm just wondering, is it standard for you to be surveying a yard after people have moved in?"

From the corner of her eye, she saw Noah watching.

"Not without a request, no."

She *knew* it. That son of a bitch. "Hmm. Is that so. How are the property lines looking?" She spoke through clenched teeth.

The guy looked at Noah, back at Grace. "I should probably write up my report for the customer before I say anything."

God damn it. If she had to pay to have the fence moved over, she was going to throw the slats at him.

"For argument's sake, what if your findings show part of my property is Mr. Jansen's?" She wasn't sure why she'd gone all professional, but it seemed like a necessary buffer.

The man shifted from one foot to the other. "It would depend on the residents but in most cases, adjustments would need to be made."

"And if that happened, who would be responsible for paying the costs?"

The guy was clearly uncomfortable. Noah disappeared into his house. Grace locked her gaze on the city worker. "Would it be me?"

"Again, it would depend but most likely, it would be the person encroaching on the other's property."

Encroaching? Noah Jansen had been encroaching on her thoughts, space, *life* since the day she'd all but stumbled into him. Never mind fences. He was crossing lines and it needed to stop.

Going around the fence, she climbed up his steps, and walked right into his house without knocking. She called his name, heading up the stairs to where she heard voices.

She took the stairs two at a time, which her thighs would regret later, finding Noah and his company in his master bedroom.

They stopped, midconversation, and stared at her, standing in the doorway, her chest heaving.

"Hey, Grace. Everything okay?" There was a mixture of genuine concern and nerves in his voice. He walked over to her, and she couldn't hold back her sarcasm. It was the only shield she had for the duality of feelings he evoked.

"Okay? Gee. I don't know. Let me think. I thought things were *okay* between us but turns out I may need to move the stupid fence after all. You paid for a surveyor? Of all the petty, childish things. You need to learn to take no for an answer, Noah Jansen. In this life, you do *not* get everything you want no matter how much money you have."

Noah put a hand on her shoulder but she shook it off, stepping back. "Grace."

"Shit," Josh muttered behind them.

"Oh my," the woman said.

"Grace. I requested it weeks ago. I forgot they were coming and I had a"—he looked back at the woman—"a thing today. Please don't worry about whatever the report says. I didn't mean for this to upset you."

She shook her head, tears cracking her voice. "Of course you didn't. You don't think about consequences or backlash for anyone else. You just think, 'What do I want and how do I get it.' Then you bulldoze your way over anything and anyone to do just that."

"Grace. That's not fair."

Tears burned her eyes. "*That's* not fair? *That's* what's not fair in all of this?"

She had to curl her fingers into her palms to steady herself. "You have no idea what fair even means. You think because you've painted a couple of boards, learned how to use a roller, you're Mr. Fixer-Upper. You're not. You're just another rich suit who'll do whatever it takes to get what you want. You'll probably get bored of this place and move on. Then none of this will matter to you. But it matters to *me*."

Noah's face went through an array of emotions: surprise, regret, anger, and hurt. Good. It was good to know he had some human feelings.

"Grace, please. Forget the report. I'll fix this," he whispered.

She leaned in. "What will you use? Your money or your charm?" She hated herself the minute the words left her mouth.

Noah reared back. "You're upset. I get that. But like I told you before, Grace, you don't know me. I don't have your story to tell but I have one of my own. Unless you know what it is, don't make assumptions about me. I'll figure out the survey thing, but, for now, you should leave."

Tears blurred her vision as she turned on her heel to go. As she went down the stairs, she heard the murmurs of conversation but not what was being said. She couldn't do this. She'd let Noah Jansen into the tiny cracks in her heart. He'd seeped in like molasses, sticking to all the empty places with the way he made her laugh, smile, and imagine.

How was she supposed to live next door to him, see him every day with the double-edged sword of wanting him and wanting to throttle him? Hopefully, her words would come true: he'd get bored, move on, and she'd pretend he never existed.

18

Noah left the bedroom, following after Grace, but Josh stopped him on the stairs.

"Think it through, man. Don't just storm over trying to fix things."

"I forgot about the land survey." He ran both hands through his hair. Damn it. He'd done what he would in any other situation, only this one was different. He'd hurt her *again*.

"We have Emily here. Let's focus on that," Josh said in a quiet voice, glancing back to the bedroom.

Emily Swanson. A former interior designer turned writer for *Home and Heart*, a world-renowned magazine featuring home renos, how-to features, and a selection of covetable houses. Several famous people's homes had graced the pages, and Josh had used a connection to get Noah's remodel in an upcoming issue.

"I didn't mean to upset her," Noah said, more to himself than to Josh.

His assistant crossed his arms over his chest, tipped his chin up and his gaze down. Surveying *Noah*. "Focus."

Emily joined them, a strange smile tilting her painted red lips.

Shit. Please don't say I've blown it. This magazine spread would be a loud and glossily clear message to his father that he'd arrived. That he'd be just fine on his own two feet. That he was paving his own path with success.

"Emily, I'm so sorry," Noah said, turning on his deal-closing smile.

"Please. Don't apologize. Is everything all right?" She walked to the curved railing, put her manicured hands on it.

"Just a neighborly dispute. I'll sort it out later. Come on. I want to show you what I plan for the guest rooms," Noah said, heading back up the stairs and leading them down the carpeted hallway.

Emily stayed rooted to her spot, so Noah turned, gave her his full attention, his body vibrating with the tension of wanting this to go well and wanting to chase after Grace.

"That woman is your neighbor?" Emily asked.

Yup. His pissed-off neighbor who just outed him for his home-reno *in*abilities. "She is."

"She's fiery. Great energy."

Josh laughed. "Noah seems to bring it out in her. Frequently."

Noah's stomach pitched at the little "hmm" sound that came from Emily. He sent a quick glare to Josh, who shrugged, his smile wide.

"I want something different for this feature. Something unique. Something that will bounce off the page." Was she just talking to herself? She was looking around his upstairs like she could see things he couldn't. "It's an incredible space. I like the old Hollywood vibe."

That was a good sign. "Yes, I agree. It's got so much potential and I plan on being part of each room."

"You have a designer?"

"In the works." Damn, he needed to make a choice. Why was he waffling?

"How about an assistant?"

Josh cleared his throat. "Right here."

Emily crossed her arms over her chest, looked back and forth between them. "The chemistry between you and the girl next door is captivating."

Shit. Could they just focus on his house?

"Oddly enough, Grace is finishing up her degree in design," Josh said.

Noah's jaw dropped. What the hell was he doing?

Emily's expression turned nothing short of gleeful. She actually clapped her hands as if Josh had just put on a show.

"This is too good."

Noah stepped forward. "Grace is a neighbor and as you saw, she's currently mad at me. We have a shaky relationship at best. She hasn't finished her degree and I plan on making this house a livable masterpiece."

"I'm going to level with you, Noah. We both have wants here. I *want* to be able to use this spread as my stepping-stone to editor in chief. I need something in keeping with the magazine's reputation but also a hook that will appeal to an audience that likes to be instantly gratified."

He did *not* like where this was going. He was done being a show pony. It was one of many reasons he'd walked away from his father.

"What are you suggesting?"

Her smile widened. "Let's finish the tour."

He wanted to believe he was in charge, but in this instance he knew she was calling the shots. They walked through the upstairs, chatting about carpeting versus laminate, the new landscape of wallpapering, and how to make it feel cozy but roomy. The entire time, his mind jumped back and forth between Emily's thoughts and Grace's hurt. This screwup was more than flowers. Something warm and unfamiliar had spread through his chest when he saw her planting those flowers in her yard. Without even trying to, this woman was weaving her way into the fabric of his life, and he was scared to pull at the threads. To see where they led.

"Oh, I love this!" Emily clapped her hands, walked straight to the window seat, and sat down on it. He'd had Kyle add it after Grace mentioned it. She'd been right. It looked perfect.

Emily beamed from the spot. "It's gorgeous. It's exactly the vibe you said you were going for. It'll photograph beautifully."

Noah's attention took a sharp turn. "You think so?" *Please think so.* He needed this. Nothing felt like it was going the way it was supposed to. *This* would make him feel like he was back on top.

Emily tipped her elegant chin up. Strands of her tightly wound bun looked golden in the light of the window. "I have some thoughts. I'd like to work with you and a designer of my choosing."

The hair on the back of his neck stood up. "Excuse me?"

"I like Grace."

He closed his eyes, counted to three, and met her gaze. "Grace is my *neighbor.* Who I'm not on the best terms with." *Who rocked my world with a kiss I won't ever forget.* "She's not some up-and-comer. She's completely green."

Emily stood. "The dynamic between the two of you will make up for her inexperience."

"I respect you, Emily. But I want a professional."

Apparently this woman had her own deal-closing smile. "More than you want this spread? Because I'm going big. *This* is big. This is the kind of thing that people will remember. It'll do more than put you on the map without your father's backing. It'll create an entirely new map. Like reality television on the page. There's no way for this not to work. It's edgy but in keeping with our brand."

Josh made himself suspiciously busy. Noah shoved his hands in his pockets, trying not to act or look petulant. "This is a deal breaker?"

She nodded. "I have good instincts. So do you."

Son of a bitch. He did, and those instincts told him that Grace would do a hell of a job on his house. That wasn't what worried him. There was something about her that made him think she could also do one hell of a makeover on his heart.

Emily pulled out her phone, brought up her camera. "I have so many ideas. The photographer can add a video element to our website. We'll get double the audience."

Josh joined them again. "Should I help her with a schedule, boss?"

Noah bit back an unfriendly retort and simply gave one hard nod. He held out his hand to Emily. "I guess we'll be working together."

Her gaze brightened. "Don't you have to work it out with your neighbor?"

Instincts. He had plenty. Grace Travis was a smart woman. There was no way she'd say no to this. No matter how much he pissed her off. Or turned her on. "I'm positive she'll be on board." Then why did he have this niggling worry it was going to take some work to convince her?

Emily beamed. "Instead of one article, which is our usual, I want to do a series. Beginning, middle, end. How a house becomes a home. Oh, that's an excellent title, if I may say so."

Noah's thoughts were running around like a dog after its tail. This was more than big. This was huge. If not for one gorgeous hurdle.

"That's incredible," Josh said, his voice nearly reverent.

"It's going to be a game changer," Emily said.

On that, at least, they could agree.

~~~~~~~~~

Noah tried to put Grace out of his mind while he sorted through logistics, emails, and contracts. Josh had left hours ago, promising to finalize the details with Emily. Noah's job, in the morning, was to smooth the path with Grace—get her on board for something that could be huge for both of them. Right after he got her to forgive him. Again.

Standing on his back deck, he stared at her house. There was a light on but that was the only sign of her being in there. *Why the hell does she feel so far away?* He wasn't sure what was going on inside of him. Maybe he needed to chat with Chris. Or Wes. Maybe he needed to take a quick trip back to New York. See some friends, hit some clubs, and remind himself that he was in the prime of his life. But the only thing he wanted to do as the California sky grew darker was figure out how to mend fences, literally and figuratively, with Grace.

He smiled up at the moon. He'd start there. Obviously, she liked the flowers but they hadn't impressed her. Grace wasn't like any other woman he'd met.

Going back into the house, he grabbed the supplies before heading to her backyard. As quietly as possible, he got everything set up and began working. With Spotify playing through his earbuds, he did something he'd never done before: he stained a deck.

Swiping his brow with the back of his arm, he realized, when he was about halfway through, that he'd put a lot of work into his real estate ventures but never into *himself.* There was a weird, tingling kind of satisfaction coursing through him. Or maybe it was just the sweat stinging his eyes.

Either way, he felt good about what he was doing. He leaned back, resting on his calves, pursing his lips as he struggled to recognize the emotion. It was what he'd strived for in every purchase, every deal he'd made for his father. He'd wanted his *father's* pride. It hadn't occurred to Noah that there was something better. Noah was proud of himself.

19

Grace wanted to throw her pillow across the room. Instead, she put it over her face and screamed into it. She was a pent-up ball of irritation and sadness. And she *hated* it. How many times had her mother lain in bed lamenting over a *man*? That was *not* who Grace wanted to be. Ever. She sat up, tossed the pillow onto the floor.

This wasn't about Noah. It was about her house, her goals, and him *getting in her damn way*. She threw the covers off her lap and got out of bed. She'd have a snack, get a drink, calm her mind, and go back to bed.

Padding through the house in her fuzzy sloth slippers, knowing the space well enough that she didn't need anything other than the natural light of the moon shining through the windows, she stopped at the threshold between the living and kitchen areas. Her heart hiccupped sharply, then lodged in her throat. *Someone's on the deck.* Panic spread, lightning-fast, through her body. *Breathe. Breathe.* Her phone was in her room. *Okay. Don't be the idiot in the horror movie who gets slashed. Think.* She tiptoed into the kitchen with her body hunched over. Leaning against the fridge, she glanced around, looking for a weapon. A knife was obvious, but she'd seen enough movies, read enough books, to know it could be turned against her easily. Nope. She needed something else. Opening her utensil drawer as quietly as possible, keeping her gaze on the window, she felt around, frowned. Turkey baster. Baking spatula. Bamboo sticks ... hmm ... no. Ladle. *What the hell? Why don't you have more dangerous kitchen equipment?* She moved a few things around, glanced at the drawer then back at the window. What if he looked through? The window over the sink would reveal her location in two seconds flat. Her hands closed around a meat mallet.

"There you go." She slid the drawer closed, smiling in the semi-darkness.

Four years of softball had given her a hell of a swing. All she had to do was connect; scare him off. In her crouch, she waddled to the door, stopping when she heard a sound ... heavy footfalls? Scraping? Her breath caught in her throat at the same time her stomach turned. Forcing air in and out of her nose, she held still. When nothing followed, she continued forward. Noiselessly, she turned the lock, still squatting. Grace eased the door open, glanced out, her heart jumping faster than Brutus for a toy. What if he heard it? Looking left, then right, she realized the deck was empty. Or, what she could see of it was. The sea-scented air wafted over her with a hint of ... paint thinner? The sound of distant waves cutting through the quiet. A creak came from the left. Around the corner. Okay. She could do this. Rising, she gripped the mallet, stepping onto the deck with a surge of adrenaline just as a dark, tall figure emerged into the moonlight. Intending to rush him with a warrior cry that would scare the life out of him, she tried to lift her foot. To move. She couldn't. What the? Her brain and her body did *not* work in tandem. She couldn't get her feet to move, but her arm did. Her brain caught up with what she was seeing as the scream left her body and the mallet left her hand. It hurtled across the deck toward ... *oh shit.*

Noah ducked, swiftly sidestepping to the left. "Grace? What the fuck?" The mallet hit the railing with a thud and a crack. Uh-oh. Slowly, he put his hands to his head, pulling out earbuds, staring at her like she was an alien.

Her breathing was too labored to speak. She attempted to run again, this time *into* the house, but her body wouldn't cooperate. What the actual hell?

Through a growl, she yelled, "What is wrong with my feet?!"

Noah didn't come closer. Grace's eyes adjusted to the pale light of the moon enough to see his deep scowl.

"You're stuck in the stain."

She looked down at her sloths. Wiggling her foot, it came out of the slipper. Grace sighed and slipped her foot back inside. "You're staining my deck at almost one in the morning?"

He shrugged. "I wanted to surprise you."

"With a heart attack?"

His sigh could almost be felt across the distance. "I screwed up. I'm sorry. I asked for the survey before I even knew you."

Her anger flickered. Dimmed. "And?"

He met her gaze. "And what?"

She rolled her eyes, trying to hang on to the last bits of her mad. It was easier to be upset with him. "What were the results?"

He paused so long, she wondered if he would answer. He looked back at his house as if he could see through the dark. When he looked her way again, she couldn't read his expression.

"The fence is exactly where it's supposed to be."

All of her muscles relaxed. What could she say? A simple explanation from him always seemed to erase her reasons for walking away.

"Can we talk?" Noah shifted, moving as if he wanted to come closer.

"Not from any closer. You owe me new sloth slippers," she said, attempting humor but sounding cranky. "That was supposed to be a joke."

"Can you get into the house? I'll meet you at the front door."

She nodded, gave her mallet one last look, and pulled her foot out of her slipper, leaning toward the house and stretching until her toes touched the threshold. She didn't want to think about how ungraceful she must look, taking a giant step, trying not to fall flat on her ass on her newly painted deck.

As she walked toward her front door, she realized she wasn't worried about her bedhead, ratty T-shirt, or baggy flannel pajama pants. She should either marry this man or make him her best friend. There were few people in life who kept witnessing her in such unguarded states.

When she pulled the door open, Noah stood on her porch, clutching a small bouquet of flowers.

Laughter and tears bubbled up, wanting to escape. She stepped back.

"I believe these are a more appropriate size," he said, passing them over.

"Maybe you should stop doing things that make you feel like you have to apologize."

He gave a wry laugh, closing the door behind him as she took the flowers. "That's an excellent idea. And my plan."

"Do you want a drink? Some warm milk? I don't usually entertain at this hour so I don't know what the etiquette is."

He followed her to the kitchen. "I'm good. I think, at this point, we've thrown etiquette out the window."

"Like my mallet?" She looked back over her shoulder.

"Is that what that was? It scared the hell out of me. I thought you were going to take my head off. You've got a wicked arm."

"Star pitcher all through school. Good thing you moved and my feet didn't."

She pulled a vase out from under the cupboard with one hand, set the flowers down so she could fill it. Her heart rate had settled but her chest felt too tight.

Using the mundane task of organizing the flowers, she avoided looking at him. He was a lot easier to be angry with, to blame for her feelings and the events of the day, when she wasn't looking directly at him. When he wasn't making her laugh or looking at her like he was dying of thirst and she was the only water around. She caught those glimpses so infrequently, she wondered if she imagined them. When she couldn't fuss with the flowers any longer, she turned, leaned her hip against the sink.

Noah was leaning against the doorjamb that separated the kitchen from the living room. With a lot more grace than she'd pulled off at his house.

"You didn't need to stain my deck."

"I wanted to do something to *show* you I'm sorry."

Her easily malleable heart went squishy.

This isn't about your heart. "Why are you here?"

"To say sorry."

Grace fidgeted with the hem of her shirt, glancing down. "You said it. You gave me flowers."

"I've never given a woman flowers."

Her head snapped up. "How is that possible?"

"I've *sent* them to my mother. That's it."

She wasn't sure what to make of that. "Thanks?"

He chuckled, making the room feel hotter. Pushing off the wall, he crossed the room so he was standing next to her. "In hindsight, I've probably done things that deserved an apology. You're the first woman who's ever made me stop and take a look at my actions. The first to make me want to apologize."

A distracting tingle that she was pretty sure was directly connected to the look he was giving her skittered up her spine. "I'm not sure that's a good thing. It'd make life easier if we stayed away from each other, Noah."

"Absolutely."

He said it with so much enthusiasm, she wished she had her mallet. Then he reached out with his index finger and ran it along the bridge of her nose.

"You're cute when you scrunch your nose up like that."

Grace swatted his hand away. "I'm not trying to be cute."

"You don't have to try. I've never met anyone like you, Grace. I'm sorry I keep screwing things up."

It was her turn to shrug. He wasn't responsible for her feelings. "Let's just put it behind us. We need to move forward. I can't keep getting caught up in fighting with you."

His body moved closer. "I don't want to fight."

She gripped the hem of her shirt in her fists. "We're like oil and water."

"Don't both of those things go in salad dressing?" He cocked his head to the side.

"I have no idea. I know they don't mix."

Closer. She refused to back up even though she was inhaling his addictive scent. The one that made her want to bury her face in his neck.

"Then that's not what we are. We mix. I don't want to screw this up. I realized, even when I'm fighting with you, other than my brother, you're my closest friend. You matter to me, Grace."

She couldn't help the smirk. "You need to widen your circle."

"Cute."

She did her best to hide her smile behind a frown.

Noah dipped his head, obliterating any chill Grace's pulse was pretending to have.

"Are you still mad at me?"

She nodded. "And myself. I'm sorry I stormed into your house. In front of Josh and your guest."

"I deserved it."

"You did. Except for the storming part. That was just rude."

"Guess you owe me some flowers."

They were dancing in circles. It was exhilarating and tiring all at once. She didn't have time or space for this even though pieces of her wanted to reach out and grab it all. Grab him. Kiss him. Could she do casual? A fling? She was almost thirty, looking to settle down. Maybe a fling was exactly what she needed. If she went into it knowing there'd be nothing more, she wouldn't have her heart broken, because she'd be saving it for someone else.

"What are we doing here, Noah?"

"Not what I want," he said, his tone low. Husky.

She swallowed. "What?"

"You have the most incredible eyes. The only thing prettier is your mouth. Especially when you smile. When you smile at me, I feel that high I only get when I go for a great run or hit a particularly good wave."

Okay. Screw forever. She wanted him now. She stepped forward, done with talking, with anger, with the cat-and-mouse games.

"Which is why working with you is going to be so hard. I've made some mistakes in my life but I've never crossed the line between business and personal. So, you can rest assured, no matter how bad I want you, I won't mess this up. I'll stop pushing. Stop flirting. I'll stop pissing you off. I need you, Grace. I need you on my team. I have a proposition for you. One that could be an incredible opportunity for both of us."

Only one opportunity was occupying her brain. "What if I don't want to work with you? What if I want to fall into bed with you, get my fill, and walk away?" *With my heart firmly intact.*

Noah's jaw actually dropped. Grace had never uttered those words to any man but it was 1:00 A.M., a magical hour for propositions and deck staining.

Lust and energy surged through Grace's blood. She stepped into him so their bodies brushed. It was like static electricity. She could almost *see* the sparks. She could definitely feel them. She knew from the look in his eyes that she wasn't alone in that.

His breathing was choppy. It cut through the tension between them. "This is either going to be the greatest or the worst decision of my life."

She could agree with that. She went up on tiptoe, and his hands came to her biceps, gripping her heated skin. Instead of giving in to the kiss they both wanted, he used his hold to move her away from him.

"Grace. We can't."

20

Abort. Abort. Curl into ball, roll out of room, pretend this never happened. Since that plan likely wouldn't work, she went with her backup. Standing by what she said.

Lowering herself from her tiptoes, she stepped back, knowing her face was the color of tomatoes. The only thing that helped was that his expression looked tortured.

"I'm not sure I've ever wanted to take someone up on anything so badly," Noah said in a rough voice that vibrated over her skin.

She cleared her throat, held his gaze. "Too late. Offer rescinded and hopefully forgotten."

"Not a chance," he said, the heat in his gaze making her too warm.

"This is humiliating," she muttered. Could she blame the whole 1:00 A.M. thing?

Noah stepped forward, touched a hand to her cheek so gently, there and gone like a whisper. "Don't. You're an incredible woman in so many ways. You might be the first woman I've properly apologized to, Grace, but not the only one I should have. As much as I'm attracted to you, I actually dig the fact that we could maybe be friends. I don't want to mess that up. Or any of the other stuff I need to talk to you about."

Part of her was proud of them for putting it all out there like adults. Yeah, so they wanted each other. They weren't going to act on it. Life was full of wants and disappointments and she'd rather face that than pretend.

"I could come back tomorrow. Maybe we should talk then."

Nope. Not ending the night like this, still shaky from equal parts desire and embarrassment.

"Come and sit down. Tell me what you're talking about."

They moved into the living room. By unspoken agreement, they sat opposite each other, him on the couch, her in the chair across from it. She tucked her feet up under her, pulled the draped blanket over her body. Shivers traveled across her skin. *From cold. Not mortification. Or rejection.*

When she stifled a yawn, Noah leaned forward, forearms resting on his knees. "The woman you saw at my house? Her name is Emily Swanson. She's a writer for *Home and Heart* magazine."

Grace sucked in a breath. "You're being featured in there? That's amazing." To be showcased as a designer, homeowner, or renovator in that publication was beyond imagination. It was one of the elite but had a down-home feel, making it one of the most popular magazines around. Grace particularly loved their "Quick Trick Design Hacks."

"Thanks. I shouldn't be surprised you've heard of it. Emily wants to make editor in chief. She wants to feature my house, my renovations." He paused, inching forward on the couch. "My designer."

Grace's pulse tripled. What she wouldn't give. She held his gaze, doing her best not to let her jealousy show.

"That's really fantastic, Noah." She meant it. She could be green with envy and still be really happy *and* proud of him.

"Grace, there's more."

She leaned forward, unsure why he looked so worried.

"Emily thought there was chemistry between us. Intense chemistry."

A cross between a laugh and a snort erupted. "Too bad she wasn't here ten minutes ago to see how right she is."

"She wants it on the page. She wants *you* to be my designer. She thinks it'll have some reality TV feel on the page and videos they upload of us working together. Emily says the dynamic between us is exactly the unique twist she's looking for."

Had she hit her head? Inhaled too much stain? Too much Noah? She pushed her feet off the chair, touched them to the floor just to feel it beneath her.

"Grace?" He leaned forward, making the couch dip.

"What are you saying?" She needed words. Recorded preferably. That way she could listen over and over again and be sure what he was asking was what he was asking.

"I want this for so many reasons," he said, resting his elbows on his knees, letting his hands drop between his legs. "In New York, I was at the top of my game. The only thing holding me back was my father. When I came here, I thought it'd be an easy transition professionally. I don't want to cash in on my father's name. I want to pave my own way but every step of the way here has been higher, harder. I don't mind hard work but I feel like I've fallen into one of two zones with my deals—those that want the illusion of my father's reputation and those that want nothing to do with me because of it."

"You work hard, Noah. You're making your way. It just doesn't happen overnight."

He shook his head, gave her a wry smile. "I know. I'm not trying to play the 'poor me' card. But this opportunity would be as big for me as any other person. It's a privilege I feel like I've earned. I want it. She wants you. For the deal to work, it has to include you."

She swallowed around the lump in her throat. "That's the only reason you're asking?" She did her best to keep emotion—hurt—out of her voice.

"Would I have asked you on my own? I'm thinking with both of us laying out the truth in the kitchen, we can handle this, too. No. I wouldn't have asked."

Ouch. She rubbed her fist over her chest. Damn, that hurt worse than she'd expected.

"Not because you're not talented. I've seen so many examples that you truly are. I think you're going to kick ass in the design world."

"But?" She could handle it. *Sure you can.*

"But I wanted to find someone with a name big enough to draw whatever cachet I couldn't."

"That makes sense, I guess. But you want the magazine spread enough to settle for me?"

His eyes went wide and he reached for her hand without a second's hesitation.

"No. I am *not* settling. If you agree, I'm getting an up-and-coming designer that is going to set the world on fire. I'm getting someone with a unique vision who sees things I don't, who makes me imagine how something could be and want it."

Cue heart flutters. "Those are nice things."

He smiled, squeezing her hand before he let it go. "I'm also getting someone who I can't stop thinking about. Someone who frustrates me and turns me on in equal measure. Someone who challenges me and makes me laugh. This could make us really good friends or it could tip us over the ledge into enemy territory."

She thought about that. Working with Noah every single day when just tonight she'd thought staying away from him would solve her problems. Being photographed and written about. It was more than a career stepping-stone. It was a freaking rocket launcher.

"I'm not who you want." She couldn't get over that part. Especially since it was the truth both personally and professionally.

"Professionally, you weren't my first choice. I won't be disappointed, though. I know I won't. Personally, you know that's not true. Truthfully, not going there with me will ensure you won't be disappointed." He gave a rough laugh.

Noah looked down a moment, like the answers to life were on her coffee table. Letting out a deep sigh, he brought his gaze back to Grace's. "I haven't been fair to you. You have every reason to be wary. The truth is, I've never met anyone like you. I'm not great at friendships. I'm shit at relationships. I don't even bother trying because I know myself too well. But I care about you, Grace. You snuck in when few people do. You're talented. Really talented. Even though I've been a jerk, I haven't missed that. I trust you. I'm asking you to take this ride with me."

The ache just below her ribs spread out, overtaking her entire upper body. She wanted those words to be about something else. About life. One they could share together. She'd never met anyone like *him*. A man who made her laugh and forget all of the things she'd focused on for so long. He made her feel like she'd finally woken up. Even when he was driving her mad, he was making her think. *Which is exactly why you should take this.* She could trust in the business side of Noah Jansen. She could not, *would not*, trust him with her heart.

"I'm honored. Truly."

"You'll do it?" He nearly bounced off the couch.

"I'd be an idiot not to. This is an incredible opportunity. I need to know all the details." She couldn't possibly work around three jobs, school, and this.

"Josh is working on all the details. He's having papers drawn up. Emily is coming over tomorrow evening, hoping we'll have a plan in place at the very least." Noah grinned the grin that made her feel like she was floating away on balloons.

"What now?"

"We brainstorm, you draw up designs, I get picky and annoy you. We shop, we create. We go all in and make these magazine spreads unlike any they've ever seen."

"I have to walk the dogs at seven. I need some sleep." Like she'd get any.

"Okay. You can come over to my place later?"

She stood, unable to stay still as she quelled the urge to jump up and down. "I can. I have to ask this straight-out because I have two jobs. It feels a bit awkward but business is business."

He nodded, like he read her mind. He stood up. "I'll be paying you very well, Grace. Count on it."

She frowned. "What you'd pay a designer." Like he felt about his father's name, she didn't want favors.

"Plus ten percent for the last-minute ask and inconvenience of you having to shift your life around."

She nodded. That was totally fair. She'd give Ellie her notice at the coffee shop. It was going to happen pretty soon anyway. Gears turned faster than normal. Could she use this as her Application of Design final project? It would be ideal if she could. She'd be able to use class time if Mrs. Kern approved it.

"Deal."

Noah reached out his hand to shake Grace's. She stood, locked her hand in his. The sparks didn't disappear, but they were easier to ignore when she knew her dreams were about to come true.

"Good night. See you tomorrow."

She walked him to the door, sank against it after he left. She was a designer. She'd hurdled about twenty milestones on her professional journey. It couldn't be real. She had to be dreaming. Looking down at her bedraggled outfit, she snorted with laughter. If she was dreaming, she should have at least dressed herself up.

Punch-drunk with excitement and exhaustion, Grace dragged herself up to bed. Surprisingly, she nodded off without too much tossing and turning. The few times she woke, she was pretty sure she did it with a smile on her face.

21

Mrs. Kern had been cautiously excited for Grace when she shared the news. She also recognized Noah's and Emily's names. She put Grace in contact with a contract lawyer she knew through the university. Grace didn't know how to broach that with Noah, but since he lived and breathed business, it shouldn't surprise him that she wanted her own eyes on the deal. Grace also needed to figure out how to ask if Noah would give a talk to her class, but that hadn't stopped her from telling her favorite teacher she'd check.

Showing up at his house later filled her with foreign butter-flies. The kind that tumbled and danced with the excitement of the trusted unknown. This was a "win-win" for her; she'd do the spreads, become a famous designer to the stars, or she'd do the spreads, no stars would beat down her door but she'd have transformed Noah's four-bedroom house into a luxury home. She was going to graduate with the kind of professional experience she'd only ever dreamed of having.

Noah pulled the door open. He was dressed in his usual jeans and a T-shirt, and she wondered, not for the first time, if the way her heart bounced in his presence would impact her work. *You won't let it.*

"Come on in. Emily can't wait to meet you," Noah said, gesturing his hand toward the kitchen.

She felt more than heard him following behind her as she traveled toward the voices. In the kitchen, Josh and Emily looked over magazines, their heads bent close. Josh and Rosie had been out once, and her friend was more than a little smitten.

Josh looked up. "Awesome. You're here. Grace, this is Emily Swanson. Emily, this is Grace Travis, Noah's designer."

Emily was the kind of polished that made her a perfect candidate to be *on* the glossy pages of a magazine: flawless makeup but a genuine smile that reached her eyes. She extended her perfectly manicured hand, shaking Grace's hand with obvious enthusiasm.

"I am so excited about this. Noah told me this is your first big job."

Grace sucked in a breath, put her customer-service smile on, and nodded. "It is. I'm incredibly honored for the opportunity to work with you and your magazine."

Emily clasped her hands together. A quick scan told Grace that this woman was more in Noah's social group than her own. Noah might dress casually but there was something about people with money—they exuded a kind of confidence that people scraping to make ends meet didn't have.

"It's a dream opportunity for all of us. You get your big break, I'm going to make editor in chief, and Noah is finally going to show his tycoon father that he inherited more than his good looks."

"Ew," Noah said, joining them at the counter. "No more comments on my father's looks or my likeness." He pointed at Josh. "Put that in the contract."

Grace smiled at him, thinking that their parents were something else they had in common.

"Let's get this done so we can get started," Noah said.

Emily slid the contracts toward Grace. Neither she nor Noah showed any concern when Grace expressed that she planned to run them by her own lawyer. As they went through pages of legalese and expectations, it all began to sink in.

It was a three-issue piece; a story that would include both Grace and Noah's backgrounds, what they brought to the table, and their intentions. There'd be photos galore plus video footage. Grace made a note to have it added to the contract that she could approve content. The last thing she wanted was to make a fool of herself and have it posted online.

They talked about working around camera crews, and about the magazine paying for part of the remodel, which seemed like a major bonus but was news Noah barely blinked at. He was likely used to perks. Grace would have her own in that she'd be paid by both the magazine and Noah. *This is going to set me up for my future.* She'd be able to redecorate her own place and afford some of the remodeling she'd planned on putting off.

Noah tipped his head back, laughing at something Emily said. He had such a great laugh. It made her heart squeeze in delight. *You're not here for your heart.* She'd spent her life choosing practical over whimsy. What she felt for Noah was just some pent-up attraction. This magazine opportunity was the real thing. The impact on her life could outlast any feelings she had about her neighbor.

"I want to ask some preliminary questions. My intention, when I take over the magazine, is to make it more connectable to the everyday consumer. They buy it for the chance to see inside stars' homes, maybe do a little DIY that allows them to feel closer to the people they admire. I want our readers to know you two. Know your stories. I want them to take this journey with you, which is why I'll be fast-tracking the information I get from you both tonight. We've got a teaser page set aside for next month's issue. But promos will go on our website by the end of the week to get people excited. They'll highlight what we're doing here."

"It's definitely got a reality show vibe," Josh said. "But in print."

They stood around the island, lukewarm coffee in their cups, agreeing. Noah's brows scrunched together. "My brother got caught up in a reality-show-type thing. It's how he ended up with Everly."

Grace's eyes felt like they popped out of her head, cartoon-style. "Why didn't I piece that together? Oh my goodness. She was the producer that ended up dating listeners. I can't believe I didn't make the connection. It was so sweet that they fell for each other."

"I love that," Emily said, her voice pitching to a croon level.

Josh's smile was almost shy. "Glad it worked out for them but I much prefer the classic boy walks into a bar, meets his dream girl, and they live happily ever after."

Grace smirked, running her finger over the edge of her cup. "Really? I thought you were a fan of next-door neighbor shows up with best friend and charming assistant makes off with said friend leaving me to paint with this guy." She hooked her thumb at Noah. Emily's head swiveled between them as Josh's cheeks turned the color of crisp red apples.

"This," Emily said, pointing at Grace. "You say what's on your mind. It's part of what is going to make this dynamic so fun."

Grace sent a look of triumph Noah's way. Their gazes held too long. Josh cleared his throat.

"Speaking of your best friend, Rosie and I have a date tonight so I'm going to head out. Good luck, you two. Try to keep the fighting and flirting to a minimum."

It was Grace's turn to blush.

"Please don't," Emily said.

"Be good to my girl. I truly don't want to have to hurt you," Grace said.

Josh laughed, squeezing her shoulder on his way by. "Promise I won't make you need to."

How could he promise that after no time at all? She always wondered about people who seemed so sure. So certain. Maybe she was missing that piece. The chip that made her one hundred percent positive she could trust her feelings.

After he left, Emily, Noah, and Grace settled on folding chairs in the wide-open living space.

"I really love that window seat," Emily said, pulling a notebook from her bag.

Grace glanced at Noah, startled that he was already staring at her.

"That was Grace's idea. She's got a great way of mixing comfort with class."

"Oh, I like that. Thanks for the opening line," Emily said, her smile widening.

When Noah's gaze met Grace's, he looked away, crossed one ankle over his knee, tapping his calf.

Emily looked back and forth between them. "Okay. I have ten questions; I'll jot down both of your answers. Say the first thing that comes to mind. We want to give readers an impression of who you two are, how this is different from what we've done before."

"Sounds easy enough," Noah said, clearly not picking up on Grace's nerves. Maybe it was easy for someone who was in the society pages, but all of this was new to her. If she focused too much on the fact that she'd be under the microscope for her very first job, she might hyperventilate.

"Hope so," Grace said quietly.

"Taking on a project like this is like entering any other kind of a relationship. There are risks and rewards for both parties. Name one risk, one reward you think you'll get out of this," Emily said, her gaze locking on Grace.

Twisting her fingers in her lap, Grace sucked in a breath. Wow. *Be yourself. Just answer the questions. Go with your gut. Risk? My heart.* Could they hear it stomping around in her chest like an angry toddler? "The risk is misreading Noah's tastes and style. Creating a look he isn't happy with. The reward is the opportunity to do this project at all."

Emily's hand flew across the page. "Excellent. Noah?"

She felt his gaze but didn't look up. Which didn't matter when his voice slid over her like a caress. "You know my tastes well. That won't be a problem. I think my risk and reward are two sides of the same coin. I want to be more involved but I don't have the same know-how as people I hire. It's one thing to know all the right people to make it look like you want it to. Quite another to have a hand in the final result."

"Great. Favorite style?"

They answered at the same time, Noah saying, "Modern," while Grace said, "Classic."

"Guess we'll see a blend of the two," Emily said. "Color you'd never allow?"

"Pink," Noah said, just as Grace answered the same. They laughed, which helped loosen the knots in her stomach.

"Room you're most looking forward to redoing?"

"This one," Grace said.

Noah nodded. "And the master bathroom. I want absolute luxury."

She could do that. Spending other people's money was way more fun than spending her own.

"Favorite room in a house?"

"Kitchen."

Noah grinned at her. "Same."

"Favorite store for furniture?"

"Pottery Barn," Noah said without hesitation.

Grace actually gasped. "What? Have you ever even been *in* a Pottery Barn?"

"Of course. Briefly. I like their stuff. You don't?"

"Sure. But it isn't my favorite." Why would a place that sold mass-market anything to anyone be his favorite when he could afford *anything*?

"What is?" Noah asked.

"There's a store in Venice Beach called Mi Casa. We'll go. You'll love it."

"I've been there. Love it. You have excellent taste," Emily said. "What's more important, cost or aesthetic?"

Noah said aesthetic while Grace answered the opposite.

Lifting her shoulders, she changed her answer. "Actually, since it's not my money, I'll go with aesthetic too."

Both of them laughed. The rest of the interview was painless and, according to Emily, a great launching point for their impending success. When she left, Noah stood by the door while Grace gathered her things.

Memories of the night before brought back tingles with a side of renewed embarrassment. She had to go. Her ideas were swirling and Noah tended to muddle her brain. The less time alone they spent together until she could stop thinking about the way he made her skin tingle with just a look, the better.

"You look ready to bolt," Noah said, leaning his shoulder against the wall.

Was it okay that he could read her so easily? *He considers you a friend. Think of him that way.* "Sort of. It was great but overwhelming."

"I might not have planned to ask but I'm really glad it's you."

The muscles surrounding her heart spasmed. "Me too."

He hesitated a second, then asked, "You ever feel like life leads you where you're supposed to be, even if you don't know why?"

Grace looked at the floor a moment, catching her breath. When she looked back up, he was still staring. "Not really. I guess I've worked too hard to get where I am, and it's felt like a grind every step of the way. Either way, I'm glad we landed next door to each other."

He chuckled. "Something I never thought I'd hear you say."

"Trust me," she said, opening the door, "I'm every bit as surprised as you are."

22

Noah pressed Decline when his father's number popped up on his phone. He didn't need to speak to him, since he knew exactly how the conversation would go. He did, however, pick up when Wes's number flashed on the screen.

"Hey, man. How's it going?"

"It'd be better if my two idiot brothers weren't screening Dad's calls. Or if I hadn't come in to the office today so he couldn't keep storming in every time one of you ignores him."

Despite the frustration evident in his brother's tone, Noah grinned. "Whose fault is that? We both told you to come out here." Noah poured another cup of coffee. Grace would be there shortly.

"I'm in the middle of three projects right now, all of which Dad lost interest in but I want to see through. Maybe cut me some slack for not having time to come surf or whatever the hell it is you do with all your time."

Noah's fingers clenched around the cup. "Actually, asshat, I'm pretty busy myself with this remodel and renovation. This place is going to be featured in *Home and Heart* magazine." Telling his brother about the three-on-three event was on the tip of his tongue.

"Shit. That's huge, man. No wonder you're dodging Dad's calls. Congrats. I'm proud of you."

It wasn't said often, so the words from someone he emulated, respected, *and* loved warmed him. "Thanks."

"Listen, the reason I called is because a friend of a friend gave me a contact for you. I'll email you the details but this could get you into some of those inner circles to do some of the networking bullshit you like."

Noah laughed. "I thought you just phoned to yell at me."

"Happy side bonus."

"Is this a real estate contact?" Noah could use a few of those.

"The guy . . . let me check my email . . . Sergio—there's a power name for you—Nakoff. He deals in corporate law, knows all the power players in LA. My friend said he could get you on the list for his club, maybe a round of golf. You could schmooze. You're better at that than painting."

Noah gritted his teeth. It was how he'd worked for a long time in New York. Networking was a huge part of building business and relationships. He didn't want to jump through the same hoops but at least this would be on his terms.

"Okay. Shoot me the email. Thanks."

"You okay?"

Someone knocked on his door.

"You didn't bite back about the painting," Wes said. Noah could hear the smile in his voice.

"I'm pretty good at ignoring the shit that comes out of your mouth. I gotta go."

Wes was laughing when Noah hung up, but Noah couldn't help but feel like he wasn't changing anyone's mind about him. *Why does it matter? What'd you tell Leo? Who cares what others think? Even your brothers.*

Gripping the door handle, he swung it open, surprised to see more than just Grace on his stoop. Kyle, a couple of his guys, and a landscaper were chatting animatedly. Grace tipped her chin up, glanced at him, but returned her attention to Kyle like they were best buddies.

Now you feel left out? He shook his head, forced a smile. "Hey." The one syllable was clipped. Easing his grip, he stepped back. "Come on in."

Grace came through first, the scent of her soap disrupting his train of thought. He needed to get that under control.

"Grace says she's doing your design," Kyle said.

"She is." Noah met her gaze, ignored the double jump of his chest. Heart hiccup. That's all that was.

Kyle slapped his hands together. "Let's take a look."

While the guys, and two women, spread out, Grace, Noah, and Kyle headed for the island countertop. Grace was laden down with two huge binders and a laptop.

"Hopefully everything will work as it should. I'm still getting used to the laptop."

Kyle glanced at it. "It's new?"

She nodded. "Sort of. It's a pay-as-you-option."

Noah frowned. Pay as you go? Was she that strapped for cash? He vacillated between saying he'd buy it outright for her or listening to her talk. *You don't need to fix everything for her.* It worried him that he wanted to.

She opened the laptop, and Noah leaned toward her, swallowing down the familiar punch of lust that came from standing too close. For the next fifteen minutes, she led them through a computer design program that made him feel like he was walking around in a virtual world. It was nothing short of amazing. She'd transformed his house; her ideas made it everything he'd thought he'd imagined but hadn't actually visualized.

"Grace. This is amazing. It's so real." He'd seen other programs like this, obviously, but never such an intimate remodeling. Buildings, offices, warehouses. Not *homes*. This would be his home. The images on the screen made a man want to check his shoes at the door and curl up on that kick-ass sectional, a beer in one hand, a woman nestled beside him—*whoa.* He shook his head. *A man. You thought "a man." Not you.*

"You seem surprised."

"I don't mean to. I knew you were talented."

Their gazes met for a few seconds longer than they should have. Long enough for those familiar feelings to stir.

"The appliances are coming this afternoon. We'll work around them since you knew what you wanted there. Plus, I'm guessing it makes it easier to take care of meals and such."

Noah didn't miss the amused glance Grace sent him but he appreciated her restraint in not laughing.

Kyle gestured to the laptop. "Looks like you want a perfectly square island instead of the rectangle?" Kyle pointed his stylus at the screen.

Grace, all business, nodded, making a note in a spiral-bound notebook. "I think, with the size of the room, and it being such a large rectangular space, adding other shapes will create more balance."

"That's why you've got the round footstool and bonus seating?" Noah asked.

"That's right. But all of that stuff is superficial. You can change whatever you want. The built-ins, though, like the island and these shuttered cupboards along the far kitchen wall beside the laundry area, those you need to be sure of."

"I'm thrilled with the way it looks."

"I like the storage in the island. As someone who has young kids running around, having extra space to store stuff is a huge bonus," Kyle said, glancing at his phone. "I need to take this."

"You're looking at me funny," Grace said.

Noah cleared his throat. "I'm impressed."

"Let's hope the magazine is. Are we done here? I have a list of places for us to check out. We'll be ordering a lot of items today so I hope your credit is good."

Had any other woman ever teased him with the confidence Grace did? He'd had female friends. Okay, acquaintances. He enjoyed *being* with women. Spending time with them, but it was a careful balance. Too much time, they wanted more. With Grace, there couldn't be more, so maybe he could have with her something he'd never had with anyone else.

"Are you worried it isn't?"

"Huh?"

Grace shoved his shoulder. "Dude. Head in the game."

He arched his brows. "Did you just call me 'dude'?"

She pressed her hands together. "Sir Dude? Please get your handsome head in the game? Better?"

Biting his cheek to keep from smiling, he nodded, then asked, "You think I'm handsome?"

She turned away before her eye roll was complete. "I'm about to Julia Roberts your credit cards so make sure you're prepared."

Kyle walked back in at that moment, a toothy smile showing through his beard. "Uh-oh. Good thing I got an advance on my part."

Noah grabbed his wallet from the kitchen counter, shoved it in his pocket. "I hope I'm not paying extra for the comedy."

Grace looked at Kyle, shrugged. "Mine comes with the package."

Hell of a package, Noah breathed through his nose.

"Same. On the house, my friend. Also, your appliances will be here around dinnertime so we need to get going."

"Come, my pretty," Grace said, waving her fingers at him.

"Wish me luck," Noah said to Kyle on his way past.

"You're shopping with her all day, you've already got it."

Clearly, Noah wasn't the only one who noticed her charms. She was funny, gorgeous, smart, and one hundred percent off-limits. Perfect. The day wouldn't be long at all.

23

Grace Travis was a machine. A nonstop, shop-till-she-dropped whirlwind of energy. It would have been fascinating if his feet weren't aching, he didn't need to sit down for six hours straight, or she showed any signs of slowing down.

"Do you always shop like this?" he asked.

She looked up from the gray towels she was petting. She'd probably call them moody windstorm or something equally weird, because apparently there were ten billion colors outside of the color wheel.

"Like what?"

He got distracted by her pretty eyes for just a moment but cut himself some slack based on his shopping-related foot pain. *A man can withstand only so much.*

"Like the world might end if we don't buy absolutely everything we see?"

Grace picked up the towel. "Don't be a wimp. I warned you."

He leaned on the display, enjoying the softness of those towels under his arm. These got his vote; he didn't know why she looked uncertain. "You said you were going to Julia Roberts my credit card. I thought you were going to buy a bunch of sexy outfits, some big hats, and chocolate-dipped strawberries."

Her jaw dropped, bringing his gaze to her lips. Her plump lower lip, in particular. "Someone knows their *Pretty Woman* facts."

Oops. "That stays between us." He blamed the shopping for lowering his defenses.

Tipping her head to one side, she picked up more of the towels. "We'll see."

Just like that, his mood notched up. Poking her in the shoulder, he grinned. "What's it going to take?"

Grace set the towels into the cart she'd grabbed—leading him to believe there were a lot more items to purchase—then *"tsk"*ed him. "You call yourself a negotiator? You folded." She snapped. "Like a twig."

Leaning his forearms on the cart, he pushed it forward, side-eyeing her. "I disagree. That's not folding. It's luring you in."

Falling into step beside him, she continued to browse, and for a minute he felt like they were a couple setting up house together. Something he'd never imagined doing with anyone. Giving it a second of thought now, he realized, everything she'd picked, *so far*, worked for him. Would they be compatible in other areas? *One, for sure.* But there were already others. This woman was special and if he couldn't take it *there* with her, he wanted something else. *Damn, Noah Jansen. Did you just grow up and decide to really be friends with a woman?*

"You're easy prey, Jansen. You think you know me," she said.

Always look for the opening. His father's words rang in his ears. He shrugged off the smidge of guilt for applying it to this moment. "Let's change that."

"What do you suggest?" She stopped in bedding.

"Every time we agree on something for the house, we take turns asking each other questions. Every time we disagree, we take turns sharing a secret no one else knows."

Grace turned away from the comforters and stepped closer, tilting her head back. "What's your game?"

It took actual effort not to brush the wisps of hair off of her forehead. "No game. I want to know you, Grace. Stranger, I want you to know me."

She looked around, leaned in a touch farther. "You really think we can make this friend thing work?" She whispered it like they were conspiring.

He played along, glancing around, then giving her a wide-eyed nod. "I do."

Her nose scrunched up. "Friends bring ice cream at any hour. Day or night."

He wanted to laugh but didn't. "Done." Ignoring the couple walking past them, he took a turn. "Friends ask each other for help when they need it."

Her eyes narrowed. "Okay. Friends hang out, have fun together. They go places together."

"We're out right now." It seemed important to point that out.

"We're working. That's different."

It was no hardship to spend time with her. "Anytime. We can go grab lunch and a beer right this second," he said.

"It's ten o'clock. You're such a wimp."

"Only when it comes to shopping. I promise."

Grace stepped back and he missed the feel of her standing close. He shouldn't, but as long as he didn't act on it, things would be fine.

"You liked the gray towels I chose. I go first." She turned, walked farther into the bedding section, and picked up floral-patterned sheets he did *not* like.

"Ask away, friend."

Grace smirked. She was actually reading the information on the plastic covering. *Fascinating.* "I'll ease you in. Where'd you go to school?"

Ha. He had this friendship thing in the bag. "NYU for business."

She started to put the sheets in the cart, but he pulled it back. "What? They're so pretty."

"Nope."

Grace scowled but said nothing as an announcement about a sale came over the speaker. When it finished, she said, "You're just saying that to get a secret out of me."

He laughed, moved around the cart, and grabbed the pale pink floral pattern that caught his eye. "These are nicer. I don't love the color green in general. It's dumb to have flowers be green when the leaves are green. It's too much, you know?"

She stared at him like he'd grown an extra head. "We both said we didn't like pink."

He shrugged, liking that she remembered. "On a wall? No. Like this? It's soft. Sexy. Sweet. It'll be good for a guest bedroom."

There was a look in her eyes he couldn't decipher, but she took the sheets from him, their fingers brushing. Her slight intake of breath was the only sign she felt the flicker of heat, too. "They are pretty." She sighed, set the sheets in the cart. "I need to spend some time thinking about how to make my grandparents' house my own. I want to bring it back to life. I wanted to be there for so long but now that I am, I've barely done a thing."

Every instinct in him had him stepping to her, pulling her into a hug, which clearly surprised her.

"Why are we hugging in the middle of Bed Bath and Beyond?"

He swallowed around the thickness he didn't understand in his throat. "Because I like to hug. There. You got a free secret out of me. Cut yourself some slack. You've been busy." The way her eyes went sad at the mention of her grandparents hurt his heart. He'd never felt that kind of connection to a place. Or wanted to.

Her slender arms wound around him. They stood like that, making feelings war inside of him. This woman was confusing the hell out of him. The only thing he knew with absolute certainty was that if ever a woman could tempt him to want something more—regardless of his own lack of faith in love—it would be the one in his arms. Anything less for Grace wouldn't work. He couldn't risk what he felt for her, this unknown desire to have her in his life indefinitely, for a night of pleasure. What else could he offer? Everyone he knew believed he had no staying power. No ability to commit.

By unspoken agreement, they stepped away from each other. When she picked up a gray comforter to go with the sheets, he nodded, then asked, "Why design?"

"I hated the cramped space of our various trailers so I spent my time rearranging what little furniture we had in different ways. Then I'd imagine how the space *could* look."

Was every answer she gave going to gut him?

"We're heading to your beloved Pottery Barn after this but I prefer the bedding here. We'll pick bedding for three rooms. I have a new idea for the second room downstairs I want to talk to you about."

They stopped in the middle of the aisle when a little girl sat right in front of their cart. The mom gave a smiley wince and crouched down. "Get up, sweetie."

The blond-haired cutie crossed her arms over her chest and leaned back. The large pink backpack made it seem like she was in a recliner. "I tired."

Noah bit his lip so he didn't laugh. With the mom crouching and the little girl sprawled, the aisle was completely blocked.

"I'm so sorry. You need to get up. We're keeping these people from shopping. That's not very nice of us."

The little girl looked like she might cry. Her bottom lip trembled. An unfamiliar warmth filled Noah's chest. He wanted to tell this little girl she could take all the time she needed.

"I sorry," she said.

"That's okay. Shopping makes everyone sleepy," Grace said. She pointed at Noah. "Even this guy. I had to promise him a treat to get him to finish."

His brows arched. *A treat from Grace*. He almost sighed out loud.

The mom smiled at Grace then looked down at her daughter. "Why don't we get some French fries when we're done here?"

"We like French fries," the little girl said, already getting up.

"You and Mom?" Noah asked.

"Nuh-uh. Me and Puggy." She turned around so he could see her pink backpack. It was fluffy and though it opened like a regular pack, it had the face of a stuffed, pink . . . bear? Dog? Animal, for sure.

"Well, hello there, Puggy. Nice to meet you. Enjoy your fries," Noah said.

After the mom mouthed "Thank you," he and Grace stood there a moment longer.

She looked up at him. "You're really good with kids."

He pretended to shudder. "I don't think so. They terrify me."

Her laughter rolled over him, making him happy from the inside out. "You really are a wimp."

As he pushed the cart forward, he admitted, "I may have lost my upper hand after all. Now you know I'm scared of kids and I've watched *Pretty Woman* more than most women."

She bit her lip, fought back her smile. It made him want to draw it out. *Or nibble on her bottom lip. Nope. Nope. Not that.*

"Your secrets are safe with me, Noah. That's what friends are for."

Well, he'd never felt like this about any of his other friends, but maybe it was time for a new adventure. One that made him smile more than he had in longer than he could remember.

24

There was no way to recover any amount of . . . well, *grace*, when she sank into the cushions of the sofa Noah insisted looked awesome. It swallowed her whole.

"I feel like I'm trapped in a foam pit. Help me," she said, reaching out her hand. Jesus. It was fabric quicksand.

Did he reach forward and yank her out? Nope. He took out his phone and snapped a picture.

"Seriously?" She wiggled around, attempting to plant her feet on the ground, but where did the ground go? "This thing is like a quicksand beanbag from hell."

Noah bent forward, laughing harder, deep, sexy, annoyingly endearing chuckles. "You have T. rex legs. They're flailing."

She scowled, turning to the side. He finally leaned in, put both hands on her hips, and plucked her out of the cushions. She smacked his chest. "Jerk move."

"I saved you."

"You took a picture first."

Why was his damn grin so infectious? It widened when he glanced at the couch. "I think you're overreacting. Soft couches are the best."

"Have a seat," she suggested.

With a cocky swagger that made him only more appealing, he stretched his arms wide, dropped down onto the couch. And sank deeper. His knees came up a bit, his brows furrowing into a wince. "There are no springs."

"Just a big mushy pile of foam." Satisfaction thrummed through her. Pulling her phone from her pocket, she snapped a quick picture, making him scowl. "Aw. What's the matter? You stuck?"

He scoffed. "Of course not."

She did her best to bite back her laugh as he wiggled and squirmed out of the seat.

"It's a good one, isn't it? The secret is the wide cushions. Even tall people have difficulty reaching the floor with their back against the cushions," a youngish salesperson said. His spiked hair was colored a deep blue. The kind of blue she thought would look good in the room she wanted to surprise Noah with.

"It's a little constricting," Noah said, brushing his hands down his jeans when he'd extracted himself.

Surprise arched the lines on the salesperson's forehead. "Oh. Perhaps I can show you something firmer?"

"Like a piece of paper," Grace muttered.

Noah's gaze sparked with amusement. "Yes, please. Much firmer. But we can actually just look for ourselves. We'll holler if we need help."

"Yes, sir," the kid said, leaving them to join another bored-looking salesperson.

"You sure about this place?" Noah asked.

"Of course. If you'd listened to me when we walked in, we'd already be ringing up our purchases. Now come on." She took his arm, her eyes scanning the wide array of couches for the one she'd researched. He'd balked at the warehouse stop, but Grace figured the rich stayed rich by taking advantage of a good deal.

"This one," she said. She stopped in front of a large, heather-gray sectional. It was a thing of beauty, with its chaise longue style, its thick, firm cushions, and its sleek microfiber fabric.

Noah rubbed his hands together. "Let's see."

"One second, please," Grace said. She crossed her arms over her chest, the strap of her purse shifting.

Noah stared at her, waiting.

"I get two secrets for that one. Your lack of faith was not only disturbing but hurtful." She couldn't keep the teasing out of her tone. If they were going to be friends, she could drop her shield. Sure, she was attracted to him, but she could stay within the friend zone while still admiring him. Nothing wrong with that. Or the knowledge that this was one of the best days she'd ever had.

Noah stepped closer, and despite the fact that they were in a ten-thousand-square-foot warehouse full of couches, Grace felt like the world shrank down to about two feet of breathing room.

"That's fair." He dipped his head. She felt the wash of his breath over her skin, making it prickle with excitement she shouldn't acknowledge. "I like to eat ice cream in bed while I'm watching television."

The image *that* created was hot enough to *melt* ice cream. Grace twisted her lips into a skeptical pout. "That's a weak secret."

"No way. No one knows that. That's quality, baby."

She laughed at his expression and tone. "Fine. One more."

His breathing shallowed and his gaze locked on her mouth. "This is the most fun I've had with a woman."

Grace sucked in air, the room in her chest restricting to an uncomfortable degree. *Damn.*

Stepping back, she clapped her hands loudly—one hard slap of her palms. "Okay. Let's try this thing out." She broke eye contact to sink into the couch. This one didn't swallow her whole, but Noah's words had already done that more than the last couch, anyway.

He sat down next to her, leaned back, letting his arms stretch along the back. "It's a good one. You know what you're doing, Gracie." He winced. "Sorry."

Looking at him, she shared a secret of her own. "I don't mind when you call me that."

They held each other's gaze as they sat there. They both felt it: the pull between them. The electricity fizzled when the sales guy strolled up, pointing both index fingers at them.

"You've found the one."

His words sank into the depths of Grace's soul. Holy. Shit. Glancing over at Noah, she saw he'd felt the ripple effect of the innocent phrase. The subtle shake of his head was enough to ground her in the moment, remind her of the future. She jumped up.

"Yes. We'd like to order this along with the oversize chair that matches it. I'd also like to order two wingback chairs in this color."

The sales guy's gaze widened almost comically. "Yes, ma'am. Let me get the paperwork."

Noah stood beside her; they both watched him go. "Grace."

"Don't. This is the biggest opportunity of my life, Noah. I'm not getting lost in feelings that won't lead anywhere."

"Hey." She didn't miss the undertone of hurt in his gaze.

She looked up at him, unfounded hurt ricocheting through her body. "Do you even want to be anyone's 'the one'?"

He swallowed, and her chest ached as he shook his head. "But if I did . . ."

"Don't." She held up a hand, following the sales guy so she could find a way to breathe again.

The tone shifted as they chose three bedroom sets, two televisions, and a variety of decorative pieces. Noah nodded approval at each of her choices. There were no more questions or exchanging secrets. The tension sucked. As they settled into a booth, a couple of hours past their intended lunchtime, she vowed to put them back on solid footing. Like adults.

The waitress took their orders of two Cokes, nachos and flatbread to share. The quiet atmosphere of the pub settled some of her nervousness. They both spoke at the same time.

Noah gestured to her then picked up his Coke. "You go first."

Good. Then she could get the words off her chest and maybe breathe again. "What you said about being friends? I want that. Today has been awesome. I can't remember one I've enjoyed more and not just because I was spending your money." She waited for his smile but it was half its usual size. "Obviously, we're attracted but there are too many reasons not to go there. The moment in the store was my fault. I'm sorry. I *do* want to find *the one*. But not yet. Not until I'm entirely sure of *who* I am. I promised myself I would never let a man change the direction of my life. I want one, eventually, who will add to it. Enhance it. I don't ever want my heart to dictate my choices." Because if it did, she'd be sitting in Noah's lap or curled up with him on that awesome couch they'd just bought.

He seemed to measure her words before he spoke. "That seems wrong. I mean, I get what you said and you're right. We can't act on anything. I don't want things to be uncomfortable between us. I like you a lot, Grace. I've never imagined having a woman in my life long-term but I can't imagine *not* knowing you. I don't honestly think I'm built for forever. Not as a partner. But as a friend? I'm loyal as hell. When I tell someone they have my word, I mean it. I do my best not to disappoint the people I care about. It's part of why I stayed with my father's company for so long. We can both admit there's something between us. But we can be in charge of the direction."

She nodded. Look at them being sensible adults. She was nothing like her mother. "Okay. Then we're in agreement. Mostly. Let's get to know each other without the games. Tell me something about you. Something a friend would know."

His shoulders lifted and dropped in a heavy sigh. It was like he'd breathed out the tension between them, shifting them back to better footing. Safer ground.

He set his drink down, folded his arms on the table. "Okay. I can do that. I grew up with two brothers and a sister. We had each other and all of us were focused on getting Dad's approval. Well, except Ari. She's the golden child who can do no wrong. She's a sweetheart but she's a bit lost. Still trying to figure out who she wants to be." His lips tipped up when he gave her words back to her.

"Aren't we all?"

He nodded, glancing around the restaurant. Music pumped softly through the speakers. A couple of waitresses laughed behind the bar. Noah's gaze came back to her own.

"I grew up trying to be like my older brother, Wes, who's all cool, calm, and statistics. He never acts on impulse. Always knows the logical next step. It didn't take me long to figure out that wasn't me. I tried to be a good role model for Chris but he didn't need that. Those two were born knowing which direction was up."

Flutters pulsed around her heart. She could relate. "And you?"

He laughed without humor. "I was born questioning if up was really up. I grasp at straws. I'm too impulsive. Sometimes I think I might be more like my father than I want to be."

"He can't be all bad. Chris seems like a great guy and you have your moments."

Noah's laugh made her feel like she'd won a prize. He picked up his drink, took a long sip before setting it down again. "That's true, I guess. Wes is a great guy, too. Ari's amazing when she actually locks down her focus. She'd do anything for any of us. She's got a heart of gold. So yeah, all his kids turned out okay. But my dad . . . there's an emotional chip missing. My grandfather wanted to build a legacy. That's what he started. We were supposed to continue it together but my dad's turned it into a Jenga game, pulling out pieces that support the whole structure. He doesn't care if it topples as long as he can build another tower. I'm babbling like an idiot. Why do you want to be friends with me? I'm a full-grown adult who's still impacted by his dad's approval."

That actually made her want to be friends with him more. They might come from different backgrounds but they weren't all that dissimilar. The waitress stopped at their table, setting down the nachos, flatbread, and small plates. Grace's stomach growled vigorously. Noah grinned.

"Can I get you two anything else?"

"I'm good. Thank you," Grace said, glancing over at Noah.

"This looks awesome. Thanks."

They gave themselves a moment to dig into the food.

"You're funny and smart." Grace said, dipping a nacho in some salsa.

Noah's brows furrowed in confusion.

"Why I'd want to be friends with you. I'm giving you reasons. You're mostly easy to hang out with. You make me think about things in a different way but we're actually pretty similar. I mean, aside from you growing up the poor little rich boy with the mean daddy and me growing up in a trailer park."

He winced, and she was about to apologize because she'd truly been teasing him, but he interrupted, pointing a tortilla chip at her.

"Don't give me your sob stories. You were just biding your time in those trailers, plotting how to take over the world."

She laughed. "While you were sitting in your ivory tower looking for fun."

Both of them laughed. "It's sad but true," Noah said.

She stopped, waited until he met her gaze. "It isn't. You could have stayed in that tower, taken the easy road, riding high on Daddy's money. Instead, from the sounds of it, you worked your ass off for your dad. When it didn't work for you, you got out, looked for something more fulfilling. *Meaningful.* I know you've had a less hands-on approach in the past but this time you haven't let what you don't know stop you from trying. You're willing to try, adapt, and change. That matters. It's brave. It's hard to go against the grain of how we were taught. The examples that were set for us."

He blinked several times. "You're an incredible woman, Grace."

She inhaled, absorbed the compliment. "We need to stop trying to prove ourselves to people that aren't even paying attention."

"That's good advice."

"That's what friends are for, right?"

They settled into an easy silence while they ate. After the waitress refilled their sodas, Grace lightened the mood. "So? Love? Hate? Must-haves in life? Favorite sport?"

Noah pursed his lips, wiped his hands on a napkin. "Love my family. Hate traffic jams. I need peanut butter brownie ice cream like I need air. Anything with a ball if I'm watching but if I'm *doing*, I prefer running or being in the water."

"Yes. I remember. You came out of the ocean like you were part of it."

"How about you? Hidden talents besides dog wrangling, decorating, and making a man feel good about his life choices?"

Now it was her turn to smile. He couldn't see the happiness bubbling inside of her from the easy way he described her. She'd spent too much of her life defining herself in negative ways. Ways she didn't want to be. But he saw her differently. Maybe one day, she'd be able to do the same.

"I'm pretty good at puzzles. I like running but prefer a treadmill to the road. I can swim but don't do much else in the water. Predictably, I love reno shows, poring through magazines, and playing with design software."

"Where are your parents?"

His phone buzzed on the table. He glanced down, but when he looked back up he didn't stray from the topic. He waited.

"Don't know my dad. Never did. My mom followed him to Vegas as a teenager. They moved around a bit, had me, he split. She kept moving on, trying to find the next one who'd make her life easier. I counted down the days to graduation and left immediately after. I settled here because even though I didn't know anything about my family, I knew where my mom grew up. Met Morty about five years ago and now I have all the family I need."

He nodded, taking it in without judgment, which she appreciated.

She gestured to the phone after crumpling her napkin and dropping it onto her plate. "Who's that?"

"Group thread with my brothers. They're razzing me about picking out furniture. I'm not usually so . . . involved."

She grinned, leaned forward. "You don't say."

"Hey."

"Hey what? You think it's a surprise to learn you usually hire a crew and come back for the reveal?"

Something passed over his features, making her sorry she'd said it so casually. She almost reached for his hand. Instead, she added, "You're making this one different, Noah. You just needed the right project."

"I hope so. I don't know why it matters that they see that. That they realize I'm not like my dad."

Deciding she'd do the same for Rosie, she reached out, covered his hand with hers, ignoring the pulse of attraction that she was resigned to believing would always just hover.

"I'm positive they know it. Didn't we just say we were going to stop trying to prove ourselves to others? All that matters is that *you* know."

He nodded, turning his hand so their fingers linked. Both their breaths caught but neither of them pulled back.

"I do. I just want them to see that I can do this. I can commit to something, see it all the way through. I came here because I was tired of turnover. I was looking to make my own legacy. To feel like I was doing something *real.*"

Grace grinned, slipping her hand out of his so she could form words. "You want real? You want to show them that this time is different?"

He leaned back, eyeing her curiously. "What do you have in mind?"

Lots. But only some of which she'd follow through on. "Just leave it up to me."

"Should I be scared?" His eyes twinkled. She could get addicted to those smiling eyes.

"Maybe. But I promise you'll have fun."

"Famous last words."

Maybe. But, *as his friend*, Grace was going to prove to Noah that he could be the man he wanted to be. One he might not even know he wanted to be. If he wanted to show he could go the distance with the house, maybe he'd open up in other areas. Maybe these requited feelings didn't have to be pushed away. At least not for good.

25

The appliances were in, the kitchen renovations looked fantastic, but the walls still needed fresh paint. The island had been altered to a perfect square with drawer storage on one side and book nooks on each side. Two stools that Grace had ordered were sitting in boxes, waiting to be put together.

"This looks fantastic," Chris said, turning in a circle, taking in the changes. To separate the kitchen and laundry areas, Grace had worked with Kyle to create a custom, rustic, white barn door with gorgeous sliding hardware. Beside it was a frosted-glass door that led to a shallow pantry. She'd thought of everything. *Because she's freaking amazing.* He'd seen glimpses of her talent but taking on this full project with her was eye-opening. And damn impressive.

Noah hadn't seen much of her in the last few days, because she'd been online shopping and arranging deliveries around her school schedule. He'd golfed with Wes's connection twice this week and agreed to a couple more outings. He realized that he missed being with Grace, missed working on the house when he wasn't doing it. He'd also arranged a surprise for his new *friend.*

"This is the kind of kitchen that could make a person want to learn how to cook," Everly said, sliding the barn door back and forth.

Chris glanced over, grinning at the woman who'd captured his heart. Noah never thought he'd see the day his baby brother fell head over heels in love. Noah didn't know how to describe it, but somehow Everly made Chris *more*. *The kind of more you want to be?* Labeling Grace as a friend hadn't stopped his romantic feelings.

Everly joined them at the island countertop, nestling naturally into Chris's side. His brother looked down at her, stroking her hair in an affectionate gesture that made Noah's stomach clench.

Everything about them said forever, but how could anyone know? It was always fun in the beginning. How did a couple avoid being just another statistic? Noah couldn't stand the thought of loving a woman enough to tie himself to her, only to have it fall apart.

"We should ask Grace about doing our place," Chris said.

Noah started to approve the idea but stopped. "Wait. Everly's apartment?"

The two of them turned their heads, similar grins on their faces.

"What?" He was missing something.

"We want to buy a place. We want you to help us find the right one," Chris said.

"Yes!" Noah rounded the counter, clapped his brother on the back. Everly was a little shy with physical affection that didn't come from Chris, but Noah knew her well enough now that he pressed a kiss to her cheek. She still ducked her gaze as a pretty pink flush crept over her skin. "This is awesome. We're not talking stupid starter home, right? We're talking rest of our lives, let's raise the kids and be here for good?"

Everly's gaze widened. Chris laughed, pulling her tighter against his side. "Slow down, man. I just got her used to the idea of moving out of her apartment. We haven't talked a lot about specifics. What do you think, babe?"

Her brows furrowed in thought. "Bigger than a starter home but we don't need something huge. I do want a kitchen like this, though. How'd you know this one was the one?"

Noah's smile didn't belie the happiness bursting in his chest. Everly believed he was in it for good. Those two words, though, "the one," kept coming back to haunt him. "Cliché as it sounds, I walked in and felt like it was home. We're going to find you something perfect. I was online last night looking for properties. I've got a few that I think would work. This is freaking awesome."

The front door bell chimed before he heard Grace's voice. "Knock, knock."

His heart rate spiked as if he'd taken a shot of caffeine. Damn it. He had to get over that. There was a big difference between finding a house to spend his life in and finding a woman to spend his life *with*.

"I brought friends," Grace called out.

She'd asked him to invite Chris, Everly, and any other people he considered friends. She'd already claimed Josh, since he and Rosie were inseparable. They followed behind her now along with Morty, who was holding hands with a woman who had to be Tilly, his fiancée. Another guy, who looked to be Morty's age, joined them. His kitchen was nearly full when Shane brought up the rear. Noah swallowed the discomfort he knew he had no right to feel. It wasn't hard to pick up on the signals that the guy liked Grace. *Which is none of your business.*

"You didn't say you were having a party, bro," Chris said, his tone sharp.

Noah glanced over, taking his gaze off Grace, who looked gorgeous in anything but particularly in the yellow tank top she wore that showed off her tan. *Shit.* He forgot how nervous Everly got around crowds. She had severe social anxiety. As someone who loved being around people, it had taken him some time to learn how large groups impacted his brother's girlfriend.

He knew she'd spoken to a professional about it and that she seemed more at ease around him now than months ago but that could just be her comfort level, having gotten to know him. He started to apologize but Everly looked up at Chris. She ran her hand over his stomach and mouthed "It's fine."

The tension in his brother's shoulders eased but he still felt bad.

"I didn't know I was having a party. Speaking of which, where's Stacey?" Everly's best friend often put her at ease.

"Rob's teaching a class. They're coming after," Chris said.

Grace looked around, coming to Noah's side. "This is not a party. It's a crew."

"What?" He was in the dark. He just hoped whatever she'd planned wouldn't make Everly uncomfortable.

"If everyone will join me in the living room, please," Grace said.

Most of them followed, but Noah hung back a moment to talk to Everly and Chris.

"Hey," Noah said to Everly. "I didn't know there was going to be a crowd. I actually have no idea what she has planned. Might end up having to apologize depending on what I've gotten you guys into."

Chris slid his hand down Everly's arm, connecting their fingers. The quiet smile she gave Chris created an inexplicable pressure in Noah's chest.

"You're sweet to worry but I'm okay," Everly said.

"I did tell you I was the exceptional one. I don't want to fall short," Noah said.

Chris rolled his eyes. "Not sure that's the word I'd use."

"Well, big words are hard for you," Noah said.

Chris's bark of laughter put him at ease. "You should maybe save the trash talk for after we do whatever it is you've gotten us into."

"Fair enough."

They were arguing over who would sit or stand. The couch would arrive in the next few days.

"Are you joining us or not, Jansen?" Grace called.

"Have I mentioned I really like her?" Chris said.

Noah frowned. "You love Everly."

Shaking his head like Noah was an idiot—which, he could admit, sometimes he was—Chris clapped him on the back. "I'll speak slower. Yes, I do love Everly. She's mine. I like Grace *for you*. And in general."

"She's waiting for us," Everly said softly, her lips twitching.

They joined the rest of the group just as Stacey and Rob let themselves in.

"Did we miss anything? Hey, Noah. Wicked place," Stacey called out, stretching her hand up to wave. Rob jutted his chin in Noah's direction.

Waving, Noah joined Grace by the fireplace. She'd pulled two clipboards from somewhere.

He leaned down, caught the scent of something sweet, like strawberries. "What are we doing, Gracie?"

Tilting her head toward him, which brought their faces closer, she whispered, "You'll see. You wanted normal. That means rolling up your sleeves, letting the people who love you pitch in. With a twist."

That weird feeling invaded his chest again. She was unlike anyone he'd ever met. "I hope I don't regret this."

"That's what she said." She bumped his hip and slapped her hand a couple of times on a clipboard, commanding attention easily. "If you guys can spread out a little, I'll introduce everyone quickly. I'm Grace. I'm Noah's interior designer and you'll have to excuse me for how big I'm smiling because that's the first time I've been able to use those words for real. I also live next door." Their friends and family laughed while stepping back. They created a loose definition of a circle.

"I won't make us play any icebreaker games or anything like that, I promise," Grace said.

"Thank you. We get enough of that in school," Rosie said.

"That there is my bestie, Rosie. Beside her is Noah's assistant, Josh." Both Josh and Rosie waved. Grace pointed to Morty. "That's Morty, his fiancée, Tilly, their friend John, who is Shane's dad."

"Noah, you introduce your team." Grace nudged him with her shoulder.

Team? Interesting. "Sure. I'm Noah. Nice to meet all of you. Right there is my brother, Chris, his girlfriend, Everly. Everly's bestie, Stacey, who some of you might recognize as the voice of 96.2 SUN radio. That's her guy and a friend of mine and my brothers', Rob."

"Okay. I'm sure everyone wonders what we're all doing here so I'll get right to it," Grace said. She looked so excited, a little zip of energy flared through Noah.

Grace passed one of the clipboards to Morty and one to John. "Hopefully, you guys have seen the show *Trading Spaces*. This is going to be a little like that with the addition of a good old-fashioned painting party. Noah and I both need some work done in our homes. He wanted to know how people do this without hiring a band of merry men who cost a fortune."

The back of Noah's neck heated. That wasn't exactly it.

"Investments falling flat, man?" Chris's voice was thick with humor.

"As if."

Grace took command again, bringing Noah's attention back to her. Not that it was ever far away. "In the short time since Noah and I have become friends, I've learned that he likes a challenge and a bet almost as much as I do. We're going to break into teams. Each team has to transform one room in the other person's house. Everything is set up and ready. We have three hours. Morty is on our team, so he'll stay here, watch to make sure there're no violations, and vice versa for John, who will hang with us. They'll be our judges. When I moved into my place, I treated my helpers to pizza and beer, which is pretty standard. So, Noah will do that as well. It'll arrive after the reveal."

"At least I'm generous." Noah was trying to absorb all of the information.

The group laughed at his surprise.

"That you are." She winked at him and, this time, lust fired through him. What the hell had he gotten himself into?

Just like that, she split everyone into two groups. His team was Chris, Everly, Rob, and Stacey. Her team had Rosie, Josh, Tilly, and Shane. They were all talking when Noah put a hand up.

Grace bit her lip. Noah wanted to do the same, but for now he'd keep his head in the game.

"You don't have to raise your hand, Noah. We're not in school." Grace's gaze sparkled with amusement.

"He never raised his hand in school," Chris offered.

Noah ignored his brother. "The groups aren't fair."

"I knew you were going to say that," Grace said, a sly smile on her lips.

"Why aren't they fair?" Stacey looked around like she was trying to figure out the advantage.

"There are two design people and Shane owns a construction company."

Grace nodded. "True, but since you and I are doing a side bet, I can't be on your team. You take Rosie and Josh. Stacey and Rob can switch to my team."

"What am I supposed to do for three hours? Think I got nothing better to do than hang out with a bunch of kids?" Morty's voice was gruff but held no rancor.

"We're adults. Also, I've met you, so, no, I didn't expect you to just sit around. You're like the foremen. You'll need to check the clipboard every so often and make sure we're following the rules. There's also a television in each house if you're not needed. You'll live, and get beer and pizza as a reward."

"That's fair," John said, looking at his friend.

"Fine. Which rooms and what's the side bet?" Noah was pumped to get started. He'd enjoyed being more involved—he liked working with his hands more than he'd expected. But some of the home-reno jobs were tedious. Grace managed to spice up even the littlest things.

"Your team is doing my office. I've ordered furniture from Ikea. We'll be taking on one of the upstairs guest rooms."

"What's the side bet?" Stacey looked back and forth between them, rubbing her hands together.

"The side bet is, if we win, I get to do a surprise room for you." Grace's smile reached all the way up to her pretty brown eyes.

"What do I get?"

"Besides more of your house decorated?" Chris asked.

"That's her job. Which she loves." He knew her well enough to know there was a reason she'd added this caveat. He kept his gaze locked on Grace.

"Whatever you want."

An actual hush fell over the group. Gracie's cheeks went a sweet shade of pink. "Within reason."

Noah spread his arms wide. "I'm nothing if not reasonable."

This brought laughter from his brother and Everly, as well as from Stacey and Rob.

"Anything else before we get started?" Noah asked.

"One thing," Grace said. "Josh contacted the magazine to approve all this. They have a photographer coming by in an hour to get some candid shots. Only Noah and I will be in them if they include anything other than the space and changes."

Grace walked up to him, tipped her head back. "You in?"

Noah lowered his head, ignoring everything but this woman who intrigued and turned him on in equal measure. "All in."

Her breath hitched. "What do you want if you win?" She asked it low, so he doubted the others heard.

"I'll let you know."

Her gaze flashed with a moment of apprehension, so he squeezed her arm. "Don't worry, Gracie. You can trust me."

Warmth filled his chest when her genuine smile came back. "I know. Plus, I can kick your ass."

He was still laughing as they split into their teams and went to gather what they needed. With Gracie, it felt like even when he lost, he won.

26

Noah stole a final glance at Grace as they left her and her team in his house. Morty lugged one of those canvas camping chairs with him, talking about how he had better ways to live his life with a hint of a smile on his lips.

"This will be fun," Everly said.

"I'm glad you think so. I was worried you'd be uncomfortable. Now, I'm counting on you to help me win."

Chris shot Noah an amused grin. "You didn't know what she was up to?"

He looked at his brother as they took the few stairs up to Grace's front door and let themselves in. "I had no idea. She's . . . something else."

Chris pursed his lips, giving a slow nod.

"What?" Noah stared at him.

Everly laughed.

Chris didn't even try to hide his grin.

"What? I didn't say anything."

"Grace has awesome ideas like this in class, too," Rosie said.

"Never updated anything in my house," Morty grumbled.

"You told her it was a shrine to a better time." Rosie lifted her brows, daring him to argue.

Morty chuckled. "Huh. Forgot about that. Okay, let's get set up so I can watch television." He moved ahead of them, clearly knowing the layout of Grace's home.

They stopped at the door to the den.

"This is tiny," Chris said.

Noah peeked around him. "The boxes make it look smaller. We're going to crush this. All we have to do is set stuff up and we're done."

Morty smacked the clipboard. "Don't underestimate my girl. Small space, big ideas. Don't be dumb."

Chris muffled his laughter behind his hand. "Yeah. Don't be dumb, Noah."

Everly leaned her face into Chris's arm, trying to cover her amusement.

"You can't do much in a room this size," Noah said.

"You'd be surprised," Rosie said.

He stepped into the room, navigating his way around the boxes to open the window that looked onto the side of his house, letting the air rush in.

"Rules are there's no using the internet for ideas but you can text with your phones. Grace has alerts set for each hour as a countdown. You have to think about what the other person would want and maximize the space. You're supposed to . . ." He trailed off as he squinted at the clipboard. "Make it functional and enjoyable."

Morty clucked his tongue. "Lot of hubbub to paint some rooms."

Noah saw that the others' expressions mirrored his own. Funny old guy. He was all bark, no bite.

"You're allowed to get other supplies if you need them but not change the furniture chosen for the room. Bonus points for creativity in design and execution. I guess I get to give those. Also bonus points for doing a theme. What does that even mean? Not my problem, I guess. You have three hours which started ten minutes ago so I suggest you get going."

Noah reached for the paint, but Rosie put a hand on his arm. "Hang on. We need a plan."

He looked around, counting the boxes. "Okay. Half of us can paint, half can start putting the furniture together?" He was enjoying a lot of the process more than he expected but he wasn't a fan of assembling his own furniture. Stupid Allen wrench.

Rosie nodded, smiling at him like he'd said the right thing. "We want to create a space Grace will love. Let's figure out color and design. Then we can split up. I need a pencil and some paper."

He'd watched Grace enough over the last couple of weeks to know that designers' minds worked differently than his own. It was fascinating to watch how Grace could make subtle changes— move furniture, switch colors, or add an accessory—that pulled her ideas together. Rosie's design was excellent. Worth the delayed start time.

They split up, Everly painting with Noah while the others assembled the furniture and shelving. Nothing was cut-and-dried with Grace. He should have expected that. She'd left two blues, a gray, and a soft yellow for paint, like she was silently testing him. *How well do you know me?* When Rosie and Everly suggested gray with an accent wall of yellow, he didn't share his agreement. But it felt like a victory to have thought it before they voiced their opinions.

As he set up the rollers, trays, and brushes, Everly tied her hair back and up.

"Sorry to rope you into this," Noah said, swiping the dripping paint off the side of the can. It was fun and exciting to him but maybe not how others wanted to spend their night.

"What? This is what friends and family do. Have you never had friends over to paint? Stacey helped me paint my whole place when I moved in," Everly said.

Noah thought about the places he'd lived in. He'd grown up in a penthouse condo in Manhattan. When his parents divorced, he'd stayed with his mom for part of the time in a luxury hotel. He'd gone to college but lived off campus in a high-rise apartment. After that, he'd bought a condo overlooking Central Park. It'd come fully furnished.

Everly picked up a brush and the tray of yellow paint. "I forget sometimes that you guys are rich. Well, I've helped others paint and asked the same of friends. No need to apologize. We're happy to be part of it."

He nodded, a little surprised at his own recap of his living situations. He'd really never done any of this until he met Grace.

"Plus," she said, "I like your friend."

He rolled his eyes. "Thank you, Everly. I hear that tone in your voice but that's all we are, friends."

"Because you're the charming, funny, hard-to-tie-down one."

His bobbed his brows at her, making her laugh. When he saw his brother in the hallway, he called out, "Chris, your girl wants to tie me up."

Chris stuck his head in the room. "Do what you have to, baby. He's expendable."

Everly's chuckle was much like her, sweet and quiet.

"Jackasses."

"I'm surprised there's no twist," Chris said. He passed them both waters.

"You should be working or the twist will be that we lose." Noah took the water, unscrewed the cap, and took a drink.

"Pretty good deal. Even if you lose, the rooms are getting painted." Chris walked over to Everly, gave her a kiss on the cheek, and whispered something in her ear that made her cheeks rosy.

"I'd say get a room but I'm scared you might and I need the help," Noah said. "Get to work. Please. Everly says this is what family and friends do. Go do."

"On it." He winked at Everly, punched Noah on his way by.

"You guys are so funny with each other," Everly said, carefully edging the wall that met up with the windowed one.

"You think? Because we beat on and razz each other?"

She nodded, dipped the brush. "Yup."

"Again, I think you have a weird idea of funny. What'd he mean by twist?"

He started rolling the gray, little splatters coming off the new roller. Good thing he put down a tarp.

"On a lot of those shows, they'll add a twist, like you have to do a feature wall, add a bonus piece of furniture, or they try to surprise someone with something unexpected."

"It's unexpected that we're doing Grace's house, too." Noah liked the fact that she took what she needed while she was doing her job at the same time. That kind of creative energy was what he craved in the final months working for his father. That kind of vision to see things and implement ideas differently.

"This is an adorable house."

It was. A little small for his tastes but she fit there. He figured Grace would fit anywhere. She adapted so well, whether she was chatting with him about design or directing all their friends and family.

He wondered how she was doing. He'd seen a new side of her through designing. She was confident in most situations but her passion for her job lit her up like a beacon. He pulled his phone out to send her a text.

Noah
Just checking in. You like the color orange, right?

He grinned, thinking of her reading it. He loved teasing her, making her laugh. The little dots popped up but he told himself the way his smile widened had nothing to do with the woman. Just having some fun.

Grace
For sure. While we're checking in with each other, you a fan
of birds?

His smile fled. *She's just messing with you now.*

Noah
Not particularly.

No response. He waited, glanced at Everly, who continued to
paint.

Noah
Grace?
Grace
Hmmm?
Noah
Birds?
Grace
Right. Birds. My bad. But flamingos don't really count, do
they?

"What?" Noah did a double take, staring at his phone.
Everly looked over. "You okay?"
"I think so. Flamingos are birds, aren't they?"
Everly's laugh suggested she thought he was joking.

Noah
YES. FLAMINGOS ARE BIRDS.
Grace
You're so fun to tease. Get back to work so you can't blame
losing on texting me.

"Brat," he muttered but couldn't stop the laugh that escaped.

"You keep chatting with her, she'll beat you for sure," Everly said.

Right. Back to work. He continued on, getting a fair amount of wall painted before his shoulders started to ache. Another twist—liking the feelings, physical and otherwise, he got from doing the work.

Music from the other room interrupted his thoughts. Thinking to take a break, he told Everly he'd be right back. Morty had taken up residence in the great room, barking orders at the others, telling them to use a drill, work together, slow down, speed up.

His bushy brows pushed together when he saw Noah. "You're not done painting yet."

"No, sir. Just coming to check on things."

Morty shifted in his chair. "Ought to order that pizza early. A man could starve."

Noah's grin came slowly, like the idea. "I'm sure I can rustle you up something."

Chris's head snapped up. "When was the last time you rustled anything?"

"Wouldn't you like to know?"

Josh made a dismissive sound. "Weak comeback."

Rosie was whipping along on the desk she was making. She didn't seem to need any help. Which meant she was distracted. Noah walked over to Morty. Didn't hurt to play to the judges, right?

"Get you something to eat? You shouldn't have to sit here with no food or drink."

Morty looked up without lifting his head. "Wouldn't say no."

When he didn't find beer in her fridge, he slipped out the patio door. He'd go to his place, grab a couple of premium beers, a little snack, and Morty would be "creatively" entertained. *Bonus points.*

As he slipped in through his own back-patio door, he heard

the movements and noises of the others upstairs. Quickly, he grabbed some chips and nuts from the pantry, then went to the fridge. He had two bottles in his hand when Stacey walked in.

"Hey! Cheater."

Noah looked around quickly. "Shhh. I'm not cheating. I'm getting a damn beer."

Stacey jutted her chin in his direction. "You guys so sure of yourselves that you can waste time on snacks?"

"Who has snacks? I want something. My blood pressure goes wonky as a turntable if I don't eat regularly."

Noah winced as John came into the kitchen area. "I don't know what that means, John. But help yourself."

He turned to leave, needing to get out of there before Grace found out he was in enemy territory. *It's just for fun. Relax.* Straightening, he pushed his shoulders back.

"How's it going?"

Stacey's jaw dropped. "Seriously? You want intel? How about this? You better make sure you do it up good because your girl is a freaking design genius."

His girl. Damn. That burrowed in under his heart. Noah cleared his throat, hoping to dislodge the feeling.

"Whatever. We're doing just fine. I gotta go."

"Hey, babe, can you grab me a . . ." Rob's sentence trailed off when he saw Noah. "Hey, cheater."

Noah groaned. "I am not cheating."

Rob crossed his formidable arms over his chest. The guy owned a gym, but Noah just scoffed at the show.

"What? You gonna bounce me out of my own house?"

John rooted through the fridge, pulling out a bunch of items, making Noah wonder if he'd need to shop when this was all over. *You mean get Josh to shop.*

"I'm leaving."

"I'm telling Grace," John said, his arms laden with pickles, yogurt, a bag of carrots, two sodas, and a container of red-pepper spread. What the hell kind of mix was that?

Noah cringed. "Nothing to tell. I'm leaving. And maybe put a puke bucket by your judge." He saluted Stacey and Rob and hurried back over to Grace's.

The tensions were running higher, giving him that rush of adrenaline. He couldn't remember a time a woman had managed to infuse him with energy when she wasn't even touching him. When he got back, Morty was snoring in the canvas chair. Chris and Josh were lifting a shelving unit upright. Rosie was securing the final shelves inside the desk Grace had purchased.

"Where were you?"

He grinned. Even his own team was suspicious. "I went to get Morty a snack. Can't hurt to keep the judges happy."

"It can if we lose because you were sneaking into enemy territory," Chris said.

Noah laughed loudly, making Morty snort himself awake. "It's *my* house."

Noah looked down at the old guy, who looked momentarily confused. "You should really get that checked out. Here, I brought you snacks and beer."

He took off back to the den to see that Everly had almost completed the feature wall.

"Hi there. You get lost?"

He hurried over to her, tried to take the roller from her hands. "Let me finish. You take a break."

She shook her head, a small smile on her lips. "We don't have time for breaks. You want to win or not?"

It stopped him in his tracks when he realized the answer normally would be a hard-and-fast yes. Now? He was just enjoying the process, the game. The atmosphere Grace had created.

"I'll catch up in no time. Just watch."

As he got to work, he heard Everly chuckle.

"You better hope cute and quick are exactly what she's looking for in a man."

He started to growl back a response but as he rolled gray paint onto the wall, he couldn't help but wonder exactly what Grace *was* looking for outside of her profession. She wanted forever, but what kind of man did she envision? She was definitely attracted to him. That was only a starting point, though. Did she see anything else in him? Did he want her to?

27

"That's time," Tilly said. "Think the others will stop? Morty's probably sleeping."

"I set timers and I'll send a text now."

Grace
Time's up, cheater.

Noah
I didn't cheat! I came over to get some food because your fridge was empty.

Grace grinned at her phone. He was so easy to rile up. She loved . . . no, not loved. She enjoyed being with him, messing with him, making him smile. Like she did with Rosie. They were friends.

Grace
Whatever you say. Meet on the lawn.

Excitement fluttered, making her feel like she could paint another room on her own. Would he like it? They'd talked about what he liked, so she was fairly confident he would, but this felt . . . important.

Rob threw his arm around Stacey. "Nice job, crew. We can do my place next week."

They all laughed. She really liked Noah's friends. She pulled her tank top away from her sticky skin. Three hours to the minute and they'd worked their asses off. She turned in a slow circle, head tilted just a bit, ignoring the photographer snapping pictures of her movements. It was amazing.

"You've got some vision, Gracie," Tilly said, patting her on the shoulder.

"Thanks. You never really know, until it's done, how it's all going to play out."

"We all finished? Is the pizza ordered?" John came into the room, took a look around. He whistled. "Well done. Looks fantastic. I recognize my son's handiwork right there."

He walked closer to the once-useless alcove between the wall and the end of the closet. Grace couldn't figure out if it was meant to store brooms and mops or if it was poor design. Either way, Shane had added shelves, making it not only useful but aesthetically pleasing.

"Let's go then," John said, leading the way out of the finished room. "Meet up on the lawn. Who ordered the pizza?"

Grace's gaze met Stacey's and they shared a laugh. "It's on the way, don't worry."

A warmth settled in Grace's chest as they all came together. Her whole childhood, she'd worried about being alone. She felt relatively safe tucking that worry away. At least, for now.

Noah wandered over, brushed his arm against her shoulder. "You okay, Gracie?"

"I'm great. You?" A subtle buzz started in her toes and moved along her body. She'd never known a man she could feel all the way down to her toes. Once again, she wondered if this was the feeling her mother had given up her family and a different life for.

"I'm pretty excited actually. Your office is kick-ass."

"If we don't eat soon, you're going to have two dead senior citizens on your lawn," Morty called out.

"I fed you," Noah called back.

Grace stepped away from Noah. "Let's wrap this up. Noah, me, and the judges will check out the rooms. You're all welcome to join but if you'd rather take a break, maybe a dip in the ocean, feel free. Pizza is on the way. It'll be here in twenty minutes along with a bunch of pasta dishes, a variety of beverage choices, and brownies."

"Wait, you can order brownies to be delivered?" Stacey raised both hands in a "stop" gesture.

"I could just buy you some on the way back to your place," Rob said, a charming smile on his lips.

"Not the same. But I'll take it."

"I, for one, want to see the rooms," Tilly said.

Grace showed Morty and John how to use the rating scale to assess the rooms. When they walked into the entryway of Noah's house, the photographer, Jack, was putting his gear away. Late twenties, he wore black pants and a black T-shirt, and kept his black aviator sunglasses on the top of his jet-black, spiked hair the entire time he weaved in and out like a silent, picture-taking ninja.

"Already got pictures of the finished product here. Going to head over to Grace's and sneak a peek."

Grace glanced at Noah, then at Jack. "But mine isn't being featured in the magazine."

"Maybe not but I still want to see it." He winked at her as he hefted his bag onto his shoulder, and then he shook hands with her and Noah, and left.

It didn't seem real that a photographer for an international magazine was taking pictures of work she'd done.

"You good?" Noah asked.

She wondered if there were stars in her eyes. "It's surreal."

He laughed, shook his head like he didn't get it. He couldn't. He couldn't know what this moment meant.

"Let's go," she said, nerves starting to swirl, making her feel like she was on one of those giant swing rides at the carnival.

Noah stayed right by her side as they climbed the stairs to the guest room.

"Says here you need to tell us the theme and intention," John said, tapping the clipboard.

Clasping her hands together, sort of glad this part wasn't being photographed, she turned to address the small group of their friends.

"Noah and I had previously discussed color themes." Her gaze automatically sought out his. "This one is ocean blue. My intention was to create an oasis where someone could kick back with a good book or curl up for a wonderful night of sleep or . . ." She grinned, trailing off purposefully.

"Or what?" Morty asked, trying to peer around Tilly's shoulder.

Grace ignored him and turned the door knob. They all entered the room. She sucked in a breath and held it while they took in the transformation. She couldn't look at Noah. She was scared to see his initial reaction.

The feature wall was an off-white with painted lines that gave it the illusion of being covered with shiplap. Shane had done an amazing job making it look like actual panels of whitewashed wood were attached to the wall. The wrought-iron bed was covered in a white bedspread, but accented with giant navy blue pillows, and a white-and-blue-striped throw decorated the end of the bed.

The shelving nook beside the closet had been painted a pale blue, the white knickknacks—a cool-looking shell, pieces of worn-looking beach glass, and a tiny replica of a ship—creating a kitschy beachside vibe. An oversize chair sat just under the window. The other walls were painted pale blue, so the dark blue of the chair really pulled everything together. This was her work and it was going to be featured in a magazine. *The* magazine. She subtly pinched the skin under her arm. *Ouch. Yup. Really happening.*

She watched Noah move around the space, taking it all in. A purposely weathered dresser, also white, sat against the wall across from the window. The room was clean, comfortable, and striking. She saw a smile tip his lips. When he stopped at the chair, his large hand sweeping over the blanket she'd draped across the back, his gaze found her own. Her heart rattled against her rib cage.

"Not a flamingo in sight," he said quietly, his eyes wide.

She laughed, but it sounded as nervous as she felt.

Touring the room, he came back to stand in front of her. "Grace. This is stunning. You're amazing." His tone was reverent, the words seeping into the cracks of her heart that she'd always covered with bravado.

"Not too bad," Morty said gruffly, patting Grace's arm. "Let's go see how he did."

"Don't you know?" Grace sniffled. She would not cry over a design or the look in Noah's eyes taking it all in. So what if it was the best moment of her professional life? And maybe her personal one.

"Nah. Thought I'd keep myself in suspense."

The doorbell rang. Morty lengthened his stride. "Damn. Pizza is here. Might need to take an intermission."

"Oh, stop it. You can wait a few more minutes. Go on, Grace. Take them over, sweetie. I'll take care of setting up the drinks and food," Tilly said, squeezing her arm.

She kept shooting glances Noah's way, and every time she did, he was looking back at her with the kind of awe she wasn't sure she deserved. He hadn't really expected flamingos, had he? Curling her fingers into her palms, she fought the overwhelming desire to slip her hand into his as they entered her house.

"Breathe, babe. Your guy may get easily distracted but we've got you. You're going to love it," Rosie said.

Your guy. Had Noah ever been anyone's guy? Did he have a bad relationship under his belt? One that had changed him, made him averse to finding forever?

John stopped in front of her closed office door, pushing his shoulders back. He wasn't using his cane today. Actually, neither was Morty. She was so happy they'd taken part. Merging the two . . . *Two what? Families?* Groups. She'd go with groups. Bringing them all together was more fun than she'd expected.

"Please state your theme and intentions toward our Gracie," John said.

Morty's laugh turned into a cough. "Maybe we ought to ask Grace's intentions toward Noah."

"Maybe we should stay on track before I deny you both pizza and beer," Grace said with a smile.

John cleared his throat, gesturing to Noah. "Go ahead, boy."

Noah was at least a foot taller than the older man and definitely not a boy, but he stepped forward. As his gaze locked with Grace's, she noted the way he shoved his hands in his pockets, rocked back on his heels. Noah Jansen was nervous. Rosie nudged her hip, ramping Grace's excitement up another level.

"I'll admit that Rosie is the genius behind this vision but we all wanted to create a space for you that was functional and eye-catching. While you're all standing here, I also want to say thank you for doing this with us. It's unconventional for sure. It's . . . special."

Grace's stomach flip-flopped with his words, the intensity of his stare.

"What's the theme?" John asked, tapping the clipboard.

"Serenity," Noah said.

"Productive serenity," Rosie amended.

"Open it up," Chris said, his arm around Everly.

John pushed the door open. Grace moved into the doorway, taking in the changes. Folding her hands together, she clasped them in front of her chest, her gaze moving over every nuance of the space they'd created for her to work in.

Soft yellow adorned one wall, while the others were a light gray. She'd so hoped they'd use the gray. Instead of standing the shelving units against the wall, they'd mounted them above the worktable she'd purchased, which gave her more room than she'd expected. A corner desk sat to the left of the window. The shelving cubes above the one side of the desk were decorated with treasures: a squat gorgeous blue ceramic vase filled with her favorite contour sketch pencils, a framed abstract color wheel, and a cool wooden clock.

On the wall opposite, next to the closet, were the photographs she'd had framed years back. They were black-and-whites of some of her favorite architectural pieces.

"You took off the closet door," she said, her voice scratchy as she walked toward the shelving they'd installed. Most of the shelves were empty, ready for her to fill up, but several copies of *Home and Heart* magazine sat on one of them.

Grace's throat tightened uncomfortably. She stared at the shelves, overcome with the fact that they'd put so much effort and thought into every little detail. It was meant to be fun. A way to show Noah how regular people got their homes painted. With a twist. He didn't have to jump in with both feet. The man was paying her to design his house, not come up with games. He'd not only jumped in with enthusiasm, he'd helped create a dream office space. She breathed in and out slowly.

Noah placed his hands on her shoulders, squeezing gently. She felt his body at her back. Everything else seemed to disappear, though she was sure the others were all still standing there.

"You like it?" he whispered.

Pressing a hand to her mouth, not trusting herself to speak, she nodded.

Noah dipped his head, his breath fanning over her cheek as he spoke into her ear. "You sure?"

A strange sound left her throat as she turned, launched herself at him, wrapping her arms around his neck. The emotions and feelings she tried to keep in check when he was near burst free. She couldn't stop them. "I love it. I love it so much."

Her voice broke but she didn't even care because his arms came around her, locking around her waist.

"Maybe we should check on that pizza," Rosie said.

Grace didn't look up from where her nose was buried in Noah's neck, but she heard the others mumble agreement. Cool air washed through the room from the open window. Noah pulled back, looking down at her with a mixture of concern and amusement.

"What's going on in that beautiful head of yours, Grace?"

She blinked, unsure if she could speak without spilling the contents of her heart all over him.

Noah's hand stroked her hair back from her face. The last vestiges of the day's sunshine flickered along the walls like diamonds sparkling. Grace's breath caught in her throat. She felt so much for this man despite her denial. The cage around her heart, the one she kept locked while she waited for the perfect moment and the perfect man, squeaked open.

"Is it what you imagined, Gracie?"

Swallowing past the lump in her throat, she nodded slowly. "I love it. I feel so selfish because we're supposed to be transforming your house. I just thought this would be a fun way to introduce you to having friends over to help out because you wanted to do things differently and I knew they would do a good job, I mean, Rosie was here. But this is so much more than I expected. I love it. While I was trying to show you how much people care about you, how they have your back and will show up when you need them to—without you having to *hire* them—I showed myself the same thing." All the words tumbled over one another, coming out in an ultrasonic stream of emotion.

Noah's expression was unreadable. She was such an idiot. Why had she thrown all of that at him? Why couldn't she just say thank you? She started to apologize but he beat her to it.

"Grace." His voice was rough. Reverent. "This friend thing might be harder than I thought."

The tip of his nose touched hers and before she could ask him what that meant, he kissed her, his arms tightening around her as he lifted her up against his body. One hand tunneled into her hair, holding the back of her head while the other arm gripped her around the waist. Grace got lost, and possibly found, in the seconds that followed.

Everything that followed was a blur; like a dream she could picture vividly but wasn't entirely sure actually happened. The laughter and voices of their friends were the soundtrack to a day and night she wouldn't ever forget.

With an unspoken understanding, Grace and Noah rejoined the others, standing apart but sneaking glances at each other. She didn't have to be touching or even standing next to him to feel like he was at her side. She wasn't sure she participated in the conversations, the debates over who won. She no longer cared. Nerves hovered along her skin with the acknowledgment of how consumed she felt with *him*. But beyond the worry, surpassing it, was a bone-deep desire to see where it could go. *You're not your mom*. She was in charge.

Noah's heated gaze caught her attention. The overwhelming urge to usher everyone out of her house caught her off guard.

No one seemed to notice that she'd checked out. No one other than Noah.

John raised a hand and announced, "Due to the transformation of such a small space, we've decided that Noah's group wins."

They cheered, leaned into one another, and high-fived. Noah

looked at Grace, then leaned in so only she could hear. "Whatever I want."

She shivered. She wouldn't think about what came next. She'd just focus on right now. One day—one minute—at a time. Even losing, she felt like a winner.

28

Fire blazed through Noah's body when he heard the click of the front door closing. He curled his fingers into fists, watching Grace come back to the living room from saying goodbye. Their gazes collided like stars. Memories of high school astronomy tickled his brain: crashing stars could combine to create a giant constellation or collapse into a black hole.

Even knowing that this could go really damn well or completely implode, he stepped forward. When she reached her hand out, he met her halfway, surprised their connection didn't create bursts of color in the air.

Grace stared down at their joined hands. "We said we wouldn't do this. That we wouldn't go here."

His heart stumbled at the thought of walking away. He'd rather get caught in the black abyss of them not working out than not try at all. He tilted her chin up with his index finger.

"It's not too late to walk away," he whispered, their bodies moving closer.

A one-sided smile tipped her beautiful lips upward. "It's not?"

Had he ever worked so hard to stop himself from taking what

he wanted? Craved? "It's whatever *you* want, Gracie. The choice is yours."

She pressed her hand over his heart, resting it there. "It's yours, too. It'll change things. I'm not a one-night-stand kind of girl. Especially with someone I care about."

God. The thought of walking away after a night with her gutted him, actually making his insides seize. He pushed a hand into her hair, inhaling the unique scent only she possessed. The one that curled inside of him, burrowed into his being. This wouldn't just change things. It would change him.

"I don't make promises I can't keep," he said, his throat unexpectedly dry. "But I can tell you I've never felt like this before or wanted anyone more than I want you. Not just for a night or two or three. I don't know what the future holds but you're all I see, Grace."

She pulled her hand from his, put both of her arms around his neck, gave him that brilliant smile that simultaneously tied him in knots and set him free. "So, we're talking somewhere between three nights and forever."

His laugh surprised him. She was the only woman he knew that could add humor to the tension vibrating between them. He let his forehead touch hers, the connection grounding him.

"Tell me what to do, Gracie," he whispered.

Her body moved against his as she began walking him backward. "If I have to tell you what to do, I'm going to be very disappointed."

Another rough chuckle escaped his lips. "I won't disappoint you. I just want you to be sure." His heart was trying to beat out of his chest as their feet slid in tandem toward her bedroom.

"You're all I see," she whispered, giving his words back to him. She went up on her tiptoes, arching against him as she brought her lips to his. Noah was lost. He scooped her up, his arms wrapping around her like a vise.

In her bedroom, the gentle light of the moon danced through the slats in the blinds. Soft throw pillows in light colors adorned her dark gray comforter. He lowered them, coming down beside her, barely loosening his hold.

He let his lips travel over her face, stopping to kiss her eyelids, her forehead, down her cheeks, along the column of her neck. She was intoxicating. Her breathing halted, started, her body shifting enticingly. Her hands traveled over him, learning his body, driving him out of his mind.

"Noah," she whispered as her hands cupped his cheeks.

He moved over her, kissing her, peace and hunger warring inside of him. Her hands in his hair, their skin touching, her mouth on his; he was drowning. For the first time in his life, he was okay with losing himself if it meant finding them.

~~~~~~~

Noah's career and life were built around measuring risk and reward. He loved that part—knowing, in his gut and his head, if the benefits outweighed the drawbacks. Lying there with Grace's breath fanning softly over his chest, tickling his skin, he realized this was different from anything he'd ever known. Because he didn't make deals or decisions with the piece of himself she'd captured. His heart had no place in boardrooms. Which meant, he didn't know where to go from here.

Acting with his *gut* was different from following his *heart*. Right now, all he wanted was to sweep her beneath him again and profess the feelings overwhelming him. He wanted to make promises and hear them from her lips. He wanted guarantees and bottom lines. Were they a couple? Would this impact their working relationship? Did she regret it? Was he the kind of man she imagined by her side? Had he lied when he told her he wouldn't be a disappointment?

Her hand stilled on his heart. "Not to be cliché but what are you thinking? You've gone quiet but it's like I can feel your thoughts buzzing around the room."

He laughed, squeezed her tighter. "You know me too well."

He sucked in a breath, realizing it was true. Grace lifted up, folding her forearms on his chest, her gaze warm and captivating. Her hair fell around her, brushing against his cheeks.

"That or we think too much alike," she said.

Noah couldn't stop his hands from tracing over her skin. "You think so?"

"More than I would have thought. Are you sorry?" Her eyelids lowered when she asked, and his heart clutched.

Noah cupped her cheek in his palm, waiting until she met his gaze. "I'm so many things right now. Happy. Sated. In awe. Crazy about you. A little hungry. What I'm not, in any way, is sorry. Are you?"

She shook her head, and he could see in her eyes that she meant it. Brushing her fingers through his hair, she looked like she was gathering her words.

"I've been fighting this since the minute I saw you on the beach. I told myself it wouldn't happen but I think it was inevitable. I don't know where we'll go from here and that in itself is different for me. I always need to know where things are going. Where I'm going. But with you, needing those things comes second to how much I need you." She took a deep breath. "And that scares me."

Noah shifted, moving so he was sitting with his back against her padded headboard. He put his arm around her, tucking her into his side. She rested her head on his arm so they could keep looking at each other.

"I'll never lie to you. I'll never intentionally hurt you. I tried to fight it, too, but it's too big."

She snickered.

"Jesus," he groaned.

She covered her mouth with her hand. "Sorry. Continue."

He pressed a kiss to the bridge of her nose. "You're adorable. I don't know how I ever thought I could fight what I feel for you. I'm going to ask Chris to cut your checks through our corporation, though, to put a little separation between the professional and personal. But even if I couldn't do that, I wouldn't take this back. I'm better at contract language than professing feelings but you're like my house, Gracie. Or this one for you. I can't walk away. The pull is too strong. I feel like I'm finally figuring out who I am right here in this place, with you by my side."

She sucked in a sharp breath, moved over him, her hands on either side of his face. "You must be really good at contract language. If you can take a leap, so can I."

His body heated with the intensity of her gaze. "There's something special between us. There're so many great things coming up for both of us. Let's jump. We'll see where we land."

He had a strong suspicion that his heart was going to land firmly in her hands. Which didn't scare him nearly as much as he thought it would.

29

HH
HOME AND HEART MAGAZINE
It's what's inside that counts

New LA Designer Joins Forces with New York Real Estate Developer on an Old Project
Story and Interview by Emily Swanson
Photographs by Jack Stein

HOW A HOUSE BECOMES A HOME; PART 1 OF 3

Regardless of how many times I've done these interviews, how many celebrity homes I've been invited into, how many amazing renovations I've had the good fortune to witness, every experience feels brand-new and unique. Every once in a while, there's an opportunity to do something with a twist. This twist? Hotshot East Coast real estate developer Noah Jansen is putting down roots in a little beach town south of LA. Helping him turn his house into a home is a new-to-the-scene designer, Grace Travis, who lives next door. I mean, *the designer next door*? I can't even make that stuff up. If this isn't reality show material, I don't know what is. Speaking of which, check out our website for behind-the-scenes footage of these two working together on a variety of projects.

Now kick back in your favorite accent chair, because this is the first of a series of interviews and stories about an amazing journey full of heart, hard work, and happy endings.

Emily Swanson (ES): I have so many questions, I almost don't know where to start. Describe yourselves in three words each.

Grace Travis (GT): Motivated. Determined. Resourceful.

Noah Jansen (NJ): Driven. Successful. Confident.

ES: How did you two meet?

(Designer and client exchange an interesting glance I want to read into.)

NJ: Grace moved in next door. I offered to buy her house.

GT: (laughs) About a half dozen times. He wanted to put in a pool.

ES: I take it the answer was no. Something Noah probably isn't used to hearing. Tell us about your background, Grace.

GT: I'm finishing up my interior design degree at California Polytechnic. I've always been interested in design. This is my first professional gig but I've planned some significant projects through school.

ES: It's a big risk, Noah. You have a reputation for closing wicked deals and turning places over. You were part of a Brooklyn development project that altered the landscape of the neighborhood. How do you know Grace is the right fit for this project?

NJ: There are lots of moments in your life, especially in business, where you have to go with your gut. You hope that your experience and history are enough to make the follow-through worth it. Listening to Grace's ideas . . . it's like seeing a young, naturally inclined athlete. You watch them play and you say to yourself, they're going all the way. I saw that in Grace.

Grace tossed the magazine onto Noah's marble-top counter. He laughed, the sound deep and sexy.

"What's wrong?"

She shook her head, backing away a step. "I don't know. I can't read anymore. It's too much. This must be how actors feel, watching themselves on the screen."

Noah stepped into her, wrapping a hand around her biceps, using the movement to pull her into his chest. "Aw. Are you shy, Gracie?"

Before she could answer, he dipped his head and kissed her, making her forget what they were talking about. Emotions ran wild like a late-night, downtown riot only it was the middle of the day. This was all so new: him touching her, kissing her, making her crave more. It was a mystery how this thing that terrified her—their relationship—also ignited her in the best possible ways.

She wasn't losing herself in him, like she'd assumed. If anything, she was learning more about herself. She could compartmentalize to a certain extent. She could miss him when they were apart but still focus on work. She could work with him next to her, and perhaps the best surprise of all was how much she liked being able to kiss him in one breath and share her ideas in the next.

"I've lost you," Noah said, pulling back, pressing his forehead to hers. "You're thinking too hard so I must be doing something wrong."

Ha. No worries in that department. He knew exactly how to do all the things. Not that they'd done all the things yet but she could imagine. *Nope. Don't fall down that rabbit hole. You may never surface.*

"I'm sorry," she whispered, the restless energy seeping through her pores.

"Don't be. Emily dropped it off this morning so we could see an advance copy. It hits stands next week. It's a good interview, Grace. You're professional, intelligent, and animated. You need to figure out what you want professionally because I have a feeling several people will reach out to you about your services."

He was serious. He was her first client and this could launch her into a stratosphere she'd never imagined reaching. When her chest tightened, making it hard to breathe, she realized it might be too much.

"Hey," he said. "Breathe, babe. You've got this. You were made for this."

"I appreciate your confidence, but it's a lot. I haven't even finished school," she said, thinking about the paper on building professional contacts that she still had to write this week.

"You will. You know what? I think we need a proper date," Noah said, leaning back against the counter, pulling her with him, his arms looped casually around her waist.

Just like that, he distracted her from her nerves. Excitement bubbled in her chest, calming her breathing. "Oh yeah? What do you have in mind? I wasn't sure the illustrious Noah Jansen actually dated."

"Hey. What's that supposed to mean? I date."

"The same girl more than once?" God. Why did she say that out loud? Just because it was a thought that had consumed her for the past three nights didn't mean she should throw it in his face.

He winced.

"I'm sorry. That was unkind and unfair."

His hand moved up and down her back. "At one time, probably accurate. Which I'm sure doesn't feel very nice from where you're standing. All I can tell you is there's never been a woman I wanted to make things work with. I had one short-term relationship before moving here. I put my all into it, or thought I did, because I thought that would cure the restlessness I felt."

"Did it?" Did she want to know? It wasn't like she didn't have a past. Mind you, hers wasn't plastered on old editions of tabloids. But still.

"No. Things started to make sense the day I was attacked by a pack of dogs on the beach."

She grinned. "'Attacked' is kind of a stretch."

He brushed her hair back from her face with a tenderness that stole her breath. "You're the only woman I want. I think about you when we're not together, and when we are, I'm thinking about how to make you smile or laugh."

"You're good at that. Both of those."

"I want to show you all the other things I'm good at," he said, hugging her tighter. "You make me want to be good at all of the things I've avoided so far."

She thought about how scared she'd always been to grow attached to someone. How she'd equated falling in love with losing herself. Not that she was in love with Noah, but she could be. She could slip down that slide so easily and never find her way back. But that didn't make her Tammy Travis. Noah wasn't showering her with promises, he wasn't asking her to change her life or who she was. So maybe she didn't know where they were going, but that was okay. It had to be, because whatever was between them was too strong to walk away from.

Stop overanalyzing everything. Just enjoy. You're allowed to have all of this. She took a deep breath, going up on tiptoes to press her mouth lightly to his. He tasted like sugar from the doughnuts he'd had Josh drop off. Noah and sugar. A girl could easily get used to that combination.

"What are you thinking? For our date?"

He smiled, lifting his brows in quick succession. "You'll see.

But I promise, it'll show you that I get you. That I want to know you better. That you matter to me enough to break a lifetime of bad habits. Trust me?"

She nodded. That wasn't the problem. It was herself she didn't trust.

30

Grace pushed the coffee toward the customer, biting back a grin because she *knew* Rosie was staring at her, just waiting to pounce. Her friend had shown up almost at the same time Grace had for her shift. She'd cut back her hours but promised Ellie she'd stay on until she hired someone new. Her date with Noah was tonight. He was at work—buying some new building or something—she was at work. Life was completely normal.

"Have a good day," Grace said, smiling at the elderly gentleman.

"You too, dear." When he walked away, Grace kept her body turned, pretending to wipe down the counter, keeping Rosie waiting.

"Excuse me? Barista? Can I get a refill please?" Rosie asked loudly from the end of the counter where there were a few stools.

Grace laughed, her eyes meeting Rosie's. She *"shh"*ed her as she walked over. "I just got you that. No way you're empty."

Rosie leaned in, pressing her forearms on the counter. "Nope. I need a refill of details. Explicit details."

Grace glanced around. The coffee shop was quiet. She had a quick, four-hour shift. But she didn't want anyone listening in. "There's nothing to tell. We're going out on a date tonight. It's . . . new. For both of us." That was an understatement.

"I thought he was going to set fire to your clothes with just his gaze the other night. What did he say he wanted for winning the bet?"

"He didn't. Not yet." She couldn't think of what he could possibly want. That she wouldn't give him.

"Where are you going tonight?" Rosie picked up her cup.

"Don't know."

She eyed her skeptically over the rim. "You didn't ask?"

Grace shrugged. "It's been so long since I went on a date, I'm just excited to get dressed up and go out. Speaking of, how's Josh?"

Rosie's eyes immediately darted away. Grace's heart tensed like her shoulders. She really didn't want to have to kick Noah's assistant's ass. "What's going on?"

Her friend looked at her through lowered lashes. "No judgment, okay?"

Guilt coated Grace's feelings. Was she judgmental? Did Rosie feel like she was hard to talk to? "Of course not."

Rosie's face lit up. "We're moving in together."

"What?" Grace practically yelled the word, drawing attention from the few customers.

Frowning, her friend set her cup down. "*Shhh.* Look, before you say anything, I know this is something Miss Cautious would never do but we're in love. This is it for me. I'm there and so is he. Why waste time?"

Grace could think of about three dozen reasons without any effort. Instead, she focused on the important piece, pushing down her multiple concerns. "You're happy?"

The look of elation that passed over her friend's face was jealousy-inducing. It was pure, unadulterated contentment. Grace wondered what it was like to be that sure about *anything*.

"I'm so happy, Grace. I didn't know this kind of happy was out there."

She covered one of Rosie's hands with her own. "Then that's all that matters."

The rest of the shift flew by, a midmorning rush, along with Rosie's news, keeping her too distracted to worry. When she got home, she saw a package on her doorstep. It was wrapped in light brown paper with pink polka dots. As she picked it up, curiosity swirled along with excitement. There were two tags, one with a company logo, BROWNIES TO GO, and the other with a message: *Looks like the rumor about brownies was true. Enjoy. See you tonight. Dress comfortably in something you don't mind getting messy. N.*

Letting herself into the house, she opened the brownies immediately. She was taking her first bite before she entered the kitchen.

"Oh my God," she murmured. The delicious taste of mouthwatering chocolate on her tongue overrode her slight disappointment that she wouldn't be dressing up. She was very curious about Noah's ideas of a date. She sort of thought he'd go all fancy. He was the kind of man who enjoyed his money without flaunting it, but she assumed he'd try to impress her with a swanky restaurant or something. Was that what he did with his other dates?

She picked up another brownie. "Doesn't matter. Those dates don't matter. You do. You get more than one." He'd promised she'd enjoy herself, and she might be a fool, but she trusted him. If Rosie could move in with Josh after knowing him three weeks, Grace could take this little leap of faith. After all, he'd had brownies delivered to her door. That was a man who knew his way into a woman's heart.

When Noah showed up on her doorstep, the nerves kicked into high gear. Taking a deep breath, she pulled the door open, a confident smile pasted on her face. He wore slightly faded jeans that looked made for his body, a light gray T-shirt, and a pair of aviators were perched in his styled hair.

"Hey. You look great," he said, taking in her pink tank top and jeans. She'd braided her hair so it wasn't in her face. Noah reached out, stroked a hand over it. "This is pretty."

Cue full-out fluttering. Damn. She could lie to herself all she wanted, saying she was breezy about this, but her heart revved like an engine. She grabbed her purse from the entryway table and slung it over her shoulder, closing the door behind her.

"So are you."

Noah grinned.

She winced. "Not pretty," she amended. "Well, you are. But also, you look great. I'm going to shut up now."

Taking her hand, he brought it to his mouth, kissed the knuckles while keeping his gaze locked on Grace's.

"Don't do that. I like your voice."

Okay. Smoothed over. First word jumble over and done. *Chill out now. It's just a date. Which you haven't been on in a while. Anyone would be nervous.*

He opened the door to his truck but before she slid in, he asked, "You really think I'm pretty?"

Looking up at him with a forced bland look, she poked him in the stomach. "Don't start."

"You make me laugh, Grace," he said, leaning in to kiss her softly.

The way he said it, the way his lips lingered against hers, made her feel like however many high-profile dates he'd been on or how few dates she'd been on in the last few years just didn't matter. She'd gotten to this point in her life by looking forward. She was learning to appreciate the moment, but nothing good came of looking back.

Noah backed out of her driveway. "Not going to ask where we're going?"

She shook her head. "Nope. I like surprises."

She got one when he reached over, took her hand, and threaded their fingers together. "Me too. Tell me something about you that no one else knows."

Whatever she'd thought he might say, it wasn't that. He really did want to know her. She thought about it for a few minutes, then turned her head in his direction. "When I was younger, I used to take any old magazines I could find or flyers and I'd cut out furniture, lamps, anything that went in a house really, and I'd glue them or tape them all on a piece of paper. Sometimes, if we didn't have glue or tape, I'd just arrange each of the items on the floor."

He sent her a quick glance before looking back at the road, just long enough for her to see the affection in his eyes. "That's really sweet. I can actually picture you doing that because you leave little sketches everywhere. I found two on the back of napkins in my house yesterday."

Grace laughed. "I don't even realize I'm doing it. Your turn. Something no one else knows."

She watched him, saw his jaw loosen, his fingers on the wheel tighten. "I've been helping Rob out with some community kids. We get together once a week to play basketball. There's a tournament coming up to fundraise for a new building and I'm trying to get some big donations together."

Her mouth fell open. "Why is that a secret?" Then she clapped her hands together. "This makes so much sense! Rosie thought she saw you leaving the basketball court when she went to pick up her nephew. He's really struggling with his parents' divorce. Lashing out and throwing attitude around. Noah, that's really awesome."

He was such an outgoing person, it surprised her to see the discomfort in his stiff shoulders and the firmness of his mouth. "I don't know. I wanted something that was my own. Something that my brothers wouldn't razz me about, saying I'd never keep up with it. As it is, Rob made me practically swear in blood I wouldn't let them down."

Grace worked to stymie her anger. When she felt like she could speak calmly, she said, "I think when people have magnetic, powerful personalities, people can make assumptions. I guess we do it for all personalities but just because you enjoy a party or socializing does not mean you're unreliable."

"Tell my brothers that. Shit. Sorry. No. My brothers are great. They just like giving me a hard time."

"Sometimes we let how other people see us color how we see ourselves."

"I agree. I'm trying to stop doing that. I'm working on making choices I want for myself rather than to make someone else happy."

Her heart squeezed tightly. "Is that part of why you left New York?"

He turned down a street she recognized but she kept her eyes trained on him.

"That and I felt like I couldn't breathe. I was always pushing for something but none of it had any meaning." His fingers tapped the wheel.

"Is that different now?"

Once again, he looked her way. "Things seem pretty meaningful."

Reaching over, she used the hand not holding his to stroke his arm. It was time to lighten the mood. "Speaking of meaningful, those brownies brought new meaning to my life."

Noah's chuckle filled the cab. "I saw your eyes widen when Stacey and Everly brought it up. "Were they good?"

Grace let out a deep sigh. "So very good."

"Did you save me one?" He pulled onto the highway, piquing her curiosity.

"There might be a few left. I could probably split it. I'll decide after the date."

"Ouch. No pressure." His lips twitched. "Fingers crossed I earn one."

They settled into an easy silence, but the smile stayed on her face. If she didn't think about how a relationship could derail all of her hard work, she'd be fine.

Noah took the exit for Venice Beach. Grace's heart rate accelerated. "Are we going to Mi Casa?"

He turned his head, a wide smile giving her the answer. She bounced on the seat. "You're going to love it!"

"Be one hundred percent honest," he said, weaving through the traffic.

Her tummy tumbled with the serious tone. "Of course."

"Would you rather visit Mi Casa or have those brownies?" He asked with such mock seriousness that Grace tried really hard to answer in kind.

"I'm not sure what kind of man would make a woman choose."

After he pulled onto the kitschy street that housed her favorite store, he found a parking spot, then turned his body toward her, pulling her close with the hand he still held.

"Obviously not a smart one."

When his mouth met hers, Grace had to remind herself that she deserved to live her life, not just wait for it to happen. It was happening now. Falling for Noah didn't mean leaving all her dreams in the dust. No other guy made her worry about her ability to keep her focus. But clearly, given the brownies and the first stop on their date, Noah Jansen was unlike any other man she'd ever known.

31

Noah hurried around the front of his truck to open Grace's door. Why was he so nervous? He'd gone into multimillion-dollar-deal meetings with less anxiety rumbling around in his gut than he'd felt today.

He opened the door, held out a hand to help her down. She was stunning. What she couldn't know, what he knew she wouldn't believe, was even in jeans and tank top, all that sexy hair tied back in a cascading braid, she was the most enticing woman he'd ever known.

"You're looking at me funny," she said, lifting her chin to meet his gaze.

He pressed a kiss on her nose. "That's better than being funny-looking so take what you can get."

Her laughter made him feel like a king. He slung his arm around her shoulders while they waited for the cars to pass so they could cross the street.

"I want to go surfing here," he mentioned as they walked across. "It's popular."

"You ever done it?"

She shook her head as she stepped up onto the sidewalk. Dozens of shops lined the street. The beach was only a block over, but this felt like a tiny world of its own, the palm trees standing like sentinels in front of the brightly colored shops.

"We'll have to change that," he said, pulling open the door to the shop she loved.

"You're a funny, funny man."

"You can't live in California and not surf." He stared at her, blocking her from stepping farther into the store.

She leaned into him and he caught the light citrusy scent of whatever she wore. His blood hummed. She was so sexy without even trying. Maybe that's what made her different from anyone else he knew.

"Don't spread it around but there are actually many Californians who've never stepped onto a surfboard. Despite the rumors, it's not mandatory."

Noah leaned down so their noses touched. She had the cutest nose, and he realized when the thought entered his head that if he was cataloguing that feature, he was probably in dangerously far over his head already.

"Is Grace Travis actually scared of something?"

She glared at him, moved around his body. "Nobody said scared."

Taking her hand, he pulled her to his side. "Our little secret."

She gave him an indulgent but exasperated look. Even that was cute. He was falling fast. "Okay, show me what you love, Gracie."

Before she could point to the first item—her arm was already in motion—the shop's owner greeted them, asking if they were looking for anything in particular. When they said no, she left them to wander.

It was an interesting setup that seemed to have no rhyme or reason. Different areas resembled different rooms in a home, showcasing items, antique, new, and used, that might be found in whatever area of the house it showcased.

"I've been thinking about getting a coatrack," she said, stopping at a dark brown, slightly scuffed rack with black iron hooks. She ran her hand over it. "This one is cool."

"Pretty old-school."

She looked up at him. "That's part of the cool factor."

"My grandmother has one like this. My grandfather would come home from work every single night at seven o'clock for dinner, even if he had to go back to the office. He'd hang his fedora on it. We used to tease him about it all the time. The hat. He said gentlemen wore hats."

Grace turned to face him, putting a hand to his chest. "Your voice sounds sweet when you talk about him. You were close?"

Noah nodded, his mouth suddenly dry. "We were. He was the glue. Well, he and my grandmother, but once he died, things changed." Noah shook off the dark thoughts, thinking he should call his mom and his grams. It'd been too long. "Let's get this for your place."

Like she sensed he needed to gloss over the moment, she nodded. "We'll come back to it. Come on, I want to show you something for the sitting area."

When she stopped in front of a fireplace mantel, he didn't get it at first. Grace ran her hand along the delicate carvings in the dark wood.

"With the white window seat, the white shelving, I feel like this would be such a great focal piece. It's modern and elegant but also warmer than the slate or brick ones that you typically see in homes these days."

Again, it brought back memories of his grandparents' home. What the hell was wrong with him? He was on a date and emotions were swamping him, making him feel twelve years old again. A time when he'd thought his father was as amazing as his grandfather. When he'd thought they'd all work together, changing homes and lives in the neighborhoods of New York. When he didn't know that life changed and not everything stood the test of time.

"Are you okay?" Grace stepped into him, settling both hands at his waist.

"Yeah. I don't know. Something about this place really reminds me of my grandparents. It's hitting me funny. That's all. It's a gorgeous piece."

"We can go," Grace said, her brows furrowing in concern.

He shook his head. "No. You were right about this store. It's great. Let's get the mantel. We'll have it shipped with the coatrack."

"You sure?"

"My grandmother would love you," he said.

Grace's surprise showed in her eyes and the way her mouth dropped open. "She's still alive?"

"Yup. She'll outlive us all."

Grace grinned. "Let me take a picture of the mantel with you in front. You can send it to her. I bet she'll get a kick out of that."

She would. She absolutely would. Somehow, Grace made him feel more connected with little pieces of himself he'd closed off. He didn't know if that should worry him or make him happy. For now, he'd go with happy. He knew how fleeting those moments could be.

───────

When they got back in the truck, Grace looked over, her gaze clearly expectant.

"What?" He started the truck.

"Admit that Pottery Barn's got nothing on Mi Casa."

Grinning, Noah pulled out of the parking spot. "I don't think it's fair to compare the two. It's like comparing a show dog to a mutt."

"Did you just call my favorite store a mutt?"

He wasn't sure how he walked into these ridiculous conversations, but they amused the hell out of him. "Not intentionally.

I think they cater to very different tastes. One for show and one for feel. Hungry?"

"Nice deflection but good description. Yes, I'm hungry. Where are we eating?"

"Can't tell you. Top secret."

She leaned back in the seat. Unlike a lot of the women he'd spent time with, Grace was entirely fine with silence. It was refreshing. It made him relax, feel more like himself.

"Have you talked to Josh?"

Switching lanes, Noah thought about it. "Texted a couple times today. Why?"

"Did he say anything about him and Rosie?"

"No. But we don't gossip and braid each other's hair."

Grace shoved his arm. "Sexist. I braided my own hair."

Noah gave her a smile. "It's sexy as hell. I look forward to undoing it later."

The heat in her eyes sidetracked him. "Don't look at me like that while I'm driving, Gracie. I'd like to get to our destination safe and sound."

"Then don't say things that make me look at you like that."

Gripping the steering wheel with both hands, he returned them to the conversation. "Josh?"

"Maybe I shouldn't tell you. It's gossip. Though, not really since it's true. You really don't talk about stuff outside of work?"

Noah cringed. "Other than the time I asked him out, no."

Grace's laughter rang out over the music playing in the background. "Oh my God. I forgot about that!"

Noah laughed along with her, remembering how awkward he'd felt.

"I wonder if he told Rosie."

"Are you going to tell me the gossip or what?"

"They're moving in together."

He nearly slammed on the brakes. "What?"

She nodded. "That's what I said. But hey, they're grown-ups.

They make each other happy and as Rosie told me, not everyone has a mapped-out plan of how life is supposed to happen. She said they don't want to waste time when they both know."

He bit down on his lip to keep from asking the cynical question that popped into his brain: How could anyone actually *know*? They couldn't. There was no way. Moving in together wasn't like buying a great piece of property. It wasn't something someone just *did* with the security of knowing if it didn't work out, there'd be plenty of others available.

"It's okay if you're skeptical," she said softly.

"Aren't you?"

She was quiet a moment. "Yes. But then I think, I've spent my life being cautious, weighing and measuring my feelings so I didn't dive headfirst into cement. Now I'm almost thirty and single. When I was little, I thought I'd be married with kids by now. What I'm saying is, there's no one right way, I guess. If they're all in, they're all in."

"That's a hell of a gamble. Nothing wrong with weighing your choices. Thinking things through and being sure."

He felt her gaze on him. He focused harder on the road, flipping the visor down to block the streaks of sunset shining in his eyes.

"Haven't you ever just gone with your gut? On a deal? A place you wanted to buy?"

He thought about the warehouses he'd purchased through his father's company. The ones he was currently trying to off-load to get his money back because his father wasn't willing to see Noah's vision.

"Sure. But that's different."

Grace's laugh didn't hold the same humor it had earlier. "Right. A deal is just millions of dollars."

Exactly. A hell of a lot easier to lose money than your heart. He kept the thought to himself.

32

Grace did her best to put the obvious skepticism in Noah's tone behind her as he parked the truck. *You feel the same way. Why judge him for something you agree with?* Because if neither of them believed in acting on their feelings or throwing caution to the wind, what were they even doing?

She looked up when Noah stopped. The Art Shop. Her smile widened when she met his gaze.

"Up for something different?"

Grace gave a quick nod. "You like to paint?"

Noah took her hand. "Walls? Not really. This is different."

"It really is. I thought we were going to grab something to eat," she said, surprised that he could surprise her so much.

"Give me some credit, Gracie. I know how to treat a girl." He nudged her with his hip.

When he knocked on the bright yellow wood door, she saw the sign in the window that said CLOSED. Before she could ask him about it, a lock clicked and someone pushed it open.

A woman, probably in her late twenties, wearing a canvas smock, with clear goggles pushed back on her head and paint smearing her hands, greeted them.

"Mr. Jansen?"

"Carrie?"

"Yup. Come on in."

"We're excited to have you. We've set everything up as requested. The back door locks automatically and I will engage the alarm remotely once you text me that you're finished. Do you have any questions?"

"No. Thank you for accommodating us."

"Our pleasure. Dinner is set up." She pointed to one room. "When you finish, in there, you can head to the back to the Sunset Room. If you need anything, you can call me."

Noah nodded his head while Grace did her best not to let her jaw drop.

She smiled at Grace, then went down a hallway Grace assumed led to the back exit.

Turning in a circle, Grace took in the walls. One was a swirl of rainbow colors with a quote by Degas in black lettering: "Art is not what you see, it's what you make others see." Another wall was a mosaic of colored tiles. Bits of evening sunlight shone through the window, bouncing off those tiles, creating a myriad of colors dancing on the floor.

She'd never been anywhere like this. Grace became acutely aware of the pressure invading her chest. It was like Noah was physically seeping inside of her heart to carve out a cozy spot for himself. One that would leave a hell of an imprint if this didn't work.

"You good?" Noah's voice was soft, the front of his body barely touching the back of hers. She turned, much like she had at her house, launching herself at him.

"This is the best date ever," she whispered into his ear.

Noah lifted her off her feet. "It's only just started."

"Still the best."

Noah's laughter washed over her skin, making her smile, but when his lips pressed against the sensitive skin of her neck, she had to bite back a heady sigh.

"Let's eat."

He led her to a large room with multiple tables. The sign above the door read STUDIO. From the shelves around the room, it looked like this was a do-all room. Paintings dried, brightly colored pottery of different sorts sat side by side, and a few sculptures littered the floor, some as large as Grace.

One of the tables was covered in a soft yellow tablecloth, a vase of daisies in the center. There were two wineglasses, several silver warming trays, and candles burning.

"How?" She could only stare at him.

Noah shrugged. "I had some help."

She was so blown away, she forgot to censor herself. "How am I supposed to not fall for you?"

He grinned. "Is that the goal?"

She tilted her head from side to side, pretending to weigh the question. "A little bit of falling would be okay."

He stepped closer. "Good thing."

"But too much seems unwise."

Closer. "Who's to say how much is too much?"

Grace took a deep breath. "I'd like to escape with my heart unscathed," she whispered.

Both of his hands came to her face, framing it, his thumbs brushing over her cheeks. "I'm afraid there's no guarantees there, Gracie. But I can tell you it's not my intention to hurt you."

God. This was too much for a first date. She suspected that the feeling running around like a wild animal in her chest was the kind of thing that made a woman run off with a boy she loved at seventeen. *Like Tammy.* Or a full-grown woman move in with a man after only three weeks. *This is different. You're going in with your eyes wide open.* Said every person who had their heart broken.

"Don't overthink it, Gracie. Let's just enjoy each other."

She could do that. Hadn't she already told herself that? She could enjoy him without losing herself. She didn't even want forever yet. But as his mouth found hers, she lost her train of thought, her convictions, and her mind. All she could do was *feel*.

When he pulled back, she gave in to his suggestion. "Let's eat. I'm starving. What's the plan after this?"

Noah gestured to a stool, waited until she sat before he lifted the lids off the silver domes. "We paint. I've heard it's a great way to get out some energy or frustration. Like, say, an annoying neighbor who's been a bit of a pain?"

"I'd say you've more than made up for it and I've had a few moments of my own."

She eyed the delicious foods—an assortment of all of her favorites. "I love everything here."

He arched his brows. "You don't say?"

She'd bet anything that he'd asked Rosie. Which made the gesture even sweeter. She loaded some rice onto a piece of naan, and took a bite.

"Want some wine?"

She nodded because her mouth was full. When she finished, she took a sip of the wine he offered, gesturing to him with her glass. "Tell me something you've never told anyone."

His smile told her he knew she was just turning his words back on him. "Pretty sure I already did that today when I told you about Josh."

The memory made her laugh all over again. "That was a great story. Tell me something else. From when you were young."

He used a fork to spear some ultrathin pieces of steak. "When I was fourteen, that show *Star Search* came back on. Do you remember it? I made a video of me rapping and sent it in."

"What?"

He pointed his fork at her. "I need something on you that ensures you never share that story."

She made a face, trying to think of something good. Her childhood wasn't built on funny moments. "I'm trying to think of something, I swear. But all I can think about is you laying down a sick beat." She didn't get all the words out before she snorted with laughter, making him laugh and toss a tortilla chip at her, which made her laugh harder.

"Tell me something."

"Okay. Okay." She took a few deep breaths, averting her gaze from his so she wouldn't break into another fit of giggles.

Picking up another piece of naan, she dipped it in hummus. "Oh. I know. Okay, this isn't something no one knows but the people who do have probably forgotten it because it was twenty years ago."

"Give it up."

"I went to a friend's house for a sleepover once. That was always a big deal for me because I loved to imagine their homes were mine. Well, I was hanging with this slightly older girl, she was eleven to my mere ten. She invited a couple of twelve-year-old boys and a few other girls. She snuck them into her basement and suggested we play spin the bottle. I pretended I knew exactly what that entailed but when we sat in the circle and the bottle pointed to me, I had no idea what was going to happen. This boy, I can't even remember his name, kissed me. It was more like he lip-smushed me. It was ridiculous."

Noah was laughing but she held up a hand. "That's not the funny party. I burst into tears and told them I wasn't allowed to get married. I thought it was some sort of ceremony or something. I got teased for months until we moved. That was actually one of the moves I was happy about."

"Jesus, you're so cute."

She glared at him. "I am not that girl anymore." She waved her hand around the table. "I'm fully aware that none of this means we're married."

Noah pursed his lips. "Maybe not this but once we paint each other, I'm pretty sure we'll be bound for eternity."

Rolling her eyes, she finished sampling bits of everything while they shared stories of growing up. It was surprising to her, given how different their financial statuses were, how much they had in common. At their core, both of them were pleasers trying to outrun the shadows of their parents. *Doing a pretty fine job of it, too.*

When Noah tossed his napkin down, he stood, stretched, and reached out his hand for Grace's.

"We'll have dessert later. You ready?"

There were a lot of things Grace was ready for in this life. Noah Jansen was not one of them. But she slipped her hand in his, going up on tiptoes to kiss him. "Absolutely."

Noah trailed behind her, his hands on her hips, down the hallway to the Sunset Room. The narrow hallway, painted a bright, fluorescent green, was hardly wide enough for one person.

"This one." He reached around her, his hand and arm brushing against the skin of her biceps to turn the door knob. It could have been the wine or the company, but the touch felt more intimate with them standing this close.

The room had rubber mats, splattered walls, and a corner station with a sink that had several shelves above it containing paints. A small, metal, rolling trolley was set up with a variety of paints, brushes, and cloths.

Noah shut the door behind him and went to the trolley. "Everything we need is on here." He turned, pointed to the two canvases that were far larger than she expected. One was nearly her height but narrow, while the other was a fat, perfect square. That would fit beautifully in the spot over the wrought-iron guest bed.

She pointed. "Are we painting our own or each other's?"

He shrugged. "Whatever you want."

"I want to paint that one for you. You paint that one for me."

Noah's mouth dropped open. "Okay. You know this is for fun, right? You've got your design face on and I can't paint."

Walking closer to him, she framed his face the way he'd framed hers earlier. "I don't have a designing face."

"You do." He pointed at her face. "It's on you right now."

"If they suck, we won't hang them, but if they're cool, this canvas is the perfect size for your guest room."

"Okay, well, fair warning, mine is going to be perfect for a dark closet."

She patted his cheek. "Have some faith."

"Fun. I wanted to have fun. Not faith."

She just laughed, checking out the colors on the trolley. They worked together to choose colors. For his canvas, which she knew she'd treasure forever no matter how it turned out, he chose bright shades of purple, blue, pink, and yellow. For hers, which she hoped he'd hang in the spot she suggested, she chose every shade of blue available.

"What are we thinking? Go in slow and deliberate?" He picked up a brush like it had the potential to bite him.

"There's nothing slow or deliberate about splatter paint. Let's get messy," she said, meeting his gaze.

He stared a second, then leaned in over the paint tray she held. "I don't know how that's hot but it is."

She shook her head, surprised by how much fun she was having. "No peeking. Deal?"

"Deal."

He worked on one wall while she worked against another. The sounds of paint splashing and sloshing against the surface were oddly soothing. About five minutes in, he called her name.

"No peeking."

"I didn't turn around."

"What's up?" She chose another blue, dabbed her brush in it.

"This is the best date I've ever been on."

Fortunately, the sound of paint splattering the canvas covered the final drop of her heart. Right into Noah's hands. She took a deep breath, her brush pausing in midair. In many cases, it was safer, and easier, to lean into a fall than try to avoid it. So, Grace let herself lean. Hard.

33

Noah turned on one of his Spotify playlists, which added the gentle beat of music to their painting sounds. It was oddly cathartic, whipping paint at a surface. Grace used a bigger brush to give the entire canvas a coat of pale blue before using the darker shades to create a variety of splatter marks. She kept most of her marks to the upper part of the canvas so she could create the illusion of water below. Her hope was that it looked like water and waves bursting from the sea. She'd use other brushes and possibly a sponge to add some texture to the bottom. She smiled, wondering how his was turning out.

"Two brothers and one sister. That's a busy household," she said over the music.

"It was, for sure. We're really close together in ages. Our parents had us back-to-back."

"How long have they been apart?" She heard him mixing something on one of the palettes.

"Mom left by the time I turned twelve. I'm surprised she stayed so long. The older we got, the more intense my father became. His life was about business and finding a trophy wife. We didn't meet wife number three until they returned from a quickie wedding in Vegas. After her, it's been just engagements. My mom made a smart choice. After my grandfather died, he changed. Not just as a person but his vision for the company."

He said it all nonchalantly, but Grace knew from experience that parents leaving or failing in their roles left marks on a kid.

"You're close to your mom?"

"I am. Not as close as Chris but we talk every couple weeks. Text every few days or so. How about you? You're not close to your mom but do you talk to her at all?"

The paint hit the canvas with a little more energy. "Infrequently at best. A few texts here and there. She's sent a couple letters recently but they're just more of the same."

"What's that look like? The same?"

She grabbed a thick brush and coated it with a gorgeous, deep shade of blue. "Her needing money. Guilt trips for not being a better daughter. Complaining about how hard life is and that she has no one to take care of her. She can't hold a job but it's never her fault. My mom's sort of a 'what can you do for me' person."

"You certainly didn't turn out like her," he said.

A strange, nearly painful, type of happiness bloomed inside of her. She turned without thinking, his simple words a solace she'd craved. Noah heard her and spun as well, pointing his thin-tipped paintbrush.

"Hey! We said no peeking!"

She stared at the vibrant colors decorating the canvas in big chunks. They crossed over one another, spreading out from the middle like a Skittles rainbow. It was so . . . happy.

Grace stepped forward. "Sorry. I didn't mean to look but I worry so much about being like my mom, it was nice to hear that maybe I'm not. Now that I'm looking, I can't unlook and it's so pretty. I love it. It's so happy."

Noah set down his brush, walked closer to Grace, but stared straight ahead at the work she'd created.

"Is there anything you can't do well?" He put his hands to his hips, studying the painting.

She had a whole list of things she couldn't do at all, never mind well. But she liked the way he viewed her. It made her want to see herself that way.

"You like it?"

He turned to meet her gaze. "It's beautiful. It feels alive. This is what that quote means. It's the perfect quote to describe you."

Grace's features crinkled. "What quote?"

"The one you were looking at out front. It's what you make others see. You make me see things I never imagined, Grace."

She sucked in a breath, overwhelmed by the emotion in his gaze. This was the kind of moment that could change a person. Depending on what action she took, she'd look back at these seconds as the ones that determined her path with Noah. *All in one hundred percent, take no prisoners, leave me the tattered remains of my heart when you go. Or door number two: Let's have some fun, tread lightly on each other's emotions, remember me fondly when we part.*

When he didn't make a move, she went for door number two. Lifting her hand, she painted a strip of dark blue all the way down the front of his shirt. His jaw dropped, almost in slow motion, then he looked down.

Grace bit her lip to keep from giggling. When his gaze met hers again, she was pretty sure he could see right through her expression, so she offered, "Oops?"

"Really? 'Oops'?"

"My bad?" She smiled, took a step back as he took one forward.

"Oh, Grace."

She knew she should be worried by the gleam in his eye, the purpose in his step, and the fact that he'd grown up with siblings so he surpassed her abilities in this area. Instead, worry and intensity fled, leaving her with a bubbly joyous feeling. She sprinted around the tray station, squealing when he didn't even chase her but instead went the other way, cutting her off. The music switched to a heavier tempo as she all but crashed into his chest. He slipped the brush from her hand with an ease she didn't have time to admire.

Squirming to get away from the brush, she arched her back over his forearm, which was wrapped around her body.

"Where you going, Gracie?" The brush dabbed her nose. "Oops."

She laughed even as she reached out her arm to slide her fingers through the palette he'd left on the trolley. She swiped a blur of colors down his cheek.

"Back at you."

Noah dropped the brush, pressed his hand into a tray of paints, and cupped her cheek. "You're so cute," he said, his eyes wide with mischief while his grip squeezed her cheek, making her laugh harder.

Grace turned in his arms, reached out to pick up a tray that had smears of red, orange, and yellow. Noah tightened his grip so she was basically back to his front but curled over. Her ribs hurt from the position combined with the uncontrollable laughter.

"Don't do it, Grace. Call a truce."

"Okay," she said, breathing heavily.

His grip tightened. "For real?"

"Yes. Yes. Truce. Here, see?" she said, setting down the supplies.

Noah loosened his grip by degrees. Grace turned in one quick motion, grabbed the bottle of red that he'd left open, and pressed the plastic so a stream of paint shot all over his T-shirt.

When she went to run, she slipped on the rubber mat, dropping the paint.

"Shit, are you okay?" Noah came down after her, realized she was army-crawling to the paint, grabbed her leg, and yanked her closer. "No, you don't."

His longer arms won out, letting him snag the bottle. He rolled them, half pinning her under his large, sexy, slightly sweaty, definitely messy frame.

"Oh. What have we here?" He grinned like the damn Cheshire cat, holding the bottle above her head.

"You wouldn't. Remember, you know how to treat a girl," she said, fluttering her eyelashes dramatically.

"That's true. Treat her like she treats you," he said, squirting out a blob of paint onto her chin. "You got something right there."

Her giggles returned with a vengeance. "Stop. Truce."

"Now, how can I believe you?"

"I swear." She only laughed harder.

"Say 'Noah is the sexiest man I've ever met,'" he said.

She met his gaze, tried to say the words but got only to the second one before a fit of laughter cut in.

"That doesn't sound like what I said." He squeezed a drop onto her forehead.

Grace scrunched her eyes together. "Okay, okay. I'll do it."

She kept her eyes shut until she heard him say, "I'm waiting."

She held back the laughter but couldn't erase the smile. "Noah is the sexiest man I've ever met." He had no idea how true that was, but she wasn't about to share.

"'He's a painting master and I've learned a great deal from him,'" he continued.

Grace snorted, taking advantage of the way his body relaxed. With one hand, she knocked the bottle across the mat while rolling so he was pinned under her. She held both his arms down, knowing full well he could dislodge her with little more than a deep breath.

"Now who's in charge?" She gave him her best menacing stare.

"It's been you the whole time."

Her heart smiled at his words. "Say 'Grace is the boss of everything, she's all-knowing and sexier than any woman I'll ever meet.'"

Humoring her, he nodded. "All true. Grace is the boss, she's all-knowing, and I've never met, nor will I meet, anyone sexier."

Ha. She started to slide off his body before she attacked him with more than paint but he moved his arms, capturing her waist. "Not so fast," he whispered, his voice going husky.

She gave in to the kiss, letting her body meld into his while his hands roamed up and down. The swells of music and the scent of paint faded into oblivion as Grace memorized the taste and feel of him.

When he rolled, bringing her under him again, he brushed her hair back from her forehead. "You're pretty messy."

She reached up, cupping his paint-covered cheek. "So are you."

"We should go."

"That wasn't where my mind was headed," she said honestly.

Desire flashed in his eyes. "As much as I want you, Grace—"

When he paused, embarrassment surfaced. Here she was throwing herself at the man. It wasn't like he was hard up, and here she—

He cut her off, clearing his throat. "There are just some places a man doesn't want to get paint."

Grace's thoughts came to an abrupt halt as she envisioned Noah covered head to toe in paint. "Good point." Maybe her voice was a little huskier than she'd intended but it was tinged with amusement as well. "I think you'd look good with a blue ass."

He pressed a kiss to her lips. "Flatterer."

She started to get up, but he pulled her onto his lap as they sat up. "What would you say to heading home? We could shower, have dessert there?"

She wasn't sure if dessert was code for what she wanted, but she figured she won either way. She got either Noah or sugar—or, best-case scenario, both.

34

Noah dropped Grace off at her house so they could each clean up and grab fresh clothing. As he showered off a rainbow of paint, he couldn't remember the last time he'd had so much fun with a woman. And that painting. It was gorgeous. He couldn't wait to hang it exactly where she'd suggested.

He'd finished his shower, changed, and set out a selection of bite-size cakes from Baked. When she knocked on his door, his stomach and heart actually clenched like they'd both been given a hard hug. This woman had the potential to wreck him. He'd surpassed the point of this just being for fun.

Opening the door, he found Grace in a pair of thin, checkered pajama pants and a sleep top that said BUT FIRST, COFFEE.

She shrugged. "I figured there was no point in dressing up."

Why that turned him on more than if she'd shown up in lingerie, he couldn't be entirely certain, but he was pretty sure it had something to do with Grace being exactly what she was: herself. She didn't put on a show, try to be something she wasn't. She didn't expect him to be anything other than who he was. It was damn refreshing and sexy as hell.

Reaching out, he took her wrist, pulling their bodies together. He forgot to ease them into the kiss. As her hands roamed over his chest, he drowned in the feel of her, the scent of her shampoo and her still slightly damp hair.

When he boosted her up, her arms and legs locked around him without hesitation. She pulled back as he shut the door with his foot.

Looking down at him, she ran her hands through his still-wet hair. "Guess you like my jammies."

He kissed a path up one side of her throat, reveling in the way she arched for him, then down the other. "I like you, Grace. Everything about you."

Their mouths met again and there were no more words.

~~~~~~~~~~~

Noah stretched out on his bed, his arm moving to the other side, which turned out to be empty. In the dark quiet of the room, he blinked a few times. They'd fallen asleep wrapped up in each other. In his life, Noah had never felt the connection he did with Grace. It got better each time and it wasn't just physical. It transcended his expectations and, if he was being honest with himself, shook him to his core. Because when it was more than physical, lives changed, concessions were made, hearts got broken like promises.

Maybe focus on the immediate problem—like, where is she? Shoving back the sheet, he pulled on boxers, ran his fingers through his hair, stifling a yawn as he padded out of his bedroom.

She wouldn't have gone home . . . would she? He thought about all the times he'd left in the middle of the night. He'd never done so without saying goodbye. Apparently, neither did she. Her legs were pulled up on one of the stools. The only light came from her phone. Her hair was tied up in a messy knot, her chin tilted down. She looked elegant and adorable at the same time. If that was even a thing.

"Everything okay?"

She squealed, tossed her phone on the island. Noah hurried over. "I didn't mean to scare you."

He pulled her close, pleased when her arms went around his waist.

"If that wasn't the goal, then announce yourself. You nearly gave me a heart attack."

Noah leaned away, ran his hand down from her neck to the upper swell of her breast, letting it rest there.

"Nope. Heart feels completely normal."

"Now you're a doctor?"

"Just making an observation. Here's another one: you're sitting in my kitchen at two A.M. instead of keeping me warm in my bed."

Grace tipped her head back, her hands moving up on his chest. She twisted her lips, staring at her own hands, making him more curious by the second.

Noah put two fingers under her chin to lift her gaze. "Grace?"

"Okay, well, I'm still not used to sleeping beside someone. I woke and had that moment of where am I? Then I looked over and I was like, *Oh, yeah. I'm right here.* I tried to go back to sleep but couldn't."

Okay. More cute. She was full of it. "Why didn't you wake me?"

She tilted her head. "To tell you?"

He leaned in, kissed her forehead. "Who says you had to *tell* me anything. You could have just let me know you were awake."

"You look so peaceful when you sleep." She averted her eyes again.

He sensed the distance she was stuffing between them. Not physically. Which was worse.

"Talk to me," he said.

Her fingers tapped against his pecs, tickling a bit. Noah had to press his hands against hers to flatten them so she didn't completely distract him.

"I convinced myself I could take it slow but my heart seems to have other ideas. We agreed to see where things go but I'm not great at that. I like answers. I like knowing."

Her thoughts echoed the ones he'd had earlier, making him more sure of this choice—this path they were on together.

"What do you want to know?" He couldn't stop touching her.

She nibbled the inside of her cheek. "We're exclusive?"

He thought of all the times his father had walked away from a relationship, blaming the other person. Noah wouldn't make those mistakes. He wouldn't take her for granted but he also couldn't assume she knew what was going on in his head. "I sure as hell hope so. Didn't you believe me when I said you're all I see? Didn't you mean it when you said it back?"

Her expression softened. "Of course."

He hated that while he slept, wrapped up in the memories of being with her, more content than he could ever remember being, she'd been running all of this through her head like a fidget spinner.

"You know what I think?" He scooped her up in his arms.

Her eyes widened before she put her arms around his neck. "What's that?"

"I think I didn't exhaust you completely enough and should rectify that."

Because they were nose-to-nose, he saw the flicker of sadness. It was so often easier to go with his gut than his heart but Grace made him happy. She deserved the truth even if it scared him.

"I also think this is new for both of us. So, we'll need to be careful to talk to each other. Everything falls apart without communication." He knew that well. "You're the only person I want, Grace."

"Okay," she whispered as he walked toward his room.

Noah waited a beat. "Now you say it."

She smiled, soft and sweet. "You're the only person I want, Grace."

He narrowed his gaze. "Cute." Tossing her down on his bed, happy to hear her squeal of delight, he covered her body. "Try it again."

"I forget what you said." Her eyes glittered with sass and sweetness.

"Hmm. How ever will I remind you?"

She pulled him close, her body aligning perfectly under his. "Say it again," she whispered.

Noah pressed his forehead to hers, held her gaze. "You're the only one I want, Grace."

"You're the only one I want, too."

His heart actually freaking soared. It felt like it was levitating in his chest.

"As long as it lasts, it's just you and me," she said, arching up for a kiss.

For some reason, her words felt like sandpaper on his skin. Did anyone think he had staying power? Did she think he wouldn't stay? Or did she know she wouldn't?

Her lips pressed soft kisses along his neck, over his Adam's apple, up along his chin. Noah did his best to push the thoughts out of his head. Focus on now. That had never been a problem for him in the past. *What if you're not the same guy you used to be?* Grace was so sure she'd be the one walking away with scattered pieces of her heart trailing after her like bread crumbs. In this moment, even as he got lost in sensations unlike any he'd known, he felt a pressing worry that it might be him.

35

Grace moved the couch a smidge to the left, laying the deep blue blanket at just the right angle across it. She was right: the couch fit perfectly in Noah's living room. The two wingback chairs sat closer to the reading nook. One side of the L-shaped couch had its back to the island, creating a natural division between the spaces. The fireplace mantel was a thing of beauty. Kyle and his guys had finished installing it this morning. Noah had been gone all morning but returned for the second magazine shoot. They'd spent every waking moment together, minus his meetings, trips into the city, her dog walking, and mandatory school days. Okay, maybe every night was more accurate.

"This looks kick-ass," Noah said, staring down at the corner of his couch. "That's going to be my spot, right there." He turned and sank into it, then frowned. He stretched out his feet, setting them on the edge of the oversize ottoman. "Nope. Doesn't feel right." He got up, moved to the part that faced the fireplace directly. Doing the same thing, only this time stretching his arms along the back, he put his feet up. They reached easier, almost touching the rustic wooden drink tray she'd placed on top. "This is it. I need some masking tape."

Grace, amused by his antics, put one hand on her hip. "For?"

He looked up at her like she'd lost her mind. "To put my mark on this cushion."

Shaking her head, she picked up her clipboard. "You're a strange man, Noah."

"Ha," he said, leaning farther into the couch. "Like that's the first time anyone's said that?"

"You two have such an easy rapport," Emily said, coming in from the kitchen area, where she'd been finishing up a call.

"That's because I'm so charming," Noah said, reaching out and snagging Grace's hand to pull her down next to him. They'd been seeing each other this way for two weeks now. When would the little belly flip she got every time he touched her, kissed her, *looked* at her, fade? *If you're lucky, never.*

Emily opened her small laptop. "Okay. I have a series of questions, just like last time, then I'd like you to walk me through the plans for the next reno." She flipped through some papers. "It's the rest of the downstairs, correct? There are three bedrooms, a powder room, and laundry area. Are you doing anything with the entryway?"

Grace answered, seeing as she had the design plans memorized. They talked through a few of the plans, some of which were already in the works.

"Okay, what's the hardest part of a design from your perspective, Grace?"

She thought about that a moment. Not quite as easy to do with Noah's thigh mashed against her own. "Listening to each other. Both the client and the designer are going to have several thoughts about each step of the process. Ideas and visions might change. You need to be able to trust in each other enough to listen to what the other is saying and to speak your mind. Everyone needs to remember they have the same end goal."

Emily nodded. "That makes sense. Noah, as the homeowner, what's hard on you?"

Noah curled his arm around Grace's shoulder. "Getting actively involved without stepping outside my own range. I've never been this close to a project before. It's never really been personal. Now that it is, I want my stamp on it but design isn't my background. Being able to communicate with Grace so my vision can come to life isn't always easy."

"Why is this the one that became personal?" Emily asked with a smile.

Grace turned her face, curious about his answer.

"I was actively seeking something different. Both personally and professionally. I moved here from New York to work with my brother and rebrand myself. I wanted a home base. I was staying not too far from here and one morning, I went for a run, took a break near this place and, this probably sounds cheesy, but, it called to me. I thought about waking up every day, seeing that same view. The idea made me happy."

"Would you say it's meant to be?"

Noah rubbed the back of his neck. "I don't know. Maybe. It's been eye-opening. There's so much pleasure to be had in going through the process. Really, it's watching it go from something simple, like this room that had a wall up there." He pointed toward the dining table that had also arrived. "It cut off the kitchen completely, except for a small doorway. The floors were dull, the walls boring. Now," he said, shaking his head, looking from the window seat to the kitchen. "Now it's magnificent and I got to see every step of the transformation. I even picked this couch."

Grace nearly choked on her own spit. "Excuse me?"

He squirmed from side to side on the cushion. "Yup. Sat on it, knew right then, it was the one. I'm still learning but I think I have an eye for this stuff."

Emily's grin suggested she knew Noah was full of it. "I'll go off the record for this for a moment because I realize it's none of my business and doesn't tie in to the article, but, you two are clearly a couple now."

Grace's cheeks warmed but Noah nodded. "She couldn't resist me. At first, it was just my handsome face and amazing physique but I think what really caught her were my designing sensibilities. She had me design a canvas for her house."

Laughter bubbled up as Grace stared at Noah. "You are utterly ridiculous today." She looked at Emily. "We are a couple now. Did you want to see the rooms we're working on this week?"

Emily stood. "Absolutely. For the record, but not the magazine one, you two are adorable together." She shut her laptop and slipped it into her bag.

Noah stood up, squeezed Grace's hand as she got up. "That's all Gracie. And for the record? So are all the wicked design ideas."

They walked through, with Grace showing Emily the front room. It was going to have off-white walls, a daybed full of luxury pillows, soft curtains, and a beautiful antique writing desk Grace found at Mi Casa when she'd gone back last week.

"I'm calling this one Vanilla Essence."

"Lovely," Emily said, writing it down.

They moved past the middle room so she could explain the third bedroom. It would be deep grays and blues with dark wood furniture. The powder room would also get an uplift but was such a small space, she had to keep it basic.

"This sounds like it's going to be wonderful."

"Why won't you tell her what the second room is going to be?" Noah leaned on the hallway wall.

Grace grinned. "Because then I'd have to tell you."

They spoke more about the second and third issues of the magazine. The first one had sold well. Grace had a list of calls to return. She'd had business cards made up and gone over the remaining projects with her teachers to see which assignments had criteria that could be met by what she was doing.

"Oh, I almost forgot. You were on the phone, Noah, when Jack left. He asked me to give this to both of you." Emily pulled out a manila envelope, passed it over. "I'll touch base and send a copy by the end of next week. Grace, if you can email me the particulars, like a website if you have it, I can include that in this issue."

Nervous excitement swept through her. They were headed over to Josh and Rosie's tonight to work on the website. She and Rosie would also finish up a partner project they had for one of their classes.

Noah tapped the envelope against his palm. "Thanks for everything, Emily."

She looked at him a moment. "You have no idea how very much I mean it when I say, it's my pleasure. Turns out my boss, who's about one hundred and four, interviewed your father back in the day. He's very excited about having the next generation featured."

Grace saw the slight twitch under Noah's eye. He didn't want praise that came connected to his father, but still, he could be proud of his legacy. Couldn't he?

When Emily left, Grace nearly tore the envelope out of Noah's hand. "What is it? What is it?"

Noah laughed as she opened it. Grace's breath got stuck somewhere between inhaling and exhaling. There was a yellow sticky note on the black-and-white photo:

Not to be intrusive but the sun was just right & this moment felt like magic. ~Jack

It was a photo of them kissing and it *was* magic. Noah's head was tipped down to Grace's, hers tilted up toward him. One hand cupped her jaw while the other sat at her waist. Their lips weren't touching, but they were close, and the emotion simmering between them, the heat she could *still* feel, emanated from the glossy image.

"Damn. We look good together." Noah curled his arms around her from behind, staring over her shoulder.

She had no words. She'd never been photographed with a man in this way. She didn't even have photos with old boyfriends. Mostly because she'd been on such a straight and specific track, she hadn't veered off for more than moments of time. She hadn't connected with anyone enough to take the relationship to the picture-taking level. Every guy she'd dated had been on the periphery. A momentary distraction from the ultimate goal.

Though it was a profile picture, she could see the depth of emotion in her gaze, feel it in Noah's. This wasn't one of those high-society glamour photo ops. This was raw and real. They were both so in the moment the world had fallen away. She'd slipped under the surface and truthfully, she hadn't even seen it coming. All that caution she'd exercised for so long? It didn't exist in this picture. This picture was Grace, all in. It was as terrifying as it was stunningly beautiful.

Noah reached up, moved the picture. "There's two. One for me and one for you."

A lump lodged itself in Grace's throat, so she nodded.

"You're a beautiful woman," he whispered against her cheek.

She nodded again. "So are you."

It took her a second to figure out why his body was shaking behind hers. Turning in his arms, she smiled up at him. "Only, you know, a man."

"Thanks for noticing. You're so sweet," he said wryly.

She didn't want to get overly emotional about a photo. She liked the fun they were having and just because she looked all wrapped up in all things Noah in the photo didn't mean he was everything. His house was proof that she'd held her laser focus. She hadn't lost herself.

"I need to go get ready to go to Josh and Rosie's."

"Right. I still can't believe my assistant lives with your best friend."

"I know. Life is full of strange things. Them moving in together, you thinking you picked the couch, and evidence of you falling hard for the girl next door." She waved the pictures, trying to sound like she was mostly joking.

"The girl next door is pretty hard not to fall for," he said, kissing her one more time. "Go get ready so we can head out. I'm starving."

"You just ate."

"I'm a big guy. I need food. We can stop and get brownies."

"You had me at brownies."

His laughter followed her out of the house. *Lean into the fall, Grace. You've got this and you're not alone.*

36

Rosie and Josh had moved into his apartment, since hers was smaller. It was on the other side of town, farther from the beach but in a nice neighborhood. Noah carried a bottle of wine while Grace held the brownies. When they approached the steps, he looked at Grace before pressing the buzzer to their apartment.

"What? Want to eat the brownies before we go in?" She bounced her eyebrows.

"I might have to stage an intervention for you and those brownies."

She held them closer to her chest and angled her body away. "Watch yourself, Jansen."

"I just realized I've never done this. I want you to know you're not the only one in uncharted territory," he said, looking down at his feet.

"You've never brought wine and brownies to someone's house before?"

He looked up with a smile. "Actually, not together, I don't think, but what I meant was, I've never . . ."

When he trailed off again, her curiosity spiked. "Never what? It can't be that bad."

"It's not bad. I haven't visited a couple as a couple." He said it like he was ripping off a Band-Aid.

Because she was having to put effort into keeping a leash on her heart, she decided to lighten the mood and his obvious discomfort.

"Does that mean I can call you my boyfriend?" She singsonged the word.

Noah's brows scrunched together and he tested out the word, making her smile wider. "Sort of feels like middle school. Girlfriend. Boyfriend."

She batted her eyelashes. "How about my fella?"

His lips quirked. "Oh look, it's 1950."

Grace tapped a finger to her lips. "My *man*. My big, strong—"

He groaned dramatically. "'Boyfriend' works fine. Girlfriend."

She leaned against him, hiding her smile. Middle-schoolish or not, she liked the labels.

He pressed the buzzer for the apartment again, but he also took her hand and linked their fingers together. It didn't matter what they called each other. She appreciated his willingness to be vulnerable more than any label he could have given to their relationship.

The apartment was on the fifth floor, overlooking the rest of the residential neighborhood.

"You've already unpacked everything?" Grace asked, looking around the living room after handing Rosie the brownies.

"I didn't have a ton of stuff and we got rid of things we had doubles of," Rosie said, passing Grace a glass of wine.

"Nice place, man," Noah said to Josh.

"Thanks. Is this weird for you? Us hanging out? Or is it everything you were hoping it'd be?"

Noah gave him a look that Grace knew the story behind. She smothered her laugh with her hand, which had Noah side-eyeing her.

Rosie glanced between them. "What am I missing?"

"Have you told her the story?" Grace asked Josh.

His surprise was clear. He clapped Noah on the shoulder. "You told her? You're a confident man. Not everyone would share that story with someone they were into."

"Tell me," Rosie said, pulling her toward the couch.

"Pretty please?" Grace folded her hands together and looked at Noah through lowered lashes.

"Dude. She does it or I do." Josh sat down on the chair that sat kitty-corner to the couch.

Noah flopped onto the chair opposite it. "Whatever. Clearly, I'm just here for entertainment."

Grace told the story, stopping when Rosie nearly spit wine out of her mouth.

"Aww, things could have worked out so differently for us," Rosie said, leaning her head on Grace's shoulder.

"That's fine. Laugh it up. Like none of you have put both feet in your mouth?"

"How about I grab us some snacks," Josh said.

Grace wanted to reach out to Noah or go curl up on his lap. She'd never craved physical closeness with anyone before. Growing up with her mom, she'd gotten used to drying her own tears, reveling alone in her small successes, and lifting herself up when she fell down, physically or emotionally.

"I think it's supercute," Grace said.

Noah rolled his eyes. "Just what I was going for." He winked at her, then looked at Rosie. "How's school going? You're on the same timeline as Grace, right?"

"Yes. Less than six weeks. It seems hard to believe. Speaking of, we can finalize the slide show after dinner," Rosie said.

Josh joined them with stuffed mushroom caps and scooped tortilla chips filled with salsa and topped with melted cheese.

"You are a man of many talents," Noah said, leaning forward to pass out the napkins Josh set down on the coffee table.

"It's just snacks." He sat back down after pressing a kiss to the top of Rosie's head.

"He's modest but he is good at everything he does," Rosie said.

Grace heard the happiness in her friend's voice. Maybe it was too soon, but Rosie had a point: Why wait if you've found what makes you happy? Too often, people waited for the perfect moment only to have it pass them by.

"What's the slide show about?"

Grace picked up a tortilla bowl, holding it over her napkin. "How to make a house a home. We had to talk about essential design elements that change a place from being walls and floors to being a *home*. We've been introduced to so many techniques, styles, and influences, it's basically a wrap-up with our preferences."

"That's a good description," Rosie said, after she finished a chip. "Grace has a fondness for marrying modern with rustic."

Noah choked on his chip, pulling all of their attention to him. He pressed a hand to his chest, coughing, but lifted his other hand as his eyes watered.

"You okay?" Grace watched him carefully.

He nodded. "Yeah. Sorry. Wrong tube and all that."

She continued to stare.

"I'm fine, baby."

The term of endearment threw her for a loop. It was like her heart took a leap in her chest.

"It might have been the word 'marry,'" Josh said, snickering.

"Bite me," Noah said, his voice rough.

"No matter how many times you ask, the answer is going to stay 'No.'"

Noah cleared his throat. "Sorry. What are you fond of, design-wise, Rosie?"

She sighed into her answer. "I love vintage. Unique patterns, heavy furniture, old parlor rooms."

"Now," Grace said, pleased he was so clearly interested in their assignment, "we just have to show how each of these things, the elements we choose, can transform a room into something more. I guess it's establishing a connection between the technical and the emotional. Because really a design only comes to life once you start putting the features, textures, and materials into place."

"We've got examples of what fabrics we might choose to create a warm sitting room or what décor we might give a modern-day library or home office." Rosie looked at Noah. "We're allowed to have a guest for our presentations. Josh is coming."

Grace glared at her friend. "Way to put him on the spot." She looked at Noah. "You do not have to come."

"Do you want me to?" His voice was flat, like he didn't want his tone to influence her decision.

The truth was, no one had ever been there for her milestones. Having *him* there would matter. It would mean something to her, she realized. But she didn't want him to feel like he had to.

She tried to match his neutral tone. "I would love to have you there."

"Then I'll be there."

She couldn't tame the excitement in her chest. "Really?"

He nodded. "Promise." He turned back to Rosie, but the warmth of his tone and his words sank into her skin.

"It's really interesting, what you do. You're obviously very good at it, like Grace."

Rosie poked her in the side. "Maybe since she's busy with your house, I'll have a chance at the internship."

"Of course you have a chance. A great chance," Grace said. She wondered if anyone in her classes felt like she didn't deserve the opportunity since she'd already been given such a huge one. *Earned. Not given.*

The rest of the visit went well. They shared a nice dinner, more conversation, and Grace and Rosie were able to finish their slide show while Noah and Josh watched sports and chatted back and forth. The website looked fantastic. It was a productive night.

As Grace was putting her notes back in the messenger bag she'd brought, Rosie leaned in, her mouth close to her ear.

"I live with a boy," she whispered.

Grace giggled. "How is it?"

They both glanced at the couch where the guys sat, staring at the television.

"It's good. Weird but good."

"I'm so happy for you," Grace said, still whispering.

"Me too. I didn't think I'd find this. I wasn't even looking."

Grace squeezed her arm. "You deserve it."

Rosie covered Grace's hand with her own. "So do you. Things look like they're going well."

"We're trying to go slow but, yeah, it's really good. I'm happy and . . . optimistic."

"There are no guarantees in life. Just chances to jump at happiness when it's offered." Rosie stood up from her chair by the desk where they'd been working. She stretched.

"You should get that put on a shirt," Grace said, also standing.

"You done?" Noah called.

Grace met his gaze, nodded. "We are. You ready to go?"

"I am. I have an early meeting," Noah said.

"Three early meetings. Your tee time has been moved to eleven," Josh amended.

"I don't like golfing with that guy," Noah said as he stood up. "He wants me to attend a bunch of events. It's too much like what I did in New York. If he doesn't commit to a donation during the game tomorrow, I'm done with him."

Grace was surprised at the frustration in his tone. Sometimes she forgot he had so many irons in the fire.

Josh, however, looked impressed. "About time. There are plenty of people who would want to work with you and be committed to the cause. If he's just holding out for a connection to your father, it's best to walk away. Also, I finally got ahold of the owner for the strip mall on Eighth. He's supposed to review your offer, get back to me."

"Excellent. It's a good deal. I want to add it to our portfolio.

Chris wants our other businesses to be in closer proximity to the station." Noah caught her staring. "What?"

Grace looked at Rosie to see if she was the only one impressed. "Oh nothing. Just my *boyfriend* talking about buying a strip mall."

Josh laughed, slipped his arm around Rosie. "He does say it all pretty nonchalantly, doesn't he? Josh, can you schedule me a dentist appointment, and there's this house on the other side of town I think I should make an offer on. Set that up as well."

The girls laughed at Josh's impersonation. Noah rolled his eyes and reached for Grace's hand. "I have never asked you to make me a dentist appointment."

They laughed harder, walking to the door and finally saying good night.

Noah lifted Grace's hand in the elevator, pressed his lips to her knuckles. "You have fun?"

"I did. You?"

He nodded. "I kind of like hanging out with a couple as a couple."

They stepped off the elevator, headed for the exit. "Kind of?"

He stopped them just before they pushed the door open. "If I had to choose, my preference would be just you and me, but yeah, if we need to socialize, it's cool to have mutual friends."

Every time he confirmed things she felt, the more hopeful she became. Maybe the other shoe wouldn't drop. *Or maybe you'll break up and have to split the friends.*

Noah ran his finger from her forehead down the bridge of her nose. "That was supposed to be a good thing, not something to make your nose crinkle."

She laughed. *Here and now. Focus on that.* "It is a good thing. A great thing."

When they got back to his place, she wondered if it was presumptuous to head to his bedroom. It'd become routine, but maybe he wanted some space, especially if he had an early meeting. Before she could ask him, Noah pulled her into a deep, thought-dissolving kiss. When he pulled back, smoothed a hand down her hair, he asked, "You need to grab anything from your place or are we good to head to bed?"

Her heart filled like a balloon. *Looks like it's okay to be presumptuous.*

She wrapped her arms around him. "I have everything I need right here."

37

Noah wanted a real office space. He loved what Grace designed, and if he was paying bills or sending emails, it worked. But he wanted to get up in the morning and *go* into the office. He finished up his second meeting of the day before texting Josh.

Noah
Keep looking for a space to lease or buy. I'm losing home field advantage every time. It's pissing me off.
Josh
On it, boss. Don't like doing it from home?

Noah liked the house a lot. Loved the way the space was coming together, but with everything else going on, it wasn't conducive to working.

Noah
It's not working.
Josh
I'll have a list of places for you by the end of the day. Did the meetings so far go okay?

Noah frowned, reminded of how similar the outcomes of both had been. He'd had these guys. They wanted his investment, his name. These meetings were supposed to be formalities, deal closers. But both companies had gone "a different direction." Was it him? Were these guys picking up on the fact that his priorities were shifting? He spent more time thinking about his house, the community center, and office space than investments. People could read passion. Was his dimming visibly?

Noah
Not great. I'm going to get ready to go golfing and hope I can get Sergio and his friends to invest in the community center. Keep your fingers crossed.
Josh
Skalifajarioelald.

Noah scrunched his eyes, brought his phone closer to his face. Leaning against his truck, he typed his response.

Noah
WTF?
Josh
That's how I text with my fingers crossed.

Noah laughed out loud. Shit. He had a good assistant. He absolutely did not feel like laughing or even smiling right now, but Josh had found a way. Weird how he'd gone his whole life thinking he had more than enough people in his circle. Now that it'd expanded considerably, he wondered how it would feel without them. Thinking of being without Grace made him feel like he was putting on a sandy wet suit. Inside out and backward.

Noah
Gotta go. Thanks for the laugh.

He got into his truck, headed to the highway, replaying the meetings in his mind. When they used the line "We've decided to go in another direction," it translated to "We found someone to give us a better interest rate, cut a better deal." The question was, who was cutting the deals, because what Noah offered was pretty great. He was trying to establish himself here in a multitude of ways, but he had a strong reputation and, truthfully, thought it would be easier.

In New York, he'd had his hands in corporate and personal real estate. He flipped properties, invested capital, acted as a liaison for purchases. Since coming to LA, his focus had shifted, downsized in a sense. He'd lost three out of four of the investment property bids he'd made. He wasn't even sure if he was pissed about the opportunities so much as that he kept losing.

He was working on a proposal to build a new community center between San Verde and Harlow Beach. He'd always wanted to find a way to honor his grandfather's vision. Under his father's watchful eye and tight fist, he hadn't been able to. That was pulling his attention hard right now, but it shouldn't be impacting his sales pitch for investments. Something else was going on.

His phone rang as he hit the highway. Seeing the ocean to his left filled him with a sense of calm. Tapping the Bluetooth, he answered.

"Hey. It's Wes. What are you up to?"

"Heading out to golf with Sergio-stick-up-his-ass."

"I was going to ask how that was going. Not well, I take it?"

"I don't know. I'm completely off my game."

"Weird. I know he's looking for people to invest with." As usual, Wes's tone was thoughtful.

Noah spoke before he could change his mind. "Maybe I read him wrong. Instead of pitching things I normally would, I've asked for help funding a community center."

Silence. He gripped the wheel tighter.

"That's unexpected."

Right. Because he was the family fun guy. Not responsible like Chris or logical like Wes. He was impulsive, acted on his gut. *I can be more than that.* He started to say that but Wes spoke.

"Why wouldn't you talk to Chris and me about this? It's an opportunity to add to our portfolio—we could think about starting a nonprofit. But more than that, it reminds me of something Gramps would do."

Like he'd punched him in the solar plexus, his brother's words stole his breath. Why hadn't he trusted them enough to open up?

"I don't know. You guys are always saying shit like I'm flighty and less reliable. I want this. It's not a whim."

"Jesus, Noah. You're in my face all the time about being a nerd. Last week you texted that my longest relationship was with my Switch console."

Noah laughed, remembering the text.

"Okay, fine.But I didn't want to joke about this."

"I saw the magazine." It was a quick shift in topics but Noah rolled with it.

"And?"

"Clearly you're finding your passion. You look and sound different. The house is gorgeous. As is Grace, but that's beside the point. We bug you because we're your brothers, same as you do. But we have your back and you know it. The house, the community center . . . you're doing what you wanted. You're finding your own path."

Noah's fingers loosened, his chest puffing out. "It's not what I thought it'd be."

"Most things aren't. You should have seen Dad's face. If he'd tried any harder not to react, he would have exploded. His face was so still it was like he'd had Botox."

"So much for making the old man proud, huh?"

"I don't know, man. I think part of him has to be. You're making your own rules and he's realizing he shouldn't have let you go."

Did he? Or was he pissed at Noah and looking to get back at him? The thought hadn't occurred to him before. "Do me a favor?"

"The very reason I phoned," Wes said dryly.

"I know you're short on time, what with all the gossiping you and Chris do about me," Noah said.

Wes laughed. The sound reminded Noah how much he missed his brother. "There's so much to dish about."

It was Noah's turn to laugh. Wes interrupted, saying, "What do you need?"

"Look into a couple companies for me. Do some digging. They said they were going in a different direction."

"Ouch."

Exactly. "I know. I want to see which direction."

"Okay. But the real reason I called is the warehouses."

Noah took the turnoff for Anaheim. "What about them?"

The final straw with his father had been when Noah fell in love with some old-school warehouses in the Bronx near the water. He'd had big plans for them that would have thrilled his grandfather. But not his father. Noah had invested his own money, thinking this would show his father how sure he was about the investment. It hadn't.

"The sale has been stopped."

"Why?" He felt bad leaving Wes with his mess to clean up, but his brother had offered to finish up the deals to sell that Noah had started before he left.

"You put Dad's company on the papers."

Noah pulled into the golf course parking lot and found a spot.

"Noah."

"What?"

"You can't guess where I'm going with this?"

He tried to reroute his thoughts, irritated with himself for thinking about all of the things he wanted to do with his girlfriend. Not just in the house either. He wanted to go to Disneyland, take her to Napa, do some hiking.

"Just tell me."

"Dad won't authorize the sale."

Noah's foot flexed, anger coursing through his body. "Excuse me?"

"Says it's his."

"It was my money. He knows that."

"I'm just trying to give you a heads-up. Don't shoot the messenger. You might have to call him and talk."

"That bastard."

"I'm sorry, man."

"I'll deal with it. Get on a plane and come out here. Why are you still there?"

"With just me and Ari here, we're the golden children now. You want me to leave my pampered lifestyle?"

Noah laughed, again when he didn't think he could. Of the three of them, Wes was the least concerned with amassing a fortune. Oddly enough, he was probably worth more than Noah or Chris. He created apps, designed software, and did a bunch of nerd stuff that ended in tons of dollar signs.

"At least come visit."

"I'm thinking about it. Trust me. Talk soon, okay?"

"You bet."

They hung up and Noah worked to ease the tension out of his body as he grabbed his clubs. Before he got to the clubhouse, his phone buzzed again, this time with Grace's number.

His heart double-bounced like a kid on a trampoline. She was becoming more and more important to him. It was a shift he hadn't expected. Work always came first, but maybe that was because no other woman was Grace. Chris made it work with Everly, and he was committed to his job. His dad couldn't make a relationship work even when he was engaged, but Noah wasn't him. And Grace wasn't just a fling. As scary as it was to admit that, it made him more determined to prove to himself that he could balance it all. He could do what he did best and have a life on top of it. But what if what he did best was changing?

Noah
Headed onto the course.
Grace
Break a leg. Or whatever you say before a game. Just wanted to let you know I invited Morty and Tilly for dinner. You're welcome to join. I'd like it if you did but no pressure.

No pressure. Why not? He could handle pressure. Besides, he liked Morty and his fiancée. And he was crazy about Grace.

Noah
I'd love to join. See you soon.
Grace
Awesome. Good luck.

He hated that he felt like he needed it.

38

Grace wasn't the best cook, but she could follow a recipe, even adding some extra spice without killing anyone. When she'd first worked for Morty, he'd been on a bland diet that consisted of a lot of rice, bananas, and pasta. She was a pro at those.

As she slipped the lasagna into the oven, she wondered if it was normal to feel this nervous. If she'd grown up, the way so many people did, with one or two parents who took care of her, guided her, and had expectations of her, would she be introducing them to Noah? Would her mom have cared? There was no man before him who had made her wonder.

For a variety of reasons, she hadn't had many boyfriends growing up. She kept her eyes on the prize—getting away from her mom. Not every memory was bad, but their life, as a whole, was something Grace had always known she wanted more than. Despite her mother's rotating door of men, they weren't all bad. But Tammy found reasons to push them away regardless. It wasn't until she was older that Grace realized the real flaw Tammy saw in every man was they could never live up to Grace's biological father. That confused Grace, since he'd taken off right after

Grace's birth. Whatever the reason, her father was Tammy's bar and no man measured up.

Part of her could understand, since she knew that if things didn't work out with Noah she'd measure all others against him. She didn't need Noah in order to be *happy*. She wanted him as a partner by her side. Yes, she wanted Tilly and Morty to like him, enjoy his company. *Approve of him? So damn what. There's nothing wrong with that. It's normal.* Was it? Her former employer turned surrogate grandfather and his soon-to-be wife were coming to dinner with her now boyfriend-neighbor who not so long ago had been her sort of nemesis. *Yeah. So many shades of normal, Gracie. Way to go.*

The doorbell rang, and she breathed a loud sigh of relief to no longer be alone with her thoughts. Walking from the kitchen through the living room, she smiled at her own additions. She'd been plugging away at her own décor and design while working on Noah's.

When she opened the door, Morty and Tilly stood on her stoop. He wore a bowler hat, which made Grace think of Noah and his grandfather. Tilly wore a pretty patterned dress with a heavy white cardigan. She carried a large, rectangular dish.

"You didn't have to bring anything," Grace said, taking the dish from her.

"People say that but it's just rude if you don't. Besides, I haven't baked my apple-peach crisp for you in far too long."

"Mm. Well, I'm not saying no to that. Come on in. Hang your purse and hat on the coatrack."

"Well look at this," Morty said after shutting the door and seeing the antique rack. "This here is a thing of beauty. I think we may have had one just like this when I was a boy."

"You find it at Mi Casa?" Tilly asked, hanging her purse on it.

"I did. I just love it there. Come on in and see what I've done with the place."

Like a sunflower turning to face the sun, Grace felt herself bloom. She stood taller, felt proud.

"Oh, Grace. I love this couch." Tilly sat down on the slightly curved sofa. Grace had fallen in love when she saw it in *Home and Heart* magazine. It had been her only real splurge so far with the money she was earning for designing Noah's place. It looked like a shallow U, like something someone would see at a swanky nightclub. It was silvery gray, and she'd added teal cushions to each end for pops of color.

"Isn't it awesome? I actually thought of going with one the color of the pillows but decided to be a bit more subtle."

Morty stared at it, standing in front like he didn't understand. "How's a man supposed to stretch out?"

"What are you talking about?" Tilly scooted over a bit so he could sit, but he didn't.

He gestured to the couch, waving his wrinkly hand from one end to the other. "A man wants to lay his feet at one end, his head at the other. What's he supposed to do? Lie on his side and curl up?"

Tilly's gaze locked with Grace's, and they both laughed at the same time. Tilly grabbed his hand, pulling him down beside her. "Like your body would take up this entire couch. You're shrinking, old man. There's no reason to worry." She moved back and forth on the cushion. "Admit it. Cozy as a bed, isn't it?"

Morty shrugged, settled in a little. "Not bad, I guess. What other weird furniture did you get?"

Grace shook her head, pointed to her two perfectly normal armchairs. They were darker shades of gray, each holding a slightly different throw pillow with splashes of white and teal. Over the fireplace, she'd hooked up the television, and because she wanted to change the mantel, there was nothing under it.

Tilly rubbed her feet on the rug. "I like this, too, honey. It's all coming together so nicely. You're making a home."

Grace spent a lot of time thinking about that word: "home." Her whole life, she'd imagined it to be somewhere to come back to, a constant, a North Star with sturdy construction and no wheels. She hesitated, her hands and heart momentarily frozen. The definition had shifted, morphed into something else that included someone rather than something. Rolling her shoulders, she huffed out a breath. *That's fine.* She could adjust her perception without changing her life for a man.

"I'm happy with how it's turned out. You two want a drink? I've got some beer, wine, and soda. Or just water or juice if you'd prefer," Grace said, glancing at her watch. Noah said he'd be here by now. She glanced out the side window. She could still see his driveway, even with the patio extension Kyle had added. She'd filed the paperwork through city hall to have it built and was crossing her fingers no one said anything about it being there before it was approved. Backward was better than not at all. Noah's truck wasn't in the driveway.

"You missing your boy toy already?" Morty asked.

"Leave her alone, Morty."

"What? She's the closest thing I got to a daughter. I ought to be allowed to ask her what's happening with him and how things are going."

"But that's not what you did," Tilly said. "You teased her."

Grace looked back and forth between them, amused by the banter that didn't seem to need her input. "Drinks?"

"I'll have a beer and so will he, honey," Tilly said. "Smells delicious by the way."

"Thanks. Be right back." She went into the kitchen, grabbed the beers for them and a soda for herself and set them on the counter. The lasagna had another thirty minutes or so. She'd bought a delicious-looking loaf of French bread and made a salad. Everything was ready. She just needed the final guest. The simple dining-room table was already set with the dishes she'd bought. Okay, maybe she'd splurged a little, but everything, other than the couch, had been a reasonable price.

She brought the drinks back, set them on coasters on the coffee table. Taking her own can, she settled in one of the chairs, bending her legs to the side so she could curl her feet up under her.

The rasp of the soda opening made her mouth water. "How's the wedding plans?"

Morty opened Tilly's beer, handed it to her, then opened his own and took a long drink.

"A nurse friend of mine has a pretty cottage near Irwin Lake. We're thinking just before Christmas. December nineteenth. Evening ceremony, just close friends. Ceremony and party right there. Simple buffet-style dinner."

"That sounds lovely. And soon." It was already mid-October, but since there wasn't much to plan, it should be fine.

"We don't see much reason to wait. Really, we only put it that far off to give people a chance to plan to come. We'll have some of Morty's old crew from the electricians' union. My nurse friends. I have one sister and two nieces. They'll come down from Oregon."

They continued to chat about plans, menus, and gifts, but Grace couldn't stop thinking about whether or not Noah was going to show. He'd been going into his last meeting hours ago. She wanted to text him but didn't want to seem . . . what? Needy? The timer on the oven went off.

"How come Noah's late?" Morty stood up.

"Probably stuck in traffic. He had meetings all day. You know how busy the roads are," Grace said, unfolding herself from the chair.

"Has he texted? Called?" He put his hands on his almost non-existent hips.

"Morty," Tilly said low, under her breath.

Grace grinned at them. "I don't know. I thought it was rude to check my phone with two of my favorite people here. While I do that, you go use the bathroom and wash your hands."

His eyes flashed with impatience. "What am I? A four-year-old?"

Grace laughed. He was so easy to rile up. "Just a suggestion. No need to be cranky."

He growled. "Like a four-year-old?"

Tilly hid her smile behind her hand.

"I'm not the one who keeps saying it," Grace said, pursing her lips and shrugging.

She started for the kitchen, Tilly right behind her, but noticed Morty heading toward the hallway. "Where are you going?"

He scowled at her, then turned to walk away, mumbling, "Have to use the damn bathroom."

Tilly and Grace dissolved into giggles as they entered the kitchen. Grace pulled the lasagna out of the oven.

"What can I do?"

"Grab the salad and dressing from the fridge?" Turning off the stove, she reached for the covered basket of bread she'd already sliced. "The butter, too, please."

"Got it. We can wait for Noah," Tilly said.

Grace kept the oven mitts on so she could bring the hot pan to the table. "I'm sure he'll be here soon. I'll check my phone soon as we get this set up."

They did it together, Tilly setting out the butter and salad.

"Morty misses having you around the house," Tilly said.

"Now why'd you go and tell her that? She'll get a big head," he said, shuffling back to the dining area.

Because she could, she leaned into him and gave him a hug. He returned it easily, making her heart happy. He was all bluster.

"I'll try not to be too unbearable now that I know. You two sit. I'll check my phone."

Grace walked toward the mantel, where she'd left the phone, but heard Tilly and Morty exchanging whispered words. Tilly crossed the room, heading for the coatrack as Grace picked up her phone.

Noah
Game took forever. They wanted to do drinks after.

Noah

Going to stop at the gym. Frustrated and not good company. Give my apologies to Morty & Tilly.

Grace blinked away her surprise, wishing she could do the same with the onslaught of disappointment coursing through her body.

He'd texted over an hour ago. That was why his truck wasn't in the driveway. Swallowing the lump in her throat, she set her phone down without replying. Walking to the table, Tilly came to her side, some white envelopes in her hand.

"No answer?"

Grace pasted a smile on her lips. "He got hung up. He won't be able to join us. He asked me to apologize to both of you." She had a quick flash of her mother forgetting to pick her up at school, of showing up late or not at all for her science presentation. Forgetting her birthday or just blowing it off.

As she joined Morty and Tilly at the table, she waited for the old man to say something disparaging. Something about today's youth, commitments, and how, when he was courting a young woman, he'd have shown up even if he'd been shot in three toes and two fingers. Grace would never know why those specific parts of his body had been shot but she'd know that when he said something, he damn well meant it.

They stared at each other. Grace wished he'd say anything to make her feel like there wasn't just an empty seat at the table but in her heart as well. *Stop being dramatic.*

"Let's eat," she said too cheerily.

"Starved half to death, I am," Morty said.

"Well, simmer down, Yoda. The food is being served," Grace said, putting a huge piece of lasagna on his plate. Tilly added some bread she'd buttered for him. He'd brought her beer to the table, set it by her plate. They took care of each other. Grace's eyes prickled with tears she did not want to shed.

"I'm glad you guys could come. Thank you," Grace said quietly, after she'd filled her own plate.

"We're always happy to visit, Gracie," Tilly said. The suspicious white envelopes sat near Noah's plate.

Morty dug in but Grace moved slower, cutting a small square out of her pasta. "We talking about those letters?"

"Not if you don't want to. Damn girl. This is good," Morty said around a large mouthful.

Tilly made an *"mmm"* sound and nodded her agreement.

"Thank you. When did they arrive?" Grace slipped her fork into her mouth but didn't taste anything. Tammy was covering her bases, sending to both addresses.

"Couple weeks ago. Back-to-back."

"Thanks for bringing them."

They ate in an awkward silence. Grace felt like there was a large anvil pressing down on the room.

Morty cleared his throat, picked up his beer, and took a long swallow. When the can hit the table, he announced, "She called, too. Left a message saying she just wants to see you. You're blood and all that."

Grace's fork slipped and dinged the plate. "When did she call?"

"Last Monday," Tilly said. "She asked who I was, wanted to know what she could but I wasn't telling her anything. She said she had a right to know. Just said we'd pass the message on."

Grace nodded, tears filling her eyes, which did nothing more than piss her off. She didn't cry over her mother.

"Only going to say this once," Morty said.

"You say that all the time and then tell me the same thing fifty times over," Grace mumbled, looking at her plate.

"Never mind your smart mouth. Look at me, Grace." His voice was hard and soft at the same time.

Grace bit the inside of her cheek hard before looking up.

"She didn't do right by you but getting old has a way of making you think about all the things you messed up along the way.

Not saying you have to hear her out, forgive her, read her letters or nothing. Just know that the same as you aren't that little girl scared and lonely in a trailer no more, she might not be the same either."

The thickness in her throat made it impossible to swallow. She looked up at the ceiling without tilting her head back, hoping that would keep the tears at bay.

"You cry, I get all the apple-peach crisp," Morty said.

The heaviness got pushed aside for the rest of the meal, dessert, and a few games of Farkle. When she walked them to the door later that night, stepped out onto the porch, she saw Noah's truck in his driveway.

"Night, sweet girl. We'll see you soon," Tilly said into her ear as she gave her a hard hug.

"Don't see why you get to keep all the leftover crisp. Tiny thing like you will never eat all that," Morty said, coming in for his hug.

"Why do you keep issuing challenges you know I can crush?"

He hugged her tight. "You can crush anything you put your mind to. Don't forget it."

She held on extra hard for another beat. "Love you."

"You, too."

She watched them walk to the old Ford pickup. Morty opened the door, waited with the patience of a saint for Tilly to climb up in. He made sure she was settled and seat-belted before he shut the door and rounded the hood. He lifted his hand as he got in.

Grace waved back, crossing her arms over her chest, breathing in the cool, nighttime, salty air. The truck rumbled to life with several loud gurgles before he backed it out of the drive way. She stood on the porch another minute, looking over at Noah's house. The lights were on upstairs. Everything else was dark. She didn't know what to make of that or the way he'd bailed on tonight.

Going back into the house, she reminded herself that she was in control only of herself and her own emotions. It would do her no good to try to figure out what was going on with Noah, playing guessing games. When they saw each other, she'd ask what happened. No big deal. She didn't need to see him every night. Didn't need him to check in or check up. She hadn't been waiting by her phone like she'd seen her mother do more times than she could count. Nope. She'd had a great night, a good meal with her family, and she was going to bed happy.

Picking up her phone from the mantel, she saw there were no new messages. She drew in a shuddery breath. Yup. She was going to bed happy. And alone.

39

What he knew about being a good man, he learned from his brothers and grandfather. All of them were men he admired, men he *wanted* to learn from. Though he was learning plenty about what kind of man he didn't want to be from his father. His father would never own up to his mistakes or make things right.

Pride didn't make a man; choices did. He picked up the stack of paint chips, held together on a ring, put them in his back pocket, grabbed the coffee he'd run out for, and walked over to Grace's house. Hopefully, she wasn't still sleeping. Though, the way she was running herself ragged lately, he doubted she would be. She was multitasking like an Olympic medalist without a complaint.

He took a few deep breaths after knocking, hoping like hell she'd forgive him for blowing her off yesterday.

When she opened the door, his pulse accelerated. How could she always look so good? She was dressed in yoga pants and a T-shirt that read NOT NOW.

"Hey," he said. *Nice opening*.

"Hi." She eyed his coffee.

He handed it over. "This is for you."

Her hesitation nicked his heart. He'd hurt her, and that freaking sucked. Reaching out, she took it from him.

"Thank you."

"I fucked up."

Her gazed widened but she shrugged. "You texted to let me know. No big deal."

"Don't do that," he said. "Don't let me off the hook. I bailed because I was in a bad mood. That was wrong. Last time, you told me the best way to apologize was to just say it. I'm sorry, Grace. And in case the words aren't enough . . ."

He pulled the paint chips from his back pocket, a rainbow of color samples, fanned them out so the words he'd written on them would appear. Her smile brightened his soul. Jesus. This woman was going to be the end of him. He couldn't focus on anything but her when she smiled like that.

The paint chips read: *I'm sorry Gracie.*

She pursed her lips, nodding slightly. A soft sheen filled her gaze. Noah stepped forward, cupped his hand around the back of her neck.

"I'm sorry."

"It's okay," she whispered, looking up at him. "For the record, this beats the small garden you bought me."

He laughed, leaning down to kiss her. "It'd be better if I didn't keep doing things I needed to apologize for."

Again, she shrugged. "Obviously, something came up. It happens. Do you want to come in?" She pointed at the paint chips. "I get to keep those?"

"They're all yours." He pushed them back into a stack and handed them over but didn't come in any farther. "I actually wondered if you'd be up for taking a drive with me. If you have time."

"We have things scheduled for delivery this afternoon," she said.

"We'll be back by then."

Grace stared at him like she was trying to read him. *If any woman could.* He hadn't wanted to rub his bad mood off on her and her company last night. He never considered that it could work the other way. She was like sunshine drying the rain his father had cast onto his life. It was a terrifying realization. And an incredible one.

"Let me grab my purse."

~~~~~~~~~~

He loved that she reached for his hand when they got in his truck and headed for the highway.

"How was dinner?"

She looked over at him. "Delicious. You missed out on my lasagna. I'm no gourmet but I've got that one down."

"I'm an idiot."

"Worse than you think. You missed out on Tilly's apple-peach crisp."

"Any chance you saved me some?" He gave her a quick glance and squeezed her hand.

"Maybe."

"What did they think of your place? They haven't been there since the *Trading Spaces* thing. They like the couch?"

She chuckled. "Morty thought it was weird. Tilly liked it. They were really impressed with everything. What happened yesterday?"

He liked that she didn't let him off the hook. As he drove, he told her about the two deals he'd lost out on, then filled her in on his golf game, which yielded nothing but a headache. Those men only wanted to put their money into things that would benefit them. They didn't think another community center was worth their time. They reminded him of his father.

"I'm sorry. That's a lot of lousy things in one day," she said.

"Yeah. I wasn't lying about my mood. I wasn't in a good one even after the gym. I thought I could sweat it out but all that did was give me time to think about how hard I've worked to separate myself from my father without getting anywhere."

He switched lanes, grateful that the traffic wasn't horrendous.

"Why do you say that?" Grace picked her coffee up from the drink holder to sip.

"Wes got back to me after my game. The two companies that turned down my bids did so because my father undercut me."

She gasped. "What? Do you think he knew? Of course he knew. Does he have any other properties in California? Why would he do that?"

There was something about the way her tone changed, hard and protective, that did something all the working out in the world couldn't achieve: it made him feel understood. Like he might be standing on the edge of a cliff but he wasn't alone there.

"All good questions. I do think he knew exactly what he was doing, and he has investments everywhere but these were very targeted. He wants to show me he's still in charge."

"God. What is wrong with people? Parents are supposed to support you, push you to be better by showing you the way. They're supposed to protect you and love you, not try to screw up your life to show you who's boss."

Taking the exit for Anaheim, he glanced over briefly. "We still talking about my dad?"

Her hand twitched under his. "Doesn't matter. It just doesn't seem right."

"It does matter. You matter to me, Grace."

"Are we going to Disneyland?"

He wasn't sure what to think of her sidestepping his declaration. *Hardly a declaration, man. Coffee matters. Surfing, getting a good deal, and hanging out with friends matter. She's more than that.*

"No. But we can another day, if you'd like."

"Never been. I'd love to."

He smiled, thinking that he'd like to experience a whole world of firsts with her.

"Then we'll make a plan. Now, back to the conversation. Were we talking about just my dad?"

She sighed, setting her cup down. "My mom phoned Morty's trying to find me. Sent a couple more letters. She asked for money when I first moved and she's texted a bunch. I haven't opened the latest letters. I'm tired. I want to move forward. I don't want to go back."

Taking a detour, he turned on Katella Avenue. "I get that." He felt the same about his father.

"People don't change," she said, so quietly he almost missed it.

Noah didn't answer right away. If he took a long look in the mirror, he wasn't entirely sure he agreed. "I think they can. Given the right motivation," he said.

She started to say something but stopped, put her hand to the window. "Disneyland!"

The excitement in her tone thrilled him. They were definitely going there together.

"Another day. I promise." The words fell from his lips as easily as they had the other night. Instead of making his stomach clench, they infused him with confidence. He would follow through. He wasn't his father. The longer he was here, the more time he spent with Grace, his brother, and even Josh, the more true it felt.

"I'll hold you to that."

They drove in silence for several more blocks, Noah taking the turns he knew well. He'd checked the lot out several times, had Josh look into zoning. He'd applied for all the permits and talked to Kyle about the build. Now he needed backing. But before he got to that, which felt far off given how badly his golf game had gone, he wanted to share this with Grace.

He wanted to hold up a mirror so they could see all of themselves but also each other. This was letting her all the way in. He hadn't even shared this with Chris, and Wes knew only pieces.

He pulled up to the abandoned lot. It was partially fenced in. The neighborhood surrounding it was middle class, with modest one-and two-story homes. It was centrally located between an elementary and junior high school. Apart from the palm trees and bright yellow shrubbery, it reminded him of New York. Of strolling with his grandfather through residential areas, looking at buildings. He hadn't realized then how special those moments were.

They got out of the car, Grace eyeing him quizzically. It seemed so natural to meet at the front of his truck, join hands. He leaned down, kissed her, his other hand moving to her hip. She fit against him so perfectly it should scare him. It would have, even a few months ago. Now it made him want more.

When she pulled back, she reached up, brushed her fingers through his hair. "What are we doing here?"

He turned, put his arm around her shoulder so they were staring at the land.

"I want to do more than buy and sell. My grandfather was more than that. I'd hoped to do something similar in New York with warehouses I'd purchased. I want to leave a positive mark." His cheeks heated. Why the hell was he embarrassed?

"You want to make the community better even if it costs you," she said, looking at him like he made rainbows appear from nothing.

"I think, whenever you have a chance to give back, you should. It's more than that, though. It's hard to explain in words but I think I've gotten more out of hanging with Rob and those boys than I've been able to give back."

"You always underestimate your impact. You're giving them your time. That's a powerful gift in a lot of circumstances."

He smiled at her, squeezing her shoulder. "You're right but it's helped clear the fog I feel like I've been walking around in professionally. I bought this land. On my own. It's the first thing I've bought without my father's or brothers' input. I want to build a community center. I thought I could get Sergio and his band of annoying men to donate but it didn't work out how I hoped. But I'm not giving up. The three-on-three tournament will raise money for the San Verde center but there aren't enough places for kids to turn to. I want to create one from the ground up. I was going to pay for the land outright with the sale of my warehouses in New York but my father blocked the sale."

"What?" She looked outraged, and it filled him with pride.

He smoothed her hair back. "Simmer down, tiger. I've already come to terms with who he is. Mostly. This isn't going to stop me."

She stiffened, visibly forced herself to loosen her stance in his arms. She touched both her hands to his chest. "Damn right it isn't. I can't wait to watch you do this, Noah. I have not one single doubt about your ability to pull it off whether we fundraise, hold charity events, or you borrow the money."

His heart snagged. "We?"

She stepped closer. "Yes. We. I want in. You need to talk to your brothers because my guess is they'll want to take part, too." She frowned.

"What is it?"

"The magazine. There's got to be ways to raise awareness and money. You're doing this, Noah. I'll be right by your side every step of the way."

Pride filled his chest so full it was hard to breathe. There was something other than pride, too, but he wasn't going to look too closely at those feelings just yet.

Noah wrapped his arms around her waist and lifted her off the ground, twirling them both. "You're the coolest, Grace." He pressed his mouth to hers, losing himself in the unique taste and pleasure only she could give.

"You're pretty cool yourself. And smart. So, I'm assuming you have a plan for how to go around your father to get the money from your warehouses?"

He nodded. "I do."

"What is it?" Her eyes sparkled with excitement.

"I have to go back to New York."

40

Grace could *not* miss him. "It's absurd," she told Brutus, who had gotten a solo walk today. "We've only been apart one day."

Maybe she just felt like she missed him because she knew how far away he was. *Or maybe you're weak like your mother and depend too much on Noah to bring you happiness.*

Brutus barked, making it feel like he agreed with her last thought. She glared down at him. "That's just cold, mister."

He barked again. Grace laughed, crouching down to pet him. "Kind of nice without the others, isn't it, buddy?"

Jumping up to her knees, he tried to give her a generous kiss. "Nope. I'm taken. Keep that tongue to yourself."

She saw the Blundstones before she heard them. From her crouch, she tilted her head back, locking eyes with Shane.

"You've probably broken his heart with that news," Shane said, reaching out a hand to help her up.

Grace hoped her face didn't show the embarrassment she felt. She let him help her up before slipping her hand out of his.

He was such a nice guy. If Rosie wasn't so gone over Josh, she'd have tried to set them up. *How do you know he'd want to be?*

"You're looking at me oddly," he said with a laugh.

"Sorry. Stuck in my own head. I haven't seen you since we did the renos. Thank you again for your help."

He shoved both hands into his pockets. "No problem. It was fun."

They stood there awkwardly for a moment, and Grace wasn't sure if she should fill the silence.

"You good?"

She nodded, letting out a sharp breath. "I am. I'm dropping this guy off and heading to class. There's a job fair today with dozens of design firms pitching to the students. It's pretty cool because it's a chance to check them all out."

His eyes brightened with his smile. "That's awesome. With the magazine, you'll have a lot of options I'm guessing. Even solo if you wanted it."

She hadn't thought much about that. She liked being around others. Rosie often pushed her creative boundaries, made her look at things differently.

"Something to think about. But it's good to know all my options. Don't want to put all my eggs in one basket so to speak."

Shane laughed, gesturing for her to go first up the stairs. "That's very true. Baskets break."

He was absolutely right, but she'd been working hard to look at the opposite side of things. The positive.

"Noah left me a voice mail. Any idea what he wanted?"

Interesting. She could guess it had something to do with the community center but it was best to let him fill Shane in. "No. He's in New York right now, though. He might have some project ideas he wants input on."

"Cool. I'm game. Tell him to call me when he gets back."

"I will."

He waved as he walked away. Would her life have been easier if she could have fallen for someone uncomplicated like Shane or was love—whoa. *Shut that down.* Were *relationships* naturally emotional cardio?

It was a bit unsettling to realize she couldn't *make* herself feel something she didn't—that she couldn't force herself onto the safe path. It made her almost understand things about her mother. *Not everything. Everything after she had me was a choice. She could have chosen differently.* Even if Grace had no control over her heart belonging to Noah, she was in charge of the rest of it and that's where her mother let her down.

After dropping off Brutus, she decided against stopping at Morty's. Smiling, she thought about how he'd tell her to call first. She took the beach entrance to her backyard, hurried inside to shower and change. When she came out of the bathroom, she heard her phone chirping.

Noah's name popped up on the screen, giving her blood an extra pump of oxygen.

Noah
Landed safe and sound. Thinking about you. Have fun today exploring the job fair.

He had a lot going on, and most of it was intricately tangled up personally and professionally. The fact that he remembered warmed her heart. She *did* miss him, but he was missing her back. It was okay to feel. She stared at the screen a minute, thinking about how much of herself to reveal.

That's it. You're done second-guessing this. Have some faith. In yourself and him. If she kept waiting for one of them to disappoint her, how could she ever be all in?

Grace
Thank you. Glad you're there safe. Good luck with all the things you have to face today.
Noah
Thanks.

Three dots showed, disappeared, showed again. Grace's fingers hovered, then typed, but he beat her to it.

Noah
I miss you.

A happy laugh left her mouth.

Grace
I was just typing the same thing.
xoxox
Noah
You're cute.
xxx

She laughed out loud, marveling that he could make her do that from thousands of miles away. Hope glimmered inside of her. She wasn't becoming Mrs. Kern, but she was becoming her own version of it, and that was even better.

~~~~~~~~~~

"I feel like a kid at a free carnival," Rosie said, her hip bumping Grace's. Tables and booths were set up in long rows in the concourse of their school. Dozens of design firms displayed what they had to offer as potential employers. Grace and Rosie both had collected a handful of pamphlets and brochures. It was almost like the college fair she'd gone to in high school.

"There are so many," Grace said.

"You won't need any of them," Rosie commented, stopping at a booth that read DESIGNED FOR YOU.

Grace smiled at the recruiter behind the table. They were located about thirty miles outside of Harlow. Most of the firms were at least that far away.

"You don't know that. Things can change in an instant. Besides, starting from the ground up is daunting."

"You're not wrong," the man behind the booth said. He wore a three-piece suit and his dark hair was slicked back. He reached out his hand and introduced himself. "A benefit of working for a firm is the losses aren't all on you. You have capital and a team behind you."

Grace thought about that as they wandered through the fair.

"Are you okay? You seem very . . . contemplative today," Rosie said when they stopped to grab fountain sodas and share a plate of fries.

"Shouldn't I be? I mean, we're literally contemplating our next life steps."

Rosie picked up a fry. "Or, in less dramatic terms, we're checking out awesome opportunities we may or may not want to explore. Your worst-case scenario is you meet several of Noah's richy rich pals who ask you to redo their mansions."

Rosie smiled through the words, but Grace's stomach dipped. "I don't want anything handed to me. You know that."

Rosie sighed, munching on her fry. She picked up a napkin, making the dip in Grace's stomach deepen. "I do know that. Think about the flip side, though: just because someone builds off of the connections they have doesn't mean they deserve it less. If I knew someone who could boost me up, help me start my own business? I'd be all over that. Would you think less of me?" She didn't wait for an answer. "Sometimes I think you're so worried about proving you don't need a hand that you hold yourself back."

Sipping her soda as a distraction from the serious tone, Grace thought about what her friend said. "I'm determined. There's nothing wrong with that. So are you."

"I am. But when I was stressed out about the paper I was working on, Josh asked if there was anything he could do. I snapped at him that unless he wanted to make sure my mother got her birthday present in time, my emails were answered, and my bills were all caught up, then no."

Grace cringed. "I'm sure he understands being stressed out."

Rosie's sigh was adorable. Grace was surprised cartoon hearts didn't float over her friend's head. "He does. He said to tell him what my mother liked, he'd grab it, he had no problem replying to emails, and if I gave him my bank number, he'd do the bills, too. He also said he'd pick up dinner. I burst into tears because I'd been so snappy and he was so sweet. But he said this is how we know what we have is real. We can see each other at our worst, build each other back up, and most important, rely on each other for anything. He said it's when couples drown in their independent misery without reaching out, that you have to worry."

Grace's stomach tumbled. "This isn't about me and Noah."

Rosie shook her head. "No. But it applies to everything in your life, Grace. You're not alone. Asking for help doesn't make you weak. Picking up the pieces for someone you care about and letting them do the same for you is a sign of strength. What I'm saying is if Noah's connections give you a leg up, own it, babe. Take it. Take it all. You're no slouch. You work your ass off and no one is ever going to say life got handed to you."

Grace clenched her teeth, then leaned forward. "But this job with Noah literally did get handed to me."

"Because he saw your potential. He didn't pity you or do you a favor. Let the people in your life help you. Stop second-guessing every step you make, because the people who love you aren't judging you for the route you're taking to the top. Which, if you haven't caught on yet, is exactly where you're headed."

Grace's throat tightened. She reached across the table, took her friend's hand. "Not alone."

Rosie tipped her head back. "Exactly!" She locked gazes with Grace, her friend's eyes dancing with happiness. "Now you get it."

"You're such a dork."

"You're stuck with me. Let's go grab some more pamphlets and then we can go through them all."

"Sounds like a plan."

Grace had spent so long being alone, even when she wasn't,

that she was scared to lean on or into anyone too hard. She didn't expect people to stay, but she didn't want to push them away quicker either. *Stop expecting them to leave. Have a little faith.*

She grabbed her phone, not giving herself a chance to second-guess.

> **Grace**
> I look forward to you coming home. I have a surprise for you.

She had three days to pull it off. As they walked to Rosie's car, she looked over and said, "You said to ask for help when I need it."

Rosie looked at her over the hood. "I meant it."

"Good. I need your help. And Josh's."

She gave herself a minute to absorb the ask. *Look at that. The sky didn't fall because you made yourself vulnerable.* She hoped that meant she could take the leap, give her heart to Noah completely, without landing flat on her face.

41

Jack laid out the photos on the table, showcasing the various transformations Noah's house had taken. In the last six weeks, they'd renovated his kitchen, the living area, two guest rooms, the powder room, the upstairs bath, and Noah's en suite. Noah had done most of the painting in his own bedroom, but Grace had helped him pick the furniture and accent pieces to finish it off. They'd discussed ideas for the downstairs room. It could be a bedroom or an office, but Grace had different plans.

"It's a lot of work in a short period of time," Jack said, moving the pictures around.

"It is. We've had a lot of help. Thanks for coming to do a few shots of this room. I have some friends arriving shortly so we'll get to work right away." She'd already painted the room a deep blue. It was warm and inviting, which she hoped would pair well with her design.

"My pleasure. I love watching you guys work. I'm going to go grab a few of the backyard now that the trees have been taken out and the yard has been landscaped."

That had happened the day Noah left for New York. A crew

had arrived and worked with a speedy efficiency good money could buy.

Josh, Rosie, and Shane showed up at the same time. She'd told Noah this was what people, friends, did—they asked for help—but she'd been reluctant to take her own advice. She'd felt little wiggles of guilt but reminded herself she'd do the same for them. Plus, they were as excited as she was—thank goodness she hung out with fellow design lovers. Grace took a few minutes to outline her vision, and then they got to work.

While Grace and Rosie put furniture together, Josh took care of getting expedited deliveries on a huge television, a mass of books, the long list of games Grace had written down, including a PlayStation, an Xbox, and a Nintendo Switch.

Jack left sometime later that afternoon. He'd take the final shots another day, when everything was done. By late that night, they sat side by side on a kick-ass cozy couch, staring at the big-screen television that was framed by the custom entertainment unit Shane had whipped up with expert wizardry. They'd installed custom lighting so it could be dimmed for movies. There were a variety of seats, including the couch, beanbags, and a gaming chair. It was a decent-size room, even with the large unit that was filled with gaming equipment. They'd used the entire wall, placing custom shelves on either side of the entertainment unit, filling them with books and cool knickknacks that reflected Noah's tastes. Board games sat on the bottoms of both bookshelves. On the wall behind the couch was a gorgeous photo Grace had blown up and framed of the New York City skyline.

"Damn, girl. When you come to play, you play hard," Rosie said.

"I don't think my hammer hand works anymore," Shane said, his head back against the couch, eyes closed.

"Not something to brag about, dude," Josh said, making them all laugh.

Grace was the best kind of exhausted. Noah texted to say he'd be home late tomorrow night. He didn't tell her how things went or were going but she thought that was probably something he'd want to update her on in person.

"He's going to love this room," Grace said.

Rosie's gaze traveled around the room. "If he doesn't, Josh and I will come over and hang out in here."

"I can't thank you guys enough."

"Two of us are getting paid, so that's a pretty good thank-you," Shane said.

Grace's laugh ended in a snort, which made the rest of them laugh harder.

"Okay, baby. We need to sleep here or get going," Josh said, getting up off the couch, holding a hand out to Rosie.

Rosie groaned. "Sleep here? There's literally guest rooms."

"I'm positive Noah wouldn't mind," Grace said.

"I was teasing. We've got our own bed," Josh said, looking at Rosie with adoration.

Grace walked the three of them to the door, locking up behind them so she could head to her own house. She said goodbye on her porch, let herself into her home, and got ready for bed. The heaviness in her limbs felt well earned.

She'd been home only ten minutes when the knock came. Hurrying to the door, that addicted hitch in her chest, she told herself it wasn't Noah. One of her friends likely forgot something at Noah's.

When she swung open the door, her smile dropped along with her stomach.

Her mother stood on her doorstep, the moonlight casting a glow around her ragged appearance.

"There's my girl," Tammy Travis said, stepping into the house without invitation. "Exactly where I thought I'd find you."

Grace's shock swallowed her words. Her mother's dark hair was brushed but thinning. There were traces of the beautiful woman she'd once been, but her eyes held the same callous cool that Grace remembered from her childhood. She had the look of someone who took too many hard knocks in life and expected nothing less. Nothing good.

"What are you doing here?"

Tammy's smile was forced. "That answers my question of whether or not you read my letters. I told you I was coming. I'm here to see my darling daughter. And, because this house belongs to me."

42

Noah let himself into his house, tossed his carry-on to the floor, and went straight for the stairs. He'd taken an earlier flight because he needed to get out of New York. Across the country didn't seem like far enough away from his father.

He'd wanted to go straight to Grace's, but it was three in the morning and she didn't need the mood he was in no matter how much he wanted to see her face, touch her, kiss her, forget about anything else in the world.

As he wearily dragged himself from one stair to the next, he thought about everything his father had spewed at him. He bypassed the bed, heading straight for the shower. Under the hot spray of water, his muscles loosened even though his anger still simmered.

He turned off the shower, feeling cleaner inside and out. He'd cut ties. Screw the warehouses. Screw the financial losses. Noah wanted more than money in his life. He wanted happiness. He'd called both of his brothers on the way home. Things were going to be okay.

As he dragged himself to bed, he stopped short when he heard the gentle sounds of breathing. His own breath hitched. Was he dreaming?

"Grace?" he said into the darkness.

The sheets rustled and his heart soared. He no longer felt the urge to stop it.

"Noah?" Her voice was sleepy.

Noah crawled into the bed, pulling her close. "I feel like I conjured you out of pure hope."

He felt her smile against his neck as he clutched her like a lifeline. She was real and warm and right there, ready for him to fall into.

"What are you doing home?" she whispered.

Home. Goose bumps trailed over his skin and not from cool air. "I came back early." He kissed a trail down her neck. Just being near her shifted his mood.

She arched into him, so giving and sweet. "How was it?"

His hands snaked down over her soft skin. "Terrible. My father said if I want the warehouses, I'll need to sue him."

She stiffened under his touch. "Seriously? That lousy son of a—"

He smiled against her mouth. He *loved* when she got all fired up on his behalf. *Loved. Holy shit.* All these feelings . . . he *loved* Grace. As his fingers danced under her T-shirt, his mouth pressing kisses to hers, he went with complete honesty. "All I wanted was to see you tonight. I didn't want to wake you, though, so I came home, but the truth is, it only feels like a home when you're in it with me."

His throat felt thick with the admission.

Grace's arms wrapped around his neck. Her gaze found his in the darkness, her breath hitching.

"I feel the same about my place," she whispered.

Energy coursed through him, and with those simple words, she pushed away all of the darkness. With Grace, he had perpetual sunshine in her touch, her gaze, her heart. It was, as he'd told her, all he could see. All he wanted.

Their foreheads touched, their uneven breaths echoing in the quiet. Her lips twitched, making his do the same. They stared at each other, which wasn't easy given how close they were.

"What are you thinking?" Her whisper was accompanied by the brush of her fingertips over his cheeks.

"The same thing you are, Grace. Say it."

"Gracie," she whispered. "I decided I like when you call me that."

He smiled, his heart pressing against his ribs. "Say it, Gracie."

She bit her lip, her fingers stilling against his face. "You first."

"Same time," he said, his heart stuttering.

She gave the slightest of nods, which he felt more than saw; then they both spoke.

"I love you." Their words overlapped. It was perfect. He couldn't get close enough as he kissed her, yanking her onto his lap, burying his hands in her hair.

As he laid her back on the bed, she pulled away from their kiss. "I have a visitor." Her tone was sad.

It took him a second. "Oh. That's okay. We don't have to have sex. I just want to hold you and be close to you."

"What?" He saw her confusion in the slivers of light shining through the blinds.

"You have your period?"

She snickered. "No."

He hoped she couldn't see his cheeks heat up. "Oh. I thought that's what you meant."

"No. My visitor is worse than my period. It's my mother. She just showed up."

Noah couldn't help but grin. "I thought I disliked my father more than you did your mother but we might be even."

"Ahh. Nothing like two adults bonding through their mutual dysfunction caused by their parents."

"Fortunately," he said, shifting over her, "there's more than that that connects us."

She smiled, pressing up against him. "Very true. I have a surprise for you."

"It can't be better than finding you in my bed or telling me you love me," he murmured against her skin. "You love me."

"You love me back."

"I really do," he said, his heart full.

She pushed at his shoulders, her grin playful. "You need to get up."

"Uh . . ."

She laughed, leaned back. "We have to go downstairs."

He groaned dramatically, still a little shell-shocked that his night had gone from the worst to the best in very little time.

Following her down the stairs, doing his best not to fixate on the way her short shorts framed her ass, he almost ran into her back when she stopped abruptly outside of the one room they hadn't decided how to decorate yet.

"I wanted to do something special for you. I think every room reflects you but this one is *for* you. Completely."

He'd never had anyone do something for him just to make him happy. *You've never let anyone in close enough so they could try.* She pushed open the door, turned on the light.

Noah stepped into the space and was immediately over-whelmed. It was incredible. It was a media room, complete with games, books, a kick-ass couch, and an assortment of cool seating. He couldn't stop staring at all the little features that showed how well Grace knew him. The basketball signed by Kobe Bryant—his heart pinched—on one of the shelves, a baseball signed by Mike Trout. Gaming consoles, some of his favorite books. He turned in a slow circle, stopping when he saw the incredible picture of the New York skyline. He stepped closer to it, seeing both of their reflections in the glass frame. She was watching him so closely. Words escaped him. He loved that skyline. He loved New York. But he realized, as he looked at it, that it was no longer home.

Turning to Grace, he pulled her into his arms. *She* was his home.

43

Grace crept out of Noah's bed far too early, but she needed to get back to her place. She took one last glance at his sleeping body and finally understood what people meant when they said someone was their other half. She'd have stopped the fall if she'd been able, but now that she was here, she wasn't sorry.

Her mom was already up when she let herself into her house.

"Ahh. More like me than you'd like to admit if you're doing the walk of shame," Tammy said, her hands around a mug of coffee.

Hurt and anger collided like bumper cars. Hard and jarring. "There's no shame in what Noah and I share."

Tammy's expression was dismissive. "He seems like quite the catch from what I've *read*."

The article. Grace's mind flashed back to the design magazines she'd found lying around now and again in the different trailers. Was it possible her mom had started that journey for her with her own interests?

"You saw the *Home and Heart* article?"

She nodded. "Imagine my surprise. I was in a waiting room,

flipping through, and there you were. With *Noah*. The son of one of *Forbes*'s most wealthy men." She looked around the little kitchen with disdain, then focused on Grace again. "This place is even worse than I remembered."

Another flash of anger ignited. Grace was proud of the kitchen. Proud of the house. Of herself. "Good thing it's not yours then."

Tammy's lips turned up in an unpleasant smile. "I've spoken to a lawyer who says I have a solid case against you. This house is rightfully mine. Of course, we have plenty of time for that."

Unease prickled below Grace's skin. "We need to talk." To steady her nerves, and her voice, she took her time pouring herself a cup of coffee.

"First, I want to meet the man who is going to stomp on my daughter's heart," Tammy said as Grace sat down across from her.

"You know nothing about Noah."

Her mother's laugh was hoarse, and Grace catalogued how much she'd aged. She'd had Grace so young, but she hadn't carried the years well.

"I know men, sweetheart. Better than you do. They'll give you all sorts of promises but they won't follow through. He won't stay. None of them do."

Grace leaned forward, hating the coldness in her mom's voice. "People stay if you give them reason to."

Tammy's brows arched, her hands clenching around her cup. *What's wrong, Mom? Did that strike a nerve?*

"You'll see." Tammy shrugged, looking away.

"Why did you keep me from my grandparents?"

Tammy stiffened in her chair. "They didn't deserve you. They wanted to control me, tell me what to do. They were sanctimonious and judgmental."

Grace told herself that as a teenager her mother probably felt those things. That didn't mean her assessment was true.

"What about over the years? They never tried to reach out?"

Tammy set her coffee down. "They said if I left, I couldn't come crawling back. So, I never did. Then when you turned five or six, they started calling me, wanting to see you. I said no."

Grace's heart spasmed. "Why?"

Tammy's glare was icy. "They cut me out of their lives. They only reached out because of you. Why would I give them anything when they turned their backs on me? You know, I said if they gave me some money, you could stay with them for a while."

Grace's brain went foggy. "Wait, you told them you'd give me to them for money?"

Her mother rolled her eyes. "Oh God. Don't make it sound so sinister. I needed cash. If they weren't willing to help me, why would I help them? They acted all high-and-mighty. I wasn't good enough but my daughter was? No way. I was calling the shots. They didn't like that."

Grace realized as she listened to her mother that she really believed what she said. She wasn't a teenager, but her vision of her parents had never matured. "Wouldn't it have been easier to come back? Stay with them? No cash but they'd have let you stay, right?" She just wanted to understand.

Tammy stood up, paced the small room, then sat down again. "When I walked out, I said I'd live life on my terms. No one was going to tell me how to do that. Not them, not you, not any of those losers who said they loved me."

Grace saw it clearly then. She didn't believe in love because she didn't love herself.

"What did that get you, Mom? A life of loneliness and heartache?"

Tammy lifted her chin. "The upper hand."

Grace laughed bitterly. "Yes. You and your kid in some dingy trailer. You really had the upper hand."

Fury crossed her mother's features. "You've always been naïve. You have no idea what I went through. You've never had everyone turn their backs on you. Maybe I wasn't the best mother but you never went hungry. I let you stay even when you were old enough to leave. Do you have any idea what it's like, thinking the love of your life would come back one day and realize he'd made a mistake? He never did and I was stuck with you, all by myself."

The words felt like embers straight from a fire, but a strange, centered calmness overtook her body.

"You need to leave. I'm sorry for what you went through as a *teen* but the choices after that were yours. I didn't exactly have it easy as a teenager either but I made something of my life. By myself. Without anyone to lean on. You gave birth to me but you've never been a mother. I don't want you here."

Tammy stood, took her time pouring out the rest of her coffee before she leaned against the sink, eyeing Grace.

"Life has a way of making a person hard. You can only fall down so many times before you develop a thick skin. Before you realize how necessary it is."

Unless you accept help from people who love you.

"That's your view of things but I don't agree. Instead of letting yourself not feel anything, you could reach out and let someone help. You could have put me before your pride."

"They could have done the same. That's on them. Even when they died, they made sure to hurt me. That's why they left you the house."

Grace could only stare, because she could see from the look on her mother's face that she really saw it that way. Her perception was her reality.

"You can't have the house."

"Fine. I'll take the money."

"What money?" Grace stood up.

Tammy lifted her hands, looking around. "The house is worth something. I'm sure it was paid off when you got it. Give me what's mine, I'll go."

A knock sounded on the door.

"I'm not giving you anything," Grace said.

"You're just like them. You said ask for help, I did. Now you're slapping me in the face, showing me you think you have the upper hand."

"Grace, babe? You up?" Noah's voice carried from the entryway.

Tammy's smile turned mean. "Looks like I get to meet your boyfriend."

"No. You don't."

Only he came around the corner, spotted the two of them standing by the sink, and froze.

"Hey, babe. Everything okay?"

"Just a little family reunion. You must be Noah. I'm Tammy Travis, Grace's mother." She walked toward him like she wore a designer outfit and not a pair of Grace's pajamas. She believed her own hype, thought she was entitled to whatever she wanted in life with no effort whatsoever.

His gaze locked on Grace's as he shook her mom's hand. "Nice to meet you, ma'am."

Tammy's laugh was shrill. "Please. Call me Tammy. Grace and I were just chatting about the house. Sure would be nice if you'd make some breakfast, Grace. It's the least you could do."

Grace was torn. She did not want to have a scene with her mother in front of Noah.

"We could go out for breakfast," Noah suggested, his attention focused on Grace. She knew he was trying to read her, figure out what she wanted, but she couldn't deal with both of them. She wanted to protect Noah from the ugliness of her mother's words.

Tammy perked up. "That sounds great. I'll get changed. I'll need to borrow some of your clothes and makeup, Grace."

No. She wasn't a helpless kid. She was an adult woman who made her own way. Noah pulled Grace into his side but she barely felt the embrace. She was tired of lying down, avoiding conflict to look like the bigger person. She was tired of holding back and holding in. Telling Noah she'd loved him last night had set her free, and right now she needed to free this part of herself. The angry, hurt girl who had always made do because she'd never had any other choice.

"No." The word came out harsh.

"You okay?" Noah said, leaning down to press a kiss to her cheek.

"No. You should go." She needed to do this on her own.

"Grace." The one word was strained.

"That's rude, Grace," Tammy said.

She looked at Noah, cupped his cheek, drawing strength from the look in his gaze, the one that said he had her back. "I'm okay. But I need to do this alone. Please."

He frowned, clearly struggling with what he wanted to do versus what she was asking. "I'm right next door."

Tammy glared at her as Noah left. But his faith in her made her stronger.

"Don't look at me like that," Grace said.

"You should take your own advice," Tammy said, crossing her arms over her chest.

"Excuse me?"

"You didn't exactly give him a reason to stay, now, did you?"

"I'm not talking about my relationship with you. We're ending this now. You're leaving."

"Like I said, I'll take whatever market value is for this place and be on my way."

A wave of nausea rolled through Grace. She leaned on the counter. "That's not happening."

"Fine. My lawyer only gets paid if I do, so even if I get nothing, I win. Your name won't be in any more fancy magazines after this."

Her stomach dropped. "Why are you like this?"

"What's that supposed to mean?"

"It didn't have to be like this," Grace said.

"You're right. It *doesn't* have to be like this. You're always talking about choices. Now you have to make one. Give me my house or give me my money. Borrow it from your boyfriend if you have to. It's pocket change to him."

"You're not getting anything from me or from Noah. You don't deserve anything. From anyone."

Tammy stepped closer until she was in Grace's personal space. The hard look in her eyes was all too familiar.

"Life doesn't always give you what you deserve. You need to learn that lesson. As your mother, I ought to be the one to teach you. What do you want more: me out of your life or a life with that man? Because I'm pretty sure my presence alone could mess that up. Even if it doesn't—and make no mistake, there are plenty of ways it could—your career will take a hit when I contact the media, when you're dragged through the mud. Social media is a beautiful thing, my girl. I can reach out to any news outlet with a simple post. Tag Noah's name to it? That's got gold mine written all over it."

Grace pushed off the counter. "I wanted to understand why you were this way but it doesn't matter. None of it matters. I can't go back. I won't. You aren't worth the fight and you sure as hell aren't worth the attention. You're nothing to me. You have no idea what family, loyalty, or love mean. But I'll get you your money. It'll come with an NDA and an agreement that you never darken my doorstep again."

It hurt, saying the words, but it also healed. She didn't want to give her the money and had no idea where she'd get it, but she wanted to protect Noah more.

"Whatever it takes." Tammy gave a self-satisfied smile.

"Get out. You can come back tomorrow morning and that'll be the last time I see you."

She shrugged it off like she was devoid of human emotions. "Fine. I'll be back tomorrow."

Grace laughed bitterly as Tammy turned to leave the kitchen.

"That's the first time you've ever said those words and meant them."

Her mother didn't even reply. Which was fine. Grace was done listening.

44

Grace felt like she'd put caffeine right into her veins. She couldn't control her jerky movements as she paced her house. Noah had phoned a record number of times but she needed to close this chapter of her life before she could go to him. She'd texted and told him to just give her until this afternoon.

After Tammy left yesterday, she'd showered off the visit, gone to the bank, and taken a loan against her home. With a check in hand, she'd drafted up the papers for her mother to sign and had them checked by the same lawyer who helped her with Noah's contract.

Now she just needed her mother to show the hell up so she could send her packing. Her stomach rolled like a ship in a stormy sea. When her phone buzzed again, she checked it, frowning. *Noah*. She missed him, wanted her arms around him, but not yet. *Soon*.

"Where the hell are you?" She went to the window to stare outside. Tammy wasn't known for punctuality, but with money on the line, Grace would have bet on her being on time. Her brain spun with possibilities: She was in an accident, she had a change of heart, she found a guy and forgot time completely.

When she saw Noah crossing his yard, heading for her place, her stomach cramped. Her body tensed. She needed to do this alone. It would be so easy to fall into his arms, curl into him, but she needed to draw on her own strength to prove to herself she could.

"He didn't take you to New York to face his father." He had his own demons. She could deal with hers.

She met him at the door, opening it before he could knock or come in. The relief that crossed his features when he saw her was echoed in her heart.

"Gracie. I'm going crazy."

She walked into his open arms, returned his embrace, and breathed him in. "I told you, I just needed some time. This is almost over."

Noah pulled back, and they went into her house. He shut the door, looked at her with furrowed brows. "What's almost over, baby?"

She shook her head, the tenderness in his tone nearly destroying the dam holding back her tears. "This thing with my mother. It's not ideal but I'm getting her out of my life. Out of *our* lives. For good. She should be here soon."

A strange look came over Noah's face and Grace's pulse sped up. "What?"

His silence made her skin itch. "Noah?"

He rubbed the back of his neck, leaned against her door. "She's not coming."

Grace's words got trapped in her throat. In the end, she could utter only a garbled "What?"

"Grace, you're everything to me."

"What did you do?" The whispered words hovered between them.

"I saw her leaving."

Grace backed away, shaking her head. "What did you do?"

He stepped forward, placing his hands on her shoulders. "We're in this together."

"No!" she shouted. She took a deep breath, closed her eyes to breathe it out, then met his gaze again. "We're not in *this* together. This is my problem. Tell me you didn't do anything."

"I gave her a check. Told her not to come back and threatened a bunch of stuff I'm not entirely sure I can follow through on but I think it scared her enough to work."

Grace pulled out of his hold. "You didn't."

"Come on, Grace. I couldn't stand by and watch her rip you apart. I've dealt with people like her my whole life."

"So have I, Noah. She's my mother."

"She's a vulture."

She nodded, her gaze widening. "Yeah. One *I* was prepared to deal with. You had no right."

He stalked forward. "No right? Correct me if I'm wrong but we're a team. We're building something together. Something we both want to last. You think I'm going to let her treat you like that? Scam you out of money? Walk all over you and hurt you?"

She leaned into his frustration. "We are a team but that means you have to trust me like I trusted you to deal with your father. You're supposed to support me not do it for me. I'm not helpless." The last few words vibrated with anger.

"This is what you do when you love someone, Grace." He folded his arms across his chest, and it made her madder.

"No. When you love someone, you listen to them. You *hear* them when they say they'll take care of it and trust them to do that. You're there to comfort them if it all goes to hell. What you did is control the situation without my input. I've had too much of that in my life already."

His lips parted, and even though it hurt every molecule in her body, she walked to the door and opened it. "I need time."

Noah walked to her, ran his hand down her hair, nearly breaking her resolve. "Gracie." His whisper was tortured. "Don't do this to us. I only wanted to help. I wanted to protect you. What can I do?"

She met his gaze evenly despite the tremor rippling through her body. "Cancel your check."

He left, and Grace felt like she'd shut the door on more than him. She rested her forehead against the cool wood, wishing it could absorb the hurt and anger coursing through her blood. It felt like part of her, and she wanted it gone. She had no idea how to achieve that. After a few deep breaths, she lifted her head, but only to turn and sink down to the floor, the door at her back.

She stared into the foyer, her heart feeling empty. The first tear fell as she realized she'd been on her own most of her life but until this moment, she'd never felt so alone.

45

Noah paced Chris and Everly's small living room like a trapped animal. He'd been there for over an hour after driving around aimlessly, ignoring all of his calls and texts because none of them were from Grace.

"You're making me dizzy," Chris said, flicking through channels on the TV. Everly had very reluctantly gone shopping with Stacey. She'd been on her way out when Noah showed up unannounced.

"Sorry my misery is irritating you."

He thought of how mad he'd been when he came back from New York. How much anger he'd felt toward his dad and how Grace pulled him out of it. Now when the devastation felt like it might suffocate him, he couldn't turn to the one person who would make it better.

"You're not irritating me. I get it. But I seem to remember a time when I felt like you do now and you said there were no problems we couldn't solve." Chris sat up, throwing the remote onto the coffee table.

Noah threaded his hands behind his neck and stared at his

brother. "Dude. We threw money at your problem. I tried to do that here."

Chris laughed, but Noah didn't know what was so funny. "We threw money at it because that helped us out of the situation and it worked in that case. What we didn't do was throw money at *Everly* and disregard her feelings."

Noah's hands dropped. "I was helping. I wasn't disregarding her feelings. I was saving her from that nightmare she calls a mom. Seriously, man. That woman ought to marry our father."

"Ew. She'd be like your sister then," Chris said.

Noah stared. "No, she wouldn't. What's wrong with you?"

Chris stood. "Me? You said it, you weirdo."

"I was just saying how perfectly matched they'd be."

"Never mind them. Think about Grace." Chris walked over to stand in front of him.

"All I can do is think about her, Chris. She's it. I can't think of anything else."

His brother clapped his shoulder, kept his hand there. "I know, man. That's how it happens. Hard and heavy."

"That's what she said," Noah said with no inflection.

Chris arched a brow. "Really, jackass?"

Noah shrugged. "It seemed necessary."

Chris dropped his hand, walked around the wall that divided the living area from the galley kitchen. Noah followed.

"We wouldn't want anyone taking care of Dad for us. We did it ourselves because it felt damn good to do it. To make that break without anyone else's help." He grabbed a couple of sodas from the fridge, tossed one to Noah.

Noah caught it, tapped the top before popping it open. "I know. I just . . . I wanted to do it *for* her. I didn't want her to have to face that alone. She did it her whole life and I needed her to know I'm in this for real."

"Yeah but you did it in a way that made her feel like she couldn't do it herself. You took the choice away."

"So I shouldn't have helped her?"

"No. You shouldn't have tried to save her."

"I just need to fix it." He hated the desperation in his own voice.

"Let her lead."

Noah stared at his brother, wondering when he'd gotten so smart.

Instead of asking, he shoved Chris's shoulder. "Mr. Know-It-All."

Chris shoved him back with a wide grin. "Which one of us is living with the love of his life? You could learn from me, young Jedi."

The two were locked in a futile double headlock when Everly walked through the door. From his awkward, bent position, he saw her hang her keys on the little hook by the door and remove her shoes.

"This is new," she said, coming into the living room.

"Hey, Evs. How was shopping?" Chris's breathing was heavy.

She stood close to them, her hands on her hips. "Crowded. How was the visit with your brother?"

"Pretty good. Except he doesn't like being told what to do," Chris said.

"Just because Everly took pity on you doesn't mean you're a relationship guru," Noah grunted.

They shuffled but neither of them gained any traction and Noah was starting to get a kink in his neck.

"Is Grace okay?" Everly asked, tilting her head to better meet Noah's gaze.

"He hasn't heard from her," Chris said, circling them around again.

Everly bent and tilted her head so she was looking sideways at them. "Do you two need someone to yell 'break'?"

"You can't yell, Evs." Noah grinned, rubbing his knuckles on Chris's head.

She gave him a wry grin, stood up, and said, "Break," at a perfectly reasonable decibel.

They released each other, both of them groaning a little as they stretched, rolled their shoulders.

Everly kissed his brother on the cheek, leaned her head against his shoulder, but looked at Noah. "You okay?"

He shook his head. "I just need to see her. Talk to her. I need to make it right."

"How did her presentation go?"

"It's not for a few more days." His thoughts started turning like gears, making him miss whatever Chris and Everly were saying.

He pocketed his keys from the kitchen table and started for the door.

"Wait. Where are you going?" Chris followed him to the door.

He turned back, unable to contain his grin. "I'm going to win back my girl and show her I always keep my promises."

46

Grace was livid at herself. She glanced around the classroom once more, taking note of how many of her classmates had brought significant others, including Rosie. Noah had left her alone for four days now, and the emptiness that crept inside of Grace's body was unlike any she'd ever known. Different from the nights she'd hidden in her closet in their trailer because she kept hearing strange noises and her mother was out at the bar. Different from hearing that the grandparents she'd never known had died. But it was her own fault. She'd sent him away, told him to respect her words, and he did. He did exactly what she'd asked and he was going to miss her presentation.

"We can reschedule," Rosie whispered, leaning over to Grace.

Grace shook her head, looking at Josh, wishing she could just ask about Noah, but if she said his name out loud, she might cry.

She'd worked toward this for so long. She would not make it less because her personal life was in tatters. *Of your own making. If you don't like how things are, change them.* She lifted her chin. She'd go to him. As soon as she finished up with the slide show.

"No. Let's do this."

She did her part, speaking the words she'd rehearsed more times than she could count. She kept her gaze on the screen to lessen the nerves of having to stare out at the audience. Of having to deal with the fact that he'd promised. *You can't hold this against him. You told him to stay away.* Rosie cleared her throat, pulling Grace back into the moment. It wasn't until the clapping started that she took a full breath, forced a smile for her teacher, her classmates, their special someones, Josh . . . and Noah.

Grace's knees wobbled as their gazes locked. He stood leaning against the wall beside Josh, focused on Grace. She pulled in a deep breath, her heart rebooting. She continued to stare, feeling the smile take over her face without any effort. Rosie nudged her shoulder.

Mrs. Kern stood, glanced back at Noah, which struck her as odd. "Fabulous job, ladies." She walked to the front of the room, turned to face everyone. "All of you did so well. I'm not sure how they'll choose an intern. I'm so proud of how far all of you have come and you should be as well."

Grace locked her hands together, unable to break eye contact with Noah. Just looking at him was refueling her energy, her breath, her *heart*.

"Now, there's one more special presentation but it's for one person only. I've set up snacks in room 310 if you'll all join me and we can celebrate your successes."

Rosie squeezed her hand. Grace looked at her, squeezing back. "What's going on?"

Her friend hugged her hard. "This is where you get the chance to choose the happiness you deserve."

Grace pulled away, stared at her cryptic friend. Everyone filed out, including Rosie and Josh, until only Noah and Grace were left.

Noah walked to her, keeping too much distance between them. She wanted to close it, fall into him, and hold on tight.

"I had a plan but I didn't account for how seeing you would scramble my brain."

She laughed, understanding. "Plans are good. I'm sorry I haven't answered your calls."

His jaw tightened. "You needed time. I want to give you whatever you need but I can't wait any longer to make things right between us."

Air *whooshed* out of her lungs. "You still want there to be an us?"

He closed the distance but still didn't touch her. "I want that more than I've ever wanted anything. I have something to show you, if you can give me a minute?"

He walked to the table. Grace realized Rosie had left her computer attached, and Noah fiddled with it, then adjusted the lights in the room. He pulled a chair closer to the screen while Grace did her best not to wring her hands. She'd forgotten how to breathe without him in her life, and now she pulled in oxygen like she'd been starved of it.

What really struck a chord was the realization she'd come to over the last few days: she'd follow him anywhere. She understood how her mother let herself ache over a man for years upon years, carrying the flame and the hope of him coming back. Because if she couldn't fix things with Noah, she'd do the same. She also understood how that could make a person hard. Closed off. Like a wounded animal lashing out in the face of more hurt. That didn't excuse her mother's behavior, but it lessened some of Grace's anger.

Noah gestured to the chair. "Can you have a seat?"

She sat, hands clasped in her lap, heart beating like a rabbit on the run.

His fingers flexed, in and out. "Six weeks ago, I didn't see the words 'house' and 'home' as different. They're synonyms, essentially the same thing."

A small smile snuck onto her lips. He was presenting a project just as she'd done.

"I've learned a lot in that time. Not just about what makes a house a home but what kind of man I want to be, what kind of life I want to live. What kind of person transforms you, much like you transform spaces." He paused, cleared his throat, and Grace could see the nerves in the way he stood. His eyes were tired, like maybe he hadn't been sleeping any better than she had.

She was transfixed by every little thing about him. The way his hair looked slightly mussed, how his shirt fit perfectly over his strong arms and chest. How his lips twitched just a little and his gaze held hers like they were tethered, like they were keeping each other afloat.

Noah pressed Play on his slide show. Her heart squeezed painfully hard when Blake Shelton and Gwen Stefani's duet "Nobody but You" came through the sound system. It was his words coming up across the screen, however, that put her back together again.

I had no idea what made a house a home.

Until you.

A 3D image of the first level of a house appeared. It was empty.

A house becomes a home when you make it your own with the person you love.

Splashes of paint colored the image, furniture zoomed in, landing in spots on the screen, transforming the room from barren and empty to full and vibrant.

It isn't paint on the walls or the furniture you buy. It's who pulls you out of the couch when you're stuck.

Grace laughed too loud, her eyes filling with tears.

The song continued to play, talking about loving no one else.

A beautiful slide with a picture of Noah's house filled the screen.

This is just a house. Without you, it's empty. Without you, I am empty. A house is a shell. A blank canvas. A home is a masterpiece.

Their paintings appeared on the next slide. The final slide was black. The words that came up made it hard to breathe.

You are my home, Grace. My everything. Nothing matters without you. I'm sorry I didn't listen but I hear you and will do better in the future. I want a future with you. Finding you helped me find myself. I love you.

Grace was so blown away, she forgot to breathe. He moved toward her as she stood up and crossed the room. Their arms went around each other, and she buried her face in his neck.

His hands moved over her like he was making sure she was real.

"I'm sorry," he whispered.

"So am I." She leaned back just enough to see him. "You want to protect the people you love. I should have been more understanding of that."

"We're both still learning." He pressed his forehead against hers, his hands pulling on her hips. "It might take a lifetime to figure it all out."

Her breath hitched. "That's a long time."

He nodded. "It is. About the same time frame for how long I plan to love you, make you happy, and keep my promises."

Emotions swirled around like ballerinas. "I didn't think you would come. It would have been my fault if you broke your promise."

"It doesn't matter because I didn't. I won't. I need you in my life. I know we have things to sort out and discuss but—"

She went up on tiptoe. "Not now. Right now there's just us. Just this. I love you, Noah. I love everything about who you are. You keep saying I make you better but you've done the same for me. You've shown me happiness is okay to grab ahold of without guilt. You've taught me there's life outside of work."

"No," he said, a silly grin on his face. "*You* taught *me* that one."

Grace wrapped her arms around his neck, hugging him tight. "We'll teach each other. We'll learn. We'll mess up. We'll fix it. But we'll do it together."

"No more time apart," Noah whispered into her hair.

With a sly smile, she pulled back. "You missed me."

He shrugged. "Only as much as I'd miss air. You miss me?"

"About the same," she said right before she kissed him.

"So, what now?" Grace asked as she laid her head on his shoulder.

Noah's arms were her favorite place to be. "Now we go home."

She looked up. "Which house is that?"

He kissed the bridge of her nose. "Whichever one you're in, Gracie. Wherever you are, that's where I'll be."

~~~~~~~~~~

Grace couldn't wait to go home with Noah. It felt like a beginning. The beginning of everything. They took their own vehicles back to their places. As she was hurrying out of her car, intent on nothing more than throwing herself into his arms, she saw he was on the phone.

His gaze heated when he looked at her, his arm extending to pull her in even as he carried on with the conversation.

"That's fantastic. I can sign the papers right now. Yes. Yes. Great." He ended the call, pocketed his phone, and framed her face with his hands.

Grace put her hands to his wrists. "What was that?"

"*That* was a foundation that wants to invest in the community center. They heard about it through Sergio so maybe the guy wasn't a waste of time after all."

She didn't know she could feel so much happiness on someone else's behalf. "That's amazing."

"It's just a start but it's something. Unfortunately, I need to go meet with them."

She saw the indecision on his face, and she wanted nothing more than to curl up with him and shut the world away. But they had time. Lots of it. Going up on tiptoes, she squealed when he lifted her, bringing her closer.

"Go, do what you have to do. I have some things of my own I need to do."

"Oh yeah?" He kissed the underside of her jaw, making her lose her train of thought.

"Yup. Just make sure when you get *home*, the rest of your day is cleared for us."

He pulled back, still holding her around the waist, her feet dangling in the air. "I love you, Gracie."

"I love you. So much it scares me."

"Don't be scared. I've got you."

She nodded, her heart completely at ease. "I know."

47

"Anything else?" Josh called as he wound the hose back up.

Grace looked around, thrilled with the transformation. Him having to run an errand turned into a blessing, and once again, her friends were right there when she needed them.

"No. This is awesome. He's going to love it."

Rosie wandered over to where she stood under the canopy. Grace eyed the table her friend had set up. "It's perfect."

Resting her head on Grace's shoulder, Rosie murmured, "You deserve this. Him. Everything."

Grace looked at her friend. "So do you."

Josh wandered over to them. "We having a moment?"

Rosie laughed. "Just appreciating life." She walked into his arms, resting her head on his chest.

"Thank you so much for this, guys. I have a few more things to do—" A car door slamming cut her short. Grace hurried around the side of the house. "I'm not ready yet, you guys need to—" She stopped short as Tammy marched toward her, anger written in every line of her body.

She felt Josh and Rosie at her back, and she had the same

urge as she did with Noah, to protect them from the hostility of this woman. Instead, she absorbed *their* need to protect *her*.

Tammy waved a check around in the air. A cab idled in the distance. "This check wouldn't cash. What the hell, Grace? We had a deal."

"I told Noah to cancel it. You had no right to take anything from him."

Tammy stopped in front of her, breathing heavily, like being spiteful stole her breath. She ignored Josh and Rosie, but Grace felt their presence like a shield. Noah's car turned in to the drive. Grace winced. She'd wanted to welcome him home with happiness, *not* with her mother.

Tammy grinned almost gleefully as Noah hurried over to them, heading right to Grace's side. "What's going on?"

Waving the check at him, she sneered. "Your stupid check was useless. Fix it."

Grace's heart burst when Noah looked right at her, love, trust, and strength in his gaze. "What do you need, Grace?"

She took a deep breath, stepped in front of him, and went with her gut, knowing if it didn't work the way she hoped, she wasn't alone. Either way, she needed to do this or she would spend her life feeling like a bad person and would always wonder if she'd done enough.

"You can stay in the house," Grace said.

Tammy blanched, lowered her arm. "What?"

"Your parents' house. You said you wanted the house or the money. You can't have either but you're right, this was your family's home so you can stay there for as long as you need."

If anything, her mom looked only angrier. "I don't want to *live* in the house. If anything, I'd want to sell it."

Grace tipped her head to the side. "Well, as I've had to say before, my house isn't for sale. But the offer for you to be there stands. You can take it or leave it but I'm done letting you manipulate me. I'm not giving you money but I'll give you something more valuable."

Tammy scoffed. Noah put both hands on Grace's shoulders and she closed her eyes a minute, letting the feel of him at her back sink in.

She met Tammy's gaze. "If you stay, maybe we can repair some of the damage to our relationship. You said in one of your letters that you wanted that. You said that family matters. There are no guarantees but I'm willing to try if you are."

The cab honked impatiently. Tammy looked back and then at Grace. She didn't even realize she was holding her breath.

Was it indecision she saw in her mother's gaze? "I can make your life miserable," Tammy said, leaning into Grace's breathing space.

How could it still hurt? "No. You can't. You don't have any more control over me, Mom." The words felt true, mostly. The hurt would fade. "It doesn't have to be like this." Hope hung by a pinkie finger on a crumbling ledge.

Tammy's jaw clenched. She ripped the check up, tossed it toward Grace, and turned on her heel, hurrying toward the cab. Grace's breath *whooshed* out of her lungs, and though her mother not being willing to try nicked her heart, she knew she'd be okay. Noah turned her, hugged her hard.

"I'm so proud of you," he whispered.

"Damn, Grace. You're amazing. It's completely her loss," Rosie added.

When Noah pulled back, started to turn toward the back of the yard, Grace grabbed his hand, looked at Josh.

"As much as I'm probably going to need therapy for that little drama, we have other things happening and I still need a few minutes." She widened her eyes in Josh's direction.

"Right. Noah, let's get you settled in Grace's house with a beer until she texts you."

He looked at the three of them funny. "What's going on?"

"Dude. Trust me when I say it'll be worth the wait to find out."

~~~~~~~~~~~

Nerves danced in her belly as Grace made the final touches. She still couldn't believe all of the things that had happened. She knew she wasn't over the hurt of her mom, just like he wasn't over the malice of his father. But right now, all that mattered was them and the life they were going to build. He loved her. She loved him. They were a team. Each other's person. He hadn't gone down on one knee, but she had no doubt he would, no doubt she'd say yes. It wouldn't always be easy, they'd fight, make up, outside forces would try to tear them down, but they'd weather those storms and stand strong together. He'd laid his heart on the line for her, and now it was her turn to do the same.

Grace
Come outside to your backyard.
Noah
Should I be dressed?
Grace
LOL I'd rather you didn't show your goods to the entire beach so, yeah.
Noah
Fair enough. Need anything?
Grace
Just you. Always you.

The back door opened, and Noah came out onto the porch. He stood on the deck in shorts and a T-shirt, his feet bare, and surveyed everything Josh and Rosie had helped her pull together in record time. Should she have told him to put on a bathing suit? The gesture was supposed to be more symbolic than anything.

His gaze moved over the canopied tent that covered the rectangular blow-up pool. Candles flickered in the light breeze, set up on a bistro set she'd picked up for the back porch. Three fully-stocked coolers rested beside the pool. Towels lay over the back of the chairs.

Grace walked forward, meeting him at the bottom of the stairs.

"You got me a pool," he said, his lips twitching.

"It's where this all started, right? You wanted a pool."

He nodded, taking her hand and walking forward. He dipped a hand inside. "It's freezing," he said around a laugh.

"We don't have to get in," she said.

"Oh, we're getting in. Those curtains close," he said.

She'd tied them open so they had the view of the setting sun over the water behind them, but maybe his idea was better. There was nothing she'd rather look at than Noah. They worked quietly, each of them taking two sides, pulling the strings so the massive canopy curtains closed around them. Seagulls squawked in the distance, laughter drifted faintly from people enjoying the beach. But inside the curtains, it was just them.

Noah glanced at the pool. "Maybe I didn't think this all the way through. That water is pretty cold."

Grace laughed. It didn't matter if they went in. She kissed him, pulled him to the bistro set. "Sit down. There's more."

She opened two of the coolers, delighted to see Noah's jaw drop.

"That is a lot of peanut butter brownie ice cream." He dug through the ice and pulled up a pint-size container. Grace grabbed a spoon from the other cooler, which was filled with a picnic. She passed it to him.

"You said you needed it like air," she reminded him.

"I did say that, didn't I?"

He opened the lid, scooped up a bite, and held it out to her. She swallowed the delicious treat. "I should be feeding you."

"We can take turns. Give-and-take, right?" He took a huge spoonful for himself.

"What now?" She whispered because the words wouldn't go away.

"For us?" He smiled at her with a quiet sincerity she knew she could trust. For good.

"For all of it." She gestured wide, meaning to include his house, her house, their parents. Everything.

"Well," he said, then paused long enough to make her breath hitch. "I was hoping we could make my house our home but, honestly, it doesn't matter where we live as long as we're together. I've never wanted all of this with anyone. I thought I wasn't built that way but that wasn't why. It was because I hadn't met you. This house is special. We did it together. I want to build a life and a family here with you. I want it to be our home."

She launched herself at him, not even caring that he held ice cream. He laughed, catching her as he promised he would, managing not to drop the ice cream. He set it down as she straddled his lap on the chair.

"I'm supposed to be making the grand declarations and you're just doing it all over again."

He laughed as she buried her face in his neck. "You can declare whatever you want to me, baby."

"I want everything you just said." She brought her mouth to his, kissing him, getting lost in the fact that this was really real.

As his hands moved over her body, sending the best kind of shivers over her skin, she pulled back slightly. "I'm second-guessing the cold water." She nuzzled against him.

"Especially when there's a jetted tub upstairs," he said against her neck where he pressed his lips. He handed her the tub of ice cream they'd been sharing. "Hang on to that." Without warning, he stood, with her in his arms.

She laughed as he carried her through the curtains, up the stairs. "What about the rest of the ice cream?"

He didn't answer. He was too busy kissing her.

48

Grace stared at the magazine, unsure if she was ready to open it.

"Why are you nervous?" Noah rubbed her shoulders as they both stared down at the shiny cover.

They'd been so busy with Noah's work on getting donations for the community center, getting ready for Morty and Tilly's wedding, *moving in together*, she'd forgotten that the magazine hit stands today.

"I don't know. It's almost like a snapshot of our relationship. This is the last one."

"But not the end," he said, kissing her cheek before resting his chin on her shoulder, his arms looping around her waist.

He'd wait patiently, content to just hold her, which was so different from when they'd first met. Both of them had been in constant motion, not stopping to recognize where the holes and emptiness were in their own lives. Until their worlds collided thanks to a nine-pound Chihuahua.

"What did Rosie say about the offer?" Noah asked, distracting her from her thoughts.

"She loves it. The internship is going to give her a solid

foundation but she's as excited as I am for us to go into business together."

"I'm so proud of you," he whispered. He touched the magazine with one finger. "Aren't you curious?"

"Of course. I just, I don't know. I'm being silly. Let's read it."

HH
HOME AND HEART
It's what's inside that counts
HOW A HOUSE BECOMES A HOME; PART 3 OF 3

Story and interview by Emily Swanson
Photographs by Jack Stein

The photo spread that preceded the article was gorgeous. Noah's home—their home now—before and after the changes. She stared at the glossy photos of the media room, the upstairs bath with the overhead rain-shower faucets. All the little details that they'd chosen together.

Noah came to her side, his hip pressed to her body. She ran her hand over the first page of their article, in awe.

"You have to read the whole thing this time," he said.

"You, too," she said, glancing at him.

"I already did. While you were getting ready."

She smiled, turning back to the magazine. She read the description of their home, how it started, little notes Emily had included in the margins, which made it such a fun article.

"Be right back," Noah said.

She got lost in the magazine, remembering every minute that the pictures shared. They couldn't possibly show how much happened behind the scenes. It looked so easy. No one would know, from the captions or words, that she'd lost her heart, found it again during the process.

Emily Swanson (ES): What is the biggest reward of taking on a renovation slash restoration like this?

Grace Travis (GT): Seeing it come together. The end product. Knowing all the hard work was worth it.

Noah Jansen (NJ): I agree. That and looking back to see how far you've come. It feels surreal.

Grace heard Noah come back into the kitchen, but her gaze caught on an unexpected photo of her and Noah looking at each other. Laughter and love clearly shone in both of their gazes. What struck her right in the heart was that she remembered the moment. It was before she'd even realized she'd fallen so hard.

She ran her fingers over the glossy photo, got lost in the rest of the article. As she read to the end, the tone changed, confusing her because she didn't remember all the questions.

ES: Noah, you've done so many projects. What makes this one different?

NJ: That's easy. Grace. I came to California to figure myself out. What I found was the love of my life. The woman who taught me that at the end of the day, it doesn't matter where you're standing, but who's standing next to you.

ES: So, you and Grace fell in love during this project. That's so romantic.

Grace's breathing grew heavy. Emily hadn't asked this in the last interview. Grace picked up the magazine, pulled it closer to her face.

NJ: It is. This house is like us in so many ways. It took time to see what we could become but the more effort we put into each other, the stronger our foundation will be.

ES: So, what does the future hold for you two?

NJ: Anything she wants. But one thing I know is that I plan to make a lot of promises and keep them all.

Grace felt Noah at her side again. She turned her head toward him, the magazine clutched in her fingers. Her smile softened when she saw the bouquet of flowers in his grasp. "I can't believe you said all of this. To the whole world. When did you do this?"

She set the magazine down, noticed him glance at it.

"I called Emily a couple weeks ago and asked for the add-ins."

"You've basically told them there'll be a white wedding with all the trimmings." Was she hyperventilating?

Noah tucked a strand of hair behind her ear. "What's the matter, Gracie? Don't you want all the trimmings?"

She exhaled, her heartbeat slowing to normal. "Honestly? I just want you."

"You already have me. I want it all with you. When you're ready, I'm going to ask you to marry me at a castle in the middle of the happiest place on earth."

She laughed nervously. "What? In Disneyland? How will you know when I'm ready?" She reached for the flowers to stop her hands from shaking. He gave them to her but stayed close. How would *she* know? She wanted to marry him, wanted everything for them, but they were just starting out. They were both forging new paths in their careers, getting used to living with each other.

Like he could see the gears turning in her head, he pressed a kiss to her cheek. "Turn the page."

Grace looked back at the magazine, set the flowers carefully on the countertop, and used her index finger to flip the page. There, nestled in the crease, was an envelope. She took it out, opened the fold, and saw two all-day passes to Disneyland.

She held them up, unable to contain her laughter or excitement. "Tickets?"

He pulled her in close. "Whenever you're ready, Grace. You're in control. You're everything I want. I have no problem waiting but I wanted you to have the promise of something with this magazine. It's our beginning in more ways than one."

Wrapping her arms around him, she held tight. "So, what if I said I wanted to go right now, today?"

His breath tickled her ear. "It'd be a tight fit with the wedding you're officiating tonight but like I said, whatever you want, Gracie."

"I love you, Noah."

"I love you, too." When he pulled back, the intensity in his gaze filled her with happiness.

Morty and Tilly were getting married tonight at sunset. Grace had been practicing her speech all week. She only hoped the words she chose would convey how happy she was for two of her favorite people.

It'd be a celebration of everything. Morty and Tilly had invited everyone Grace and Noah loved, because they said 'what's a party without all of your people?' Grace stared at Noah. *What is anything without all of your people.* He was hers. Her person. Her home.

"I can't believe you put it all on me," she said, setting the tickets down.

Noah arched his brows. "Bet you wait at least six months."

Her lips quirked. "I see what you did there."

He gave her an innocent look. "What?"

"Six months, huh. Bet you it's sooner."

"I'll take that bet." He kissed her again. "Because either way I win."

Before they got too lost in their kiss, Grace eased back, hoping her gaze conveyed all she felt for this man. Her throat felt tight but her heart was full.

"Thank you," she whispered.

"For what?"

"For showing me that happiness isn't about where you live or what you achieve. A home isn't walls, a roof, and a floor. It's a *feeling;* it comes with being seen and accepted for who you are. It's finding the person who makes you feel alive no matter where you are or what you accomplish. The person who makes you feel like you could have nothing and still have everything. It's unconditional love."

He swallowed, his gaze bright. "It's you."

She shook her head. "It's us."

The end. But really, the beginning.

Acknowledgments

Even as I write the acknowledgments for my second book with SMP, I can't believe it's real, and I'm this lucky. I might spend a lot of time in my own head, but I'm far from alone, and for that, too, I am grateful.

Thank you, Alex. You're more than an editor. You're a wonderful human being, and I feel honored to know and work with you.

The nice part about having a second book is adding in any thank-yous I left unsaid in book one. If I forget again, there'll be a book three. ;)

To DJ and Mary. Thank you for working so hard to get my book in the hands of so many people. Because of you, I've not only had my book read but made some lifelong connections and friendships. Thank you, Mara, St. Martin's Press, and all of the people who took part in making this book shelf-ready.

To Fran. Like Alex, you are more than just a person helping me on my journey. You are a constant, a supporter, an advocate, and someone I am deeply happy to know.

To Matt, Kalie, and Amy. You guys. I love you so much. I know

I tell you eight thousand times a day, but now, here it is in print.

To Brenda, Tara, Christy, and Sarah for being patient, thoughtful friends who push me to do better and sit with me when I'm too tired to stand. To Cole and Stacey for your endless enthusiasm and belief in me.

Special shout-out to the people I've met because of *Ten Rules*: Addie. You're so cool. To Shay, Kelsey, Jessica, Stephanie, Chip, and Sydni Ellis. Thank you for your enthusiastic and kind support. To all of the people who have loved and shared my first book and are looking forward to this second one, thank you.

To Rachel Lynn Solomon for not blocking me after my zillion messages and for agreeing to read my book after I fell in love with yours. To Lyssa Kay Adams, who is always available when I randomly message, who always responds with kindness and encouragement. You are awesome, and so is the wonderful writing group I've become part of because of you.

To all the people who are afraid to jump because the landing is uncertain: I hope you find the courage to take the leap. Even when the landing hurts a bit, it is so incredibly worth it.

Ten Rules for Faking It

Can you fake it till you make it when it comes to love?

Don't miss Sophie Sullivan's first charming rom-com!

Available now from

HEADLINE
ETERNAL

**Look out for Sophie Sullivan's
next escapist rom-com!**

**Coming soon
from**

HEADLINE
ETERNAL

HEADLINE
ETERNAL

FIND YOUR HEART'S DESIRE...

VISIT OUR WEBSITE: www.headlineeternal.com
FIND US ON FACEBOOK: facebook.com/eternalromance
CONNECT WITH US ON TWITTER: @eternal_books
FOLLOW US ON INSTAGRAM: @headlineeternal
EMAIL US: eternalromance@headline.co.uk